APATHETIC GOD

Apathetic God

IAN WITHROW

Ink & Quill Press

Contents

<u>Foreword</u>

As with my other works of writing, a portion of the proceeds of this book will go to support suicide prevention efforts and research. I want to thank each and every one of you for buying this book, and for helping support a cause that is very near and dear to me.

Furthermore, I want to encourage all of my readers to look into other ways they can help, whether that means starting a dialogue locally, or simply taking better care of your own health. Together, we can make a difference.

Acknowledgments

It is hard to imagine that three short years ago I had only just begun writing the Tragedy of Power. Dozens of friends, family members, and a plethora of kind and generous readers helped make the dream of becoming a novelist a reality.

I'd like to thank my beautiful wife, who supported me every step of the way. You really are the most gracious person in my life, and I wouldn't have made it this far without you.

To Dan, who tirelessly quarreled and bickered with me night after night, you helped me become a better writer. Thank you from the bottom of my heart.

I want to thank my readers. To everyone who helped make the Tragedy of Power a success, I hope you'll find the sequel even more fulfilling. I can't possibly thank you as much as you deserve.

Finally, dad, this one's for you.

Chapter 1

Weyland listened, committing the sounds around him to memory. Waves lapping at the shore, birdsong, the rustling grasses of the Greek countryside.

He listened to the whisper of the low-burning oil lamps providing light in his opulent chambers.

He listened to the gentle breathing of the woman sleeping next to him. Her graceful curves softly rising and falling with each nearly silent stirring of her lungs.

Her slumber was a sight to behold. Not a single line of worry creased her alabaster face or furrowed her light brown eyebrows. He often spent these morning hours staring at her as she slept, drinking in her curves as she lay beside him.

Inevitably though, the urge to wake her and have her fully with him would become unbearable and he would either succumb to it or be forced to walk away.

Today he chose to leave.

He slipped from beneath the silk sheets of their massive bed, his feet warming the cold tile as he touched it.

He padded along with a silence that seemed impossible for a man his size. He towered over his peers, yet he moved as quietly as some great cat.

He didn't hurry, but his long legs took him quickly into the hallway. The empty stone passages were still quiet, the tapestries on the walls not yet touched by the morning sun.

Rounding a corner he surprised a pair of servant girls. They dropped immediately to the ground, prostrating themselves before him. He could hear their heartbeats quicken as he passed, but he paid them no mind.

They were beneath him.

The grand temple had no door, only an archway leading out into the cool mediterranean morning. The sun crested the horizon just as he crossed the threshold.

The scratching of a straw broom across the paved courtyard intruded on his treasured daily ritual. He looked around with irritation. A servant boy some twenty yards distant was diligently sweeping dust, his back to Weyland.

As though alerted by the heat of Weyland's gaze, the boy froze and turned slowly around. Upon seeing Weyland glaring at him, he prostrated himself as the others had.

With the annoyance gone, Weyland returned to the sunrise. His favorite part, when the city first felt the light of the sun, had already passed.

Ruined.

His temper, always simmering just below the surface, flared for a moment. The faint smell of ash wafted into his nostrils and he calmed himself.

Taking a deep breath, he continued walking until he reached the edge of the Acropolis.

Weyland looked out over the bustling roofs and busy streets of one of his favorite cities; Athens. People filled the streets, ebbing and flowing like the current from some massive, sluggish river. From his place upon the plateau all the sounds, sights, and smells of the city were diluted, reduced to a soft hum nearly 500 feet below. He closed his eyes, soaking in the warm summer sun. The shining rays warmed his deep brown skin and filled him with peace. He breathed deeply of the salt air blowing in off the coast.

A dull thump sounded in the depths of his mind and a tremor flickered through the ground. He opened his eyes, startled by the unfamiliar sensation.

The people down below didn't seem to have noticed.

His brow furrowed. Certainly if he had felt it then the masses before him should have. He looked around, trying to find something, anything out of order. But the gulls drifting in the sea breezes kept their lazy course, the waves on the distant shores kept their steady beat, and the hustle and bustle of the city went on undisturbed. His paradise was unchanged to his keen senses.

The soft sound of rustling feathers drew him from his contemplation, making him turn.

She was as radiant as he had ever seen her. The woman standing before him was tall, lean and tan. Her golden hair looked like rays of sunshine brought to earth, her eyes were the deepest emeralds flecked with bronze. A cream colored silk dress accented her most noticeable feature; A pair of snow-white wings, covered in broad, sleek feathers. She flashed him a dazzling smile from across the marble courtyard.

The sight of his beloved against the backdrop of the massive stone columns of their estate cleared all worry from his mind. Truly she was a goddess, and a worthy companion for his own station.

He stepped towards her, his own face breaking into a smile from her infectious grin. As he crossed the smooth stones of the courtyard he reached a hand out to her.

Thump.

This time the sound hit him like a fist in the gut. He stumbled from the blow and shook his head to clear the ringing it had left in his ears. Worried, he looked back up at his bride.

She looked different, the smile on her face seemed more forced, less warm. The air lost a bit of its heat as the sun seemed to pale for a moment.

But she was there, still waiting for him.

He struggled towards her, his legs growing heavier with every step. His temper rose, and he shook himself. His powerful muscles flexed and suddenly he was free of the unseen burden upon him. The sun was once again warm and bright, he could move just as easily as he ever had.

The sweat dotting his brow and his heavy breathing were the only physical side effects of the strange momentary weakness he had experienced.

He looked down at himself, but everything appeared in order. His towering, seven-foot physique was as muscled and strong as it ought to be, his dark skin tight over sculpted flesh.

He recoiled when he again laid eyes upon his wife. Her shining gold hair had been replaced with wild, lightly curling darkness. Her eyes matched her new hair, as did her wings. The snowy feathers that he was used to looked like they were fresh dipped in the deepest black he had ever seen. Her smile was a faint, cruel curl at the edge of her lips. Her arms were outspread, waiting for him, but he felt no welcome there.

He took an involuntary step backwards.

As he did so, she spoke.

"Weyland please, I need you."

Her voice was velvet to his ears, enticing him.

"Weyland."

As she spoke, she returned to the form he was used to. His shining maiden was again before him. She sounded desperate, like she needed his help.

A mere 20 feet separated them.

He sprinted towards her, driven by a sense of urgency he couldn't quite explain. His strong legs propelled him at inhuman speeds but the distance between them seemed only to grow.

Frustrated, he pushed himself further, running harder and harder. She was speaking, but the wind rushing past his ears drowned out her words.

Thump.

This time, the sound was like a clap of thunder directly on top of him. It drove him to the ground and cracked the marble stones around him. He looked around in a daze. He was at the center of what looked like a small impact crater, surrounded by a spider web of cracked stone.

He closed his blurry eyes, drew an unsteady breath and composed himself.

When he opened them again, there was blood running between the cracks in the stone around his hands. But it wasn't his own.

He looked up, shocked at the sight of his bride's broken, crumpled form in front of him. Her wings stuck out at odd, impossible angles, her feathers cracked and matted with dark blood. Her once pristine features had shattered like a china doll.

It could not be; it simply was not possible that this could happen. Not here, not in this protected place.

Steeling himself, Weyland turned inward. He began the unfamiliar but not forgotten work of unmaking the paradise around him. The lush sounds of the Grecian landscape faded, the brilliant warmth of the sun grew distant, his senses dulled until he was floating in nothingness.

Weyland returned to reality with a frustrated snap, his head was pounding and his joints felt stiff.

He opened his eyes and was annoyed to find his chambers unlit. Still, he had no trouble seeing in the pitch blackness of the ancient temple.

From his perch upon his throne he could see the dense layer of dust and detritus that coated everything in the room. It was several inches thick and lay equally upon the fallen, once-proud columns of broken stone, the disintegrated furniture, the long-decayed tapestries, and the ornate marble floor.

He must have slept for decades this time, centuries even to have been so thoroughly ignored. Grumbling his discontent, he slowly stood and stretched the kinks out of his joints.

His movements sent a cascade of dust pouring off of him and swirling out into the crypt-like silence of the decrepit building.

The entire temple was in a state of disrepair, many of the rooms had fully collapsed.

This will not do.

The ancient fabric of his clothes disintegrated as he strode confidently towards the exit, but he didn't mind. It was clear nothing had disturbed these halls in many lifetimes. Turning a corner he saw that the stairs that had once led upward to the surface had collapsed as well, replaced with a wall of fallen stone and dirt.

Well, that explains that.

No matter.

Weyland concentrated; he hadn't done this in ages. Thick veins stood out on his arms, a fierce orange glow emanating from them as he focused his long-dormant powers. A split second later he vanished with a sizzle, leaving only smoldering stone behind.

A few hundred meters away, a patch of bare stone high in the mountains reddened with heat, unnoticed by the occupants of the small camp nearby.

The brisk mountain air did little to stifle the heat in Natalie's cheeks as she lost herself in a trashy romance. The confines of her tiny tent seemed overly warm as the book heated up.

Janessa wiped a tear from her eye and turned away from her lover. She took a step across the pearl-white beach of Isla Pasion and towards the waiting boat.

"Wait, mi amor!"

Ricardo grabbed Janessa's arm, pulling her close to his smooth, muscular chest.
"Don't go, I cannot bear to live without you, not even in this paradise."

His thick latin accent lent a sensual feel to his words, and Janessa found herself unable to resist him. His large powerful hand snaked up her back and into her hair, pulling her head towards him.

She let him move her without any resistance.

Their lips met and Janessa felt her legs go weak. The heat between them was a rival for the volcanoes rising in the background. Her passion built until she felt she might erupt, she had to have him...

A loud crackling boom startled Natalie Schreiber from her book with such suddenness that she let out a terrified squeak. Clutching her novel to her chest, she slowly crawled out into the Changbai Mountains of southern China.

Natalie had been enthralled by her book when Weyland arrived, but now it slipped forgotten from fingers numb with shock. Just a few feet away from her stood a total stranger. The tallest, most muscular, most handsome man she had ever seen. Stranger yet, he was standing in a smoldering crater, a few inches deep, that certainly had not been there the day before.

The junior archaeologist stared dumbfounded, blinking at the naked Adonis in front of her.

Weyland inspected his new surroundings. A collection of smallish tents and piles of digging tools, tables covered in maps, and mounds of excavated dirt filled a clearing about 60 feet across.

Good, these servants clearly understand my importance since they are digging out my temple.

Taking his time, he looked more closely at the camp. The materials were all foreign, not the leather and animal skins he had seen when last he walked the earth. One of the mortals was looking at him from within a tiny shelter, clearly petrified.

"Child, what century is it?"

He spoke in perfect Korean, but the young woman furrowed her brow, clearly not understanding.

Hmm.

He tried again, cycling through Welsh, Breton, and finally Latin before he got the reaction he was looking for.

"You speak Latin?"

The girl's words were sloppily pronounced, and her grammar imperfect. More importantly, she was asking him questions, rather than providing the answer he required.

"As do you, poorly. What is the century?"

He repeated his question, his annoyance building.

"Um, the 20th, er sorry the 21st century. Who are you?"

Weyland hid his surprise well, he had slept more than a millenia. No wonder this girl couldn't speak properly. More likely, it was he who was using outdated language.

His first question answered, he set about getting more information from the girl. Weyland took a step towards her, causing her to scurry slightly backwards.

"Do not fear, child."

She was still afraid. She looked like a cornered mouse, her breathing erratic and her eyes darting to and fro.

"Come out here."

Natalie's curiosity overtook her caution.

Come on Nat, you're a scientist.

Slowly, she crawled out from inside the tent and approached the giant before her.

Weyland took a look at the diminutive figure in front of him. She had the look of an intellectual. Certainly she could be no warrior.

"I need to know if you have seen something. But first I must show you what to look for."

She was furrowing her brow again.

"I don't understand."

Weyland reached out a hand, eliciting a flinch from Natalie.

Slowly, delicately, he placed his index finger on her temple.

Natalie found herself standing in a courtyard in the middle of magnificent temples and marble statues. She recognized the place immediately. It was the Acropolis in Athens. What she didn't understand was why it was new, filled with servants, and not a crumbling ruin like it should be. She spun in a slow circle, breathless at the impossible sight.

Could it be a dream? If it was, it was the most realistic she had ever experienced. She could feel the ocean breezes, hear gulls in the distance. Sights, sounds, even the stone beneath her feet felt more real, more tangible, than she could have ever imagined. Her desire to explore nearly overcame her.

"Focus," Weyland's powerful voice rang out in her mind.

His words drew her eyes to a low throne across the stones. A woman sat in it. As Natalie approached, she could see the woman was being fanned by handsome men and beautiful women. They held large peacock-feather fans and wore the finest silk garments, but around their ankles were golden chains. They were slaves.

She felt compelled to go to the woman, as though beckoned by some unseen power.

Her eyes widened the nearer she got.

There was no mistaking it, the woman in the throne was Lauren Corvidae, the miracle who had so upset the balance of the world. She was laughing brightly at some unheard joke, conversing quietly with her servants.

Even chained, the people around her seemed filled with joy and adoration, as if it were truly a blessing to serve her every whim.

"You know this woman?"

Weyland's voice again intruded on her mind.

Natalie didn't have time to respond before she was again standing in China. Disoriented for a moment, she could swear she still felt the warm Mediterranean sun on her back.

Natalie looked around, her eyes wide. Sure enough, she was back at the excavation site she'd called home for the past year. Her bleary-eyed fellow scientists were beginning to emerge from their own quarters, drawn by the unexpected commotion outside.

"Nat, what's up? Who's this?"

Weyland paid them no mind. His attention was entirely on the still bewildered young woman before him.

"I asked you if you knew that woman," Weyland insisted, this time in Natalie's mother tongue of German.

Her mind scrambled to make sense of what was happening. She settled on an unexpected revelation.

"How can you... how do you speak my language now?"

Natalie was amazed. The being, for he was certainly no normal human, seemed to have pulled the language from her mind.

"Answer me!"

Weyland's voice rose with impatience. The faintest smell of cinders wafted into Natalie's nose and she grew warmer, as though Weyland was exuding heat. Some uncharted, primal part of her mind sensed unquestionable danger.

"Y-yes, That's Lauren Corvidae. She's, well she's a miracle. She heals people."

So she is real, and not merely a product of the Dream.

"Where is she?"

Even here, in this remote corner of the world, news of Lauren's exploits were widely known. However, it had been several days since she'd heard anything. Natalie wracked her brain, what had she heard most recently?

"I-I'm not really sure. Last I heard she was headed to the States, Chicago I think."

"This land, Chicago, Where is it."

Natalie was caught by surprise; she very nearly laughed. That this mighty figure could appear out of thin air, pluck a new language from her mind, and be unaware of such a well-known place was oddly comical.

"You've never heard of Chicago?"

Weyland did not enjoy being the subject of humor.

"Do you mock me?"

His tone spoke danger and the smell of ashes grew stronger, until it filled the air between them. The veins in his arms, neck, and chest swelled and darkened before her eyes.

Natalie watched the powerful man's eyes begin to glow a deep red and felt terribly afraid.

"No! No sir, I'm sorry. Chicago is in the United States of America."

Another new name. Weyland was growing frustrated. How would he find her, with so little information to aid him. No, better to go to a place of learning, where the scholars would certainly be able to provide him context.

"You will accompany me."

Without waiting for an answer, he focused inward. In a flash he had once more disappeared, this time taking Natalie with him, leaving only smoldering stone as evidence.

Natalie felt as though her insides were being ripped out through her skin, and then as if up was in several directions at once. The sensation seemed to last an eternity, and yet, in the blink of an eye she was laying face first on warm stone. The world was spinning violently, and she had little warning before she was emptying her stomach on the pavement.

"Get up."

Weyland's voice held no sympathy, no concern, only con-tempt.

Weyland was satisfied the mortal was going to survive, she was moving and groaning on the stones of the courtyard. He was less satisfied, however, with the sight in front of him. The once proud monuments and splendid temples of the Acropolis were in ruin. Thousands of men, women, and children were running around wildly, oohing and ahhing over his favorite vacation spot. A thousand years ago none would dare enter this place without his good graces.

Crowds were gathering around him. The people, all dressed in foreign garb, pointed tiny boxes at him and spoke animatedly in some unknown tongue. His brain began to pick through the languages. Some he could almost recognize, others were entirely new to him.

This was not at all what Weyland had expected.

When last he walked the earth he had been met with fear, respect, and worship. The people before him were surprised, certainly, but they were far more excited than afraid. They crowded around him, creeping closer and closer as they shoved each other out of the way to see him more clearly.

Frustrated, Weyland realized that the whole world was almost certainly like this. He had been forgotten. His legacy was long gone. He had nothing to present to his bride, to his Lauren Corvidae. One thing the world still seemed to have in abundance was mortals. They had built monuments in his name before, they would do so again.

At the moment though, they lacked respect. Lacked discipline. Lacked humility.

Spare the rod, spoil the child.

So be it.

Weyland's entrance, and the events that followed, would on any other day have been headline news. But attentions were already focusing 5,000 miles away.

"This is Kent Dailey, reporting live from downtown Chicago. Lauren Corvidae, controversial healer and religious figure, has just been spotted flying above Michigan Avenue!"

Kent's excited face filled the frame of his news crew's camera for a moment until Lauren came into sight.

"Clark, there she is! Zoom in right there!"

Lauren was wearing a sleek black evening gown, her hair whipping wildly in the turbulent air of the Windy City. Her serene, expressionless face was captured for the world to see as the helicopter neared her position.

"As you can see from our vantage point up here in the chopper, she's well over one thousand feet in the air right now. We're being told she has been staying at a nearby hotel, where our sources tell us she broke out of a window near the top of the building. It's possible she's attempting to escape from the government agents who allegedly kidnapped her earlier in the week at O'hare International Airport."

Billions of eyes around the world were glued to computer screens, cell phones, and television sets. Every news network that had reporters in the area scrambled to get a scoop on their competition.

"She's been the subject of increasingly divisive debate over the past several months, which came to a bit of a head in Rome just a few days ago where her father was the latest victim of the violence that has followed her since - Wait, something is happening!"

Lauren's rising form was suddenly swan diving towards the streets below.

"She's falling now, um... she seems to be dropping quite low... I'm not sure if..."

Kent stumbled into silence as she fell faster and faster.

The world held its breath.

The camera followed her streaking form all the way to the pavement. Lauren impacted the ground with bone-shattering speed. The footage was eerily silent except for the rotor-wash of the aircraft. The unblinking gaze of the telephoto lens caught every detail as a growing pool of red spread out from the pale form below them.

"I... I don't know if.. it's impossible to say what caused her to fall."

Habit forced Kent to speak through the silence and say something, anything.

"She's um, not moving though..."

Instantly, footage of Lauren plummeting from the sky was on a non-stop loop on every major network in the world. No amount of viewer discretion warnings could dissuade people from watching her crash to the pavement over and over. The heartbeat of the world seemed in tune with the steady thump of her televised impact.

Seconds turned to minutes and people flooded into view of the TV cameras pointed at her from helicopters circling the scene as Lauren's unmoving body was portrayed from every possible angle.

Lauren's wings stuck out at odd angles, her snowy feathers soaking up the dark blood covering the asphalt where she was lying. Her body was quickly surrounded by black vehicles with dark windows. Within a few minutes she had been covered with a sheet and was no longer visible to the clinical stares of the cameras.

Already tens of thousands were taking to the streets where her crumpled form lay in the heart of Chicago. Police forces were quickly augmented with elements from the National Guard and a perimeter was established as medical and religious personnel filtered in and out of the large, green, multi-purpose military tent marking her resting place.

Could she survive such an impact? Had the world finally seen the limit of her miraculous gifts? The uncertainty of the moment seemed to stifle the more violent urges of the people, at least in the city. Vigils sprang up as the hours lengthened without a sign of life. First around the city, then the country, and eventually all over the world.

Chapter 2

Caroline Adams hit the edge of the traffic jam leading into Chicago more than 100 miles from the city, and it was nearly fifteen hours before she was able to actually reach her goal; The Central Church of the Immaculate Child, the humble headquarters of her faith.

By the time she arrived, around 50 of her fellow believers were already there, downtrodden and grim, but determined.

"Are we ready?"

Her tired voice got no verbal response, only solemn nods.

The group set out on foot, the only reasonable method of travel left in the crowded city. Many of her companions were elderly. Hours ticked by as the small band moved through Chicago at a slow crawl. Finally though, somewhere around dawn, their pilgrimage was complete.

People filled the street for blocks in every direction. Some were camping in tents, others in cars, some simply crawled into sleeping bags on the sidewalk. Stale smoke from cold campfires drifted in the air, lending the urban sprawl an uncharacteristically outdoorsy feel. A sleepy peace blanketed the area. Caroline and her fellow travellers were among the few people awake at this hour. They picked their way carefully through the sleeping forms.

In light of the peaceful nature of the gathered crowds, the National Guard had been recalled, and the police had brought the barricades inward, allowing people to get fairly near to the tent holding Lauren's body.

Caroline looked at the drab, olive green tent and strengthened her resolve. She grounded herself in her faith and approached a pair of officers chatting behind the bright orange temporary barriers.

"Excuse me sir, my fellows and I have travelled a very long way to see Ms. Corvidae," she began.

"I was her caretaker after her return, you may have heard of me? Caroline Adams?"

The officers looked relaxed when faced with the harmless looking group of older folks in front of them. They had in fact heard of Mrs. Adams, she had been a flash-in-the-pan celebrity after news sources had tracked her down at Cherry Hills. Her fame had been short lived, mostly because she refused to cooperate with the media. Her statements had been limited to unconditional support for Lauren, testimony of her divinity, and scripture. Within a few weeks most news outlets had determined she was boring, old news.

"Um, yes ma'am, I've heard of you and it's a real pleasure to meet you," the younger of the two officers spoke while the older one disappeared into the bundle of tents within the barricades.
"It's just that all religious personnel are required to go through our executive liaison prior to entrance."

Caroline nodded.
"Of course, we don't want to cause any trouble for you at all officer. Could you direct us to them?"
No sooner had the words left her lips than the older officer reappeared with a tired looking lady in tow.
"Good morning," the woman yawned.

Caroline began again.
"Good morning ma'am, I'm Caroline Adams, an elder with the Church of the Immaculate Child..."

The woman didn't seem to be terribly interested in the details, instead she simply pushed a battered clipboard into Caroline's hands.

"That's nice ma'am. Please sign yourself and your companions in. We are currently only allowing bona fide religious personnel to see the body-"

Caroline interjected.

"You mean Lauren. To see Lauren."

The lady sighed.

"Yeah, sure. You'll need to provide identification and proof of your organizational affiliation. If you meet the criteria you'll be allowed in groups of no more than ten. Please do not attempt to touch the body. Please do not take any photography, flash or otherwise. You will need to consent to a search and will not be allowed in with any kind of weaponry..."

The officers began checking the small business cards that the elders carried with them, comparing them to unseen lists on grey tablet computers. Next came a brusque, but impartial search. In short order they were being separated into groups.

Caroline, as one of the longest serving women in the church, found herself in the first group.

The man escorting them was a walking stereotype, his clean black suit and dark shades were straight out of every spy novel ever written. He didn't say a word as he led the clerics to the large tent. When they arrived, he held aside the large flap, allowing them to enter.

The plain exterior hid a complex suite of medical equipment. Wires, tubes, and hoses led directly to the center of the room where a large cushioned table dominated the space. Lauren's body was there, she had been clothed in something akin to a hospital gown. The garment left her arms, her face, and her legs from the knees down bare. Deep purple and black splotches covered every inch of her exposed skin, a testament to the incredible damage done to her. Her hands, fingers, jaw, feet, ankles, even her knees were splinted with thick metal wires. Her wings, similarly caged with pins and wires, were extended out to either side of her, drooping limp towards the floor.

Other changes had been wrought by her impact as well. Just as dramatic were the differences in her hair and wings. Her golden locks had been turned a shiny opalescent black. The way it fell around her face, it looked as smooth and dark as refined oil. Her feathers were black as well. Though, to describe them as simply black seemed somehow blasphemous. Each feather was indistinguishable from the next, they were distilled night. Not simply dark, but the utter absence of light.

Caroline tried and failed to stifle her shock.

One exhausted doctor in bloody scrubs was leaning on a heart rate monitor wiping her brow. The flat green line on the screen captured Caroline's eye. Other doctors in surgical gear were passed out on cots around the room, and they barely stirred at the group's entrance.

"Is she... alive?"

Caroline whispered the question to the doctor, who seemed surprised to see them. The woman opened her mouth to speak, seemed to change her mind, and then tried again.

"No, but then again also yes. Honestly, ma'am, I'm not sure what she is."

Shrugging helplessly, she cast a confused look at her patient on the gurney.

"She's got no pulse, she's got less electrical activity in her brain than a wrist watch, she's got 112 broken bones and her organs are soup."

Caroline was taken aback by the blunt assessment, but the lady wasn't finished.

"But that's just it. Corpses don't bruise. It's a mechanism that the body uses to repair damage, it just... it just doesn't happen to dead people. We operated for more than ten hours and I've

never seen damage like that before. Never. If I was in medical school I'd say she was as dead as you could get."
The group of believers huddled closer together, a wave of sadness washing over them.
"But."
Hope returned to the weary travellers.
"She's getting better. I can't explain it, none of us can, but her body is repairing itself. We've all seen the news, heard the stories, but she isn't healing as quickly as we expected. I was surprised we could even operate, but... maybe there's just too much damage for her, uh, powers to keep up. There's no telling how long it will take either, she's sustained almost every kind of impact injury you can sustain. Frankly, we don't know if she will wake up, or who she will be if she does."
Caroline nodded, it wasn't the news she wanted but she would keep the faith. After a few minutes of prayer, the group was ushered out of the tent and back to the edge of the barricades.

By the time the whole congregation was able to see their savior, the tent city surrounding them had begun to wake up.

She was humbled by the kindness and solidarity she saw. Kids were playing, burning off the restless energy of youth. Parents and friends gathered around small propane stoves and grills. A compelling sense of community pervaded the entire area.

Caroline breathed easy for what felt like the first time in years. Here was the power she believed in, here was the evidence of Lauren's Truth. All of these people brought together from every social status, every religious and ethnic subgroup of the city. It was a peace that had eluded her since Lauren had flown away from her tiny church so long ago.

Unfortunately, her duties could not wait. She and her congregation would minister to these people, would help them understand the gift that Lauren represented. Not simply as a healer of bodies, but as a healer of souls.

After an hour or so of searching, the group found an area large enough for them to put down roots. A trash-filled alley that had been largely ignored would certainly suit their purposes, and at less than a block away, it was the closest open space to Lauren. After setting up a small camp, the group took to the streets in teams, walking from campsite to campsite looking for people who would listen to their gospel.

Most people were fairly accepting, some had their own deeply held convictions, and an unfortunate few were openly hostile. Caroline's band learned over the next several days which areas to avoid, and which would be more receptive.

"We're standing here on Michigan avenue, the site of Lauren Corvidae's heartbreaking fall, with some of the thousands of people who have turned out to see what many still see as their savior. Excuse me sir, would you like to tell us why you're still here, after all this time with no real sign of life?"

Kent was braving the chilly Chicago air, trying to drum up ratings by walking among the followers still gathered around Lauren's resting place. In the past week his ratings had been tanking. Even the normally tunnel-visioned American viewers were tuning in to the unravelling mystery taking place in Greece.

"You're good Kent, we're not live. They're cutting over to Cyprus again."

Kent threw his hands up in frustration.

"Are you kidding me?"

His cameraman, Clark Reynolds, shook his moppish blonde head.

"D-do you still need me to say somethin' or nah man?"

"No! Fuck, man, obviously not! Did you not notice the camera pointed at the goddamn ground?"

Kent's off-screen personality shone brightly as he caustically dismissed the citizen he had roped into an interview just minutes ago.

"Did they say what's going on over there?"

Clark shook his head again, pausing a moment before he spoke.

"Well, Valerie–"

"Damn it! I *knew* you were gonna say Valerie. How the hell is she getting these stories over me? This is my beat, I invented this topic. I made this shit what it is. And now I'm stuck covering a damn vegetable."

Kent cast a wrathful look at the small but growing shrine a few dozen yards distant. Since the police had fully vacated the area, pilgrims had begun construction of a small temple. Depending on what particular brand of crazies you asked, it was called all sorts of things. The one thing these people could agree on was that it belonged to the "Interfaith Council," a collection of crackpot mystics, priests, and reverends. The council members, led by a tight-lipped woman named Caroline, claimed that only through cooperation could Lauren's powers be shared fully.

What a crock.

"C'mon, pack up your crap. We're not sticking around here."

Clark and Kent began tearing down their cameras, microphones and other gear in preparation to leave when a loud rumbling interrupted them. It had been general practice since day one that vehicles were expected to avoid the area, and no one had tested the unwritten rule yet.

Nonetheless, Kent could hear what must be dozens of motorcycles approaching. People were shouting and scrambling out of the way as a roaring pack of cyclists worked their way through the camp.

Kent had enough journalistic chops left to smell the change in the air, the electric feel of potential energy building.

"Start rolling. Clark, start rolling right now."

As soon as the lead motorcycle came into view Kent knew he had struck gold again. The man riding the chopper was decked toes to collar in black leather and shiny chrome studs. A large, winged tattoo adorned on his bare chest, visible through a part in his jacket. The man wore no helmet on his shaved head, which was similarly covered in tattoos.

By far the most striking feature of the imposing figure was a bright red armband with a stark white and black swastika on it. The man laughed as he rolled over a tent, a pair of children barely scrambling from within before he crushed it under his tires.

"Get out of the way!"

Motorcycle after motorcycle roared by, every rider with the same bright band of hate on their arm.

"Tell me you're getting this..."

Clark kept his lens fixed on the leader, but gave Kent a solid thumbs-up as answer.

"Good. Call the studio and follow me in."

The group of motorcyclists was forming a loose mob at the edge of the shrine, where the old police barricades halted their progress. The bright plastic wall sections had been colorfully decorated with messages of peace and faith, and in a show of solidarity the city had left them there when they pulled their people out.

Kent shoved through the gathering crowd, only slowing down when he got within a few feet of the riders.

Jesus, there must be fifty of them.

He steeled himself against the potential dangers, but his narcissism would not allow him to hold back.

"Excuse me! Kent Dailey, WNG-TV can I get a statement?"

Kent shoved his microphone out like a sword as he pushed closer and closer to the leather-clad brutes in front of him. The pack had assembled in a rough semicircle around their leader, the roar of their engines drowning out even Kent's loud voice.

Kent was so fixated on the leader, now standing on the seat of his motorcycle and addressing his comrades, that the steel-toed boot of the rider next to him caught him totally unprepared. He felt the blow in his stomach like a baseball bat and doubled over in pain.

It had been many, many years since he'd received more than a papercut or a stubbed toe, and the unfamiliar feeling of pain kept him on his knees. The woman dismounted her bike and placed a spike covered boot on Kent's hand, grinding it slowly into the sharp asphalt as she bent to retrieve the microphone he had dropped.

Her prize retrieved, she left Kent there whimpering. Clark followed her movement as she walked through the gathered bikers and handed the microphone to the ringleader.

"Alright! Cut 'em!"

As one, the bikers cut their engines, leaving behind a silence that was nearly as deafening.

"Where's the fuckin'- Ah there we are. Hey fatty, get the fuck over here!"

The man pointed at Clark, and a pair of goons stepped up and led the cameraman into the crowd. He did his best to keep the camera steady as he was shoved and jostled on the way to the stranger. He was stopped several feet away by the two bruisers flanking him, and he knew better than to move any further.

"We live?"

Clark nodded, the camera shaking as he did so.

"Good, cuz I got some things to say."

The man straightened back up, his piercing blue eyes scanning the crowd around him.

"Good morning sheep!"

His clear, powerful voice perfectly matched his stage presence. His audience was utterly captured.

"We, are the wolves."

A dark chuckle rolled through the bikers. The citizens who had not yet fled looked uneasily at each other.Kent was able to stumble to his feet in time to see a cruel smile on the speaker's face.

"Consider yourselves evicted! If you remain in this area, I will-"

"You are unwelcome here."

Eyes widened everywhere as a small voice rose to match the man. A woman had stepped forward from the shrine. The woman was known to the crowd, she spoke softly but with authority. Her hawkish features told of a strength beneath her frail form.

"Oh imagine that, one of your kind that doesn't know how to listen."

The man gestured rudely at Caroline, eliciting some cheers from his gang.

"Something about that dark skin make you deaf? That it?"

"As I said before, you are not welcome here. This is a place of peace."

Tension clouded the air like poisoned gas and the whole crowd held its breath.

"Bring that mouthy ape up here," he growled.
Eddies of discontent swirled through the onlookers, but no one made a move as a group of men grabbed Caroline and dragged her forward.
"You will call me Sigurd," he was again addressing the crowd. "We are the Sons of the Valkyrie, chosen soldiers of the glorious Fourth Reich. If that don't sit well with you, then you're welcome to join this animal up here."

As he spoke, Caroline was brought next to his motorcycle. He looked down at her, a sneer of pure hatred on his face.

"You wanna beg for your life?"

She opened her mouth to speak but he spit in her face, forcing her into shocked silence.

"Don't bother. You're nothing. Killing you is like breaking a lamp, in a civilized society I could just go buy another."

As Caroline moved to wipe the spit from her face, Sigurd reached down and grabbed a handful of her hair, yanking up on it as he did so.

She cried out in pain as her tiny frame was hoisted up for the crowd to see. With his free hand, Sigurd ripped open his jacket. A massive tattoo dominated his powerful chest. It depicted an armored angel, clearly styled after Lauren, holding a burning sword in one hand and a flag bearing the Swastika in the other. At her feet was a world on fire.

"Your time is up! All of you! All the homos, the little rat-jews, these animals!"

He cast Caroline down to the pavement.

"When The Valkyrie rises again, it will be with the banner of the Iron Eagle! We, her soldiers, will execute her will, and clear the filth as we were meant to do!"

The assembled bikers dismounted and pulled bats, brass knuckles, and chains from their saddlebags.

"Clear it out!"

At Sigurd's command, the marauders began tearing apart the camp. Any tent that had survived the motorcycles was torn to shreds, campfires were kicked into sleeping bags, and anyone who didn't immediately run was shoved to the ground and beaten.

Kent made to run, his eyes wild with fear.

"Kent! Kent, don't leave me!"

It wasn't that he didn't hear Clark, but Kent was far more concerned with his own safety at the moment. Unfortunately he was surrounded. He curled into a ball and sobbed, hoping that they wouldn't notice him.

"Hey, get me that little news guy, bring him over here!"

Sigurd's command was answered instantly, and Kent was roughly dragged across the pavement until he was laying beside Caroline.

"Stand up."

Sigurd's voice was low, deadly, and Kent dare not disobey.

"Good boy, you a jew? I know all them jews own hollywood."

Kent shook his head.

"Even better. We're gonna do an interview, got it?"

He didn't wait for an answer, instead he slipped down to sit on the seat of his bike and motioned for Clark to get closer to them. He was relaxed, immune to the violence around them.

Sigurd pulled a small tube from his pocket, unscrewed the cap and poured a pinch of white powder onto his hand where his thumb met his forefinger.

He sharply inhaled the powder, holding his breath and then shaking his head to clear it.

"Nothing like it, want a hit?"

He offered the tube to Kent, but he carefully shook his head no.

He settled more comfortably into his seat with a shrug. As he sat, he placed his right boot upon Caroline's head, keeping it pressed to the ground. Kent tried not to look at her, his stomach churning.

"So, ask me some questions! You're supposed to be a hot-shot right, if I gotta do this my damn self what am I keeping you here for?"

Kent jumped, barely holding back a scream.

"Right, um, yes. S-Sigurd, is it?"

A nod.

"Sigurd could you, ah, tell us more about your organization?"

A loud crackling explosion interrupted them. This time Kent couldn't help himself, he let out a terrified squeal like a teapot boiling over. He could feel warm liquid running down his pant leg but was too scared to be ashamed.

A smoking crater had appeared a short distance away. A motorcycle that had been occupying the space had been re-duced to slag, only the front wheel remained untouched at the edge of the circle.

A giant of a man was standing in the crater, he was wearing nothing but a kilt and a pair of gold bracelets. His skin was deep black, and his eyes glowed a dull orange for a moment before cooling to a dark brown.

The commotion in the street came to a screeching halt in light of the strange man's appearance. People stood still and more than a little afraid, unsure what was happening.

"Well, I'll be a son of a bitch..."

Sigurd stared a moment before he could compose himself.

"You're a big one ain't ya, boy."

Weyland ignored him, taking stock of his surroundings instead. He could sense his prize was nearby. As he laid eyes on the shrine, he knew he would find her there.

"Hey, I'm talking to you!"

Weyland took a long stride toward the building when a loud bang and a tiny projectile interrupted him. It flattened against his chest and fell to the ground, already half melted when it landed.

His gaze turned to Sigurd, who was standing slack-jawed pointing a tiny metal device at him.

Several motorcycles filled the ten feet between Sigurd and Weyland, but to Sigurd's eye the distance was far to small.

He fired off another round, and then a few more, watching in awe as they crushed themselves uselessly against the bare skin of Weyland's chest. Sigurd's eyes widened with horror as Weyland continued calmly walking towards him. The motorcycles between them caught fire, and then melted as Weyland approached. As he stepped across the puddles of smoldering plastic and molten steel, his skin darkened and cracked. It looked like fresh lava, deep jagged breaks in his flesh revealing a red-hot glow beneath.

It was the eyes though, that captured Sigurd. The deep, white-hot coals stared into his soul and held him motionless in fear. As Weyland approached the mortal he could see the stark, senseless terror in his eyes. He lowered the intensity of the heat surrounding him as he drew near.

Good.

Sigurd felt the waves of heat washing over him as Weyland came within arm's reach. Even dialed down, the heat was like a blast furnace against his exposed skin.

Weyland's skin cooled and sealed itself back together, until he resembled a mortal man once again. The only telling sign of his power a dull and fading glow in his arms and chest.

Sigurd tried to speak, but found he had no words.

"Sie wagen mich zu schießen?"

The accusation was barely more than a whisper.

Weyland's hand shot out with lightning quickness, his fingers wrapped firmly around Sigurd's throat. He plucked him from the ground with the effort a man might need to lift a small child. Again the dull red spread through Weylands powerful arm, creeping slowly towards his tightened grasp.

Sigurd tried to scream, but the air in his lungs was too hot. Instead, his mouth worked silently as steam and then smoke poured from between his lips.

To the onlooking crowd, it was the stuff of nightmares. Sigurd's body flopped like a hanging man as his throat and chest slowly darkened and the foul smell of burning flesh filled the air. Eventually, the body stopped moving, leaving only the grisly sizzle of cooking flesh to fill the air.

Weyland dropped the upstart and peered around, testing the waters to see if anyone else would be so foolish as to challenge his rule.

No such challenger presented himself.

The silence in the street was absolute. Even the wind seemed to freeze in deference to his power.

"Natalie!"

Weyland's voice dripped with irritation.

Natalie, until now unnoticed, lay huddled on the ground in the crater that Weyland had created upon his arrival. She struggled to her feet and rushed to Weyland's side, keeping her eyes dutifully downward.

Natalie's movement spurred action within the crowd. Stunned silence gave way to screams of terrified disbelief. More than a few onlookers vomited as the smell of burnt meat reached them and lent credence to the grisly sight. Only those bystanders too terrified to move were left behind as the people dispersed.

Weyland didn't care.

His chosen aide at his side, he resumed his interrupted walk. Inside the shrine he found her at last. The pins and wires that had held together her splintered bones had been removed before the physicians left her to her followers. In the time since they had left she had very nearly finished healing her body, the deep purple bruising remained only in her hands and feet now. Everywhere else it had given way to the palest porcelain skin.

To his keen eyes, Lauren was a vision of beauty. Raven hair cascaded down around her youthful face and slender neck. Her ebony wings were tucked gently in at her sides. The hospital gown she wore couldn't hide the sleek, trim figure beneath it. Weyland drank in the sight of her. His heartbeat quickened at her presence.

He was careful to keep his face expressionless as he approached her. By the time he was standing beside her he could barely keep his hands from trembling. How long had he waited for this moment? What countless lonesome centuries has passed?

He reached out, gently sliding an arm behind her knees and across the back of her shoulders. Her skin was cool to the touch, and she didn't react at all to his attentions.

He lifted her slowly. She was as light as a feather in his powerful arms. With a careful step he strode back out into the sunlight of the street. The scene was mostly as he had left it; people stood around in a daze, minds reeling at what they had seen.

Weyland gestured with his head, indicating to Natalie that she should stand closer while he prepared to transport them. She set a non-confrontational look upon her face and braced for the horrid, twisting feeling of his abnormal method of transit.

Chapter 3

Lauren curled her exposed toes at the unexpected caress of a cool draft. She snuggled deeper into the silky blankets surrounding her, struggling to slip back into slumber. The cold had kick-started her mind, however, and her efforts were in vain. She remained willfully in denial, trying to convince herself if she just lay still enough she could be dreaming in no time.

She had almost drifted off when a irksome noise interrupted her. The light scuff of a servant's feet against the stone floor of her room.

Sitting up, she let out an exaggerated sigh.

"Your Majesty, I am sorry to disturb your slumber."

The servant before her was little more than a girl, she was holding shiny silver tray and a decanter, her eyes dutifully downward.

An oddly familiar smell reached her nose, causing Lauren to narrow her eyes. She sat up straighter, tucking her wild blonde hair behind her ears.

Pancakes?

Something stirred in her mind. A nagging sensation she couldn't explain.

"Girl, what did you bring me to eat?"

"I-it's a tray of fruits and cheeses your Majesty, a-as you always have?"

Lauren shook her head, already wondering what she had been thinking. She didn't like pancakes. Why would she like pancakes? These summer mornings were much too warm for food that heavy.

She must have had very strange dreams.

Lauren waved a hand at the young girl, who set about preparing her breakfast. When she was finished she bowed low and left the room. Lauren looked at the silver tray. With it's cover now off, she could see it was laden with succulent fruits and berries, artisan cheeses, and fresh bread.

Despite the bounty offered, she couldn't help but feel an unusual disappointment at the meal.

Still, she was famished. Her stomach growled as though she hadn't eaten in a week. Lauren rose, keeping one sheet wrapped around herself to cover her unclothed form. Walking to the edge of her bed, she stepped down onto the marble floor and walked to the table. Her hair fell in waves down to her shoulders and her feathers rustled softly as she stretched out the kinks of the night before. She felt cramped and sore, like she'd been still for too long.

That's new.

Lauren cast a suspicious look at her bed, it was nearly a dozen feet square, a massive pile of silk, down, and satin. It dominated her large circular bedroom, and would have been the envy of any queen.

"Ellian!"

"Yes, your Majesty"

The response was instantaneous. A young woman appeared through the curtain-covered archway that led to the rest of the palace. As soon as the handmaiden entered, she knelt and waited for instructions.

"Have my bedding replaced, today."

"Your will be done, your Majesty."

Lauren was inexplicably annoyed with Ellian's total subservience.

"Get up, Ellian."

Her frustration must have crept into her voice, because Ellian seemed nervous when she answered.

"Y-your Majesty?"

If anything, her servant's fear made her even more frustrated.

"Just... have my bath drawn, prepare my clothes, and clear this food away."

"Your Majesty, you haven't eaten anything. Is everything ok?"

"I'm fine, Ellian!"

The girl flinched.

"Thank you, Ellian, I'm fine..."

Lauren gently rubbed her suddenly throbbing temples.

"Have the cooks prepare pancakes, I'll take them after my bath."

Ellian nodded, bowed, and scurried away. Lauren was left alone in her massive bedchamber. She felt awkward, uncomfortable, as though she had forgotten something very important. She looked around for something to stir her memory. Her eyes slipped across the massive silk tapestries decorating her walls, the exquisitely tiled floor, and the simmering jeweled oil lamps, but none of them yielded the answers she sought.

She could feel her temper simmering just below the surface of her thoughts, not unusual if she was painfully honest with herself. It felt different though, hot, dangerous, unstable. She cast off the silk sheet she was wrapped in. It felt restricting and warm, where it had been cool and soft a moment before. She let out a low growl and, determined to improve her mood, headed off to the palace baths.

Guards snapped to attention as she passed through the flowing curtains separating her quarters from the main corridor that ran the length of this wing of the palace. Chloe, her other handmaiden, quickly fell into step behind her as her long, lean legs carried her quickly past the statuesque soldiers.

They were consummately professional, their gaze never wavering as her naked form passed them by, reflected in the mirror-bright surface of their armor.

The palace was nearly silent this early in the morning, only the occasional patrol of guards or stray servant interrupted her brisk trip. Everyone she met hastily stepped clear of her path and kept their eyes respectfully downcast.

Despite no one meeting her gaze, Lauren couldn't help but feel like she was travelling in a spotlight. Some malignant gaze seemed to bore into the back of her skull. She could feel this unseen presence leering at every inch of her body. She tried to shake the feeling, but failed.

By the time she reached the bathhouse she was trembling. She didn't realize she was holding her breath until she finally passed through the hanging silk doors and into the privacy of the baths.

"Chloe."

"Yes, your Majesty?"

Lauren tried to keep her voice from cracking. She took a deep breath to calm her racing heart.

"Fetch my apothecary."

She didn't turn to see if the girl had gone, she knew she had.

Alone at last she felt some of the tension leave her shoulders.

She was standing a few yards from the edge of what amounted to a heated swimming pool. Given the unique requirements of her wings, the artisans from the city had crafted a massive, shallow brass basin for her to bathe in. It was close to 20 feet across, and it sloped to just over four feet deep in the middle. Large diameter pipes delivered steaming water into the basin, and above it a complicated cage of brass piping could let forth a steamy rainfall, if she desired.

The pipes were flowing, but the basin was not yet full, and it would be several minutes until it was ready. Instead, Lauren walked around the outside of the bath and strode to the thin sliding door that separated the steam room from the main chamber.

The steam room was one of Lauren's favorite places in the entire palace. It was smaller, only 20 feet to a side, but it was covered floor to ceiling in pink granite from Corsica. A low bench wrapped around the outside of the room, and a beautiful brass sculpture of a maiden sat on a raised dais in the center. The statue held a large decanter, from which steam would pour at the turn of a cleverly hidden dial. Lauren had never been quite sure how the steam arrived to the statue, some byproduct of heating her bathwater, she supposed. Her still-sore body was grateful for it though, however it came to be.

Lauren turned the dial and sighed contentedly as the decanter let loose a steady column of steam into the air. Satisfied that the room would soon be to her liking, Lauren moved to the bench to lie down.

She must have dozed off, because she was suddenly aware of a soft tapping at the door. The room was thick with steam, and the door was sweating as much as she was.

"Enter," she called out sleepily.

"Your Majesty, you called for me?"

Lauren recognized the soothing voice of her apothecary, Peggy.

Lauren stood, and walked to the door. It was uncommon for her to go to a servant, rather than the other way around, but Peggy was a special exception. Peggy had been in Lauren's life for as long as she could remember. The plump little blonde woman carried herself well, especially for being in her late sixties, but having her stand in a room this hot would be rather cruel at her age.

"Your Majesty, how can I serve you this morning?"

Peggy bowed low as Lauren opened the door.

"Good morning Peggy. I... slept poorly. I was hoping you had something for a migraine, or for stiff joints, or... I guess anxiety?"

"Well now, that's unusual isn't it, your Majesty? Stiff joints? Migraines? In all your life you haven't needed any of my help dealing with those."

Lauren managed a weak smile. But Peggy was right. Lauren's powers had always seen to her perfect health. Soreness, stiffness, pain, these had always been exceptionally temporary.

"Don't you fret though, your Majesty. I have just what you need in my bags."

Lauren followed Peggy further into the main bath chamber, noticing excitedly that her bath was ready as well. The strong scents of citrus and lavender wafted up from the steaming water. Her servants must have added some of her favorite essential oils.

Peggy sat at one of the low stone benches beside the basin and reached into a white handbag with a big red cross on it. For some reason the bag and the symbol comforted Lauren, though she didn't recognize them.

"Here we are, this should help with your symptoms your Majesty."

She pulled a small bottle from the bag and handed it to Lauren, who looked it over. It was small, filled with amber liquid, and had fancy gold script on it. She couldn't read the language, but she noted a number at the bottom; 60.

Lauren had no reason to doubt her friend, but she felt hesitant. The tiny bottle seemed much heavier than it ought to be, and it filled her with unease. Still, she uncorked the bottle and took a sniff. It smelled of oak and plums. Her sense of Deja Vu returned.

"Thank you, Peggy, that will be all."

"Your Majesty."

The woman stood, bowed, and walked away. Lauren was left staring at the bottle in her hand. She decided to test the waters of her bath before committing to the medicine. Lauren set the bottle down at the very edge of the basin, and dipped a toe into the steaming liquid below.

It felt sensational.

Thrilled, she sat down and eased herself fully into the tub. It was a nearly religious experience. The hot water rose up her legs, relieving tension in her calves and thighs as she entered. Wading towards the center was like walking into a lover's embrace. The surface rose to meet her hips, her stomach, and finally her chest, stopping just below her breastbone when she reached the deepest parts. Her wings, still held aloft, had not yet touched the water, but she would soon fix that.

Lauren took a deep breath and then sat abruptly down in the center of the basin, immersing herself fully and plunging her wings beneath the still waters.

The incredible sensation of her feathers rippling beneath the surface was unlike anything she had experienced. The unusual resistance mixed with the oddity of buoyancy was mesmerizing. She felt herself smiling as she sat on the bottom of the basin, gazing up to the rippling surface just above her face.

She laid back upon the bottom of the basin, floating a few inches off the bottom for as long as she could. She relished the weightless feeling and the deep heat soaking into her.

Finally though, she had to come up for air.

She laughed out loud as she stood, bursting through the surface of the water. She brushed her hair back behind her ears and relished the electric feel of the cooler air against her wet skin. She stretched her wings high and wide, giving them a gentle shake to clear them of the heavy water droplets that were trapped between her feathers.

"You are beautiful."

Lauren let out a tiny shriek of fright at the unexpected

interruption. She spun around, sending water flying around the room. Instinctively, Lauren covered her exposed body with her arms and wings.

A tall, powerfully built man was standing at the edge of the basin, next to where she had left the bottle Peggy had given her. His coal-black skin was tight over his rippling muscles. He wore only a short kilt, and his attraction to her was impossible to hide. Not that he tried.

"Did I frighten you, my love?"

Lauren tried to still the pounding drum in her chest. For a moment she hadn't recognized Weyland, but how could that be possible?

"N-no, I was just surprised. That's all."

Weyland had a deep and obvious hunger in his eyes, and it made Lauren more uncomfortable than she could rationalize. *What's wrong with me?*

Lauren flashed a cautious but convincing smile at her husband, but she couldn't bring herself to uncover her body. She felt the familiar love she had for him, but it was accompanied by a strange, unnameable hesitation.

"Your water is cooling down my dear, let me fix that for you."

Without breaking eye contact, Weyland undid the ties at his hip and let the kilt fall to the tiles. Lauren blushed uncomfortably and looked away, but not soon enough to avoid seeing his desire for her.

She flushed at what she had seen. It was... attractive in an objective way, certainly, but she was conspicuously unaroused. She found herself hoping he would stay where he was.

He didn't.

Weyland stepped confidently into the pool, the water hissing on contact with his skin as he did so. He took slow, purposeful strides towards her, his eyes never leaving her face. She couldn't meet his gaze until after the water had risen above his hips.

With every foot closer, Lauren felt the urge to run building in her mind. Her legs tensed, her wings quivered with the need to be somewhere, anywhere else. She was unable to fight the strange hold he seemed to have on her, though. She was rooted in place.

"Are you hiding from me, my little bird? You were so free and... open a moment ago. I was rather enjoying watching you, actually."

Lauren's skin crawled. Weyland was right next to her now, walking around the perimeter formed in front of her by her wings. He circled her like a predator stalking injured prey. As he did so, he drew nearer. She screamed at herself internally to turn, to follow him, to keep her wingspan between them.

But her body rebelled.

Instead, she stood still as he moved behind her, close enough that she could feel the heat from his body against her back.

"Much better. Now smile, little bird, you're so much prettier when you smile."

Weyland reached a hand out, touching the side of Lauren's neck and causing her to flinch.

"Oh you seem so... tense! Let me help you relax."

His hands were massaging her shoulders. His skin was painfully hot, and she struggled against the urge to pull away. His half hearted massage gave way to his fingers tracing patterns down her back. His grasping fingers slipped lower and lower, reaching around to caress her hips as well.

Revulsion built within Lauren like a lake behind a dam, waiting for the single drop that proved too much. She found it when his touch made it's way forward, his fingers trying to slide between her legs.

With a sudden speed she wormed her way out of his torturous embrace. Turning swiftly, she faced him as she backed away. She fought back tears, hiding them behind a bright, smiling face as best she could.

"Lauren?"

Weyland looked annoyed.

He's accustomed to getting his way, as he deserves. Who are you to deny him?

Lauren was beginning to doubt the wisdom of her inner monologue.

"I... I'm not feeling well m-my l-love."

She stumbled over the last words. They felt foreign in her mouth.

"Well, come here. I'll make you feel better."

He was a beacon of arrogance, his arms widespread as if he expected her to fall into them.

"I think it's because I didn't have breakfast," she blurted out.

"Your servants didn't bring you breakfast? I'll have them executed."

The water around Weyland flashed into a rolling boil, turning Lauren's skin pink from the sudden heat.

"No! I mean, no I told them I wanted to eat after my bath. I think I may have overstayed though, I really need to eat."

The waters calmed. Somewhat.

"You're sure that's all?"

No.

"Yes, I'm sure."

"Very well, little bird. Let us eat."

"Oh no no, I can manage. It would be a shame to waste this wonderful bath, wouldn't it? C-come find me when you're finished."

Lauren, still backing up, bumped into the edge of the basin. She turned and climbed out as quickly as she could without acting suspiciously. Lauren scooped up the bottle and hurried towards the door.

She hoped he wouldn't follow her.

Lauren picked up the pace as soon as she cleared the curtains. She kept her head down and her pace brisk as she headed back for her bedroom. The hall was no longer welcoming. The guards she saw seemed menacing, though they still treated her with reverence.The walk that had taken her only a few minutes this morning seemed to last an eternity, but she finally made it to the curtains that marked her own private domain.

Passing through to doorway she noted that her clothes were not, in fact, set out for her. The discomfort she felt at wearing nothing but her own skin intensified.

"Erin!"

No answer.

"Erin!"

She yelled out again, trying to keep the hysteria out of her voice. Something was terribly, terribly wrong here.

"Y-your Majesty? Are you calling for me?"

Ellian poked her head around the corner.

"Yes! Why didn't you answer me?"

"I am so sorry, your Majesty. I-I thought you said 'Erin?'"

Erin... why is that name so familiar?

"I... I'm sorry, I think you're right. I meant to say Ellian."

"You seem, ah, disturbed by something your Majesty, is everything ok?"

"I'm ok, I think. Help me get dressed."

Why am I not ok?

Ellian dutifully ducked out of the room and returned a moment later with Chloe in tow. Both girls had their arms full of silks.

"A short dress today, your Majesty? Something to battle the summer heat?"

"No."

Lauren felt the need to cover herself.

"No, um, something longer. Floor length please."

Chloe produced a flowing brown satin dress. It was strapless, and had a slit from her ankle up to her thigh, but it would do.

Lauren stepped into it, holding her chest as the girls slipped it up from her feet and secured the clasps along her back.

"You look very beautiful your Majesty,"

"Thank you, Eri- Er... Ellian"

Seriously?

Would you like to take your breakfast here in your chambers, your Majesty?"

Lauren cast a paranoid look over her shoulder, but the doorway was clear. Still, she couldn't quite shake her discomfort from the bathhouse.

"No, thank you Ellian. I would prefer to eat outside. Perhaps the East Courtyard."

Ellian bowed low and headed out.

A few minutes later found Lauren seated on a low, wrought-iron chair overlooking the shimmering ocean. Her handmaidens sat quietly on the stones nearby. Chloe was humming softly while Ellian read a book. Lauren was sipping fresh apple juice from a crystal glass, sighing contentedly while she basked in the brilliant sunshine. An empty plate and a silver fork were all that remained of the most marvelous batch of pancakes Lauren had ever tasted.

Lauren set the glass down on the small round table next to her chair, enjoying the sparkle of the amber liquid for a moment before closing her eyes and leaning back against the cushions on her chair.

"Chloe, will you sing for me?"

"As you wish, your Majesty."

She cleared her voice softly before beginning a soft, melodic rendition of a familiar song.

"Amazing grace how sweet the sound
That saved a wretch like me.
I once was lost but now I'm found.
Was blind but now I see.
'Twas grace that taught my heart to fear..."

A gentle breeze tugged at Lauren's feathers and rustled the hem of her dress. It brought the unfamiliar scents of a deep forest, fresh rain, and wildflowers. She lost herself in the comfort of that breeze while Chloe sang, lost herself in the music, dozing in the warmth of the day as it built.

"Marvelous."

Weyland's voice stole her breath away. The hairs on the back of her neck pricked up and her relaxed posture tightened like a bowstring.

"A burlap sack would look stunning on you, my little bird. In this dress, however, you outshine the sun."

She could feel him there, standing at the archway just a few yards behind her. The memory of his hands pawing across her body made her shiver with fright.

"Leave us."

"Yes, your Majesty," the girls spoke in unison, and headed for the exit.

"Wait!"

She cried out just a little too desperately, stood just a little too quickly. She knew she was caught as the chair toppled over with a dull clang. Lauren wracked her brain for something to ask for. For any reason at all to keep them here so she wouldn't be alone with him.

She turned, hoping to find inspiration somewhere as she did.

The girls were frozen mid-step, unsure of what to do.

"Um, b-bring me some... um."

"Wine. It seems my little bird needs some wine. You may bring it to my chambers."

Weyland's voice had an uncomfortable edge to it. Chloe nodded while casting a furtive look back at Lauren. Was that sorrow in her eyes?

Lauren watched helplessly as the two left.

They were alone.

"You're avoiding me, little bird."

"No, I-"

"Enough!"

Weyland's voice went from playfully dangerous to an outright yell, shocking Lauren into silence. She took an involuntary step backwards at his sudden anger. He mirrored her movement, stepping closer to her.

"Now... my little dove. You know I despise that word. No one has the right to deny me, not even you. You understand this, yes?"

He took another step.

The walls of the courtyard felt like they were closing in around her. Lauren fought her claustrophobia and looked for an exit. But there wasn't one, she was cornered.

Or am I?

Lauren had no sooner thought to flex her powerful wings than Weyland's hand shot out and gripped her forearm. She felt her skin blistering at his wrathful grasp. Heat cascaded from him in waves.

"I asked you if you understood me."

She could do nothing but nod. Her eyes watered with pain, but he didn't seem to notice the tears on her cheeks.

"Good."

A moment of dizziness preceded a loud crackling bang that sent Lauren sprawling to the floor. She was no longer in the courtyard, instead the cold stone beneath her outstretched form was smooth black marble tile.

The floor was both familiar and utterly foreign to her. She knew it was his bedroom, she could see every inch of it laid out in her mind. But, in the same way, she knew she had never been here before. Primal instincts were stirring inside her, rebelling at what she simply could not believe was happening.

She was still disoriented from appearing here when she felt his large hand grabbing a fistful of her hair. An acrid burning smell filled her nose and tears streamed down her face as she hissed in pain.

"P-please, you're hurting me!"

"Little bird, it's you that is hurting me! Do you think I like to do this? Don't you think it pains me to see you act this way?"

Weyland's belief in his words was evident from his tone, and the injured look on his face as he dragged Lauren to her feet.

"Don't you think it's cruel to strut around naked in our house, to flaunt this beautiful dress and then to deny me my right?"

Lauren's wild eyes flitted back and forth, focusing sharply on the myriad details of the room. A massive, black-sheeted bed was immediately beside them, polished mahogany furniture was accented by gold trim and brass fixtures.

Lauren's terrified vision was obscured as Weyland pressed his lips forcefully against hers.

She let out a stifled scream, pushing against his bare chest with all her might. It was no use, he was stronger than her by miles. All she got for her effort was blistered hands. She felt his other hand wrap around her back and crush her against him. His body rubbed against hers, his bare flesh held at bay only by the thin fabric of her dress.

He slid his hand up her leg, riding the slit in her dress and hiking up her hem as he did so. Panic gripped her, and lent her sudden clarity. She clawed at his eyes like a wildcat, digging at them with all her strength.

It worked.

For a brief moment he let go of her, instinctively jerking away to protect his eyes.

Trapped between him and the dresser behind her, Lauren leapt onto the bed. She scrambled across the silk sheets, hoping to cross it before he recovered. She nearly made it. Just inches from freedom, she felt his vice-like grip on her ankle.

"What a cruel, selfish thing to do."

Weyland's tone was flat, with no hint of remorse.

With an effortless yank, he slid her back across the bed towards him. She tried to squirm away but he pinned her beneath his bulky frame. His weight, mostly centered on her hips, was crushing.

"I don't know what happened to you. What brought this sudden disobedient, disrespectful streak."

He shifted slightly forward, resting on her diaphragm and knocking the wind out of her. Her lungs empty, her screams were barely more than whispers. Weyland reached down and grasped the front of her dress with both of his hands, ripping it open and exposing her chest to him. His eyes widened with desire. A heartless, lustful smile was plastered on his face as his fingers traced her collarbone and lower. Screwing her eyes shut. Lauren reached out desperately for anything to defend herself. Her desperate fingers found a heavy wooden box on the nightstand. She locked her hand onto it and swung it as hard as she could.

Her clumsy swing was easily countered. Weyland struck the box from her hand with such force that it exploded into splinters. Lauren's eyes widened with surprise at the sudden piercing pain she felt in her chest.

Looking down, she could see a large splinter impaling her chest, just above her left breast. Weyland paused, exchanging a startled glance with her.

Blood welled up around the wood, pouring off either side of her chest and staining the brown satin tatters of her dress.

I remember.

Flashing red and blue lights washed over the pair as the room started to darken and spin. The smell of vomit and strong liquor flooded the bedroom. Only it wasn't a bedroom anymore, it was cold asphalt covered in tiny shards of wood and glass.

Waves of memories washed over Lauren as reality flickered in and out. The events of the years before her fall from the tower in Chicago, compressed into a few heartbeats, flashed before her eyes too quickly to process. Weyland was gone, the bedroom and the palace were gone, replaced by a tornado of sights, colors, and sounds from her past.

Lauren sat bolt upright, gasping for air like a drowned man returned to life. She thrashed around for a moment, fighting the blankets that lay upon her.

Wherever she was, it was dark. She was in a large, comfortable bed of some kind. Aware that she was lost, and that she had just made a considerable amount of noise, Lauren froze and tried to listen for clues as to where she might be. She could hear the distant rumble of machinery, but it seemed to be far away. The room smelled of incense, but also fresh concrete. More than that, she had no clue. She focused on herself instead.

She was clothed, sort of. She was wearing what felt like lingerie, some sort of lacy bra and panty set with a short kimono that was loosely belted at her hips. Other than the unorthodox wardrobe, which brought its own set of uncomfortable questions, everything seemed to be in order. She was stiff, a little cold, and felt bruised all over her body, but she was intact.

A faint light approached, leading her to duck back into the covers with her eyes barely cracked. She tensed, preparing to defend herself as the light drew nearer. Eventually, she could see that it was not so distant as she had expected. Rather, it had been behind a screen of hanging beads marking a doorway.

A young woman appeared from the darkness. She was pretty, a tiny blonde woman with bright blue eyes and thick glasses. In her hands she held a small, battery powered camping lantern. She moved very quietly, and Lauren was sure she wouldn't have woken up from her presence if she had still been asleep. Lauren couldn't make out much more about the woman until she came nearer to the bed. She was wearing a sheer, cream-colored dress and an intricate gold choker-style necklace. Her fancy clothes made the drab, pocket-covered bag slung over her shoulder much more noticeable.

Lauren didn't get a threatening feel from the girl, but decided it was better to be safe than sorry. She waited, frozen, while the girl cast a furtive look around and then set her lantern at a small table next to the bed. She dug in the bag for a moment, and then produced a small jar of something. After another cautious look around, she sat on the bed next to Lauren.

The woman pulled the covers back, exposing Lauren's body to the dim light. It was all Lauren could do not to flinch, or to look down and see more clearly what she was doing.

Her composure lasted only until the woman dabbed something cold and wet on her inner thigh.

She sharply inhaled at the unexpected sensation, revealing herself. Her visitor let out a tiny squeak, and covered her mouth with her hands.

Lauren sat up like a rocket, gripping the girl before she could try to escape. Surprisingly, the woman didn't even try. Instead she embraced Lauren, crying silently into her shoulder as she squeezed her tight.

"Lay back, my lady, I need to tend to your burns."

Burns?

Lauren looked down at herself. Her inner thighs were covered in deep burns. They were healing before her eyes, but they were still quite serious. Lauren wondered at how fresh they might be. Her stomach, breasts, neck, and from the feel of it her back and buttocks were similarly burned.

"How did this happen to me?"

The woman burst into tears. She cried herself hoarse, unable to speak as she embraced Lauren in the darkness.

Chapter 4

Lauren's stomach churned as Natalie told her what had happened in the two months since she'd tried to kill herself. Weyland had picked her up in chicago and brought her here, to Athens, where an army of slaves was rebuilding the Parthenon in honor of her "rescuer."

She had nearly recovered when he induced the dream-state in her mind, and he had kept her that way ever since. Natalie revealed that she too had been taken into the strange vision-realm, albeit for only for a few minutes at a time. Even now, parts of the dream felt more real than some of her memories. It was a confusing blur of disjointed information that had her questioning what was real and what wasn't.

There were other things, darker things, that Natalie refused to speak of. Like why she applied burn cream to Lauren's body every morning.

Hours passed in the pre-dawn morning and a sickness grew inside Lauren while Natalie spoke. It was a toxic mixture of rage, self-loathing, humiliation, and guilt.

"I have to be going soon, Lauren. He visits you each morning after the sun rises. He enjoys watching it and then ah... he comes and looks at you while you sleep."

Lauren shook her head no.

"You have to get me out of here."

It wasn't a question.

Natalie reached a hand to her throat, absentmindedly touching the choker around her neck. Lauren could see the fear in her eyes as she considered her command.

"Lauren I... I want to help you but I've seen what he can do. He sets his rules and he follows them. But he can be very cruel to those who break them"

Lauren knew she was right. She could feel it in her battered flesh that he was indeed cruel. But she would not stay.

"Then I'll figure it out on my own."

Lauren stood unsteadily. Her legs wobbled, but her gift had kept her from losing too much muscle while she was bedridden. She peered in the semi-darkness, locating a dresser and sliding the drawers open silently. Thankfully, they were full of clothes, so she wouldn't have to run around quite as exposed as she had in the dream.

No. Not a dream. And not a nightmare either. More like the perverted desires of an apex predator. She shook her head, refusing to acknowledge what she knew. The twin comforts of shock and denial cushioned her mind. They helped her slip into a dress in the darkness and make her way to the door.

"Wait, Lauren."

Natalie's hissing whisper was like a shout in the quiet room. Lauren paused, she looked back at Natalie, her face illuminated softly in the light she had brought with her.

"I wish I could help you."

Lauren said nothing.

She was running through a maze of corridors. Some of them were very old, they had velvet ropes cordoning off areas and were filled with small placards bearing explanations of what she was supposed to be looking at. Other areas looked new. Fresh concrete and stone married up perfectly with the existing architecture.

The buzzing sound of power tools seemed to echo from several directions at once. Every time she passed an intersection it seemed she went deeper into the labyrinth. Finally though, she saw someone. A man in blue overalls. He was covered in bits of plaster, carrying a large bucket in one hand and a short ladder over his shoulder.

Lauren wasn't sure if she should approach him and ask for help. What if he alerted someone? What if he turned her in? Did she have a choice?

"Excuse me!"

she hurried towards him, her bare feet tapping lightly against the stone floor.

He looked around for a moment, confused, and then he saw her. His eyes widened and he dropped to the floor with a clatter. Well, it was a better reaction than she had feared.

"Get up, please. I need to get outside. Do you speak English?"

The man looked at her dumbfounded. He answered her, but she had no clue what he was saying. Lauren wracked her brain. She didn't know any greek, it's not like her rural high school had a course after all.

Wait. Maybe that was it! She tried to think of latin words she had learned in school. Anything that might relate to the outside world at all.

"Ahh... H-Helios?"

She pointed upwards, trying to pantomime a sun by making a fist and wiggling her fingers near it. He looked like a game show contestant who had run out of lifelines.

"Helios...?"

He mulled the word over, scratching his chin for a moment.

"Ah! Ilios? Ilios!"

He stood, pulling up his shirt sleeve to reveal a tattoo of the sun and pointed at it excitedly.

Lauren nearly burst into tears right then and there. She nodded.

The man gave her a big smile and a little bow. He turned and started walking off down the corridor. Lauren pulled up next to him. He was talking as he walked, gesturing at the new construction. He was clearly very proud of his work. Lauren tried to get him to hurry in every way she could. She walked a bit ahead of him, she made impatient sighs and made a show of looking down the hallway ahead of them.

He was totally immune.

Rounding a corner, they met another group of workers. The new people greeted her companion after bowing to her. They gave him sideways looks but he seemed to be explaining to them what had happened.

At great length.

Lauren tapped her foot, but the men didn't seem to notice at all. She had no watch, no method of knowing the time, but these men were certainly just showing up for work. That had to mean Weyland would come for her soon.

She could take it no longer.

"Hey!"

She snapped her fingers, and, when that didn't work, she loudly clapped her hands.

"Hey, God damnit!"

The men looked at her, cowed by her tone. They stood quietly staring at her.

"Ilios. Take me to ilios now!"

Her original companion gave a low wave to his friends and muttered something. He held out a hand, indicating that Lauren should proceed. She did so, and the two of them continued at a much more acceptable pace.

Finally, Lauren could see daylight. The pair entered a large foyer. The room was filled with half-finished frescoes and the marble floor was still littered with construction equipment and paint-covered drop cloths.

Lauren tapped her guide on the shoulder and thanked him profusely. He didn't understand her words, of course, but the big hug she gave him seemed to break the language barrier.

Turning, she sprinted across the room and out into the open air. It was just after dawn, and the sun cast long shadows across the courtyard before her. A dull rumble shook the ground. He must have discovered her absence.

Lauren wasted no time taking to the skies. Even so, she was barely 30 feet off the ground when Weyland appeared with a crackling bang.

"Lauren!"

Was that concern in his voice? It was hard for Lauren to tell, she was too focused on getting away from him. She rose another twenty feet and pulled into a tight circle. Risking a glance she saw he was still earthbound below her. The feeling of freedom she had when she flew intensified. She was safe, untouchable, a leaf in the wind.

"Lauren, where the hell are you going?"

With every passing moment Lauren felt her strength growing. Her body was whole and complete once more. The early rays of the sun charged her body and renewed her courage.

"Leave me alone!"

He looked... shocked. Hurt, even.

"What? Why? Come down here so we can talk."

He seemed frighteningly genuine. Confused, frustrated, but also concerned.

She hovered a while, struggling internally. At last she decided she would fly lower, but she couldn't bring herself to land and be within his grasp. He looked annoyed as she dropped to 30 feet but no lower.

"Lauren-"

"Stop. Stop it, you don't talk."

His eyes narrowed and his already dark skin sank a few shades darker.

"What did you do to me?"

"I put you into a dream state so your body could continue to recover. It's harmless."

"Harmless? You call what you did to me harmless!"

She was shouting now, and the workers who happened to be in the courtyard had all frozen to observe the spectacle.

"Lauren, my little bird, you're over-"

"Don't call me that."

"You're overreacting. Come down here and we can talk more over breakfast. I'll have the servants prepare pancakes for you, your favorite."

Lauren was flabbergasted.

"D-do you really think pancakes can fix this? Can make up for what you... did to me?"

"I'm honestly not sure what you're mad about. The dream state reflects, in some ways, the desires of the dreamer. Obviously the framework is my design but most of the details were drawn from things you subconsciously desire-"

Lauren swooped to the ground, overcome with rage. She marched up to him and jammed a finger in his face. Her body trembled uncontrollably as she confronted him.

"How dare you. How dare you say I wanted... that."
"Well, why shouldn't you? You, like me, are unique. You were born for me, can there be any question about it?"

Lauren opened and shut her mouth several times. She was shocked at his arrogance.

"You're a monster."

"No, I am a God. You would do well to respect that, my love. You have the incredible privilege of being born the natural queen to my kingdom-"

He was cut off by an audible smack as Lauren slapped him hard across the face. The courtyard fell utterly silent. Lauren ignored the blisters on her palm, she regretted nothing.

"You're sick. You don't own-"

Weyland whipped a hand out, taking Lauren by the throat and lifting her bodily from the ground. She struggled in his grasp, but her buffeting wings did nothing to lessen his steely grasp.

She could feel deep burns forming underneath his fingers, and when she cried in pain the air in her throat seemed to burn as well.

"You are mine by right. I have waited millennia for you, and I will not be denied."

Lauren stopped her struggling. Her vision was starting to blacken at the edges, but she made steady eye contact with Weyland.

"I'd rather die."

His eyes widened at the conviction in her voice.

"Would you? Truly?"

Weyland's aura of heat intensified. Lauren's exposed skin turned pink and then cherry red. Her lungs felt like a blast furnace, every breath more agonizing than the last. Her gift fought valiantly against the damage to her body, but it was a losing battle.

She tried to respond, but was unable to get a word out around the blazing pain in her lungs.

"What's that? You have an answer for me?"

She nodded.

He turned down the heat enough for her to croak out a single word.

"Yes."

An expression of genuine confusion fought it's way past his anger. He dropped her to the ground. She lay there, steaming, while he spoke.

"How? How can it be that you so reject your rightful place at my side?"

She was in too much pain to respond. Instead, she stayed still, kneeling on the ground and gathering her strength.

"No matter, perhaps a reminder of the consequences for your disobedience will... encourage you to see things my way."

Weyland closed his eyes, a look of great concentration on his face. Deep glowing red cracks appeared on his body. First on his chest, and then spreading to his arms, his neck, and his head. The cracks widened, revealing what looked like molten steel beneath his flesh.

The only warning the citizens of Athens had was a moment of dull rumbling in the ground. Within seconds a massive explosion sent ash and broken stone rocketing into the sky in the middle of the city. Lauren heard the explosion, and seconds later she felt the shockwave roar past her. She stood, looking out over the edge of the Acropolis. A geyser of liquid flame poured upward in the heart of the city. Through the smoke and debris still raining down she could see lava pouring into crowded streets from a newly birthed volcano.

She couldn't help but be awed by the power that he demonstrated. He met her gaze, his eyes white hot coals as he smiled at her.

"There you are, little bird. The price of your temper tantrum. Satisfied?"

Lauren stood, making a show of doing so unsteadily. She gave her singed wings a flex, they felt alright from what she could tell.

"You have my answer."

With that, she leapt into the air faster than he could react. As soon as she was clear of the earth she pulled another tight circle, coming to hover above him.

Her new vantage point gave her an even clearer view of the blazing city. Once upon a time her heart would have shattered at the wanton destruction. She was inwardly ashamed that the most she could muster was a short pang of guilt. But she had given enough, she had died for those people. And what had they done to save her from this man? To save her from... no, she refused to acknowledge it.

He looked surprised at her answer, but also in a twisted way, impressed.

"You are right to scorn them, what have they ever done for you? You are above them Lauren! You should be worshipped as I am. Worshipped as a goddess!"

His words echoed her thought uncomfortably, and rather than stay and listen she turned to fly away, ignoring his calls.

"Don't worry, little bird. You have all of immortality to come back to me."

The thought sickened her.

She turned out over the city, making her way North. She tried to ignore the screams and devastation below her as she passed over the wreckage from Weyland's display.

You've given enough, You don't owe them anything.

Lauren repeated her mantra over and over, wielding it like a shield.

She headed higher, gaining altitude until she could no longer see their faces.

The hours passed as Lauren continued to head inland. She allowed her body to move on autopilot while she mulled over the events of the morning. She tried to sort out what she should do now. Weyland's words kept gnawing at her thoughts.

Was it true? Was she immortal? Was she stuck here, in this life where everything she did seemed to go horribly wrong? He must be telling the truth, he had no reason to lie about it. Besides, she had clearly survived the thousand foot fall she had taken. Lauren thought back to the peace she had felt as she thought she was about to die. The certainty that at last it would all end.

She sighed wistfully.

So what, he was right about her immortality. That didn't mean he wasn't lying about the rest. Right?

Her relaxed face turned into a scowl as she considered his words. The dream was based on her subconscious desires he had said. The... things he had done were *her* design, *her* intention. Lauren knew it was wrong, but the seed of doubt found fertile ground in her psyche.

She could feel her pulse quicken as thoughts started to pierce the veil of her intentional denial. She tried to stomp them back into the dark, unseen corners of her mind but they were reluctant to move. Lauren knew she would have to process them eventually, but she was afraid to face them. Afraid to face who she was, and who she would never be again.

Instead, she distracted herself by looking at the landscape below. The sun was high in the sky, telling her it must be close to noon or even after. Cities dotted the foreign landscape below her, mixing with the greenery of pastures and forests. The sight of the trees below gave her some comfort.

And an idea.

Lauren tucked her wings, accelerating rapidly as she dove earthward. Wind rushed past her, leaving a high whistle in her ears as she streaked to the ground. The speed was exhilarating. Her eyes watered and her hair whipped wildly as she dove faster and faster. The ground raced up to meet her, small dots and shapes resolving themselves into terrain features as she closed the distance.

Lauren waited until the last possible second to pull up. She held out her hand and let wildflowers tickle her fingers as she blazed across an open field just a few feet off the ground. She could see the treeline approaching in the distance. With a slight adjustment to her broad feathers, she was upright and slowing down. She touched down into a graceful trot with a few hard flaps of her wings. Her heart was pounding again, but this time from exertion. The rush of adrenaline cleared her mind. Mostly. She relished the high for as long as she could.

How long has it been since I went running?

She knew what Dustin would have said, that she needed to do this more. He had always encouraged physical exhaustion as a healthier alternative to drinking.

Hmm, drinking.

Lauren was surprised that alcohol hadn't been the first thing on her mind. She licked her lips subconsciously. Not that it was an option, but Lauren felt less... need for it. The thirst was still there, but not like it was before. Maybe a few months sober had helped?

Erin would be so proud; Here she was, finding silver linings after all.

A cool breeze dried the sweat on her brow and carried the fragrant cypress trees to her nose. It wasn't the pine and oak of her youth, but it was wild, untamed, home. Lauren sorted through her feelings while she walked, reaching her hands out absentmindedly to brush against the trees as she passed.

Everything felt distant.

Her memories, her life, the events before her fall. It all seemed like someone else's story. Like she was reading it in a book, rather than it being her own life.

She stopped, sitting cross-legged against a large tree. She closed her eyes and tried to clear her mind, to be fully in the moment. The soft loam of the forest floor made for a comfortable resting place, and the dappled shade and sunlight danced across her eyelids. She took deep breaths, holding them a moment before releasing them.

A snapping twig startled her. She froze, holding her breath and listening as hard as she could. She had just convinced herself she was imagining things when a brightly colored shaped flitted behind a tree a few yards away.

"Hello?"

Lauren stood and self-consciously brushed dirt and leaves from her dress.

Her wings flicked open and stayed there, twitching, ready to carry her skyward in a heartbeat.

"Wait!"

An attractive young woman, three or perhaps four years Lauren's senior, peeked out from behind the tree in front of her and waved.

"Sorry, I'm so sorry to intrude. I happened to be out here taking photographs and... well I saw you fly in."

The woman's soft, clear voice had a pleasant british accent. Her short, walnut brown curls stood out against the lime green tank top she was wearing. The low cut garment showed off a tight, curvy frame that perfectly accented the snug khakis hugging her softly flaring hips. She had a small bag slung over her shoulder and an expensive looking camera in her hands.

Lauren relaxed.

"You speak english?"

The woman laughed and stuck a hand out to her.

"I *am* English dear. Valerie Chatwick, and it's a pleasure to meet you, Ms. Corvidae."

Lauren accepted the firm handshake and smiled. The woman had an aura of trustworthiness. Her genuine smile was infectious and her mannerisms put Lauren instantly at ease.

"So you're a photographer? Are you here on vacation?"

"You could say it's a combination of work and recreation. Preferably more of the latter and less of the former. I actually took some shots of you earlier, I hope you don't mind. I could show them to you?"

Lauren nodded shyly, she couldn't help herself. She had never been asked to look at candid photographs of herself. Not since her wings came in at least. She'd done plenty of planned publicity shoots with her crew while she was touring, but nothing this candid and unexpected.

Valerie came over and flicked a switch on her camera. The clear display on the back of the device showed frame after expertly composed frame. Lauren found herself blushing. She looked *good*.

One shot in particular captured Lauren's attention. She was silhouetted against the clear blue sky, backlit by the sun. She really did look like an angel.

"You like that one?"

She nodded.

"Good, I'll get a print made up and framed for you."

"Oh you don't have to do that...."

"Oh nonsense, it's my pleasure. I've got most of my equipment in my lorry up the way, if you want to join me? I know you've got those gorgeous wings and all but if you want a lift I'd be happy to offer my services?"

"Uh, lorry?"

Valerie laughed and started off through the trees.

"A lorry is a truck, love! You'll have to pardon my Britishisms!"

Lauren hurried to catch up, mirroring Valerie's laughter. The humor was not at Lauren's expense, at least it didn't feel that way. It felt more like, well, genuine happiness at being in Lauren's company.

The rugged vehicle that Lauren found waiting for them was an impressive sight. It looked like it could handle anything from the mountains of Colorado to the Serengeti in Kenya. The over-sized truck had a roll cage, a few big military looking jugs of water and extra fuel, even a shovel bolted to the side of it. In a word, it was awesome.

Lauren had to use the sideboard to climb into the cab and was pleasantly surprised with how much room she found inside. A thin layer of starbucks cups, crumpled papers, and protein-bar wrappers littered the inside, but it was otherwise very well organized. Valerie had three separate laptops, including one that sat in a mount on her dashboard and seemed to be displaying weather data and a stream of related numbers.

Radio equipment, a big first aid kit, and several changes of clothes lent the impression of a secret agent meets tomb raider lifestyle that intrigued her.

"So, you're a...?"

"Photographer, mostly. Generally landscapes, sometimes wildlife, and when I see someone truly magical, I do people."

She winked at Lauren, who blushed a bit at the compliment. Any immediate follow-up question was drowned out as Valerie fired up the beast's engine. It roared like a lion and carried the two off over the rocky Greek hillside.

The two chatted idly as the afternoon passed. Lauren was shocked at how comfortable the conversations were. The women swapped travel stories for the first several hours. Lauren was impressed to learn that her host had seen more of the world than she had. Valerie had been to 87 different countries in her career, and had excellent stories from every single one it seemed.

Lauren's stories were less fanciful, more directly related to her gifts. Still, Valerie made her feel accomplished in her own right rather than turning it into a competition. When she spoke about the Vatican though, that was when Valerie truly made her feel special.

"You've been *inside* the papal apartments!"

Valerie was staring at Lauren, her sparkling emerald eyes green with jealousy.

"Yes, but only for a day!"

"Even so, they must have been magnificent. Tell me everything, oh please I insist!"

The truck chewed on loose gravel as they drifted towards the edge of the narrow country road. Valerie made a nonchalant adjustment and put them back on course. Her driving had been this way since they started and Lauren was slowly growing accustomed to the careless wandering of the large vehicle.

"Alright, but keep your eyes on the road will ya?"

"Oh where's the danger, I'd like to think I'm fun enough that you'd make sure I stuck around, no?"

Valerie regretted her words the moment they passed her lips. Lauren fell quiet and looked out the window.

"Lauren, I'm sorry. I didn't mean to presume that you'd use your gift. Or to make light of it. I... know you've lost people, people you couldn't save. That was very insensitive of me."

Lauren couldn't help it. She was reminded of the very real limitations on her power. Of the times it had failed her. She drew a shaky breath and tried to smile convincingly at her new companion.

"It's ok, I know you didn't mean anything by it."

"No, Lauren, it isn't ok. More than that, it's ok to not be ok. You're only human."

Suddenly it clicked. Why Lauren felt so at ease with this near-total stranger. She treated Lauren like just another person. Like she was human. This simple revelation, this singular consideration for her humanity, touched Lauren in a way she hadn't felt in far, far too long.

"Hey... hey, you're ok. You're safe with me."

Valerie pulled the truck over to the side of the road and reached across to give her crying passenger a hug.

"I'm sorry I'm such a wreck. It's ok we can keep going."

Lauren sniffled and tried to dry her eyes, feeling foolish. Valerie's expression held nothing but concern and understanding. Her new friend's acceptance only served to encourage her embarrassing waterworks further.

"You sure? We can rest a while, I could make some tea?"

"No, please. Let's keep going."

The pair rumbled off in silence. It took a while for Valerie to strike up conversation again, leaving Lauren to wonder at what she must be thinking.

"So. Have you ever been to Macedonia?"

"Macedonia? No, where is that?"

Lauren looked at Valerie, who had burst out laughing.

"What's so funny?"

"Macedonia is where we are about to be. It's one of the countries just north of Greece."

She pointed out ahead of them. Lauren hadn't been paying attention but sure enough there was a small border checkpoint visible a few miles distant. She panicked a little, how would she get across without being seen? What if Weyland was looking for her?

"They can't see me!"

Valerie was surprised at Lauren's vehement objection, but took it in stride.

"Oh, um, alright then. Hop in the back, there's a kind of bed set up back there."

Lauren wasted no time scrambling out of her seat, past the second row of seating and into a sort of loft area. she was confronted with a small mountain of pillows, blankets, and clothing.

"This is a bed? It looks like a disaster area..."

"I know, I'm so embarrassed! What on earth would my mother say? But it will have to do love, just uh... burrow down as best you can!"

Lauren wormed her way as deep into the pile as she could. It was at least two feet before she hit what felt like a mattress of some kind. It was impossible to tell if her wings were fully covered, so she simply hoped the border guards wouldn't look too closely.

The truck rattled to a stop and Lauren waited with bated breath. Between the thick layers of cloth piled on her and the powerful engine she couldn't hear anything. Time seemed to stretch on and Lauren grew more and more nervous. Finally, though, the truck started moving again. Lauren waited, unsure of her surroundings. She debated whether or not to emerge but decided to trust that Valerie would let her know when it was safe to come out again.

A few minutes passed and the truck slowed down again. The next thing she knew Valerie was calling her name.

"Lauren, we're good to go! You can come out now."

Lauren clambered from the pile with an impressive lack of grace, and scowled at the gales of laughter that Valerie struggled to stifle.

"Oh I *am* sorry about that."

Somehow, Lauren wasn't sure that was entirely true. To be honest though, it felt good to laugh. Lauren found herself giggling while Valerie untangled her from bits of clothing that had gotten wrapped around her.

"Oh!"

Valerie's cheeks turned scarlet.

"Ahem, ah. Sorry!"

Lauren turned to see Valerie's slim fingers working to extricate a lacey, red and black thong from her left wing. A hundred things to say crossed Lauren's mind, but none of them seemed quite right so she simply bit her lip and tried to cover a smile.

"Oh goodness, I'm mortified! It's a proper English Woman's worst nightmare."

Valerie was fumbling with the garment and blushing hard as she failed to untangle it. When she was finally able to get it clear of Lauren's feather she balled it up and threw it back into the bed area. She fanned herself with her now free hand and smiled nervously.

"Well! It's rather hot in here yes? Better get going!"

She didn't wait for an answer, bouncing back into the driver's seat and firing up the truck instead.

"You know, they were actually pretty cute."

Lauren teased her friend, and got a playful shove on the shoulder for her efforts.

"You don't strike me as the shy type."

Valerie laughed and gave a grudging shrug.

"Generally love, I'm not. Doesn't do to be overly proper in my line of work. That being said, there are things you pick up being a Brit, and they can be hard to shake."

"And untangling your lingerie from a friend is…"

"Definitely one of them! How bout some music?"

She jammed at the console and a wild, raucous tune burst forth from the speakers. Lauren didn't know what to call it, honestly. It certainly didn't fit any genre she could identify, and the words were completely foreign to her as well. It was also incredibly loud.

"Valerie."

Her companion didn't hear her over the explosion of electronic polka madness blasting through the cab. The console was covered with too many buttons and knobs to try to adjust it herself, so she tried again.

"Valerie!"

She looked over, wearing a pained expression on her still-flushed cheeks.

"This is really, really bad music!"

She laughed and sheepishly turned the volume down to a more manageable level.

"It really, really is, isn't it?"

They exchanged nervous laughter and Valerie pointed out a binder filled with CD's for Lauren to choose from. In no time they were singing along to 90's pop while the miles ticked by. Music took the place of conversation, and the awkward encounter faded into the comfortable afternoon.

"So, where to?"

Lauren was caught off guard by the question. After all, Valerie was driving, she'd assumed she had a destination in mind.

"Where to? Like, right now?"

"Well, yeah. Where to for the evening, and where to after that?"

Lauren hadn't considered where she would sleep for the night. That wasn't something she'd had to worry about in a very long time. The idea of finding a town with a hotel was attractive in that it meant a comfortable bed, but Lauren had no desire to be seen, recognized, and harassed. She hadn't shaken the fear that Weyland might find her, either. The bed in the back of the truck wouldn't make a bad option, it was big enough for both of them certainly, but she didn't want to impose either.

"Well..."

Valerie cut her off.

"If you want, we could sleep in the truck tonight? It'll be a tight squeeze perhaps but I've got running water, heat, even a camp shower for the morning?"

Lauren nodded gratefully.

"Yeah? Honestly I won't be offended if you'd prefer a hotel or something."

"I think this'll be perfect."

Every now and again they would pass through some small town, but Valerie was careful to avoid larger cities whenever she could. As the sun started to set, it filled the cab with a rosy glow that matched the warmth they felt within. Somehow, against all odds, in this giant metal behemoth Lauren was starting to feel like she was home again.

It was after nightfall when Valerie slowed the truck and turned off road. She flicked on floodlights and rumbled into an overgrown field, rolling to stop inside a small stand of trees.

"Aren't you worried we'll get in trouble? What if somebody owns this land?"

Valerie's voice took on a conspiratorial whisper as she replied.

"We'll be out by daybreak, and honestly in most of Eastern Europe there are a lot of gray areas if you catch my meaning."

Lauren didn't, but she nodded anyway. She turned the floodlights back off and plunged the clearing back into darkness. Valerie's truck continued to surprise Lauren. Along with the tiny stove that Valerie had promised, it had a battery bank to provide light, music, and warmth throughout the night.

The two were relishing each other's companionship over a dinner of canned soup when Valerie fell quiet. Lauren looked up from her chicken and dumplings. Her friend had a strange, hesitant expression on her face.

"You ok?"

"Yeah... yeah I'm alright. I just. I'm not used to having company, that's all. I'm really glad you're here."

Lauren flushed. She couldn't remember the last time someone had expressed gratitude at her presence without actively trying to get something from her.

"I envy you, Valerie. You have this... this freedom. You go where you want, do what you want. This monster-truck, this home of yours; it's a sanctuary you can take wherever you wish."

Valerie's cynical smile told Lauren that she had her own difficulties. Her own unrealized wishes and dreams. She set down what remained of her dinner and held a hand out to Lauren.

"Come with me, I want to show you something."

Lauren obliged, setting her own soup can down in one of the cupholders and allowing herself to be led out of the cabin. Valerie brought her outside and motioned for her to wait a moment. She ducked back into the truck and emerged a moment later with a rolled up blanket and a small camera bag under one arm, and a wine bottle in her free hand.

Lauren eyed the wine bottle hungrily, feeling a familiar thirst well up inside her. She blinked and looked away, hoping Valerie hadn't noticed.

"We're sleeping outside?"

She laughed and shook her head.

"Come here, I think you're gonna love this. It won't take long."

She walked around to the front of the truck and, using the cattle-pusher on the front as a ladder, she climbed onto the hood and started to spread the blanket out on the broad surface.

Lauren got the gist, but rather than help she caught herself admiring her host in the dim light of the crescent moon. Her khakis were snug already, and bending over to arrange the hood of the truck made them hug her body even closer.

"Distracted?"

Lauren jumped, her eyes flitting from Valerie's shapely behind to her face, which was looking back over her shoulder with an amused grin.

"Sorry, just uh, wondering what you're up to! Let me give you a hand."

The two made short work of setting up the blanket. Valerie held her hand out and Lauren gripped it firmly, climbing onto the hood with her friend's help. Valerie scooted back up against the windshield and laid back. She patted the blanket beside herself, indicating that Lauren should join her. The windshield and the hood formed a perfectly reclined seat.

"So..."

"Shh, look."

Valerie pointed skyward. Lauren looked up and what she saw took her breath away. A billion stars filled the sky. The thin slice of moon couldn't compete with the blazing pinpoints that filled her vision. Lauren was swept away, back to her childhood. She hadn't seen the stars this clearly since camping in the Grand Canyon as a kid with her parents.

The spiral arm of the Milky Way was clearly visible against the vivid black night.

"Wow."

What else was there to say?

The two sat in silence, lost in the splendor, for what must have been an hour. Lauren felt Valerie shift beside her. Her pulse quickened a bit when she brushed against her arm.

Was it an accident?

She didn't have to wait long for an answer. Valerie cautiously scooted closer until they were leaning against one another. Lauren risked a glance at her, and saw that Valerie was staring at her.

"W-what?"

"I'm sorry, I know it's rude to stare. You're just... beautiful, you know?"

Lauren looked back at the sky. She hadn't felt beautiful in quite a while.

"Can I-"

"Yes?"

Lauren mentally reprimanded herself. Valerie hadn't even finished the question before she blurted out the answer.

"I was going to ask if I can take your picture? Here, in the starlight."

Valerie had surprised her again. Lauren gave a shy nod. "Yeah? Ok, um... let me think. You sit here, on the hood."

She jumped up and grabbed her camera bag, slinging it over her shoulder as she slid off of the vehicle. She fiddled with lenses and a tripod while Lauren fidgeted shyly.

When she was finally ready, Lauren looked obediently at the unblinking eye of the lens. This one was different. Older and worn, it looked more at home in some kind of museum than here in the 21st century.

"Won't it be too dark?"

"No, I can set my camera for a long exposure time. It means it'll stay open for an extended time so you have to be very, very still. Ok?"

Lauren had no real choice but to trust her.

"How do you want me?"

Lauren regretted her word choice.

"Uh, to sit I mean. How do you need me to sit."

"You're perfect. Just like you are now."

Lauren sat up, her wings half-folded and her legs crossed. She stared at the camera while Valerie adjusted some final setting.

"Ready?"

Click.

Lauren wasn't sure how long she had to stay put so she sat as still as she could. As if to spite her, a light breeze struck up and her ebony hair waved in the wind. After what felt like ages, she heard a soft whirring noise and another click.

Valerie didn't move, she just stood there staring at Lauren and smiling.

"Oh shit, I forgot to smile! I'm so sorry Valerie."

Seriously? How do you not smile for a photo.

"I... Can we redo it?"

Valerie shook her head.

"Sadly my dear that's not how film works, and this isn't a digital camera. We'll just have to see how it turns out."

Valerie climbed back onto the truck, this time settling in against Lauren right away. Lauren did her best to act naturally, and it seemed Valerie was determined to do the same.

"Would you like a drink?"

Valerie sat up and leaned across her companion, reaching past her to pick the bottle up. Sparks flew between them as their chests nearly met.

"S-sure."

Valerie smiled and started to unscrew the cap on the bottle. She got the cap off and moved to take a swig, but paused. she set the bottle down in her lap and scooted around to face Lauren directly.

"Come to London with me," Valerie blurted out.

Chapter 5

London.

Valerie had immediately laughed the request off, but Lauren couldn't shake the idea. The two spent the rest of the night making small talk, drinking wine, and staring at the stars. But something had changed. Their delicate ballet across safe topics did nothing to stem the deep undercurrents of the evening.

Even now, when she should be sleeping, Lauren's mind was abuzz with energy. Should she go? London was huge, there was no way she would be able to hide her presence. Not unless she was willing to live the rest of her life inside, anyway. There were other problems, dozens of them. Lauren wrestled with them silently, unwilling to disturb Valerie's slumber.

In the near-total darkness Lauren couldn't see well enough to make out the details of Valerie's face, but if she squinted hard she could see the vague outline of her sleeping form. Restless, as if she knew she had Lauren's attention, Valerie shifted in her sleep. She unconsciously snuggled closer, resting against Lauren's side and tucking her head against her shoulder.

Valerie's body was warm and light and soft. It was as though Lauren had taken a muscle relaxant. Valerie's touch drained tension from her shoulders and temple and she found herself breathing easier. Lauren let out a sigh, listening to Valerie's heartbeat beside her own. The innocent, intimate act distracted Lauren from her worries. suddenly the obstacles in her path, in *their* path, seemed more conquerable.

Her mind at ease, the fogginess of sleep crept up on Lauren. She returned Valerie's sleepy embrace, wrapping her arm around her and lightly rubbing her back as she drifted off.

Alright then, London.

Lauren woke to a gentle shaking. She cracked her eyes, squinting in the early morning sun. Valerie's face was just a few inches away, relaxed in deep slumber. Lauren stifled a laugh when she noted the light snoring of her companion. Her arm, still under Valerie, had long since fallen asleep and was a mass of pins and needles. Her discomfort was offset by the adorable line of drool from Valerie's slack jaw.

Lauren blinked blearily, maybe she had imagined the shaking. She was nearly convinced when it happened again. The whole truck was shaking. The revelation brought her to full wakefulness. She jerked upright, her thoughts turning immediately to what had happened in Athens.

Her forehead met the unyielding roof of the truck with a resounding bang.

"Ouch, damnit!"

Lauren glanced down at Valerie, who showed no signs of waking. Lauren wiped a circle in the fogged-over window of the truck and peered outward. Her vision was immediately obscured by a massive bovine head and a huge pink tongue.

Lauren let out a tiny scream, clutching her chest to still her pounding heart.

"What? What's wrong? Are you ok?"

Valerie woke at the sound and was rubbing the sleep from her eyes and looking around with concern. Lauren took a moment to calm herself before she was able to speak.

"Yes, sorry. Holy crap. This freakin' *cow* just scared the hell out of me!"

"Cow? What cow?"

A low mooing sound vibrated the truck walls and the women shared a confused look.

"Hang on. I'll open the sunroof."

Valerie clambered over the seat and up to the front of the vehicle. Lauren appreciated her friend's decision, not least because it afforded an unobstructed view of her in a tiny pink camisole and a pair of short blue shorts. Valerie toggled a switch and the sunroof slowly rolled itself open. She stood in the center seat and poked her head out of the top of the vehicle.

Lauren was surprised to hear Valerie start laughing hysterically.

"What? What's going on?"

"Come here, you're not going to believe this."

Lauren climbed over to her friend and squeezed herself up through the sunroof beside her. It was tight quarters, and they were squished against one another, but she made it through without embarrassing herself too much. As Lauren's eyes adjusted to the brightness, she couldn't help but laugh as well. The truck, which Lauren had thought of as so massive up until this point, was a tiny island in a sea of cattle. At some point in the night, or perhaps this morning, their resting place had become the gathering point for what must be one hundred cows or more.

"I told you so," Lauren teased.

"You certainly did not!"

"I did! I told you we'd get in trouble barging into someone's field. Here we have it, Karma."

Valerie scowled at her, but had no retort.

A distant, shouting voice interrupted their fun. A farmer, silhouetted against the sky, was yelling something at them from a nearby hill.

"Shit!"

They both tried to duck back into the cab at the same time and wound up jammed together. Valerie's face was buried in Lauren's chest, her hair was tickling Lauren's nose.

"Oh, sorry! I'm just - let me, uh"

Valerie's auburn curls kept catching Lauren's mouth as she tried to speak. Valerie pushed back upwards, her head catching Lauren's chin as she simultaneously made another attempt to go down. Lauren reflexively moved her hand to cover her freshly-bitten lip, but it got caught, trapped between her side and her wings.

Both women were laughing too hard to speak. Time was running out, the man on the hill was working his way towards them. Valerie took charge, she grabbed Lauren's waist and abruptly moved to sit down.

They plummeted through the sunroof at last, loose feathers falling all around them. Lauren was straddling Valerie's lap, who had yet to remove her hands from around her companion. Both women were flushed and laughing hysterically. They settled into silence with wide, loopy smiles on their faces. Valerie had a stray strand of hair hanging down in her face. Her smile broadened when Lauren tucked it behind her ear.

The women were interrupted by a loud thump. They both flinched as a fist sized rock impacted the metal siding.

"We gotta go, Valerie!"

Lauren scooted back as Valerie scrambled into the front seat and fired up the truck.

"I can't believe that asshole threw a rock at my truck!

Valerie jammed the horn, sending the cattle into a startled rush to get away from them. She rumbled off towards the road as quickly as the herd would allow, leaving the farmer angrily pelting them with stones behind.

It wasn't until they were several miles down the road that they had finally stopped laughing enough to carry on a normal conversation.

"So, where are we headed next? Perhaps a hen house this time?"

Lauren's companion was an encyclopedia on this part of the world and soon they were laughing and smiling again. Valerie regaled her with everything from local folklore to impromptu history lessons.

"Eventually, this route will take us through Kosovo and Montenegro and then it's up to Sarajevo-"

Lauren tensed at the name.

"Sarajevo? Why are we going to Sarajevo?"

Valerie seemed confused.

"Well, Bosnia and Herzegovina is on our way back to Central and then Western Europe. All of the major highways run through and from the capitol. Not going through Sarajevo would add hours and hours to our trip."

Lauren brooded on the information. Of course it was the quickest route. Her scowl made Valerie fret until she realized what must be bothering her.

"Ooh, right."

Lauren cast her a pitiful look.

"Well, that settles it then. We'll go through Serbia instead."

"Are you sure?"

"Lauren, it's about time you start writing your own story. We can go anywhere in the world as far as I'm concerned."

"Seems like the life of a photographer is pretty open-ended... Don't you have to go to work or anything?"

Valerie winked conspiratorially.

"I'm a very, very good photographer."

A fierce wanderlust caught hold of Lauren. Here was the travelling companion she had always dreamed of. Here was the crazy, responsibility-free trip that filled the imaginations of young people everywhere. For once in her life, Lauren felt free of the cage of her self-imposed duties.

"S-so is Serbia also on the way to London?"

Lauren asked the question as innocently as she could, but she couldn't stop her cheeks from burning or a grin from forming on her face.

Valerie tried and failed to contain her excitement. She didn't trust herself to speak, so she nodded vigorously.

"Will it be safe?"

Valerie lost her smile. It was replaced by a look of... regret?

"No, Lauren, it won't. I'm not going to lie to you. Will it be safer than here? In some ways. Will it be free of angry mobs and religious fanatics? Hopefully."

Lauren mulled over the uncomfortable truth. She opened her mouth to argue but Valerie continued.

"Look, if your handlers promised you you were going to be safe, if they told you that everything was under control, then they lied to you. I'm sure they meant what they said but the simple fact is the world doesn't work that way."

"So I'm fucked," Lauren retorted bitterly.

"No, little stormcloud, you're growing up."

Lauren scowled at her, but Valerie's gaze stayed steady on the road ahead. She scanned the horizon, one hand on the wheel and the other resting on the center console between them. Lauren was annoyed. Annoyed by her slender jaw line, her button nose, the wild, unkempt mess of deep brown curls partially obscuring her frustratingly beautiful face. She tried to stay mad, to deny within herself that Valerie's words were true, but it was a losing battle. She was right, and the sooner Lauren came to grips with it the better.

"Lauren, I'm sorry I tend to speak my-"

Lauren slipped her hand into Valerie's and gave a gentle squeeze. Valerie squeezed back immediately, entwining their fingers gently.

"So what comes after Serbia?"

They hit the Serbian border within an hour, and this time they were considerably better prepared. Valerie helped Lauren get situated beneath her mountain of clothes and blankets a few miles from the checkpoint and they passed without incident. Lauren caught herself dozing off as Valerie drove, lulled to sleep by the soft rock coming in over the radio.

She must have needed the rest, because the next thing she knew she was being gently shaken by her friend. As she stirred, she picked up the mouthwatering smells of onions, garlic, beef, and pork.

"Rise and shine sleepyhead."

Lauren cracked an eye open. Valerie was waving a loosely wrapped package in front of her nose. The mysterious item was roughly hamburger-sized, which was good enough for her. Her stomach growled in agreement.

"What time is it?"

"It's nearly noon. We're just outside of Belgrade, the capital of Serbia. What better time to try some traditional Pljeskavica?"

"Gesundheit," Lauren joked.

"Very funny dear, it's the national dish!"

Lauren sat up and stretched, taking the package she was offered. Beneath the paper wrapper was a delicious looking burger. Or was it a sandwich? The not-burger consisted of a seared meat patty, pickled peppers, and fresh onions between two pieces of warm, crusty bread.

"You're not going to tell me this is like, horse meat or something right?"

Valerie looked positively horrified.

"Good heavens, no! What a dreadful thought."

Lauren smiled at her distress and bit into the sandwich. It was amazing. Grease and pickle juice covered her fingers and threatened to run down her chin as she devoured her prize.

"I take it you were hungry then."

Lauren stopped mid-bite. Her bulging cheeks made it hard to laugh, but she managed.

"Shuddup."

Valerie, for her part, was eating her sandwich in a way that could only be described as dainty. Lauren's cheeks flushed, but she stubbornly continued munching away.

When she had finished, Lauren took the opportunity to observe her surroundings more carefully. They were at the edge of a small town on the side of a hill overlooking a large sprawling metropolis. The city was dotted with large, gothic looking buildings. Lauren stared wistfully at it in the distance, but she feared that to go would be to end her adventure.

"Did you want to visit the city?"

Valerie had once again read her like a book. But she shook her head.

"Do you suppose someday it will be different for me? That I'll be able to just visit places? See them like a normal person?"

Valerie finished her own meal and put the truck back in drive.

"Hope springs eternal, Lauren. I truly hope so."

Belgrade to budapest, Serbia to Hungary, the pair chased the sun across the map. Lauren felt young in a way she hadn't since she'd left Cobden. She was a starry-eyed nineteen year old at last. Valerie was a seasoned traveller, and her passion for it bled through in everything she said and showed her passenger. As the sun set on the second day of their journey, Lauren wondered whether they would bed down in the truck again. She found herself hoping they would indeed share the small, intimate nest of blankets once more.

"You alright love? Your cheeks are quite red, are you feeling feverish?"

Lauren jumped, she'd been caught. She couldn't suppress a smile as her cheeks glowed several shades redder.

"A bit warm," she lied. "But I'm fine. Just wondering where we were spending the evening tonight."

Now it was Valerie's turn to look curiously blase.

"Ah well, I thought perhaps Vienna?"

Lauren narrowed her eyes suspiciously. Valerie's entire tone had changed. Was she was hiding something? Wasn't Vienna huge? Lauren contemplated pressing the issue, but she decided to simply trust her companion instead.

She waited impatiently, expecting any moment to arrive and find out just what Valerie had in store. Hours ticked by, the sun set, the moon rose, and still they hadn't stopped. Finally, Lauren could contain herself no more.

"How far is it to Vienna?"

Valerie flashed another fetching smile.

"We're nearly there, about an hour away actually."

Lauren checked the clock, an hour would put them arriving close to midnight. Maybe she had been wrong. Perhaps she had misread her friend, and there was nothing special in Vienna for them. Lauren couldn't rationalize why it so disappointed her, but she did her best to shake the feeling.

The view of the city as they approached it helped in her efforts considerably. The sea of lights amidst the darkness of the highway was magical in its own right. Lauren half expected them to take a side road and skirt around the city as they had done all day, but they drew closer and closer with no sign of turning or slowing down.

Shortly, they were in the city. Lights flashed past on either side and masses of young people wandered the streets. Lauren imagined what it would be like to be one of them. To be bar-hopping with her friends. To be leaving a late showing of the newest hollywood blockbuster. To be taking a date to a late dinner.

"That was a heavy sigh, everything ok?"

Lauren nodded, pushing her wistful longing back into the corners of her mind.

"You said we were going to sleep here, won't I be seen?"

"I've got a place in mind where I think we can have a pretty good chance at privacy."

With that, Valerie turned off the main thoroughfare and took them down a few side streets. They were nearly out of the city when she finally pulled down a long dark drive. The shadowy forms of broad trees lined the drive, hiding the city that lay just behind them. The trees gave way at last to a wide clearing.

Before them was a small dock and an empty parking lot that could hold a dozen cars or so. Lauren's interest piqued. She peered around for a house that they might be staying at, but aside from a small building that looked like a restroom there was nothing to see.

Valerie parked the truck and hopped out. She walked around and pulled a few bags out of the rear of the vehicle and then continued around to Lauren's door. She tapped playfully on the glass.

"Coming?"

Lauren raised an eyebrow and stepped out as well. She glanced around, afraid that someone might see her in the low light of the parking.

"Don't worry, this is a friend's place. There's no one here to see us."

Valerie walked briskly down to the dock, Lauren in tow. She went all the way to the end, where a large vessel was bobbing gently in the river. It had a big dusty cover on it, which Valerie wasted no time in removing. Lauren gasped in awe at the beauty beneath the unassuming exterior. The boat, around 40 feet long, was all exquisite walnut with shining brass accents. It was a houseboat, with a wide flat deck and a set of stairs leading down into the cabin. The wheelhouse and the hull of the craft were both painted white, in stark contrast to the dark wood that panelled the rest of the ship.

Valerie was beaming at her, her eyes bright with joy at Lauren's reaction.

"Welcome to the Liebeslied, our home for the night."

"Oh Valerie how? How can we stay here, whose boat is this?"

"A very, very dear old family friend gave me a standing invitation. An invitation I'd like to extend to you."

Valerie stepped lightly onto the vessel, set her bags down beside the stairs, and came back to offer a hand to Lauren.

"Are you sure?"

"Positive. Give me your hand and I'll help you up."

Lauren accepted her aid and stepped onto the boat feeling like a princess. Valerie untied the two ropes holding the boat to the dock and settled herself at the helm. She looked a wild sight standing in the starlight at the wheel. Two small but powerful inboard motors powered up and the craft slide seamlessly through the stillness of the water. They cruised away from the dock and into the middle of a small bay leading to a large river.

Lauren admired her host. She looked strong, capable, and as comfortable on the water as she had been in her massive truck. The air around them was cool and refreshing after spending so much time in the confines of an automobile. She closed her eyes and listened to the dull rumble of the engines as they carried her into the night. She opened her eyes when the engines died again, turning around to look at Valerie.

"We're stopping?"

Valerie nodded and flipped a switch, sending an anchor plunging into the dark waters below.

"Do you, do you mind if I stretch a bit?"

Valerie looked pleased.

"Of course not, that's half the reason I brought you out here!"

Lauren smiled and stretched her wings wide. Conscious of her audience she leapt into the sky with a little more flair than usual. She enjoyed the appreciative gasp of her companion as she rocketed upward. She left the now gently rocking boat below and frolicked in the sky. She lost herself in the unmatched joy of turning, diving, and climbing through the air. She finally leveled off, breathing heavily and sweating lightly in the breeze. Far below her was the boat and her companion. She felt guilty, unsure exactly how long she had been goofing off.

It must have been a while, because when she reached the boat again she could see that Valerie had been quite busy. A large comforter had been laid out on the flat deck of the boat, and a small feast of breads, sliced meat and cheeses were piled in the center. Valerie was nowhere to be seen, so Lauren reasoned she must be below.

Lauren alighted softly on the boat and set it gently rocking again.

"Valerie?"

"Coming!"

Valerie emerged from below decks, a pair of wine glasses in one hand and a bottle in the other. Lauren missed a step and stumbled. Valerie was wearing an emerald green bikini and a thin colorful wrap around her waist. The top artfully covered just what it needed to, and nothing else. Her petite, well-proportioned bust was held at bay by a small shining clasp from which three tiny jewels hung. The gems led Lauren's gaze down her flat stomach to her smoothly curving hips.

Valerie's laugh made Lauren turn a deep scarlet. She hoped Valerie would mistake it for the flush of exertion from flying.

"Sorry, I hope you don't mind. It just seemed right, you know? Being on a boat after all?"

Lauren shook her head maybe a bit too vigorously.

"No no, it's absolutely fine."

She felt suddenly very aware of her own attire. She was still wearing the thin dress and lingerie she had taken with her when she left Weyland's.

"Do you, um, have anything I could change into?"

"Yes of course! I've left a bag downstairs with clothes for you. There's a swimsuit as well if you wanted... as well as some other things that should fit you."

Lauren stepped quickly down into the belly of the boat, keenly aware of the heat she felt in her face and elsewhere. Most of the cabin was taken up by a bed and a small kitchen area. The bed had a variety of clothes set out and a suitcase. Well, perhaps set out was a strong way to describe it. It looked like a miniature version of the back of Valerie's truck.

Lauren slipped out of her clothing and caught sight of a mirror. She did a double-take at the black-haired woman she saw there. She took a moment to really examine herself for the first time since she had woken up. Her ebony feathers and deep black hair accented her pale skin and newly darkened eyes in a sensual, dangerous-looking way.

The runway-thin look of her childhood had softened into the form before her now. Her stomach wasn't as chiseled as Valerie's, but it was fit. Her hips and bust had widened a little over the past few years, but she was still trim and athletically built. Lauren brushed her hair back and ran a hand down her side. She felt an unusual confidence in her naked form as she turned back and forth, examining herself from different angles.

"Lauren? Everything alright?"

She started, afraid that Valerie might come down and see her.

"I'm alright, just finishing up!"

She dug through the clothes, struggling to decide what exactly she wanted to express to her friend. Her time with Valerie, though short, had already emboldened her. Her example of strength and surety started to rub off on Lauren. She held up a red bikini top not unlike the one Valerie was wearing. She tied the thin strings together and looked herself over. The garment was small for her, and there was just enough string to tie it properly behind her back. The bright cherry color screamed for attention and complimented her dark shoulder-length hair. She found the matching bottoms and was suddenly less sure of her choice. If the top was revealing then these were scandalous. All told, the strappy fabric wouldn't have been enough to make a decent sized glove.

Lauren took stock of herself in the mirror.

What do you want?

Her mind wandered and as she pondered the question she felt her cheeks flush and warmth building within her. She stepped into the bikini bottom and slid the delicate item up to her hips. As a parting thought she grabbed a wide black shawl, twisting it around her hips to make a short skirt like her host's.

Lauren took the steps two at a time, rushing to get back to the deck. Valerie was sitting with her back to the stairs, looking out over the water and sipping a glass of white wine.

She glanced back over her shoulder and spit out her wine at the sight of Lauren.

Lauren flushed with pride, her confidence magnifying tenfold. She tried to look innocent but she put an extra sway in her hips as she strode over to her speechless companion. Valerie followed her, slack-jawed.

"Cat got your tongue?"

Lauren reached out and gently lifted Valerie's still-dropped jaw, closing her mouth for her playfully. Valerie recovered, shaking her head and smiling sheepishly. She didn't stop staring.

"Well, that was very classy of me. Lauren, you look stunning."

The warmth inside her spread from her cheeks to her chest and lower. Lauren reached across her friend and grabbed the bottle of wine and wine glass waiting for her. She intentionally mirrored Valerie's actions from the night before, getting close enough that she could feel Valerie's breath on her neck.

The women sipped wine and flirted as the stars spun above. The drink flowed freely and the two had a light buzz in no time. The air between them felt like a thunderstorm, and Lauren couldn't wait for lightning to strike. She turned to Valerie to speak, but her friend was already moving.

Valerie stood and walked to the edge of the boat, staring out into the dark waters surrounding them. She cast a playful look over her shoulder and made a show of taking off the colorful wrap adorning her hips. She tossed it at Lauren and stepped off into the river, plunging into the water with a tiny splash.

She stayed down just long enough that Lauren started to worry before surfacing again. She leaned on the edge of the boat and wiped her slick hair out of her eyes.

"Join me?"

Lauren crawled to the edge of the boat, laying down a foot or so away from Valerie and resting her chin in her palms. She twitched her wings.

"Have you seen these things?"

"Suit yourself."

Valerie splashed her lightly and then jetted away before Lauren could retaliate. She looked as at home in the water as Lauren felt in the skies. Lauren was content to watch her swim about in the blackness. She wondered if Valerie had done the same while she flew about. Lauren couldn't help but feel a twinge of regret that she couldn't join Valerie. More than just the water looked inviting.

At last Valerie swam back over.

"The only bad thing about this boat, no ladder. Can you give me a hand up?"

Lauren pretended to think about it a moment before sticking her hand out. Valerie grabbed hold and she hauled her up into the boat. Lauren fetched a towel from the bag nearby while Valerie sat down on the deck beside her.

"Thanks."

Lauren took a seat as well.

"No probl-"

Valerie cut her off by planting a deep, passionate kiss on her lips. Valerie's full, plump lips lingered against her own for several heartbeats before she pulled away. Lauren was shocked, but her body responded hungrily. Lauren raised herself up and straddled her companion, a torrent of emotion bursting through to the surface. Putting a hand on either side of Valerie's face, she returned the kiss with vigor. Valerie's hands slid up her back, tickling her bare skin and sending sparks along her nerves. She pulled her closer, pressing their bodies together in the growing heat of the night.

"Lauren," Valerie breathed the word through parted lips.

Lauren was an uncaged animal. She sucked Valerie's bottom lip between her own and bit down gently on it, eliciting a gasp of excited pleasure. Her partner's response only further aroused her. She kissed her way across to Valerie's neck and up to her ear. She was heedless of their surroundings, responding only to the cues she felt from Valerie's body and her own hunger.

Lauren nibbled on Valerie's earlobe. She could feel Valerie's hands move from her back to her bare thighs. Delicate fingers slipped under the hem of her makeshift skirt and up towards her hips. Valerie's touch lit a fire inside of her unlike anything she had ever felt before.

But the placement of her hands, the slowly rising fabric at her hips, it was too familiar. Lauren's mind cruelly reminded her of Weyland. Of the cavalier manner in which he had handled her body in the dream and afterwards. She tried to focus, but try as she might Valerie's soft touch felt unnaturally like the rough heat of Weyland's skin.

She pushed back, her passion cooling with the humiliating thoughts of his abuse. Valerie could feel Lauren hesitate, and she stopped immediately.

"Are you ok? What's wrong? I'm sorry I shouldn't have-"

Lauren scooted back onto the blankets. She felt her hands shaking and tried to calm her breathing. She couldn't yet bring herself to speak, but she gave Valerie a forced smile and a nod.

"Look, Lauren, I'm very sorry if I overstepped my bounds. I- I must have misjudged the mood. I... I understand it may have been awkward or out of place for you. It won't happen again."

Lauren couldn't put into words how much it mattered to her that Valerie was so concerned about her consent. Her words broke through Lauren's carefully crafted emotional walls and a flood of tears threatened to pour out.

"Please, don't apologize. You didn't overstep. Honestly, it was wonderful. I'm just... not ready."

Lauren was kicking herself internally. She wanted desperately to tell her. But she couldn't. What would Valerie think of her if she knew? Her newfound friendship was too precious to risk. She settled beside her companion, looking for answers in the darkness around them.

"Can we talk about something else for a while? Please?"

Valerie nodded solemnly.

"Anything at all, I'm all yours."

Despite her offer they sat in silence for several minutes before Lauren finally spoke.

"How far is it to London?"

"We've around 18 hours of driving left. In all likelihood we could be there by this time tomorrow... if you wanted."

One more day.

Lauren pondered her predicament. How would London change things? Did she really want to go to London, or simply stay with Valerie? Valerie's hand slipped into hers and eased her worry.

"Do we have to go straight there?"

Valerie furrowed her brow.

"Lauren, I meant what I said. The world has stolen your youth from you. You've been kicked back and forth from place to place by people always demanding more from you for *years*. I know a few things about growing up too soon."

She put her arm around Lauren's shoulders and drew her close.

"You deserve to live. To breathe. To be alive for yourself instead of just existing for the good of other people. For once in your life, live by your own schedule."

Lauren was flooded with relief, she laid her head on Valerie's shoulder and stared out into the night.

Three magical days on the Liebeslied, eight more spent zig-zagging through Europe, and the old truck was finally rumbling across eastern France an hour or so from the English Channel.

"So explain this to me again. How are we getting across?"

Valerie smiled thinly, she wasn't a huge fan of the plan either, but it was the best she could come up with.

"So, I'll drive the truck onto one of the vehicle transport cars."

"Right."

"Then I'll get out, get my passport checked, and head to the passenger cars."

"Mhmm."

"You'll be hidden in the truck, where you'll stay for the twenty-seven minute trip across the Channel. Meanwhile I'll ride in the passenger area..."

"Right. See, that part. Not thrilled."

"Well, Lauren, I'm sorry but I just don't see another way to do it. Not unless you want to risk flying. It's 50 kilometers at the Chunnel, longer elsewhere. What if someone sees you?"

"What if the train breaks down! Or catches fire! Or the freight transport cars are filled with horrible fumes and toxic gases that are kept out by the passenger cars!"

Valerie chewed on her bottom lip, the laundry list of horrible things that could go wrong *was* fairly extensive.

"Ok. Say you flew, and managed to make it across without being seen. How would I find you again? Folkestone is no small town, and neither is Dover."

Lauren could tell that Valerie was getting worked up, she was fidgeting while she spoke and her eyes darted nervously around the road.

"Hey, hey I'm gonna be ok."

"But, what if I can't find you?"

"You won't have to, I'll ride on the train ok?"

Lauren's worry proved to be unfounded, as the freight cars were state-of-the-art and even climate controlled. They shared a laugh at their unnecessary fretting while they departed the Folkestone terminal and headed into Britain.

The countryside was filled with lush greenery and Lauren adored the rolling hills of green and fences made of stone that zipped past them on the M20.

"So you live in London then?"

"Well, Farningham actually."

"Never heard of it," Lauren joked.

"Yes well, I should think not. There's only a thousand of us after all!"

"Is it close?"

"To London?"

"No, to Paris, of course to London!"

"Sassy from your train ride I see. Yes, it's in Kent, Seven Oaks District.

Lauren Raised an eyebrow.

"Well, we don't have states, so to speak. We have countries, which have regions, which have shires or counties, which have districts, which have towns."

"You're kidding."

"Afraid not."

"I could never live here."

Valerie gripped her hand tightly.

"That's a shame, I was rather getting my hopes up."

Lauren was caught off guard and blushed deeply. She couldn't think of a witty response so she simply squeezed back and tried to stifle the huge, goofy grin that appeared on her face.

Chapter 6

The bulky truck turned off of the highway and down a narrow path, rumbling into a sleepy town nestled in the countryside. The winding cobbled streets and timeworn buildings were straight out of a fairy tale. Lauren craned her neck this way and that, trying to soak in every charming sight the quaint little village had to offer. She caught sight of an old-timey butcher shop, a young woman on a park bench reading, a tiny village newspaper office, and a few statues that might have been a thousand years old. In the blink of an eye they were emerging on the other side, once again staring at rolling hills and open fields.

Valerie turned right on the last street in town. They followed it to an old farmhouse sitting on a modest acreage surrounded by a short stone fence.

"Well, here we are. Home sweet home."

Lauren was impressed, the place was unassuming but elegant. The yard was trimmed, and the house looked taken care of, as did the outbuildings sitting on the property. It could have been any farmhouse in the midwest where she had grown up, and a wave of nostalgia washed over her.

"All this is yours?"

"Yes, well it was my parents anyway."

"How do you keep it so well taken care of if you're gone for weeks at a time?"

"I've a fellow in town that takes care of things around here, sort of a tradition between our two families that stretches quite far back."

"Like a butler?"

Valerie cringed at the word.

"No, not like a butler. A very stubborn old man who insists on helping me with my housekeeping and whom I try desperately to pay appropriately for his services. He's not overly fond of accepting my money, as it turns out."

They approached the house on a long winding crushed gravel path and Valerie pulled her truck into one of the barns. She parked and hopped out, indicating to Lauren that they could leave their belongings for the moment. Not that Lauren had any.

Lauren stepped free of the vehicle and saw a veritable wave of white fluff rounding the corner of the barn and heading their way. She yelped in surprise and then burst out laughing as a small herd of sheep surrounded Valerie, bleating for her attention.

Valerie was red in the face and trying to evenly distribute chin scratches and head pats to the needy animals.

"Sorry, they miss me terribly when I'm gone!"

Valerie had to shout to overcome the noisy gaggle.

Well, that explained how one stubborn old man could keep the grass looking so neat. It seemed he had a great deal of hungry, four-legged help.

"You didn't think to tell me you were Little Bo Peep while we road-tripped across the entire continent?"

Valerie look strangely embarrassed.

"Yes well, ah, it never came up."

Lauren waited patiently until Valerie sighed and continued.

"We're shepherds and weavers, or were. It's the original source of my family's... holdings. Chatwick wool has been highly regarded by English weavers for a few centuries. My grandfather and my father took us global."

Lauren nodded, it was obvious that her wealth was a source of embarrassment for Valerie.

"It's just, it all looks like rather a lot compared to so many other people. I don't want to give the impression that I'm some kind of stuffy British landowner, you know?"

Lauren could understand. She'd seen a great deal of crushing poverty and slum-living in her short life as well. This idyllic country home, with its ancient stone fence and rolling fields, was far from ostentatious though. To Lauren's eyes it looked like heaven.

"I can't imagine ever leaving. It's wonderful here."

"Well just remember you said that when we get inside. The house creaks like an old man and is only slightly less drafty than this barn."

Valerie led the way across the yard, stopping to look around for anyone who might observe them before waving Lauren onward. They slipped unnoticed into a moderately sized foyer that opened into a sitting room.

Valerie began a thorough tour of the property. Wide doors and high ceilings prevented Lauren from feeling her usual claustrophobia while inside. The large sitting room formed a hub from which the rest of the house radiated. Sleek granite counters and teak cabinets elevated a large but otherwise un-remarkable kitchen that, along with the sitting room, a guest bathroom, and a small but well-stocked library formed the bottom floor of the house. The wide spiral staircase leading to the second floor was a work of art in its own right. Masterful carpentry made the glowing hardwood look like flowing water as it wound upward to a long carpeted hallway.

The majority of the upstairs was taken up by what Valerie called the 'Weaving Room,' a clean but obviously unused space with a few large bales of wool fiber, jars of dye, and an exquisite wooden loom among other things.

There were also three bedrooms upstairs. The first two were draped in white cloth, as though nothing had been moved in many years.

"And this is the master suite, such as it is."

Valerie pulled open a large, six-panelled wooden door revealing a massive four-poster bed set atop a plush purple carpet. She indicated that Lauren should enter, and then followed her as she did so.

Lauren was transported back a hundred years. Every piece of furniture was an antique. Not the untouched, museum replica style of antique, but rather the warm, "lived-in" sort of old that exuded love and light. The most eye-catching feature of the room was a series four of large, framed photographs that sat in a row beside a deep bay window.

"What are these?"

Lauren approached and examined the pictures. The first was of a woman, she looked very much like Valerie, but older. The woman had longer hair, and was smiling shyly at her feet while holding a lacey parasol. The photo was a little blurry, and had faded through the years, but Lauren judged from the sundress the woman wore that it was taken at a beach somewhere.

"That's my mother. Angelica Scott. It's one of the first photographs I took as a child. She bought me my first camera that summer. This one here is my father, building a model airplane with my older brother."

Sure enough, the second photo was of an older man and a young boy assembling small wooden pieces at a desk. Lauren immediately recognized the library downstairs. The man had his back to the camera, but his sensible vest and trousers gave a businesslike appearance quite at odds with his unkempt hair. The boy standing next to him was in profile, and shared the slender jawline of his little sister. His eyes sparkled with obvious joy that matched his wide smile. Lauren chuckled at his funny school uniform.

"He was in his second year at Hamilton's Academy, just home for the summer."

The third photograph was the whole family, save Valerie. They were assembled in front of an old church. They were all several years older than the previous picture as well. The boy was wearing a crisp, military uniform and the man had a cane that seemed to perfectly suit his round glasses and bowler hat. The woman looked thinner, and she wore a broad bandana on her head. Her smile was less carefree, but just as beautiful.

"St. Agnes. My family is very religious."

Lauren sensed a great deal of bitterness in her tone, and decided not to press for details. Still, the cold response stuck out in her mind.

"And this?"

The final photograph was a confusing, almost abstract display. It was severely overexposed, little more than a white blur with a few faded figures in it. Dark cracks filled the frame, giving the viewer the impression they were looking through a broken window.

Valerie was silent. Lauren looked back at her and was surprised at how angry her companion appeared. She slipped a calm, passive expression onto her face but not before Lauren saw her anguish.

"Valerie?"

"You could call that a mistake, rather than a picture I meant to take. I... dropped my camera. I covered it, but not before I ruined the whole roll of film. That's the only frame I could salvage. I won an award for that photograph, ironically. In fact I owe my career in large part to it."

Lauren shifted uncomfortably in the awkward silence that followed her terse reply. She cast around the room for something else to discuss. She took note of a doorway that led to a large bathroom, and another that she presumed was a closet.

"Is that a walk-in? I've always loved walk-in closets..."

"Let's get a drink. I'll show you the wine cellar?"

Valerie didn't wait for a reply, but turned on her heel and headed back out of the room. Lauren rushed to keep up with her, catching up as they got to the stairs.

"Hey, I'm sorry if I offended you."

"Hmm? Oh, of course not love. Just the nostalgia that comes from a dusty old house full of memories, that's all."

Lauren remained unconvinced.

Valerie led her outside and around the back of the house. The rear of the structure was much the same as the front, save another small outbuilding with a curious glass roof on it. She didn't dwell on the structure, though, as she was busy scanning the horizon for someone who might see them.

Lauren's midnight-black feathers seems to swallow the bright sunlight of the afternoon and she felt incredibly conspicuous after hiding for so long. She glanced around nervously while Valerie fiddled with an old lock on the door to a storm cellar. Finally, the rusty mechanism loosened it's grasp and she heaved open the broad wooden doors.

Lauren was nonplussed at the mess of cobwebs before them. Her skin crawled at the thought of spiders in her feathers, nestled in where it might be impossible for her to get them out. She shivered at the realization that this gruesome event may have already occurred. That even now she may be playing host to tiny, eight-legged terrors.

"Lauren? Are you ok? You look really pale."

Lauren gagged a little, and held her finger up.

"I just. I'm suddenly horrified to think of how my wings and spiderwebs might mix."

Valerie shared her look of concerned disgust.

"I'll go first. Furthermore I shall personally uh, preen your feathers to put your mind at ease."

Preen.

Lauren laughed out loud at her word choice. She felt for an instant like an expensive macaw. She took a deep breath and nodded, steeling herself to follow Valerie.

Valerie made good on her promise and led the way, brushing away the thick webs as she did. Fortunately, it seemed the highest concentration of webbing was at the doorway, and the cellar itself was surprisingly clean. The brick walls and clay floor were dry and clear. A pair of old dim light bulbs with wild, spiral filaments provided illumination, revealing boxes filled with odds and ends and a large metal rack filled to the brim with dust-covered bottles.

Lauren kept her head ducked and her wings close to her body as she made her way across the room. So intent was she on the ceiling and it's potential pests, she stubbed her toe on a low wooden crate on the floor.

"Ouch, ow ow ow."

She hopped up and down for a moment on one leg until the sharp pain in her foot subsided, and cast a wrathful glare at the offending hazard. The container in front of her was filled with military paraphernalia. Uniforms, buttons, ribbons, and the like were stacked in neatly folded piles within it.

"Alright there?"

"Yeah, yeah I'm ok. This must be your brother's?"

"Ah yes, that's Colin's. I'd thought he had taken most of this with him when he left for Australia."

Lauren picked her way more carefully towards Valerie, who was already standing by the wine-rack.

"Australia?"

"Yes, he moved there when he left the military. That was years ago, just after our mother died. Perhaps I'll write him, tell him he still has some things here."

Something in her tone told Lauren that she wouldn't.

"Anyway, this is the selection. My father's second proudest achievement, next to my brother. Anything suit your fancy?"

"I've got to admit, I don't really know much about wine."

"Oh, I thought since- Well nevermind what I thought. Let's give you a treat shall we?"

Lauren's cheeks burned as she wondered what Valerie had heard in the news. What reputation she must have.

"Château Lafite, circa 1865?"

Lauren shrugged.

"Sure, sounds great."

Valerie nodded and grabbed a pair of bottles. She hesitated a moment and, to Lauren's surprise, picked up a third before heading back towards the door.

Lauren was happy to leave the confines of the cellar and return once more to the open air. She shook her wings vigorously, dislodging dust and cobwebs as she did so. Despite her best efforts, she looked like an antique that had been forgotten in an attic for years.

Valerie laughed a little at Lauren's expression of displeasure.

"Let's get you cleaned up, shall we?"

"Yes please."

Lauren followed Valerie back inside.

"Alright love, you remember where the shower is? Edward will have set towels out I'm sure, but just in case they are in the cabinet to the left. I'll get dinner together while you freshen up."

Lauren watched her partner prance off into the kitchen before heading up to find out what sort of shower she might be able to manage upstairs. To her slight disappointment, but not surprise, the shower in the master bathroom was a little cramped for her.

The water was hot, and the pressure strong, and despite the tight quarters Lauren felt infinitely better for it. She rinsed as much of the dust and dirt as she could, and then stepped out and wrapped herself in a plush purple towel she found hanging there. She was drying off when she realized that her clothes were still covered in debris.

"Right."

She stood dripping in the steam-filled room and pondered her options. She was hesitant to try searching through Valerie's dresser drawers without an explicit invitation, but she wasn't exactly comfortable running around nude either. At the risk of looking like a bad sitcom character she decided the towel would have to do. With her new garment securely wrapped around her she slipped back downstairs.

Delicious smells drew her to the kitchen, where she found Valerie humming softly and flitting back and forth between several steaming and sizzling pans. She turned and smiled as Lauren approached

"Oh, well hello there. You look ravishing in purple. Did you enjoy your shower? It must have been terribly cramped for you."

Valerie poured a glass of deep red wine from one of the dusty old bottles and offered it to her guest.

"Oh no, it was great thank you. I just, I don't have any clean clothes."

"Not to worry, we will get you straightened out. I think we've already demonstrated you fit my clothing *quite* nicely after all. But, if you'd prefer we could eat first?"

Lauren's mouth was watering. Savory rosemary and thyme, as well as other less recognizable scents filled the air. She didn't mind the towel, and in fact found herself pleasantly surprised at Valerie's reaction to it. She graciously accepted the wine being offered and strolled over to the stove, taking a closer look at what was cooking.

"I think dinner. What's on the menu?"

Valerie tutted and playfully swatted at Lauren's hand as she reached for the lid to a pan.

"Now now, my mother would spin in her grave if I let a guest touch cookware in this house. Sit there and sip your wine and continue to dazzle me with your conversation."

Lauren laughed and did her best to look suitably chastised. She took a seat on the counter and took extra care in crossing her legs, keenly aware of the shortness of her towel.

"Oh? Are you?"

"Am I what?"

"*Dazzled.*"

Lauren asked the question a little too passionately, with more energy than she intended. She found herself nervous for the reply. Whatever she expected, Valerie's sincere, equally serious answer made her smile.

"More than you know."

Lauren hid her blushing cheeks by taking a sip of wine. It was velvety, smooth and incredibly complex. She could, without hesitation, say it was the single most delicious drink she'd ever had.

"Wow. What is this, and where do I get some?"

"The Lafite? Oh you can't just buy it anymore. It's a very rare vintage, bottled in 1865. I think when my father purchased these they ran him around three thousand pounds each."

Lauren choked on her wine. She did some quick mental math.

"Valerie! That's like five thousand dollars! What the hell are we doing drinking it?"

Valerie laughed again, a rich melody that made Lauren's heart flutter.

"Because Lauren, it was bottled to be drank, not to sit forever in a dark basement. One of many fundamental difference I have with my father. Wine, like life, is meant to be experienced, to be enjoyed, to be lived in a way that makes one happy. The people who toiled in a field a century and a half ago to bottle this had no intention of letting it sit wasted in a rich man's basement."

Lauren raised an eyebrow. Valerie was as compelling as ever, and her philosophy struck a sympathetic chord in Lauren's heart. She couldn't stop smiling at the fierce, willful woman that fate had brought into her life.

Dinner turned out to be delicious. Valerie produced sizzling, pan seared chicken breasts with steamed asparagus, and fingerling potatoes, all smothered in a thick mushroom and cream sauce. The meal was anything but rushed, and the two women laughed and chatted casually while the wine slowly disappeared and the shadows lengthened across the tiled floor.

By the time they finished eating they were deep in the second bottle of Lafite, and a pleasant buzz filled Lauren's mind as she helped her host clean the dishes from their shared meal.

"So domestic, who would have guessed."

Valerie teased Lauren as she handed her the last plate to dry off. Lauren, for her part, played along. She wiped the plate down with a soft towel and placed it carefully back in the cupboard. She adopted a silly, faux-british accent as she had done so often as a child.

"Yes marm, happy to repay your kindness marm."

"Are you *mocking* me?"

"Oh certainly not, I could never."

Valerie rolled her eyes at Lauren's awful accent and turned back to the sink. After fishing around a moment in the soapy water to ensure no dishes had been left behind, she pulled the plug and started to rinse out the sink. She reached back towards Lauren without looking.

"Could you hand me the towel?"

Lauren looked her up and down. Valerie's shapely rear-end was unguarded, so she rolled the towel she was holding and snapped it playfully against her cheek. It made a satisfying crack and Valerie jumped, splashing water down the front of her floral-patterned apron.

"You little shit!"

Lauren howled with laughter, at least until Valerie retaliated by splashing her.

"Hey! I already got a shower, no fair!"

Valerie scowled in mock anger and tutted to herself.

"Well it would serve you right to have to take another."

"But who will *preen* my feathers for me?"

Valerie smirked and held out a hand to Lauren.

"Come with me."

Lauren's heart fluttered as she accepted. Would she ever get used to being able to freely touch someone? Valerie picked up the remaining bottle of wine as they exited the room. She expected that Valerie would be headed upstairs, so she was surprised when they turned instead for the front door.

"Where are we going?"

Valerie ignored her question, and simply led her outside and towards the back of the house again.

"Oh no. We aren't going back down there are we?"

"Oh ye of little faith."

Lauren grumbled to herself. She looked around at the countryside in the waning light. The setting sun painted brilliant colors on the clouds above, and set fire to the fields around them.

Rather than take her to the cellar, Valerie led her to the curious outbuilding she had seen before. It was a round structure, like some kind of low silo about ten feet across. The oddest feature was certainly the glass roof, which was made of several panels that appeared to be able to open and shut independently.

A moment spent fiddling with keys, and Valerie was opening the one door set into the side of the building. Lauren peeked inside and couldn't help but gasp.

It was heaven. It had to be.

Almost the entire floor of the building, save for a perimeter of about two feet, was a gigantic in-ground hot tub. Lauren wasted no time ducking inside. Valerie followed her in, laughing at her overjoyed reaction.

Lauren stepped carefully around the tub, the entire interior wall was covered in gorgeous photographs of landscapes all over the world. They were clearly different places, but Valerie had masterfully blended the changing colors and lines so that each photo seemed to flow directly into those around it. It was like looking at a quilt of the world, and made the tiny space feel massive and grand.

"Valerie this is beautiful, it must have taken you years."

Lauren moved slowly along the wall, poring over the photographs.

"A labor of love, I'm afraid. Every time I think it's finished I find something even more beautiful to photograph."

The tub itself had a low bench and several recessed lights that, along with the fading sunlight filtering down from above, provided illumination for the room. Half-burnt candles of various sizes were dotted around the walkway, as were an assortment of books. Lauren picked one up at random and turned it to the cover. She was a little surprised to find that it was a romance novel. Two women were ballroom dancing across a cover that read "Two Lips in Summer." She'd expected something a little more cerebral from her friend, but she was far from put out. She still had her back to Valerie, so with a mischievous grin she began to read in a dramatic, passionate voice.

"Two young women in the antebellum South discover forbidden love amidst fields of flowers in this sensual romp through America's past…"

"Ahem!"

Valerie coughed loudly, and Lauren turned with a big smile on her face. It was Lauren's turn to be speechless. While Lauren had been poking through the books and candles, Valerie had quietly slipped out her clothes and was sitting naked at the edge of the tub across from her.

"Wow."

Valerie's casual strength and vibrant confidence seemed more fragile in the dim light. She held the same straight-backed, self-assured posture that Lauren had come to know, but her eyes were open windows of longing and nervousness.

"Lauren, tonight could end right here if you'd like. We could walk away, go to bed, and never speak of it again... if that's what you want."

Lauren stepped hesitantly to the edge of the tub.

"I would understand, I really would. But I spent too much of my life denying who I was, and not speaking up for what I wanted, to not tell you how I feel."

Valerie's voice cracked a little as she spoke, and Lauren could sense a great deal of pain within her. She wondered, not for the first time, at the foundation that had built such a strong woman.

"But these past few weeks have been some of the brightest memories I've ever made. So, this is me. Valerie Prescott Chatwick. This is me telling you that I want more. That I want you."

Lauren's heart was pounding, her head spinning as Valerie made her confession. She'd never directly confronted this part of herself. Romance had always been a confusing, disordered, secondary concern. She never had a chance to figure out who she was, what this part of her life could be like. But now she had a real, grown-up choice to make.

This would be more than a stolen kiss. More than a lingering hug or a fantasy in her mind.

She stared at the water below her feet. She'd told herself for years that she wished for a real relationship. Or even for the ability to have one. She had pined away countless hours in high school pondering her looming spinsterhood. But here it was, a dream come true, and she was suddenly terrified.

The edge of the hot tub became more than just a step into warm water. It was a gut-check that held Lauren frozen as she weighed her options. She looked up and saw Valerie staring at her. Her heart did a backflip and her mind was made up in an instant. The raw emotion in her companion's eyes resonated inside her and gave her strength.

"Valerie Prescott Chatwick, it's a pleasure to meet you."

Lauren untied the towel she wore and let it fall to the walkway around her ankles. She took a deep breath and stepped down onto the bench in the tub, and then further to the floor. The water rose to the middle of her chest.

"This is me, Lauren Elisse Corvidae."

Valerie paused a moment, and then slid into the tub as well, wading over to Lauren and wrapping her in a bear hug. She rested her head on Lauren's shoulder and the two held each other tightly for several minutes before speaking.

Lauren tried to push back the doubts and fears in the back of her mind. She couldn't help but dwell on the people she had lost before.

"I... have to tell you that I don't think this will be easy. That I have a long history of hurting the people around me."

Valerie didn't answer at first, just squeezed her tighter.

"Lauren, if you're not sure about this...."

"I do! I mean, I am. I want to try."

Lauren felt an electric thrill as they pressed their bodies together. The heat between them put the water to shame. Her skin felt impossibly sensitive. She was aware of every inch of contact between them. Lauren's wings instinctively curled around them, her feathers skimming the surface of the water.

"I think that I need you to do something for me first though..."

Valerie stiffened ever so slightly and pulled her head back. She looked into Lauren's eyes and scanned her face curiously.

Lauren leaned in close, her cheeks scarlet, and whispered softly.

"I believe there was some discussion of preening?"

Lauren rolled over in the large bed, caught somewhere between waking and sleep. The night before was a fiery blur of passion and pleasure. She could feel the rays of the morning sun across her bare leg and back. She retreated, cuddling deeper into the silky sheets and basking in the afterglow of her evening.

She wasn't sure what time they had actually gone to sleep, they'd been too distracted to care. Visions of Valerie filled her mind, the taste of her still lingered on Lauren's lips. She could still feel the memory of her thin fingers entwining themselves in her hair. She couldn't stop thinking about Valerie's velvet touch. Drowsiness was replaced by other, more active desires and she came to grips with the idea that she was not going to get back to sleep.

Her eyes still closed, Lauren snaked a hand across the bed, reaching out for Valerie. She hoped to find her companion similarly interested in picking up where they had left off, but found nothing except more bedsheets and blankets.

She sat up, confused, and blinked in the morning light. Valerie was nowhere to be found, but a folded piece of paper with a big heart drawn on it was sitting on the bedside table with a glass of water and a cellphone.

Lauren, got called into the office in London. Turns out I do have to work occasionally. I wish I could sleep in, especially after last night. Don't worry, I'll be back this evening. Make yourself at home! Help yourself to anything in the house. This is my personal cell phone, consider it yours until we can find a way to get you one, I can just use my work phone.

· V

P.S. Don't be worried when Edward stops by, he's the epitome of British discretion and I told him I have a guest.

P.P.S. If you need anything from town just ask Edward, he can get it for you.

Lauren smiled and picked up the phone, a blinking icon indicated that there was an unread text message. She activated the touchscreen and the note appeared.

"Lauren, this is my work cell -V"

Lauren tapped a reply and smiled at the giddy, overly happy feelings flooding her body.

"Good morning, thanks for last night... - L"

She couldn't describe it. She felt an unabashed joy inside, like she was going to burst into song. She slipped out of the bed and stretched widely, resisting the urge to dance. She caught sight of herself in the bathroom mirror and laughed out loud at her messy, wild hair. She looked like she'd just been electrocuted.

Ding.

"The pleasure was mine, sorry I had to work today."

"/sigh/ I suppose I will survive."

Lauren ran her fingers through her hair in an effort to tamc it.

"You still haven't given me any clothes. Is this part of your plan?"

"Sorry! I had a rather distracting evening... anything in the dressers is fair game."

"Thanks"

"Not a problem, I'm heading into a staff meeting, I'll write when I get out, k?"

Lauren pouted a moment before moving to pick through the clothes available. She settled on a pair of khaki cargo shorts and a tank top and headed downstairs to address her next concern, breakfast.

The creaking of the wooden stairs covered the quiet sounds of cooking, so by the time Lauren saw the man in the kitchen it was already too late.

"Good morning ma'am! I am Edward Warvington, at your service."

Lauren jumped. An elderly man in a dress shirt and slacks was addressing her from behind a pair of thick spectacles.

"I took the liberty of preparing eggs florentine for you this morning. How do you take your tea?"

He seemed harmless enough, particularly considering he wore the same floral apron that Valerie had used the night before.

"Um, hello. Lauren Corvidae, nice to meet you, sir."

He beckoned her to follow him to the kitchen and she did so.

"The pleasure is no doubt mine. Your tea, madame?"

"Oh right. Is it like, green tea? I don't usually put anything in it."

He looked askance at her.

"N-no my dear. It's a proper black English tea. I'll just get you some cream shall I?"

She shrugged.

The man puttered around the kitchen and produced a cup of tea as promised, complete with a saucer and a tiny spoon. He brought over a tiny pitcher of cream and poured a dab into the cup. The end result looked like a cup of coffee to Lauren, who nonetheless thanked him.

She took a sip under his watchful gaze, and was pleasantly surprised at the taste.

He nodded with satisfaction and continued cooking.

"So you're Edward. Valerie told me you've helped her family out for a long time."

"Ah well, it's something of a family tradition. I recall when Mr. Chatwick was just a baby, and so naturally I've continued to look after our mutual friend, Valerie."

"Mr. Chatwick? You knew her father as a *baby*? That's incredible."

"Well, I hesitate to describe my age as incredible, but I do appreciate that my dear."

Edward set down a plate in front of her with a neatly folded omelette filled with spinach and fresh tomatoes. It was picture perfect, and Lauren devoured it while he spoke.

"Yes, well, caring for Valerie hasn't been easy. She had some rough times, and she's responsible for a great many gray hairs on my head. But she's the granddaughter I never had, and I love her very dearly."

Lauren nodded.

"Which brings me to my next question, and I do apologize if this seems indelicate. I... have never questioned Valerie's lifestyle, nor her choices. I knew she was different ever since she was a baby, whether her father wanted to admit it or not. Now, I say that to say this - I know you have your secrets, and what you do with them is no business of mine. But now you have one of her secrets too, and that *is* my business."

Lauren sobered as he spoke.

"You must be very careful with her, ma'am, she cannot heal so easily as you."

"Sir, Mr. Warvington, I have no intention of hurting Valerie. I care very deeply for her, in a way I didn't think I'd ever be able to."

He gave a relieved nod.

"Well, good, then I wish you both all the happiness in the world. I do apologize for being dramatic, but I have seen her in pain and I do not think my old heart could take it again."

Lauren smiled, she felt like a prom-date getting 'the talk' from a nervous father.

Ding. Ding-ding-ding-ding.

Valerie's phone was inundated with messages.

"*Are you at the house?*"

"*Is Edward there?*"

"*Nevermind, call him, tell him you need a ride right now. Tell him to take you to the Lake House.*"

"*Don't turn on the TV*"

The messages came in as fast as she could read them.

"*What's wrong V, are you ok?*"

A loud pounding at the door startled them both and set Lauren's heart thumping.

"Well how rude, we have a *doorbell* for heaven's sake. Please wait here ma'am, and I shall send whomever is at the door on their way."

Edward headed for the door and Lauren tried to shake the terrible feeling she had. The hair on the back of her neck stood up as she ducked around the corner and out of sight of the front door.

Lauren felt her chest tighten uncomfortably.

She pulled the white lace curtains open over the sink in the kitchen, only to be confronted with the lense of a large black video camera.

"She's over here!"

Lauren jumped back, her mind racing. How had they found her here? Someone must have seen them outside. She kicked herself mentally. She should have known better.

"Ms. Corvidae, Ms. Corvidae will you make a statement?"

Lauren heard the front door slam shut and Edward returned, a stony look on his face.

"Ma'am, you have my deepest apologies. I want you to know you may shelter here as long as you like. I will do my best to deter our unwelcome guests."

"No, thank you. This is my problem."

Lauren slipped her phone into her pocket and gave a defeated sigh.

"P-please tell Valerie. I didn't mean for any of this to happen."

Edward nodded solemnly and stepped aside as Lauren passed him on the way to the door.

Lauren reached for the doorknob and paused, her hand hovering a few inches away from it. She thought about bolting. Could she make it out a window upstairs and into the sky? Would she be able to evade the cameras? For how long?

Ding.

The phone in her pocket felt like it weighed a thousand pounds. The weight of Valerie's safety fell heavily on Lauren's shoulders and she steeled herself for the frenzy to come.

Someday, she reassured herself.

Lauren wrenched the door open and braced for impact. Sure enough dozens of reporters were crowded around the doorway, all jamming microphones at her. Their garbled shouting made it nearly impossible to distinguish a single question amidst the flood.

"Stop, Stop!"

Lauren held her hands up and silenced the unruly group. Recorders and microphones hovered near her, waiting for her to speak. In the distance she could see traffic pouring into the tiny town.

"Please let's... let's try to keep this somewhat organized."

She thought back to the press conferences she used to do with her State Department escorts. Lauren cloaked herself in borrowed bravado, copied from Valerie's casual confidence.

"I'll answer a few questions, but then that's it. Got it?"

The crowd grumbled, but seemed to assent.

"You, um, with the glasses there."

"Yes ma'am, Daniel Jay, BBC Wales. What brought you to Britain?"

Lauren was surprised at what felt like a softball question. But then she realized she didn't have a good answer.

"I... wanted to get away. I needed some time out of the spotlight, to sort things out for myself."

"So it had nothing to do with your romantic relationship with Valerie Chatwick?

Chapter 7

Lauren was a fish out of water. How could he have possibly known about that? The sharks before her smelled blood in the water, and she was once again bombarded with questions.

"How long has your relationship been going on?"
"Is homosexuality the root of your feud with the Catholic Church?"

"Did you know Ms. Chatwick was a reporter when you began your sexual relationship?"

What?

Valerie was a reporter.

Not a photographer, a *reporter.*

Lauren stood frozen, her mind reeling. She had never before felt so truly betrayed. Lauren clutched at her chest, physically stunned at having her heart so completely cut out.

The voices of the reporters blended into a high-pitched whine, like steam escaping a kettle.

Ding.

The tiny, almost inaudible sound of the phone in her pocket broke through the cacophony and snapped every one of Lauren's senses into a state of hyper-clarity.

Lauren reached out and roughly grabbed the collar of the reporter who had broken the news.

"A reporter for who."

Her voice trembled with rage.

"I-I beg your pardon?"

The man stuttered with shock at her violence.

She shook him roughly and shouted her reply.

"Who does she work for!"

"Th-the BBC."

"Where."

"BT Tower, in London."

Lauren shoved him back into the crowd. She clenched her fists with rage and snapped her wings violently open. Her buffeting limbs knocked a few reporters over, but she paid them no mind as she leapt into the sky.

Lauren's eyes narrowed and a scowl fixed itself firmly on her face as she blazed towards London's towering skyline.

She wanted answers.

The tower was easy enough to find. It was, after all, more than 500 feet tall and had 'BT' on it in large blue letters. Lauren angled herself downward, ignoring the crowds gathered below her. She pulled up at the last second, landing forcefully in front of the doors to the building.

People began to crowd around her immediately. The look on her face must have clued them in though, because they kept more distance than usual.

Lauren gave the ornate glass doors a violent push, shattering one and badly cracking the other as they banged off of their respective doorstops.

Bystanders shared alarmed looks as she strode through the glass and into the lobby. A small contingent of security guards rushed towards her but seemed hesitant to actually apprehend her.

"Valerie!"

Deep down she knew it was ridiculous to be screaming at the top of her lungs in the lobby, as though Valerie would be there to hear her, but it was cathartic.

"Ma'am, I need you to calm down now alright?"

She threw the guard a poisoned look and continued calling for Valerie.

The crowd in the lobby gathered as curiosity drew people in despite the shouting and broken glass. So far, her anger kept them at bay.

She headed towards a desk helpfully labelled 'information.' Her tiny bubble of security personnel traveled with her, still unwilling to engage.

"You. Where does Valerie Chatwick work."

The secretary, a blonde with wide, horn-rimmed glasses looked nervously back and forth between Lauren and the nearest guard.

Lauren felt a strong hand on her shoulder.

"Really Ma'am, you're disrupting-"

Lauren shoved the man with her wing, hard, and sent him sprawling on the tiles. She spared a glance over her shoulder to see he was a police officer, and promptly returned her attention to the woman at the desk.

"Now."

Lauren growled the word and the young woman ducked her head and started typing furiously. The phone at her desk rang. She seemed unsure how to react, but when it didn't stop she lifted the receiver.

"BT Tower this is Joyce. Y-yes sir."

A series of high-pitched whistles could be heard from outside, no doubt policemen on their way to intervene. People in the crowd were murmuring and pointing upward, drawing Lauren's eyes. A series of massive television monitors lined the walls above the plate glass windows wrapping the lobby.

Lauren's face was plastered all over them beside Valerie's. The screens cut back to a panel of news anchors who were animatedly discussing the images.

"Hey. Hey, turn that up."

Lauren slapped her hand up and down on the desk when Joyce didn't move swiftly enough.

"...Our very own Valerie Chatwick, renowned photographer and long time BBC correspondent. We received this security camera footage from the private dock of Reginald Metzger, an executive producer and family friend of Ms. Chatwick."

Lauren turned sheet-white, then blazing scarlet as the monitors filled with a high-definition video of her and Valerie sitting on the deck of the Liebeslied in their skimpy bikinis. Lauren watched herself straddle her companion and the kiss of passion they shared on-screen hit her like a punch in the gut.

The video repeated several times, while the posh newscasters commented on every lurid detail.

"We were able to sit down with Mrs. Chatwick today for a brief interview that unfortunately experienced several technical difficulties..."

"Ma'am, I need you to calmly turn 'round if you please!"

A stern, authoritative voice shouted from behind her.

She turned and saw four policemen standing fanned out before her. Behind them the crowd inside the lobby had grown considerably.

"Thank you ma'am. Now, you need to exit the building. We'll have to bring you 'round the station for vandalism of private property."

Lauren narrowed her eyes. She saw laughter and judgement in the eyes of the crowd. She watched them look back and forth from her to the screen and whisper to each other while they pointed. She bristled with anger.

"Now, ma'am."

She took a sudden step towards the officer, and smiled internally when he flinched. She drew closer, until her face was just inches from his own. She squared her shoulders and lifted her wings slightly, overshadowing the man before her.

"Suppose I say no," she threatened.

He took a deep breath and put a hand on the handle of a short black baton at his waist.

"Please ma'am, don't."

Lauren turned, calling his bluff, and stepped back to the secretary.

"I believe I asked you a question."

"Ma'am, I've been told to have you escorted from the building."

The girl was whispering, visibly terrified.

Strong hands grabbed Lauren's arms from behind. She could feel the officers try to wrench her hands together behind her back and she struggled violently against them. The crowd, excited by the sudden change in energy, pressed in against the tiny struggling group.

Lauren's face was pressed against the polished surface of the desk as she pushed against the men holding her down. She could see the reflection of the side of her face not crushed against the cool glass. Her ebon hair partially obscured the wild look of hate on her face, but the bottomless black depths of her eyes reflected the darkness of her anger perfectly.

Lauren couldn't help but think of all the times she'd exhausted herself trying to help people just like these. How many hours of sleep deprivation and hunger and exhaustion she had spent for them. The cost in blood and tears and years of her life. A debt unpaid. An equation unbalanced.

No good deed goes unpunished.

So be it. Lauren wished she could take it back. She wished deep in her heart that she could take back the gifts she had so freely given these ever-hungry scavengers that were clinging to her. But the people holding her were too strong, and her struggles were in vain.

Lauren screamed at her own impotence. A feral, ear-shattering cry to the heavens that somehow, miraculously, cast the room into total silence.

She felt the hands holding her go limp and release their hold and she returned shakily to her feet.

Her heart was pounding so hard she could feel it in her eyes. She felt *different*. Like someone had pumped her full of adrenaline and then hooked her up to a power outlet. Every muscle in her body was taut and flooded with energy.

Lauren stared at her hands and arms, nothing had changed physically, but she felt a pump in her muscles like she'd just finished an intense workout. Her vision blurred in and out of focus with every heartbeat.

The TV in the background seemed overly loud, blaring out against the silence of the room. Why was the room silent?

She focused her attention on the secretary in front of her. She was slumped face down on her desk with the phone still hanging off the hook. She wasn't the only one, everyone in the room was laying out on the floor in a heap. Their bodies, once pressed together in fevered excitement, were now limp ragdolls littering the floor.

Lauren's confusion took some of the fire from her temper. Her vision was lurching back and forth between what she would call 'normal' and a sort of magnified, incredibly sharp image. Like she was looking through a telescope.

"Hey. Hello?"

She tapped the desk, leaving a spider web of cracks in the glass unintentionally. She looked at her fingers in surprise and then back at the secretary's head. No response.

"Hey! Wake up!"

Fed up, she lifted the woman's head by her ponytail. She was surprisingly light, almost weightless, causing Lauren to lift her much more forcefully than she intended.

The woman offered no resistance, and when Lauren finally got a look at her face she let go immediately. The secretary's face showed the same fear and confusion as a moment ago, but her unfocused, lifeless eyes took Lauren by surprise. As if to confirm her condition, the girl's face bounced off the desk and she slid out of her chair and onto the floor.

"Oh my god."

Lauren's heart was still thumping, pounding like a jackhammer as she tried to sort out what exactly had happened. She pushed back from the desk, inadvertently sending it squealing several inches across the polished floor.

People who had been standing outside and trying to get in were starting to react to the sudden turn of events. Sirens were going off in the distance and dozens of cellphone cameras were snapping away furiously. In contrast to the roar of a few moments ago, everyone's voice seemed reduced to a frightened whisper.

"...Getting word of some sort of event now. They are encouraging the staff here to shelter in place. We will stay on the air until required to halt our broadcast. We have Erika Severns reporting live from the base of BT Tower here in London. Erika?"

Lauren looked up to the screens and saw herself from a third person perspective. She cast around for a moment until she identified the two-person news team standing outside with a camera trained on her.

She rushed to the cracked doorway and pulled it open. The metal handle tore off in her hand, eliciting a gasp from the gathered crowd. They kept a healthy distance from her, with the exception of the cameraman and newscaster. Still, the woman seemed genuinely frightened, kept in place more by fear than confidence.

"P-please, don't kill me," she whispered.

Lauren shook her head, her oddly heightened senses were disorienting.

"*Kill* you?"

The woman nodded, crying wide-eyed as she looked past Lauren and into the lobby.

"I didn't. I mean I never..."

Lauren's emotions were a roller-coaster. One moment she felt pure, unadulterated joy, and the next crushing despair and sadness, then envy, rage, fear, and more. She took a deep breath, trying to steady herself.

"I don't understand, w-why would you do this?"

Lauren had no answer.

She hadn't meant for it to happen, and the side effects were clouding her mind and making it difficult to think straight. She opened her mouth to respond, second-guessed herself, and then began again.

But what could she say? The urge to run built until she could fight it no more.

She spread her wings wide and for once the crowd surrounding her gave her extra room rather than pressing closer.

A perverse sense of relief flooded her heart. Now at last she had the space she craved so deeply. Her scowl settled back into place as she leapt skyward and raced to the clouds.

She spent several minutes gaining altitude, hoping to blend into the overcast sky hanging low over the city. Within seconds she was hundreds of feet in the air. She felt light as a feather, and her muscles propelled her much faster and more easily than ever before. She took one last look at the city below, then dove into the cover of the clouds.

Cold, wet wisps of condensations surrounded her and she couldn't help but shiver. Her wings were still pumping, and she could feel the air rushing past her face, but the unchanging haze of the cloud bank made her feel as though she wasn't moving at all. She picked a direction at random and sped away. The weather suited her just fine, so she carried on until the creeping feeling of lostness became unbearable.

Lauren dipped downward just long enough to catch a glimpse the land below of her. She was over a body of water between two rocky coasts. Her vision remained altered, and if she focused she could see the land below with hawk-like precision. She marvelled at the patchwork of farms and small villages, stunned at the clarity. She was certainly a far cry from London, she couldn't even see it in the distance behind her. There was land ahead, so she slipped back into the clouds and tried to sort out what exactly had gone wrong back at the tower.

She played the events over and over in her mind, trying to pick out what had been different from a hundred other times she's been stuck, surrounded by an impenetrable press of people. She recalled the raw surge of power she had felt. It had subsided only very slightly, and she couldn't deny the intense pleasure and strength that had flooded her system. Even now she felt like she could bench press a truck.

But what had she actually *done*? Was it really her, or some other force acting upon her? She tried to convince herself that maybe it was an outside force and that her gift had merely protected her. But then why would she be so... charged up? No, this was almost certainly some new development of her own.

Lauren continued drifting through the sky, bitterly reminding herself that she was, once again, essentially alone. She struggled to feel more guilt than relief. Lauren lost track of time and the miles slipped silently past.

She wasn't sure how long she'd been wrapped up in her own thoughts when she first heard the crashing waves in the distance, but the roar of the ocean was impressive enough to pull her back to reality.

Lauren looked down, pleased to see that the green landscape below her was devoid of people. She had allowed herself to drift lower, only a few hundred feet above the ground now. She was floating above a dazzling line of cliffs stretching as far as her keen eyes could see. A small footpath had been worn in the grass, stretching lengthwise along the coast, but there wasn't a soul in sight.

Lauren touched down lightly on the slope, taking a moment to marvel at the raw beauty surrounding her. The ocean roared a hundred feet below, and the land melted away into a rolling green carpet behind her. The rich scent of saltspray mixed with the tickle of wildflowers and she took a deep, calming breath.

"Ok," she said to no one in particular. "So maybe you can, y'know, kill stuff."

A tiny frown sprouted on her face as she said the words. She didn't like the way they sounded, the heavy manner in which they hung in the air. At the same time, she felt... excited? It seemed too strong a word, but her heart skipped a beat at the implied power of the statement.

Lauren stepped to the edge of the cliff and sat down, her legs swinging out into the open space beyond. She sighed and lay back against the soft cool grasses and wildflowers covering the ground, content to clear her mind and stare at the skies rather than face the consequences of reality.

Her mind was not so easily pacified as her body. It was mere minutes before she was sitting up again and plucking at the grass dejectedly. The tiny, supple blades snapped easily in her fingers and found themselves cast helplessly into the turbulent currents below.

Lauren's idle hand found the thorn-covered stalk of a short thistle and she pulled back in surprise. The tiny spikes, so perfectly suited at prickling the unsuspecting passersby, had bent and broken rather than pierce her skin. She furrowed her brow. Lauren was no stranger to the bite of a thistle, stepping on them as a child had been the unavoidable consequence of insisting on running about barefoot. She'd never been so lucky as to touch one unscathed like this.

Morbid curiosity took root, as she stared at her uninjured palm. Hesitantly she reached out to the plant once more. She pressed gently at first, and then harder as she found herself immune to the tiny barbs. Again she inspected her hand, her eyes wide as she realized that her skin seemed totally impervious to the sting of the plant.

Lauren balled her hand into a fist and slammed it down on the flower, crushing it into the ground. She laughed out loud at her total lack of pain. Moreover, her simple gesture had left a sizeable divot in the ground, much deeper than she would have expected from the blow. Her muscles were no more strained than if she had lifted a piece of paper, but the impact looked like a sledgehammer.

She felt a giddy high building in her mind at her newfound strength. This must be a side effect of what had happened in London, there was no doubt in her mind. She rolled over in the grass and lay back down, her elbows propping up her chest and head. She reached a slim finger out to the battered remains of the thistle and tried to concentrate. No response. Lauren scrunched her eyes shut and stubbornly focused her mind, demanding the powers within her bend to her will. She felt a brief stirring in her stomach, or had she simply imagined it?

A few moments passed with no apparent change and she peeked outward from behind a half-closed eyelid. Her eyes snapped open at the sight of the thistle standing healthy and strong in the depression left by her fist. Every leaf, every spike perfectly healthy and lush. There was no evidence that she had ever injured it aside from the dent in the ground.

Lauren shivered, her mind racing with possibility. Her face broke into a half-wild smile as she sat up on her knees, both palms placed flat on the ground in front of her. Again she closed her eyes, her brow furrowed in concentration. She dug deep inside, reaching for the power she had felt earlier, and found it within herself. She shivered internally at the dark, oily feeling that came bubbling to the surface of her mind.

The power radiating from her core was irresistible.

She felt a low electric buzz in her fingers slowly building into an steady hum of power that filled her arms and worked its way to her chest. She opened her eyes to see the greenery before her wilt and wither.

But it wasn't just under her palms. She rose to her feet in the middle of a swath of decayed vegetation several yards across. Her body was again filled with unfamiliar strength, though it was a tiny fraction of the power she had felt this morning.

Lauren couldn't help laughing giddily at the euphoric high that flooded her mind. She marvelled at her hands, inspecting them closely. In doing so, she noticed that faint silvery lines criss-crossed her arms. After a moment's thought she realized what they must be; faded scars from her destructive self-medication. They faded until they were almost indistinguishable from the rest of her skin.

So, she could control her healing after all. Moreover, she finally had a weapon to defend herself from the predatory world she'd been forced to live with for so long. A part of her, some distant voice within her mind, registered concern as her thoughts immediately turned to the revenge she could seek. But it was drowned out by the brightly burning lure of her newfound power.

Lauren looked out over the broad, rolling hills once more. But where a few minutes ago she had seen only beauty, she now gazed hungrily at untapped power. She licked her lips and dropped to her knees again, plunging her hands into the soil and reaching within for that dark strength simmering in her heart. It came more easily this time, and she relished the cool smooth feel of it. Within moments she was leeching the life from the ground around her in an ever-spreading circle of decay.

She was mesmerized by the silvery lines pulsing brighter and brighter on her arms as she drained the hills. But it wasn't enough. She felt like a light bulb flickering in the face of too little power. She felt good, yes, but it was like eating steak and following it up with crackers and water. No matter how hard she pushed, it wasn't enough.

She hungered for more.

Finally she sat back with a frustrated growl.

Ding.

Lauren jumped at the sound.

Rather than check the phone in her pocket, Lauren seethed with sudden anger. She stood, barely noticing that the ground around her was darkened for hundreds of feet in every direction, and leapt into the sky like a bullet.

The memory of her first flight came unbidden to her mind and she raced across the skies. The timid girl who had been a slave to every current and eddy of the wind had been replaced by a sleek savant, capable of driving easily through the strong headwinds she faced as she tore across the open seas between Ireland and Wales.

Her newly strengthened wings carried her much more swiftly than she anticipated, and before long she was nearing London. She had every intention of facing Valerie, of demanding an explanation, of venting the rage and pain she felt.

Until she passed over Farningham, that is.

She pulled a tight turn as she passed the Chatwick estate, unsure of what she had seen. Sure enough her keen eyes had not deceived her. The tiny home was surrounded by news vans and clamoring reporters, but her eyes were focused through the bedroom window. Edward was gently holding Valerie, whose shoulders shook with painful-looking sobs. What little of her face Lauren could see was red with pain and suffering. In that moment a tiny light in Lauren's heart rekindled and she hovered a moment, suddenly unsure.

But the darkness within her demanded an outlet. It stoked the hatred in her heart back into a blaze and Lauren found her fists clenched and her jaw tight.

She couldn't land. Couldn't face Valerie or the horde of reporters. She couldn't go home, even now she didn't think she had the strength to cross an entire ocean. She discarded idea after idea, growing more frustrated by the second until she settled on a course of action that brought a gleeful smile to her lips.

Unnoticed by the tiny people below, her dark shadow slipped silently southeast, heading for the channel and mainland Europe.

Weyland hadn't moved in several days. A permanent scowl seemed to have taken up residence on his chiseled face as he sat atop a massive gilded throne in the heart of the newly restored Acropolis.

Natalie entered the grand chamber softly, dreading disturbing her master while he... did whatever it was he was doing during these long periods of sullen silence.

"Y-your majesty, Lauren has been seen in London."

He stirred.

"How long ago."

"Just this morning. A few hours ago. The news is saying that she had some sort of fit and killed a bunch of people."

Natalie, for her own part, didn't believe the reporters on television. She'd heard about Lauren's gifts for most of her own life, and she had never once heard of Lauren committing such an act. Lauren had been selfless to a fault up until now.

"A few hours ago?"

His tone was deadly calm. Natalie braced herself for a blow.

"Hours!"

His rage was sudden and violent. He went from sitting across the room to towering over her in a flash of fire and smoke. Natalie cowered, biting her lip until it bled to keep from crying out as the heat from his skin blistered her exposed skin.

He took offense when she expressed pain in his presence.

Natalie stammered a response but Weyland ignored her. The smooth stone below his bare feet sizzled with heat and it was all Natalie could do to stay put. But her fear of him was greater than any pain she might endure. Natalie had seen him incinerate people for far less than bringing him late news. She trembled, sure of her imminent death. So it took her by surprise when he began to pace the marble floor of the chamber instead.

Weyland muttered to himself as he wore out the stones with his relentless movement. Had he forgotten her? Was she free to go? Natalie didn't know, but respect for his power kept her firmly rooted in place. After a few minutes of listening to his heavy footsteps she found the courage to sneak a peek at him, ignoring his preference that she keep her eyes dutifully downcast.

The wheels in her mind spun freely as she witnessed the first instance of indecision she had seen him express. His endless self-confidence appeared vulnerable as it never had before. He was clearly wrestling with a difficult choice, but Natalie dared not guess what it might be. Still, the scientist within her grew more curious with every passing second. She decided it must be something related to Lauren.

The thought made her heart swell with hope.

Natalie had taken a massive risk by waiting to inform Weyland of his prey's movements in London, but she had resolved to make up for her lack of action when Lauren had needed her most. She held desperately to the hope that Lauren would somehow rescue her.

For Weyland's part, it was as if Natalie had ceased to exist. She was only human, after all. After several minutes she shuffled uncomfortably and he finally stopped pacing. He looked surprised to see her still standing there.

"Leave me."

Weyland watched his servant scurry from the room and returned to his introspection. Weyland had expected Lauren's tantrum to last a few hours, maybe a day at most. But here it had been nearly two weeks and not only had she not returned, she seemed to be actively avoiding him, keeping her whereabouts hidden from the world.

What are you playing at, little bird?

He sighed uncharacteristically and cast about the room for inspiration. The throne room, with its splendor of artwork and abundance of gold and jewels, did nothing to excite him. He huffed at the trinkets, tribute from the various museums and collections of the world delivered by the hands of terrified mortals to his uncaring possession.

Nothing caused his heart to stir or his blood to burn except for her.

His powers had returned fully with his waking and his unchallenged might reminded him why he had slumbered so deeply in the first place.

Boredom. Boredom and disappointment.

A flash of fire and Weyland was standing in his bedroom suite. The charred black stones of the floor were the only evidence of his frequent visits, his servants kept the room immaculately cleaned in his absence. A bevy of gorgeous women, all sporting thin silk garments and heavy golden circlets around their necks, lounged on pillows around the room. A few of his concubines let out out gasps or jumped with surprise, but all of the lingerie-clad women dropped obediently to their knees.

Surprising, generally it took new girls a few days to fully grasp their place and proper behaviour, and by that time he was almost always done with them.

But even the buffet of flesh in front of him didn't ignite his passion as it had in ages past. Each of the women paled in comparison to the object of his desire. He must have scowled, because he could smell the fear in the room rising above the odors of rosewater and the faintest hint of ash and burnt skin.

The trembling, terrified women in front of him were worlds away from the defiant angel that had struck him in his own courtyard. That knowledge burned in his heart and stoked his ever-raging temper. Knowing that he could not have thing thing he wanted most only further fueled his obsession.

Heat waves poured off of his clenched fists as he scanned the girls until his gaze found a dark-haired, pale-skinned girl about Lauren's height and build.

"You."

He pointed menacingly and locked his eyes with hers. The rest of the women fled the room and tried to avoid looking at the girl they were leaving behind.

Hours later, when he left the room, he did so on foot. The girl had taken the edge off of his frustration, but he had been rougher than usual and it was unlikely she would be useful to him again for many months, if ever. A shame, her resemblance to his prey had been... useful.

More importantly, his head was clearer. Weyland would wait no longer. Enough was enough. It was time to resume his post at long last.

He smirked as he passed his guards. To their credit they didn't flinch at his passing. Weyland strode out to the court-yard and took a deep breath of the still, smoky air before disappearing in a blinding explosion.

Moments later the timeworn stones of the old Covent Garden Market shuddered and cracked as Weyland crossed the two-thousand mile gap in the space of a heartbeat. The busy shopping center exploded in screams of pain as Weyland ar-rived with a blistering heatwave. Pain-wracked citizens writhed on the ground, unable even to stand as their skin sizzled and popped in the wake of Weyland's power.

It was music to his ears, a validation of his complete and utter omnipotence. He didn't have to wait long for his errant subjects to come to him, begging for mercy and trembling with fear. After a few hours he was standing before a kneeling crowd of soldiers, officers and government officials.

"Hear this, mortals. Let is be known that any nation who harbors my bride without informing me will be considered my enemy and will face my wrath..."

Chapter 8

Kent Dailey was smiling so hard it hurt his face. His nose was pressed against the glass of a small window in the side of a massive gray C-130. The large military aircraft was descending rapidly. As they broke through the cloud cover, a spectacular view of Venice appeared before him.

Valerie Chatwick was AWOL, and had been since her very public scandal hit headlines worldwide. Her misfortune was a godsend for Kent, as he was once again the foremost expert on all things Lauren Corvidae and, by extension, Weyland.

Athens was still a hotspot, and planes had been avoiding England since Weyland's display in London left more than a thousand people dead and injured. He'd managed to hitch a ride into Venice with the United States Air Force, but it was only a refueling point between Chicago and wherever they'd be headed next.

Kent and his cameraman had jammed as much equipment as they could fit into a pair of large backpacks and crowded on-board with 70 or so tight-lipped soldiers armed to the teeth.

A helmeted member of the air crew worked his way between the huddled troops and over to Kent's side.

"Mr. Dailey, we touch down in five. We're staying long enough to refuel and then we are popping smoke. You've got until then to change your mind."

Clark was giving him a nervous look, but Kent knew he wouldn't get another chance and he'd be damned if he was going to pass it up. He was scared, terrified of being closer to the monstrous man he had witnessed in Chicago a few months ago. But he gritted his teeth and tried to swallow the lump in his throat.

"Not a chance sir," Kent replied.

Sure enough, the moment their wheels hit the tarmac the pair were escorted from the aircraft amidst a flurry of activity by the crew.

"Good morning, Mr. Dailey!"

A portly fellow with a melodic italian accent was flagging them down and waving his arms to get their attention.

"Welcome to Italy, Mr. Dailey. I'm Fernando Rilleri with Senator Fafoglia's office. It's a pleasure to meet you sir. If you'll follow me, he's waiting for you."

Kent was surprised, but hid it well. Roberto Fafoglia did not often grant audiences to the media. The controversial Cardinal was the subject of a very violent and public witch hunt after leading the Catholic Church into the Second Great Schism. As the furor over the Schism started to fade in the wake of Lauren's fall, Fafoglia found himself abreast of a popular swell of support for the heroine and had secured a seat in the Italian Senate with it.

That wasn't the only reason Kent was taken by surprise, however. Fafoglia had been an unshakably outspoken advocate of Lauren's within the Church as well as the government. A stance that seemed at odds with Kent's less-than-loyal approach to her fame.

Maybe the morbid events of the past few days had finally changed his mind?

A small black car was waiting outside the airport for them, guarded by a singularly menacing looking man in a dark suit. He couldn't have been more than 25 years old, but he had a prematurely aged face. As though he'd seen or done terrible things in his short life. A large scar, no more than a few months old, ran from his left ear to the middle of his throat and added to his threatening appearance.

"This is Kaspar von Silenen, a former member of the Swiss Guard and a dear friend of mine. He generally sees to the security of the senator and will be escorting us during your interview."

Kent exchanged a handshake with the guard and tried not to wince at the pressure of the man's strong grip. Kaspar didn't speak, but the glare he was giving Kent indicated his strong dislike of the reporter and his cameraman.

"So we'll be granted an interview? On Camera?"

Kent climbed into the car, leaving Clark to heave their baggage into the trunk alone.

"A brief one, yes."

"You'll have to forgive me Mr. Rilleri, I didn't realize my editor had contacted your offices. To what do I owe the pleasure?"

"Your agency didn't contact us, quite the opposite in fact. The senator reached out to your network this morning and requested this meeting."

The man exchanged a few words in Italian with Kaspar and the car rolled off with a purr. The ride only lasted a half hour, but the awkward silence seemed to stretch the time out inexorably.

By the time the car pulled up in front of a run-down apartment building in the heart of the city, Kent was painfully aware of how his brow shined with nervous sweat and the seemingly thunderous sound of his own breathing. The moment the vehicle stopped he reached for the door handle and took a deep breath of the humid mediterranean air.

The apartment overlooked one of the narrow canals that were the hallmark of Venice, but still managed to look a bit decrepit. An unlikely home for a senator at the very least.

As the group ascended a small brick staircase Kent began to wonder if he was being led into some kind of trap. It was too late to back out now though. Kaspar was behind them and the stairs weren't wide enough to give Kent any hope of slipping past him. With nowhere to go but up, Kent did his best to appear confident and calm.

They reached a landing and a dark wooden door opened beside them.

"Welcome Mr. Dailey, please come in."

Kent jumped, but recovered quickly.

"Hello Senator, thank you so much for seeing-"

"Yes, yes, Mr. Dailey. Inside please."

Kent took the hint and the group moved inside. The apartment was small, but pleasant. His host compensated for a heavy limp with a sturdy cane and indicated they should follow him to a small kitchenette. After waving a hand at a small wooden table, Roberto turned to the stove to grab a small carafe and a handful of ceramic mugs.

Kent sat dutifully and motioned for Clark to begin setting up the equipment immediately.

Roberto looked very different from the man that had been plastered on television's the world over. Who had defied the largest religious institution and led what could only be called a revolution from within. Kent expected the fiery orator, the larger-than-life caricature of bravery and conviction that he had been portrayed as. But the Roberto that was smiling genially and pouring strong black coffee into mugs for them seemed more like a grandfather or a beloved uncle than a revolutionary.

Clark gave Kent a subtle cue.

"So, Senator Fafoglia, may I ask what you brought us here for?"

"Please, call me Roberto."

He took a slow sip and stared deeply into Kent's eyes.

"You do not care for her, do you Mr. Dailey?"

"I'm sorry? I don't understand."

"Saint Corvidae. You have mocked her, ridiculed her, extorted her good will and abused her trust. All of these things you have done, for what? For money? For vanity?"

Kent wasn't sure what to do, he glanced nervously around the room for some way to shift the conversation. A small blinking light on the front end of Clark's camera reminded him that he was trapped. He was about to make an excuse to put off the interview, but the senator spoke again.

"So please, Mr. Dailey, let us talk."

His tone had turned jovial and innocent and he looked expectantly at his guest.

"I, um. Alright sir. Ah, can you - would you care to tell the people a little bit about the past few months? Why you continue to support Lauren Cor-"

"*Saint* Lauren Corvidae," Roberto corrected him gently.

"Sure."

"We have not lost faith in her, and I believe she must still have faith in us. Otherwise God would not have sent her back."

"But what about all the trouble she's caused? War between Pakistan and India, chaos in North Africa, martial law in Russia? And that's just in the past year!"

Roberto nodded and waited for Kent to finish before responding.

"Do you recall what God said to Adam and Eve in the garden?"

"I'm not sure I follow."

"The lord said 'But of the tree of the knowledge of good and evil, thou shalt not eat of it: for in the day that thou eatest thereof thou shalt surely die.' God's children chose the path of wickedness when they listened to the serpent. As a result of that choice, they were punished, and knew good and evil, and were ashamed of their own nakedness before God."

"So you believe that these terrible things are our fault, humanity's fault, rather than a result of Lauren's meddling?"

"I do."

"Well that's a very convenient answer, isn't it? We just blame all our problems on other people and not the person stirring up trouble?"

"It is really quite simple, isn't it? The answer is faith. I have met her, I have felt her power and seen the pain she bears for the good of us all."

"Well I'm sorry, but I have a hard time trusting someone who kills people because she's be outed as a lesbian on international television."

The quiet that followed his inflammatory comment was palpably uncomfortable. Kaspar muttered something unintelligible, but Roberto gave him a low wave without breaking eye contact with Kent.

"Mr. Dailey, I would caution you against blasphemy in my presence. I am a tolerant man, but my companion, Mr. von Silenen, is not. His dedication to God and our lady has been proven in blood, both his and that of others."

"A-and God approves of bloodshed, does he?"

Kent shifted nervously as another long period of silence filled the room.

"God allows us to experience the consequences of our mistakes. In many cases that manifests as bloodshed, yes. But as the scripture says, we reap what we sow. Mankind has sown the bitter seeds of violence for many, many years

"Senator, you're dodging my question. The world wants to know why Lauren killed those people. What gives her the right to murder a crowded room full police officers and innocent bystanders! Furthermore, how is she connected to this 'Weyland' figure that has the whole world trembling?"

"Do I appear to be trembling, Mr. Dailey? If so then you have the wrong impression entirely. I trust that God will deliver me."

Indeed, the stony Senator and his bodyguard were utterly unmoving.

"Even in the face of a being who kills tens of thousands at a whim? Who will defend you then, Lauren Corvidae?"

"If God wills it."

Kent laughed bitterly. The stubbornness of the old man made for as perfect an argument against established religion as he could imagine. By the same token, he was getting nowhere with this impromptu interview. He needed to push the envelope.

"So God willed that those folks in London should die, that their families should be torn apart. He willed that a man made of lava would burn a hole in the center of Athens and then London, *specifically* because of the actions of Lauren Corvidae?"

"The scripture is full of wicked men being destroyed by the glory of God. Perhaps, Mr. Dailey, you are so afraid because you know you have wronged her? Perhaps it is because of your wickedness that you fear her, and I do not."

Kent put on a brave face, but could not deny the terror inside his soul.

"Faith is my shield, Mr. Dailey. What is yours?"

Kent cleared his throat loudly and stood to leave. He motioned to Clark to grab their gear and contemplated another handshake, but discarded the idea almost immediately.

"Well Senator, I can't say it's been a pleasure."

"Of course, Mr. Dailey. May I ask where you will go now? To Athens, I presume?"

Kent paused with a hand on the door.

"No, actually. We're headed to Rome and the Vatican. Our audiences want to know what the opinion of the real Catholic Church is."

Lauren wasn't bothering to hide anymore. Her sleek black feathers cut through the warm air above Italy like a knife, propelling her to her destination like an arrow. She wasn't familiar with the geography of the country, so she had to drop close enough to read highway signs. It was easy enough to decipher her target, 'Roma' wasn't very different from 'Rome' after all.

After more than a day of flying, she had yet to come down from the high she felt coursing through her. She smiled at the idea that her increased strength might be permanent.

The sun was just starting to set when the city appeared on the horizon. The phone in her pocket had long since gone silent, though whether from a dead battery or Valerie giving up she hadn't yet checked.

Good.

Her confused frustration with Valerie clouded her mind, and threatened to erode the singular purpose that consumed her. Revenge. Lauren had long ago accepted that she could not replace the people she had lost, or fix the damage she had done to the people she loved. Now though, she had a tool to even the score.

As the city grew larger, she was accompanied once more by helicopters and throngs of people congesting the highways below her. Their gawking eyes and flashing camera-phones stoked the anger inside her. She knew they saw not an individual, but a symbol of their own selfish desires.

By the time she reached the outer walls of the Vatican, she was a seething ball of anger once again. She landed with enough force to crack one of the ancient stones in the courtyard and her wingbeats sent plumes of dust into the air.

More than a dozen soldiers ringed the courtyard, staring down the sights of their assault rifles at her and reminding her of the last time she'd seen this courtyard filled with armed men. The day her father had been murdered.

Lauren's eyes fell on the spot where he'd died. The stones had been washed clean but the blood was still fresh in her mind. Lauren's blood pumped in her ears and her breathing quickened until she could hear nothing else.

Lauren's wings and shoulders heaved as she panted with exertion from her long flight. A thin sheen of sweat covered her exposed skin as she slowly cooled down in the soft breeze. Deep within her a small voice told her she should warn the men, give them a chance to drop their weapons or flee.

She ignored it.

A gnawing hunger gripped her and she clenched her fists. The voice grew more insistent, a nagging pressure on her conscience that became a frustrating buzz.

Sighing with exasperation she shook her head and forced herself to unclench her whitened knuckles. Lauren opened her mouth to speak and took a small step forward.

The world stopped with a bang.

Smoke curled slowly from the barrel of the rifle held by the man in front of her. Lauren clutched her side, and gritted her teeth against a searing pain. She took stock of her injury. The bullet was lodged in one of her ribs, near the center of her chest. The bone was cracked, and the wound bled freely, but her newly empowered body had resisted the bulk of the damage.

All thoughts of mercy were chased from her mind as a hot, flattened piece of lead slowly emerged from her rapidly healing side and fell to the ground with a dull clink.

The nervous looking man's eyes widened as he realized what he had done, and the barrel of his weapon drooped with disbelief. But it was too late, his errant bullet started a hailstorm of sizzling metal.

Lauren's wings snapped up into a protective barrier around her and she sprinted towards the terrified man. Bullets punched through her ebony feathers with little sprays of blood and impacted her body. But they could not stop her.

She crossed the stones in a matter of seconds and snatched the man up by his collar, lifting him from the ground and letting the darkness within her consume him. Once again,

Lauren's veins flooded with a metallic silver and the man's eyes rolled into the back of his head as her power drained his life force. Lauren watched in detached pleasure as the man's skin turned papery and pale. His hair turned gray and all the color left his body. When she finally dropped him to the ground again, he was a shell of his former self.

Lauren's body flooded with strength and her pulse quickened as it had before. The high was as powerful as she remembered and she could feel the welts and bullet holes in her body healing faster and faster. Lauren snapped her wings open and propelled herself across the courtyard in a flash, snatching up another guard, and then another.

With every life she took, her power grew. She worked her way through half a dozen guards before the rest broke and ran. The men retreated inside behind a large wooden double door, leaving her alone in the courtyard once more.

Lauren's senses were deliciously heightened. She could smell a sweet, cloying smell that she instinctively knew was fear. It poured from the windows and doors around her, the testimony of fearful onlookers. A wicked grin appeared on her lips as her ears picked up the rapid heartbeats of cowering mortals nearby.

Perhaps the most striking difference was the incredible detail and vibrancy of her vision. Every mote of dust in the air, every hairline crack in the stones below her, every grain in the wood of the door that protected her prey stood out in high definition.

How had she gone through life so *blindly* before?

No matter, she'd never be powerless again.

Lauren sauntered to the door and put her hands against the ancient beams. They were rough and complex. Fossils from a time before her home country had even been born. Every fiber of the wood stood out with subtle differences in texture beneath her splayed finger tips.

The skin of Lauren's hands shone a mercurial silver, as though she wore skin-tight armor up to her wrists. From there, her veins ran brightly beneath her pale skin up her arms and into her chest. Her keen eyes picked up the faint pulse of each heartbeat as it pushed the blood through those veins, the faintest ripple that ran through her.

She was aware of some small part of herself that called within her to be cautious. A drowning voice that told her she should be concerned, that she wasn't herself. But Lauren was drunk with her own strength and high with the wild exhilaration that flooded her mind.

With a violent shove the centuries-old door exploded into fragments, filling the hallway beyond with splintered wood. Two of the men must have been bracing against the door, because they were now sprawling on the floor. The other four opened fire in a desperate but futile attempt to defend themselves. The bullets still hurt, and they drew ragged welts and shallow cuts through her skin, but they were no longer able to penetrate more than a few millimeters. The smell of their fear was delicious, and her chest growled with the same gnawing hunger she had felt before. The small voice within her was finally silenced as she strode over to the men still struggling to stand. The band of men spent their last precious moments of life scrambling to evade her, but she was too strong, too fast, and too unforgiving.

When the last man's cries of anguish finally ceased and she dropped his lifeless body to the floor, she took a moment to relish the stillness. It didn't last long, her ears picked up the sounds of sirens, of running feet, of the flapping of birds wings high above the building and the skittering of mice in the tunnels below as well. The overload of sensory information was nauseating. A migraine blazed across her mind like a brush fire, but she shook her head and focused as hard as she could.

There.

She could tell it was him, though she wasn't sure how she knew. It didn't really matter to her, frankly. For the better part of an hour she stalked him through the once-hallowed halls of the Vatican, consuming those unlucky enough to cross her path. She never wavered from the scent of his terror, and when she finally found him cowering in an armoire on the third floor she couldn't help but grin.

"Good evening, your Holiness."

The terrified pontiff fell to his knees before her, his hands clasped in front of him and his head bowed low. His pitiful display did nothing but add disgust to her anger.

"Please, please forgive me Lauren. I-I have sinned, forgive me. Show mercy and I will praise your name. I swear it."

"Beg."

The short, simple command was heeded immediately. The man grovelled, clutching at her ankles and kissing her feet, babbling incoherently for her to forgive him and denouncing the error of his ways.

Lauren sent him sprawling with a casual backhand. He lay where he landed, weeping. She took the two steps needed to reach him and crouched down. Her wings cast an ominous shadow over both of them and she reached a hand out to cup his chin and forced it upward.

"Look at me. I want to see your eyes."

Her heart skipped with wicked glee at the terror she saw in the man. Here was one of the most powerful men in the world, so frightened at her presence that he could not even speak.

"You want my forgiveness?"

He nodded silently, his eyes closing and tears pouring down his face.

Lauren slowly squeezed. Her hand, still wrapped around the Pope's jaw, tightened until the man's eyes snapped back open. He struggled, but couldn't break her grip.

"Look. At. Me."

He tried and failed to speak through her fingers. Instead, the only noises in the room were his desperate squeaks of pain followed by a sudden crack, like a walnut breaking beneath a hammer. Lauren smirked as his jaw broke like a dry twig and she felt his teeth tumbling inward as she tightened her grasp.

Lauren loosened her grasp, allowing her powers to heal the poor man.

"I'm sorry, I'm so sorry," he sobbed.

The pope started praying softly in Italian. The beautiful sounding words did nothing but irritate Lauren. She gripped him by the collar and shook him, hard. He wept, but screwed his eyes shut even tighter and continued his prayers.

"Do you think God can hear you now? Do you think he will forgive you?"

Lauren dragged the man to a window overlooking the court-yard and tossed him through like a ragdoll. He hit the stones feet first, his legs breaking with an audible pop amidst a throng of guards and first responders. Lauren leapt out and swooped down to land beside him. The crowd parted and many of the police and guards drew their weapons.

Lauren kept her eyes locked on the man who had murdered her father. He was trying to crawl to a nearby medical team, his shattered legs sticking out at odd angles behind him. She strolled lazily over to him and rolled him over with her foot. Lauren knelt beside him, leaning down to whisper in his ears.

"If there is a heaven it is not for men like you. Cowards that kill in the name of God. Let me tell you a secret."

She leaned back and stared into his eyes, one hand on either side of his face.

"There is no god."

With that, she drained his lifeforce. Lauren smiled, enjoying the sight of his eyes sinking back into his skull and his skin turning papery and white. Perhaps it was the length of his life, perhaps it was the pleasure of exacting her revenge, but his death tasted particularly sweet to her darkened heart.

Bullets tore across the courtyard as policemen and the Swiss Guard opened fire. The bullets stung like angry hornets and Lauren raised her wings protectively once more. With a mighty downward beat Lauren leapt into the sky, black feathers falling like rain as she ascended.

She was a thousand feet in the air in the matter of a few heartbeats, her strong wings propelling her easily through the skies. She looked down at the city and felt, for the first time, utterly unafraid.

Dreadful clarity brought an icy peace to her heart and mind as she contemplated her next move. Her options had always seemed so limited before, and now the entire world seemed so... inviting.

Unfortunately, her thoughts turned immediately to Valerie and a tiny farmhouse outside of London. A queasy feeling gripped her stomach and dampened the rush of strength and emotion coursing through her veins. It triggered a chain reaction and she felt her emotions begin to tumble uncontrollably like they had before at the BT Tower. She tried to clear her head, to regain the clarity of a few moments before, but she was overcome by the flood inside her brain. Her stomach was twisting itself into painful knots and she felt like she might be sick.

She turned herself northward and flew by instinct. Her head felt like it was splitting open and the pain was so intense she found it hard to see straight. She alternated between incredible pain and intense, exhilarating euphoria. One moment her stomach was churning, the next she felt fine.

Lauren made it a few miles outside of the city before she was forced to land. She impacted the ground a little harder than she intended, and fell to her knees at the base of a grassy hill.

The world seemed to spin around her and she heard a dozen screaming voices ricocheting within her skull. Each voice brought with it a flood of emotion. She found herself laughing hysterically while tears streamed from her eyes, sobbing uncontrollably while smiling so wide it hurt her cheeks, and everything in between.

Her roiling stomach finally proved too much, and she could no longer keep herself from vomiting until her empty stomach had nothing to produce. She heaved so hard that stars popped in her vision. She felt her fingers digging into the dirt as she gripped the ground.

What the hell was happening to her?

Lauren punched the ground, her fist sank several inches below ground level with a thump. The noise was overshadowed by a crackling bang like a peal of thunder. Lauren had only heard the sound once before in her life, but it was burned into her mind nonetheless. She stumbled to her feet, blinking away tears and casting terrified looks around herself.

"Hello, Lauren."

She froze.

The hairs on the back of her neck stood up and she trembled with fear. She was frozen, rooted in place like a rabbit beneath the shadow of a hawk.

Lauren's body finally began to behave. She raised her wings and turned slowly to see Weyland standing a dozen feet away. His musclebound frame was covered only by a dark red kilt and a wide leather belt.

"Lauren, please don't leave. We need to talk."

His voice was soft and he held his hands out palm up, as if to beg her to stay. But his hands held no promise of safety to her. Her skin crawled at the memory of those hands dragging her across fine silk sheets, of them stripping her of her dignity.

Lauren narrowed her eyes, her pulse quickening. She balled her fists and tensed like a tiger ready to pounce. Her steely new muscles bunched as her fight-or-flight instincts kicked into overdrive.

"Get away from me."

Weyland closed his eyes and dropped his hands to his sides where they solidified into fists. Lauren could see that Weyland was trying to control his temper, but the air around him began to shimmer with heat. When he spoke again it was through gritted teeth.

"Lauren, you don't understand."

"Oh don't I?"

Lauren spat the words at him, and he flinched as though she'd struck him.

"No!"

Lauren took an involuntary step backwards at the sudden ferocity of his voice. He seemed to take note of it and dropped his tone immediately. Too late though, his temper triggered her own and a decision was made deep in her brain.

Fight.

Lauren lunged, driving her fist towards his proud chin. He sidestepped her easily and she skidded to a halt several yards beyond him before whipping around to face him once more.

"No. No you don't understand. This... this isn't your path. This is where you are supposed to be. I am your destiny. It is fated. Don't you see that?"

"You mean I belong to you."

She lunged again. This time he didn't move and her hand collided with the chiseled stone of his face with a resounding thump. The blow would have powdered concrete, but he barely moved. Lauren felt her bones groan and buckle painfully but she ignored it. She followed her poorly thrown punch with another, and then another, pummeling uselessly at Weyland's face and chest.

She could see his temperature rise as heatwaves poured off his body and burned her skin, but he kept himself in check.

Lauren's battered hands were leaving bloody fist-prints on his skin when he finally crackled out of existence again and re-appeared a few feet behind her.

"Lauren, we aren't like these... these mortals. We are above them! Their affairs are nothing to us but the idle buzzing of bees of the toil of ants."

Lauren tried to catch her balance after his sudden relocation and stood there, her shoulders heaving and sweat dotting her brow.

"So you're here to what, lecture me for killing the men who murdered my father?"

"What care I for the lives of a few men?"

"Oh, then maybe you intend to claim me as your trophy and lock me away in your palace like some brainless damsel, to be used at your convenience and for your pleasure?"

"Am I truly so poor a match?"

Weyland opened his arms, displaying his impossible phy-sique. He wore a cocky, self-indulgent smile that made Lau-ren's blood boil.

"Or perhaps you have a better offer. Maybe there is some other God you seek to bed."

Lauren could feel the oily darkness within her coiling like a viper, baring its fangs defensively.

"I deserve a choice! You cruel, heartless bastard-"

The sound of approaching aircraft interrupted their shout-ing match and Lauren turned her attention back to the skies. Several helicopters were approaching their position, but they looked unfamiliar to her.

These aircraft were different from those she'd seen before. They were sleek, dark, and flying just above the treetops. The helicopters were still several thousand feet away when she heard a distant buzzing noise and watched plumes of smoke appear in front of them.

A heartbeat later found Lauren crouching down amidst a torrential downpour of steel rain. Bullets pockmarked the ground around the two of them, throwing dirt skyward all over the side of the hill.

Lauren screamed as a round found its mark in her wing. The second joint in her left wing, the one that controlled its opening and closing, exploded in a spray of bone fragments and bloody feathers. Another tore into her right thigh and she dropped to her knees clutching her broken limbs.

She felt a shadow cast itself over her, and while the rounds were still chewing up turf around her there were no more blows to her body. She looked up to see Weyland's muscular back. Sparks flew as bullets shattered on his chest, leaving him unmoved.

"Are you alright?"

Weyland's powerful voice cut through the roar of the machine guns. Lauren was in too much pain to be shocked at the concern she heard, and she could do no more than whimper.He glanced back over his shoulder and she nodded at him as her body began to stitch itself rapidly back together.

Weyland's eyes were already brilliant orange coals, and the burned even hotter at the sight of her pain. He turned his attentions back toward the helicopters and clenched his fists. Unfortunately, as Lauren was well aware, Weyland could not reach them.

Weyland turned to face Lauren and offered her his hand. She couldn't help but flinch, and as her wounds healed and her mind cleared, she took note of the pain on his face. It only lasted a moment, then his hurt expression returned to stony indifference.

"Take my hand, I will get you out of here."

She didn't want to. Every part of her wanted to stay as far away from him as possible. But as he shielded her from a torrent of gunfire she couldn't help but feel grateful.

Lauren reached up, and the moment she grasped his outstretched hand she felt herself twist inside out. In an instant it was over, but her stomach still felt tied itself in knots and she barely resisted the urge to vomit once again.

Lauren was standing next to Weyland at the top of a massive peak. The air was cold and thin, but all around them was a breathtaking landscape of snow-capped mountains and wide fertile valleys. There wasn't a sign of human habitation as far as the eye could see.

They were still holding hands for a moment before Lauren yanked hers away. She wrapped her arms around herself and stood awkwardly at his side. She was grateful, but couldn't bring herself to hate him any less.

"Lauren you *belong* with me."

"Stop it. Just... stop saying that."

The stood silently staring at the land around them for several moments before Weyland spoke again. When he did so, his voice was soft.

"It's beautiful isn't it? The last time I walked this island it had never before been seen by the eyes of men. It was one of many such places. The world was younger then. Now mankind has spread to all corners of the globe."

Lauren hadn't the faintest idea of where she was, let alone when it was discovered, so she kept her mouth shut. It didn't stop Weyland from speaking. In fact, it seemed to encourage his monologue.

"I have tried to lead mortals for centuries, millennia even-"

"Stop... leave me alone."

He stopped mid sentence and snapped his mouth shut.

"What *do* you want Lauren?"

What did she want?

"I want my dad back. I want my best friend back. I want to stop hurting all of the time. I want to stop feeling like every breath I take is a burden."

Lauren's words were barely above a whisper, but she was certain he heard her clearly.

"I cannot bring them back from the dead. That is beyond even me."

"Then kill me."

He was startled by her matter-of-fact request.

"Are you truly so ready to die? So willing to leap from a cliff with no idea of what lies at the bottom? How is it that with all the power you possess, you can think only of throwing it away?"

"Well? Are you God or aren't you? Can you do it?"

He seemed to consider his next words carefully.

"Do you *fear* death, Lauren?"

"No."

She was lying. Her heart fluttered at the idea of being truly, irrevocably gone, but she hoped he could not tell. Maybe he could see it in her eyes, maybe he lacked the power to destroy her, but whatever the case he simply turned and looked away from her.

Her cheeks burned. From anger, from rejection, from the shame she felt in being forced to be grateful to him, and from the desperate need for answers she felt inside.

"What am I?"

He shifted his footing almost imperceptibly. Long minutes passed before he cleared his throat softly and spoke at last.

"We are Gods, Lauren. Destined to be together since long before your birth, before mine even. I fought to rule this world, and I won. I've waited so long for another chance, and here you are at last. The natural queen to my kingdom."

Lauren inched away, frightened by the realization that there was nothing here to protect her from him. The need to flee built in her chest, pushing her heart into her throat until she could bear it no more.

"Where are we?"

"I'm told the people of today call it New Zealand, when I knew first it, it had no name but beautiful."

New Zealand? Damn, an island in the middle of the ocean. That left Lauren with precious few options. She was certain he'd chosen this place for just that reason. She shuffled farther away and looked at Weyland out of the corner of her eye.

"Why here?"

"This is the farthest point on earth from Italy. I could think of no safer place for you."

The answer was matter-of-fact, as though jumping across the planet in the blink of an eye were no extraordinary task. He didn't even turn to look at her when he said it. It wasn't until he noticed her staring at him that finally turned.

"What?"

"Thank you."

It irritated her to say it, but she couldn't deny that he had aided her.

"You are welcome."

"I... I want to go home now."

She tensed, waiting for him to display the latent aggression she knew was lurking in the monster beside her. She found herself surprised once more when he simply nodded and held his hand out.

Chapter 9

Natalie hated heels, but here she was half-running and half-stumbling down a long marble hallway, clicking like some insufferable clock. In her hands she carried several thick folders and dozens of loose papers, none of which she dared drop. For the first time since entering Weyland's service she was wearing something approaching business professional wear.

When her master had returned from Rome three days before, it was as though he were a different person entirely. Gone in a heartbeat were the hallmarks of his incredible age. His clothing was modernized, as was her own "uniform." He'd moved out of the Acropolis and had taken up residence in London, much to the dismay of his eight and a half million new neighbors.

Natalie wasn't thrilled about her new job as the Devil's secretary, but at least it meant she got to spend time away from him. It also meant time to sort out the latest in a series of distressing changes in her life. Theoretically, at least.

Functionally, it meant she was rushing to meet yet another dignitary who wanted an audience with Weyland. By the time she made it back to her offices on the 28th floor of the Gherkin building, she could tell her guests had been waiting for quite a while.

Rebecca, her secretary, was serving coffee to two stern-looking men. That was another thing, how the hell had she ended up with a secretary?

"Good afternoon ma'am, allow me to introduce our visitors. This is Lieutenant General J. Malone, and this is Under Secretary for Diplomacy and Public Affairs P-"

"Presley? Oh my God, Presley Weiss!"

"Natalie? What the hell are you doing here?"

Natalie ran over and gave her friend a hug. The tall, handsome man in his mid 30's, wrapped her in a bear hug. Natalie felt relieved at the presence of one of her oldest and truest friends. For a fleeting moment she was able to forget her troubles.

"Natalie seriously, this is *not* a safe place for you. I thought you were doing field work in Asia!"

He held her at arm's length, eyes full of concern.

"I know, *trust me* I know. This was not my first choice of day job. I was working a dig in China and he just... appeared out of nowhere."

"Weyland?"

Natalie nodded, a chill running down her spine as she remembered her first meeting with her new master. Natalie fidgeted with the golden choker around her neck. The thin chain was heavy against her soft skin, an ever-present reminder of her station.

"He picked me, God knows why, to translate for him. At first it was just that, then it became tending to Lauren. Now I'm running around in heels and a pencil skirt trying to organize meetings with world leaders."

The general cleared his throat softly and Presley gave her a sympathetic look and took a solemn step back. The man took a thin folder from his associate and offered it to Natalie.

"Right, I suppose that brings us to why we are here, after all. I have a statement prepared by the President for Mr. Weyland, as well as a few documents I'd like to go over with you."

"Becky, can you file these please?"

Rebecca nodded curtly, took the pile of paperwork from Natalie, and walked softly out of the room to file it. As soon she shut the door behind her, Natalie took the red folder and flipped through its contents.

"So Pres- Err, Secretary Weiss, what exactly am I looking at here?"

"Well, effectively, the United States, in conjunction with the United Nations and NATO, would like to welcome Mr. Weyland to our planet, as well as identify his current and future goals. We're also requesting an idea of how long he intends to stay, and we would like to know if he plans to contribute anything to the humanitarian and peacekeeping missions popping up all over the world as a result of his and Lauren Corvidae's... activities."

Natalie looked over the documents with a slight frown on her face. She pushed her glasses up on her nose and considered her response carefully.

"Presley... a lot of this is not going to go well."

"I was afraid you'd say that. Is there anything you can do for us?"

Damnit.

"I'll see what I can do Presley, I promise."

She managed a weak smile, but was sure her friend was unconvinced. Her anxiety kicked into overdrive and her brow creased as she thought through her options.

"Natalie, are you in some kind of trouble here?"

Presley reached a hand out but pulled it back when Natalie flinched. She gave the tiniest, almost imperceptible nod.

"Hey, are you ok?"

No, fuck no.

"Sorry! I'm fine! Sorry, just stressed out a bit. Don't worry I will take care of it, ok? Actually, I have to take these proposals to him, but let me give you my number."

Presley seemed taken aback at the sudden close of their meeting, and he exchanged an unsettled glance with his military counterpart.

"I uh, does that mean we're... done here? I was really hoping for more of a-"

He stopped speaking and rose a quizzical eyebrow when Natalie gave him a very pointed look. Natalie grabbed a spare piece of paper and scribbled a number on it before folding it in half and handing it to Presley.

"I'm sorry, Presley, I wish there was more I could do. I will pass this information along to Weyland and, if he desires, he will send a response."

Natalie held her arms out for another hug and Presley accepted. As soon as they embraced, Natalie began to whisper fervently into his ear.

"Find Lauren Corvidae. I don't know how but she's the key to stopping him. She's the only thing he seems to care about, or fear. You have to find her, Presley!"

She didn't linger, but as she pulled away he kept her at arm's length a moment longer. He looked into her eyes, trying to convey his concern non-verbally.

"Do you have time to catch-up *away* from the office? Maybe over dinner?"

Natalie's composure almost broke. To be so close to her old confidant and yet utterly unable to unburden herself was killing her. All she could do was shake her head no and turn away before he could see her start to cry.

"Becky, can you please show these gentlemen out?"

"Yes ma'am!"

"Natalie..."

Natalie kept her face hidden, her back turned, and her eyes tightly shut to hold back her tears. She tried to think of something, anything that she could say to help him understand.

"Presley, do you remember the petroglyphs, three years ago? That promise?"

He was silent a while. Almost to the point that Natalie turned just to see if he was still there.

"I do."

She let out a breath she didn't know she'd been holding.

"Take care of yourself, please."

"You too."

She stayed put until the door clicked softly shut behind her exiting guests, and then for several minutes thereafter. She took a few deep breaths, re-adjusted her ponytail, and tried to compose herself before walking toward the large black double-doors that separated her offices from Weyland's. As her hand touched the polished silver handle she found herself praying he wouldn't be inside.

Weyland was sitting in a massive black chair behind a wide glass and metal desk. He was facing outward from the tower, looking over the bustling city, but Natalie knew from the faint scent of ashes that he was here, and angry.

Another unanswered prayer, then.

Natalie took three steps into the room and knelt down, waiting to be acknowledged. Since she'd withheld information from her master in Greece, she was on a much tighter leash, and he expected a great deal of obedience.

"Another groveling diplomat, I assume."

His voice was distant, laced with indifference. He'd shown little interest in geopolitics, in anything really, since moving to London. Other than obsessively tracking the whereabouts of his most desired prey, Lauren.

"Yes your majesty, it was an envoy from the United States this time."

"Show me."

Natalie shuddered, but dutifully stood and approached him as he slowly turned around to face her. She walked up beside his high-backed leather throne and knelt beside him. She didn't flinch when he raised a hand and put it on her forehead, but she trembled like a leaf.

In the space of a few minutes Weyland strip-searched her memory of the brief meeting with Presley. She could hide nothing from his probing mind, and she shuddered with revulsion as he traced Presley back through her life, sorting through every detail of their relationship for the dozen years they had known one another. She felt him pause on her college years, carelessly shuffling through her strongest memories with Presley. He spent some time branching out along other connections, ensuring he had the full context of every nuance of their meeting before finally relinquishing control of her mind.

Natalie felt bile rise in her throat but choked it down. Colors faded and popped in her vision and she felt the too-familiar migraine building until it felt like it would split her skull. Flickering after-images of nameless lands and far-off places strobed in front of her and she tried to remain as still and steady as she could. Already she could feel her memories as less... personal. More distant. Like a movie or a TV show she had watched, rather than experiences she had lived.

Weyland was silent for a long while, processing the information he had gathered.

"You may go. Meet your friends for dinner."

Natalie was stunned. She stood unsteadily to leave but stopped at the door when he spoke again.

"The Petroglyphs. Such an interesting memory. Oh, how the threads of fate weave..."

His words carried the weight of an iron chain. The light golden choker she wore suddenly felt tighter and she caught her breath.

Weyland watched his servant slip out the door, the sounds of her rapid heartbeat fading behind the heavy door as it swung shut behind her. He stewed restlessly a moment before standing and walking to the large glass windows that lined the outer wall of his offices.

He didn't need to read the paperwork she'd brought him. He'd known what it said since before she set it down. It seemed that much had changed since he was last awake. A few centuries ago no one would have dared *negotiate* with him. His word would have simply been law, as it was in man's earliest days. He seethed internally, sending smoke curling from the fabric of his designer suit.

He had seen the birth of men. Guided them, nurtured them, tried to lead them into peace and enlightenment. But every time he turned his back, every time he left them to their own devices, they disappointed him.

Every. Time.

At every turn they disrespected him. They worshipped others, false Gods and idols. They destroyed each other in his name, squabbled over nonsense. It seemed they were eternally bent on disobedience. As in ages past, the only thing they respected was power. So he would remind them what true power looked like.

This new breed of mankind was particularly defiant. Already he had done more to punish them than had been required before and rather than yield they sent their dignitaries to *negotiate*. As though their mortal institutions should have some sway over him. As though their opinions were equal to his own. Weyland would not abide it. Could not. Though it pained him, it was his responsibility to bring them back to heel by whatever means necessary.

He looked out over the city, his powerful eyes flitting from person to person. How utterly unconcerned they were. In three short days they had gone from terrified at his sudden presence in the city to continuing their daily lives as though nothing had changed. He felt a grudging, frustrated pride.

His wayward children were resilient, to be sure.

As was his wayward bride, it seemed.

Lauren was drifting restlessly over central California. She'd been airborne since Weyland dropped her off in Chicago three days before. She'd leapt wordlessly skyward, unwilling to share a single second with him that she didn't have to, and turned westward.

The sparkling pacific coast stretched out to her left and right as far as her augmented sight could see. Million-dollar homes slipped past underneath, tucked into the hills around the dense urban sprawl ahead of her. The hot dry winds of the West Coast kept her aloft with only a minimum of effort.

She'd never been to Sacramento, and she was certain that if she'd been less distracted she would have loved the colorful city. As things stood, she was trying to shuffle through the events of the last few days.

Focus.

Lauren took a deep breath and futilely attempted to clear her mind once more. It was no use, every time she closed her eyes she was bombarded by a clashing maelstrom of disjointed images, sounds, even smells. Snapshots of experiences she'd never had and people she'd never met. Equally frustrating was the gnawing hunger that gripped her stomach.

It seemed that no matter what she ate it was always there, nagging at her, making her antsy to the point of being nauseous.

Her less pleasant symptoms stood in stark contrast to the immense power she felt coursing through her veins. She was incredibly strong, faster than she'd ever been, and she could see and hear at an astonishing distance.

Finally, with a long sigh of frustration, she swooped down low and landed atop a tall billboard overlooking a crowded highway. She no longer cared if she was seen, and for their part the people seemed to give her wide berth. She was followed everywhere by a contingent of aircraft but they never got close enough to be construed as a threat.

Lauren paced the small catwalk in front of the sign for several minutes, trying to push the cacophony of voices and visions back into the darkest corners of her mind, before plopping herself down and dangling her legs over the edge as she had done in Ireland.

Fine, let's do this.

She closed her eyes and fully embraced the visions.

With her mind open and receptive, the visions came in much more clearly.

She was in a park, sitting at the top of a short metal slide and looking down at a woman who held outstretched arms to her.

"Come on down sweetie, don't be scared I've got you!"

Her perspective moved as she slid down the narrow metal path and into her mother's waiting arms. As she neared the woman she realized she must be a child, so great was their difference in size.

The moment she reached the woman the image shifted.

Now Lauren was sitting at a small, candle-lit table set for two in an intimate upscale restaurant. She glanced down at her watch: 7:35. The dark suit jacket sleeve and the coarse black hair on her wrist besides the expensive gold timepiece took her back a moment. She must be living a man's memory?

She could feel his sadness, his date was nearly an hour late and hadn't called. Lauren's host let out a dejected sigh and reached for his half-empty glass of wine. His hand froze, hovering over the table, when he saw her walk in. The object of his attention - Lauren searched for the name - Cassidy, was stunning. Her long blue dress and sparkling silver heels matched her silver hair perfectly.

The man could do little more than wave when they finally locked eyes. His suit looked like the clothes of a peasant in comparison to Cassidy's beauty.

It went on like this for what felt like hours, days even. Memory after memory, story after story slowly unfolded before Lauren's eyes. Dozens of lives playing out before her with crystal clarity.

Deep down she knew what was happening, but she denied it as long as she could. It wasn't until she saw herself walk through the doors of BT tower through the terrified eyes of a young secretary that she could no longer stomach it. She tried to pull out, but realized too late that she didn't know how.

She experienced her own death dozens of times, screaming internally as she was carried, a helpless passenger, through the last moments of her victims. In her desperation she reached deep within herself, seeking the darkness that had saved her before.

It responded hungrily and the visions flickered and faded. Rather than disappear entirely, they appeared washed-out, surreal, like film that was overexposed and burning.

Moreover, as the memories were consumed, her hunger was sated. The throbbing need within her subsided and she was able to think clearly at last. She dove hungrily back into the memories, realizing quickly that they "tasted" differently depending on their nature. She avoided bitter sadness and sour pain and focused on the sweet taste of joy and the savory flavor of happiness.

Then she stumbled on love.

The rich umami of it was addictive, she craved it. She tore through the faded memories and sought out every scrap, discarding the rest thoughtlessly. Soon she could find no more and the hunger returned, stronger than before.

She wanted more, *needed* it.

"If you're just tuning in, we're here live in gridlocked Sacramento where the being known as Lauren Corvidae appears to be in some sort of trance above interstate 80."

Kent Dailey was beaming into a camera some 30 feet below the subject of his broadcast.

"Once believed harmless, Corvidae has been responsible for the slaying of more than 50 people in the last week, including police officers, women, children, and even the late Pope in Rome. Department of Defense officials advised Sacramento PD this morning that her projected flight path would put her over the city, and citizens have been advised to remain indoors."

He gestured behind himself at the massive crowd that filled the streets as far as the eye could see.

"You can clearly see here that the residents of the city have not heeded that advice. On the contrary, it seems the entire city has turned out to see what she will do next."

Clark gave him the thumbs up and he broke his on-screen smile. He pulled off his light gray blazer and fanned his face.

"Jesus Christ it's hot. How long is this chick gonna sit here."

Lauren had been sitting like a statue for almost 6 hours. It provided the perfect opportunity for Kent to catch up to her, but he was more than a little miffed at what he'd found. They'd been following her from the ground for days, broadcasting where they could and trying to keep the story fresh and interesting.

To be honest, fighter jets circling Lauren as she drifted across the heartland wasn't very compelling footage after the first day. That being said, it beat the hell out of her sitting uselessly on a billboard.

And what a billboard it was, too. Kent scoffed at the massive photo that covered it. The picture, which depicted Lauren backlit by the sun against a clear blue sky, had reached worldwide popularity within hours of it's release two days ago. Now it was everywhere. Billboards, online, magazine covers, people were going mad over it. Kent had heard a rumor that the negatives, for supposedly it was captured on real film and not digitally, were being valued at several million dollars already.

The photographer was anonymous, but that didn't stop Kent from suspecting his rival. It would be just like her to pull a stunt like that.

Kent's growling stomach reminded him that he hadn't eaten since they'd arrived on scene. He cast another glance upward and decided it was worth the risk. Lauren wasn't going anywhere anytime soon.

"Come on, let's get lunch. Somewhere with air conditioning."

Kent and Clark wandered the streets, passing regular patrols of California National Guardsmen. It had been this way for months, soldiers on street corners didn't phase either of the two men anymore. The uniforms and guns took Kent back to his earliest days of reporting. Back to his time spent in the Gulf. He looked at his cameraman. Clark would have been what, in high school maybe?

That was back before terrorism was a word on everyone's lips, and certainly before 'Gods' were playing tug-of-war across the world in broad daylight. Back then you had to travel to a warzone to see armed men in the streets. Now it seemed the warzone was coming to them. Half a dozen conflicts had sprouted up in the past year, and the rest of the world seemed poised to follow suit.

He tried to remember the feeling of security that he knew as a youth. It was funny to think that when he was Lauren's age he'd never seen a TSA checkpoint or police in riot gear.

He shivered in the chill of a passing shadow. The blazing California sun seemed to lose its heat at his dark line of thinking.

The shadow didn't move.

"Hello Mr. Dailey."

Kent froze.

Goosebumps broke out along his arms and the hairs on the back of his neck stood straight out. A chill gripped his spine and he barely had the strength to turn around.

Lauren was standing there, wings raised to blot out the sun, a look of icy hatred on her face. Kent was taken aback, it had been a long time since he'd seen her face to face, but the innocent young girl he had met had been replaced by a terrifying, hauntingly beautiful woman.

Her eyes were black pits without a hint of either color or white. Inky orbs of malevolence drilling into his heart. Her skin was crisscrossed with hundreds of tiny, nearly invisible scars. Hallmarks of her fall, the surgeons attempts to repair her, or left over from the stray bullets of useless guns perhaps. Her fists were clenched at her sides, radiant silver lines followed her veins from her chest, down her arms, and culminated in a deep metallic tinge that covered her hands.

He tried to speak but couldn't.

The gathered crowd was hushed. They stood, silent witnesses to his terror, none willing to intervene on his behalf. But what could they even hope to do? Kent had seen the aftermath in Rome. No man could stand against her fury.

As he stood trapped by his fear he heard again the words of senator Fafoglia.

His rise had been predicated on her fall from grace. He recounted in his mind every time that he had chosen his career over her welfare, her sanity. How many times had he slandered her to get ratings? A deep and pervasive guilt filled his heart. He'd denied it for ages, but he knew his contributions to the tragedy of her life. And he knew there would be a reckoning.

He'd always known.

"At long last, you find yourself speechless."

Her words cut him like a knife.

"Too late to save my father, of course. Too late to save my family, my friends."

"Ms. Corvidae p-please..."

"Oh no, Kent, *please* call me Lauren. Let's not stand on formality now, after all."

He raised his hands, palms facing outwards, pleading with her.

"L-Lauren I... I was just doing my job. Please it's not my fault."

"It is!"

She barked out the words, pushing the crowd backwards as those in the front began to rethink their position.

"It *is* your fault! You destroyed my family! People died because of the garbage you passed off as news. Because of the *lies* you told."

Lauren took a step closer. She was only a few inches away from him now.

"But in a way, Mr. Dailey, I have to thank you."

Kent's eyes darted furtively around as he looked for a way out. He grasped at her gratitude, drawn in by the sudden quieting of her tone.

"I.. f-for what?"

"Because in destroying me, you gave me the tools to survive. I have no family, nothing left to lose. I have no reason to live at all, save one."

They locked eyes. Kent could feel himself drowning in the bottomless pools of black. She leaned even closer.

"Do you know what that reason is, Kent?"

She was whispering so close to his ear that he could feel her breath on his skin. He shook his head no, a movement so small as to be nearly imperceptible.

"Revenge."

Kent's knees gave out.

Lauren gripped him by the collar of his shirt and held him in place effortlessly. Bright silver pulsed in her veins and she felt the exhilarating power of the darkness rise inside her.

"Oh Kent, you have no idea how *good* this feels. This.... this strength inside me, this power, it's *delicious.*"

Kent shook his head, his lack of understanding written in terror on his face.

"Don't worry, I don't understand it either. But the difference is *I don't care.* You are going to die, Mr. Dailey, and there is nothing anyone on earth can do to save you."

He whimpered, babbling terrified nonsense.

"Shh shh shh, it's ok Mr. Dailey. You don't have to die *today.* Would you like to live? "

Kent nodded fervently as Lauren dragged him close again.

"P-please, please forgive me, I'll do anything. I don't want to die."

Lauren reached out with her spare hand and gripped the back of Kent's head, pulling the skin so tight that he couldn't close his eyes.

"You cannot have my forgiveness, Mr. Dailey, but I have a different gift for you. A much... sweeter one."

Lauren tore through the fragile curtains around Kent's mind like a tornado, ripping apart his memories, his hopes, his dreams, all with reckless abandon. She could feel his pain and it fueled her drive to destroy. She dug through his psyche, searching out every nugget of love, every moment even remotely pleasant or joyful and devoured them. When she was finished, she destroyed everything that wasn't dripping with sadness, pain, rejection, betrayal, loneliness, or doubt. She left him with nothing but his worst experiences, condensed, distilled, and crystal clear.

She was preparing to leave, casting one last look around, when something caught her eye. One of the fragments, a small one that stunk of fear and shame, looked familiar to her. She stepped into his memory and found herself in Chicago.

Kent and his cameraman were tearing down their equipment amidst a crowd of tents and despondent looking citizens.

She could hear the low roar of several motorcycles approaching from down the crowded street, and saw the crowds parting angrily as a gang of cyclists appeared.

They crushed tents and belongings beneath themselves as they approached the large green tent that stood at the center of the small tent city.

Lauren gasped when she saw Caroline appear from within the shrine, and seethed with anger as she witnessed Sigurd's treatment of her old caretaker. Lauren lived the memory through to completion. Once more she found herself uncomfortably grateful to Weyland, this time for destroying Sigurd in a manner that satisfied her violent urges. She replayed the memory several times, casually aware that she was forcing Kent to do so as well, committing every detail of the bikers to memory.

Lauren found herself distracted from her original intent and scoured the rest of Kent's memories. She retrieved a few more from the mass of despair and sadness she had left him.

"We're here in Silt, Colorado today to bring you tragic news. In a scene reminiscent of Jonestown, hundreds if not thousands have died. We're here with Detective Holliday of the Denver Police Department."

Lauren was standing beside a highway that cut through an idyllic little town in the midst of a massive mountain range. Small shops dotted the side streets and wild, untamed beauty stretched as far as she could see. The most unsettling aspect of the scene, however, was the seemingly endless rows of sheet covered bodies.

"On behalf of the Denver PD, as well as the governor, we'd like to express our condolences to the victims and their families in this difficult time."

A burly man in a brown police outfit was addressing the camera, his eyes wet with tears.

"The incident is the subject of an ongoing investigation, but so far from eyewitness accounts here is what we know. At approximately two o'clock this morning a group of approximately one hundred individuals armed with knives, axes, and machetes began forcing their way into the homes of the residents here. At four thirteen the County Sheriff's office received a report of several bodies lying beside the interstate. The call, which lasted two minutes and seventeen seconds was terminated from the caller's end following what sounded like an altercation. At four thirty-five, two officers arrived on scene and found multiple victims, including the family who made the initial call. They came under small arms fire, radioed for backup, and neighboring counties were called in."

The detective drew a ragged breath, unable to continue for a moment.

"Officers Grenetz and Holmes were both killed in action. The 322nd Military Police Battalion was activated and responded at approximately six forty-five. They declared the city cleared of hostile targets at ten o'clock this morning. The vast majority of the attackers died of self-inflicted wounds, and four people were taken into custody."

Kent nodded.

"Do we know anything about the perpetrators? Why they would do this?"

"At this point the department is considering this to be the work of religious extremists. The Sons of the Valkyrie have taken responsibility for the attack on social media."

"Is there a preliminary death count?"

"At this point it is too early to tell. We've confirmed roughly 2,700 dead as of right now. I'm sorry sir that's all I have right now."

The officer walked away and Kent turned back to the camera. Lauren could see from his reflection in the cool black glass of the lens that he had a somber expression.

"There you have it folks. Another attack by the self-styled crusaders of the Sons of the Valkyrie, just one of the myriad of homegrown terror cells now plaguing the streets. We will continue to bring you details as this story develops. Hansen, back to you."

Lauren stewed over this development, a twinge of guilt flitting across her mind as she pondered her role in the attack. The darkness recoiled and crushed that guilt almost immediately. She jumped through a few more memories, similar events had played out in several major cities across the globe.

So?.

She cast one last look around, content that there was not a single mote of happiness or pleasure left to consume.

Lauren withdrew from Kent's mind, unsure if her meddling would kill him and, frankly, not caring either way. She was pleasantly surprised to see he was still alive when she returned to herself.

A look of thoughtless, uncomprehending horror and anguish was plastered on Kent's face and his eyes were wide but unseeing. So, it was indeed possible to selectively feed. She smirked, pleased with her creative punishment. She was even more pleased to see the terrified onlookers muttering and backing away from her.

Lauren whipped her wings open wide and laughed out loud at the gasps and shrieks of fear from the crowd. Her smile faded swiftly as she tore skyward.

She had unfinished business to settle, it seemed.

The glittering city on the coast fell swiftly behind her. Her purposeless drifting into California was replaced by a driven, arrow-straight trajectory back to the heartland.

Hour after hour ticked by, the sun rising high into the sky and then falling silently behind her.

When the sky again lightened with the dawn, it revealed the familiar skyline of Chicago.

Chapter 10

Lauren felt goosebumps dot her arms and legs as the looming skyscrapers of the dense, urban jungle closed in around her. Her throat felt dry and her face flushed. Fog blanketed the city, giving refuge to the ghosts of her past that flitted at the edge of her vision.

Her pulse quickened as she dwelt on the memories of everything that had happened here. From her first interview with Kent Dailey to the day she fell from the sky, so much in her young life had revolved around this wretched city.

The darkness within her sensed her hesitation, and wrapped itself comfortingly around her heart. She warmed from the freshly stoked sparks of anger and narrowed her eye, confidence renewed. Lauren slowed her pace and circled the blocks below like a vulture, keen, unblinking eyes searching for her prey. As the morning droned on she began to grow frustrated. The city was massive, and even from her vantage point it would take ages to search it all.

By noon she could take it no longer. She swooped down to the street, landing softly outside a grungy looking bar with a dozen motorcycles lined up in front of it. A pair of heavy-set, leather-clad old men were standing outside smoking when she arrived. The nearer of the two held a forgotten cigarette between loose lips, ash accumulating unnoticed as he stared wide-eyed at her. They were frozen in place, unwilling or unable to move as she strode up to them.

"I'm looking for the Sons of the Valkyrie."

They were deer in headlights.

Snarling, Lauren gripped one of them men by the front of his shirt and lifted him into the air.

"I said-"

"P-please. I don't know anything about them!"

Her now talkative captive blubbered his innocence. It was strange, coming from a man who was old enough to be her father, perhaps even grandfather. But she could find no sympathy in the darkened corners of her heart.

"Do they come here? Do you know where they go?"

He managed to shake his head no.

Lauren dropped him with a sigh and approached the door. With a light shove she sent the heavy steel door, frame and all, flying into the bar. She heard the startled cries of the patrons as she stepped inside. As her unmistakable shadow fell across the floor of the bar it fell silent again.

She dropped her voice to a low, menacing tone.

"I'm looking for the Sons of the Valkyrie..."

Natalie was sprinting, again.

For a woman who hated running, she seemed to be making a habit of it in the service of her employer. Was she technically employed? Did slavery count? She supposed not.

Nonetheless, her heels were clicking across the marble floor as swiftly as she dared lest she trip. She didn't slow down until she was almost to his door. Taking a moment to slow her breathing and adjust her glasses and tuck back the loose strands of her hair, she reached out and knocked firmly on the massive door.

"Enter."

She did so, closing the door softly behind her and keeping her eyes downcast as she had been taught. Natalie could feel the heat of his gaze. Damn, that meant he was in a worse mood than usual.

"My lord, Lauren is in Chicago."

She flinched in anticipation of a blow, but it didn't come. Instead she was met with pensive silence. She risked a glance upward and saw that Weyland was leaning back in his chair with his steepled hands in front of him.

"What is she doing?"

"My lord?"

"What is Lauren doing in Chicago?"

This was... new.

"My lord she seems to be, um, well she's going to motorcycle bars. Witnesses say she looking for the Sons of the Valkyrie."

Weyland nodded slowly, mulling over her answer. His understanding of the modern world had deepened, in no small part from his rummaging around in Natalie's mind.

"Hunting then, perhaps. Or maybe seeking her throne at last."

Natalie waited, unsure what was expected of her, until he spoke again.

"Prepare a gift befitting my bride. Return to me when you have done so."

Natalie gave a stiff bow, her mind racing, and turned to leave.

"Natalie."

She stopped and turned once more.

"Yes, your grace?"

"Do not keep me waiting."

Her heart skipped a beat as she left him behind.

Lauren couldn't contain the wide, manic grin on her face as stood over the bodies of a dozen dead bikers. She'd spent the better part of the day tracking down small groups of the gang but this had been her biggest catch yet. Her heart was pounding a powerful two-step in her ears and her muscles swelled with vigor.

She cast a look around the dimly lit bar and turned to make her way back onto the street when the tiniest of noises caught her ears. A scuff, like a boot against the wood floor, came from behind the bar.

Her eyes sparkled and she approached her hiding prize. She could hear his breathing as she drew nearer, and she leaned in close to the bar, pinpointing him before making her move.

Lauren drove her closed fists through the veneer of the bar and grabbed hold of her struggling prize. With a heave she dragged him through the jagged hole she'd made and into her sight. The broken wood and metal cut deeply into his body and she heard his bones snap as they struggled to fit through the opening.

The wheezing, gurgling wreck in her blood-covered hands was barely alive, so she gave him a little jolt of healing. Just enough to let him speak to her. Flecks of blood spattered her face as the man struggled to breathe. Lauren took note of the leather vest he was wearing and the valkyrie motifs decorating it.

"Where are your friends?"

Her voice was disturbingly pleasant and upbeat.

He struggled to respond, but finally croaked out an answer.

"Th-thirty-six thirty-seven mountain terrace road, that's where we meet."

Lauren was draining his life before he could even finish his sentence.

"Thanks."

Finally, the answer to the question she'd been asking all day. Unfortunately, she had no clue where Mountain Terrace was. She pondered a moment before a compelling idea came to mind, and caused her to burst out laughing.

Lauren stepped out into the street in front of a passing taxi and motioned for the man to stop. He slammed on his brakes a few moments too late and crashed headlong into her hip. Lauren grunted softly from the blow, but remained largely unmoved. The front end of the car was crumpled like an accordion and the engine was making a high-pitched keening noise that irritated her ears.

Lauren walked to the driver's side of the vehicle and ripped the door off.

"I need directions to 3637 Mountain terrace."

The babbling cabbie blinked at her, then feverishly jammed the address into his dashboard GPS.

The tiny computer announced that it had found the most direct route a few moments later.

"Is that battery powered?"

He nodded.

"Good."

Lauren reached past the cowering man and ripped the device from it's mount before leaping into the air. A thin robotic voice rose above the winds.

"Recalculating."

Lauren rolled her eyes and dropped back down to a few dozen feet above street level before proceeding. It took less than 15 minutes for Lauren to arrive. When she did, she was surprised at how nice the neighborhood was.

The white, three storey home she found had a pair large of unattached garages, a medium sized yard, even a pool in the back. The entire property was clearly in good repair and well taken care of. The only unusual feature was a tall chain link fence that enclosed the property.

Lauren wondered for a moment if she'd been lied to, but a gunshot from within the house confirmed that she was in the right place.

She heard the bullet whizz past like an angry bee, missing her head by a few feet at most. The single shot was followed by a dozen more as the windows of the home lit up from within.

Lauren didn't even bother to move, opting to hover noncha-lantly above the street. The small caliber weapons barely ruf-fled her feathers, and felt like raindrops against her skin.

Within moments the gunfire sputtered to a stop as the people within realized the futility of their assault. Lauren, with her bullet-riddled clothes, touched down lightly on the grass and took a deep breath, relishing the fear she could smell from the house.

She would enjoy this, the hunger within her promised.

It was right.

Lauren turned and gripped the handle of the gate in the fence behind her, she gently squeezed the metal together enough to make it inoperable, trapping her prey within the confines of the property.

she spent the next twenty minutes or so playfully tracking down and draining the unfortunate inhabitants of the house.

Unsurprisingly there were people that were clearly not members of the actual gang there as well. A number of hysterical, scantily clad women, for example. But it didn't bother Lauren, their lives tasted just as sweet.

They made their choices.

Lauren burst into the last room of the house with a grin only to be confronted by a young woman standing in front of a huddled pair of children. The woman let loose two slugs from a shaking 12-gauge shotgun, eliciting screams from the youngsters behind her.The rounds hit her leg, ripping Lauren's jeans in the middle of her thigh before ricocheting off into the wall.

Valerie's phone slipped from her torn pocket and dropped to the floor beside Lauren's foot, jarring her as much as the sight of the children had.

Slowly, unthinkingly, she bent to retrieve the fallen device. But she couldn't look away from the children.

The crying woman was speaking, but Lauren's ears had stopped working. She was lost in the piercing blue eyes of the blonde, curly-haired kids behind her. Their terror cut her to the bone, pierced her heart as surely as a blade.

"...don't hurt them. I'll do anything. Please just take me instead."

The woman was on her knees, begging.

Lauren's stomach churned and her vision swam. She shook her head violently, trying to clear the thumping from her ears or the bile from her throat. She turned and rushed from the room, barely keeping herself from being sick. The house was suddenly claustrophobic, the walls crushing in around her.

When she finally burst out into the yard she could see the house was surrounded by police. Dozens of officers leveled a variety of firearms at her from behind the hoods of their parked vehicles. The flashing lights made her nausea worse, so she shut her eyes and tried to breathe as slowly and carefully as she could.

The officers were screaming at her, instructing her to lay down with her hands in the air, but she knew she had nothing to fear. Instead she stood clutching her stomach, trying to calm herself. She could feel the inky blackness struggling to regain its grip on her heart, but the wound from seeing the children would not be sealed.

She'd nearly succeeded in returning her breathing to normal when a loud explosion shook the yard. A blast of hot air and ash announced Weyland's arrival like a trumpet, and Lauren's stomach flipped again. She gagged, but managed to keep her composure.

Weyland was wearing a tailored suit, charcoal grey with ruby cufflinks and a silver tie. Beside him Lauren could see Natalie. She'd changed considerably since Lauren had seen her months ago. For one thing, she was wearing a smart black skirt and a loose salmon blouse and heels, rather than the archaic garments she'd had on before. The only accessory that hadn't changed was the golden choker around her neck.

In her hands, Natalie held an exquisite wooden box wrapped in a silver bow.

"Lauren, my love. I've brought you a gift."

Weyland motioned for Natalie to move forward, and she did so, bowing low and presenting Lauren with the box.

It was all Lauren could do to remain standing. She scrunched her eyes shut.

When Lauren didn't react, Natalie glanced nervously at her master. He had a strange half-scowl on his face. Natalie improvised and opened the box for Lauren, revealing an exquisite gold circlet. The thin crown was shaped to resemble a string of feathers and was studded with dozens of small, sparkling diamonds.

Natalie lifted the circlet out of the box and held it up to Lauren.

Weyland took a few steps towards Lauren, his hands out to his sides.

"Lauren by now you must realize your place is-"

He froze.

Lauren cracked one eye open, taking in the sight of the crown and the half-frightened, half-wild look on Weyland's face. The slack-jawed expression on his face drew her attention and she gazed at him in alarm. He wasn't meeting her eyes, so she followed his line of sight. At first she thought he was staring at her chest, after all it was fairly exposed from the bullet holes in her clothing. But she realized his gaze was lower, firmly fixed on her stomach.

Aside from her normally flat stomach being a little puffy, Lauren could see nothing that would have so captured his attention.

Slowly his eyes tracked back upwards until they locked with hers.

"You're *pregnant*? Why didn't you tell me!"

Lauren's eyes opened impossibly wide. Her stomach would be silenced no longer and she heaved the last of her dignity out onto the yard.

Weyland stepped towards her but she managed to hold a hand out, motioning for him to stay back. She wiped her mouth with the back of her arm and straightened up as best she could.

She wanted to speak, to deny it, but all she could hear was her heartbeat in her ears. The same two-step she'd been listening to for days. Only now did she realize it was more than just her own heartbeat she was hearing.

She heard a snap and looked down at her fist. The screen of the cell phone she was carrying had a large crack down the center. The black mirror of the phone showed her pale reflection and Lauren hardly recognized herself.

Her ebony hair soaked in the afternoon sunlight and provided contrast for her pale skin and the radiant silver veins crisscrossing her skin.

"Lauren, this changes everything. You have to come home now."

Weyland was unusually soft-spoken, but this kinder, gentler mask was just as ugly as the monster Lauren knew lurked beneath.

When she didn't respond his voice rose and was tinged with the familiar violence she knew he was capable of.

"Lauren, enough of this! You are carrying my child now, you have a duty to me. I don't want to be angry, so why do you insist on testing me like this? I have been more than patient, enduring your little... vacation. Your absurd denial of your place, of *my* place."

His swelling anger manifested as waves of heat billowing outward from his body, driving the onlooking law enforcement back and forcing Natalie to kneel and shield herself as best she could.

Lauren ignored him, both of her hands resting gently on her stomach. She willed her heart to calm, mesmerized by the second beat. How could she have missed it before? It occurred to her that only by virtue of her empowered senses could she hear it at all. Sure enough, the more she focused the more clearly she could hear the rapid pitter-patter of the life inside her.

Weyland had continued speaking but she'd tuned him out, so when he roughly grabbed her arm and shook her it startled her.

"You *will* listen to me, I demand it."

The truth of her situation hit Lauren like a meteor, unfiltered by the wild surprise of Weyland's revelation. She was pregnant. She was pregnant with Weyland's child. She could no longer deny what she knew had been done to her while she slumbered under his spell.

Lauren locked eyes with Weyland, an act that he mistook for obedience.

"Better. Now, you will return with me to London and we will be bonded before the eyes of Gods and men-"

She jerked her arms free of his rough grasp, causing him to pause in disbelief.

"You still defy me?"

Lauren opened her mouth to speak but before she could utter a single syllable Weyland backhanded her with such incredible force that it drove her to her knees. Lauren felt her jaw crack and several of her teeth loosen from the blow, but in an instant the damage was repaired. The ringing in her ears and the spots dancing before her eyes took a few moments longer to resolve.

She looked up at him, her vision still swimming a bit. She stood unsteadily and spit a mouthful of blood into his hate-filled face. Weyland took a surprised step backward, wiping the sizzling fluid off of his face.

"How dare you, you ungrateful-"

Lauren's anger burned as brightly as her rival's and she shouted over him.

"How dare I? How dare I? What in your perverse, sick mind makes you think I should be grateful to you?"

Lauren shoved him and took a great deal of pleasure in seeing him stumble. Her strength emboldened her further and the look on his face as he realized how strong she had become was priceless.

"You think I want your child inside me? Did I ask you to do this to me? To... to violate me?"

"I have no need to ask! I took what was mine," he roared back at her.

The grass around them crumbled to ashes and the paint on the house started to peel, but still Lauren stood her ground.

"You, this world, these mortals? This is *mine*, all mine-"

With every word Weyland jammed his finger downward, gesturing to the blackened and cracked ground beneath their feet.

"I am not a thing to be owned!"

Lauren's voice shook as she unreservedly declared her freedom. Her breathing grew heavier and she could feel energy pulling into her body from the ground beneath her.

"You," she pointed menacingly at him, taking note that her arm up to her elbow was engulfed in bright silver.

"You *stole* my innocence, you *took* something irreplaceable from me. Something that was mine to give, and no one's to take, and you... you stole it."

Hot tears streamed down her face, blurring her vision. This would be the first time she said it out loud, made it real.

"You raped me."

Her accusation hung like an ax above the yard, casting it into silence but for the roaring flames from the now burning buildings and the wailing of sirens.

Was that... fear in Weyland's eyes? Lauren couldn't be sure through her tears.

"If it is true that I will live forever, and worse, that I am trapped in this hell with you, then know this. I will never be yours. I will never love you, or care about you. I could walk this earth until the sun burned out and you would still be nothing to me. Less than nothing."

Lauren cast her eyes upward, to the freedom of the skies, and took to the air.

"Lauren."

She hovered, staring down at him.

"This isn't over."

Lauren turned away again and headed south.

"Yes, it is."

As she gained altitude and more of the city revealed itself to her, she felt... wrong.

Something was different, but it took her a moment to place it. Every yard, every tree and bush, every errant blade of grass between sidewalk cracks had turned black and dead. Worse, the streets were littered with hollow, drained corpses. Men, women, pets still tethered by leashes to their lifeless owners. The devastation stretched for block after block, all radiating from the house she'd just left. It was several minutes before she again saw signs of life. Her resolve threatened to break, but there again was the darkness to comfort her. She gladly let it wrap itself back around her heart and pushed herself further, faster, and higher into the skies.

With weather as ugly as this, Caroline was glad to be indoors. The unseasonably cold thunderstorm that engulfed Southern Illinois had sprung from nowhere and had steadily worsened throughout the day.

Caroline was working her way towards the kitchen of her church. She could hear the tea kettle just starting to boil and was glad for the promise of warmth on this chilly summer night. The tiny whistle barely pierced the pounding of the driving rain that had been dousing the area for most of the afternoon.

Her depth perception had not yet fully recovered, particularly in the dim twilight, so it was difficult for her to pour sugar in her drink without spilling it on the counter.

Then again, she chuckled to herself, with only one good eye I only see half the mess, I suppose. Beverage in hand, she retired to her small bedroom. The television remained off, she'd had quite enough of the circus that was the news cycle, and instead she reached to retrieve a blank-covered black leather book and a small pen from her bedside table.

She'd just started writing when she heard a faint knock at the back door.

It was awfully late to be a parishioner, and besides the doors to The Lady's House were always unlocked, even in these troubling times. No, it must be a guest then. Someone unwilling to enter uninvited. Well, she would not keep them waiting. Caroline slid her feet into a pair of soft house slippers and shuffled to the door.

"Hello? Please come in it's unlocked. All are welcome here."

Her aging heart skipped a beat when the door swung softly open to reveal that last person she thought she'd ever see again.

"Oh my Lord in Heaven, Lauren! Oh how I have prayed for your return."

Something in Lauren's face seemed different, broken and defeated. Caroline wasn't sure she'd ever seen someone look so... crushed.

"My lady, a-are you ok?"

Lauren shook her head no, and Caroline could see her face was wet from more than rain. She was clutching something small in both her hands against her chest, and her clothes were ragged and torn, hanging off her body like an afterthought. Even her sleek black wings hung low and dejected.

Caroline stepped aside to let Lauren in, but was instead engulfed in a soaking wet hug. Lauren gripped her tightly, almost to the point that it hurt, but she was sobbing so hard the Caroline couldn't bring herself to say anything at all.

After a tense few moments, Caroline managed to reach a hand around behind Lauren and push the door shut. She guided her weeping friend further into the church, a trail of water following them across the dull linoleum flooring.

Loathe though she was to admit it, her own quarters were a bit of a mess, so she opted to bring her charge into the worship hall to sit a moment while she straightened up. Caroline sat Lauren down on the furthest back pew and moved to retrieve a few towels.

"D-don't go, please. Please don't leave me alone."

Lauren wrapped her arms tighter around Caroline, who acquiesced and sat beside her. Lauren cried for more than an hour, her head buried in Caroline's shoulder and her arms tightly around her. Caroline ran her fingers gently through Lauren's sopping hair and tried as best she could to comfort her. She knew that when she was ready, Lauren would speak.

It was only after Lauren started shivering that Caroline broke their shared silence.

"Let me get you a towel dear, and some dry clothes."

Lauren nodded with a sniffle and finally revealed her tear-streaked face, complete with runny nose and puffy red eyes. The change in her features was so startlingly clear, so close to Caroline that she couldn't help but gasp. Lauren's eyes were black pools streaked with bright silver threads. That same silver seemed to radiate from the veins around her eyes, giving her a look somewhere between angelic and menacing.

Lauren looked up into Caroline's face, afraid of the judgment she expected to find. All she found was grace and concern, and ugly scars running down one half of her face.

She didn't have to ask how they'd gotten there. She'd seen enough of Kent's memories to remember Sigurd's cruel boot grinding her face into the rough Chicago pavement.

Her throat felt tight, and her eyes were still blurry as she struggled to thank the woman cradling her so gently. She gently reach a hand out and brushed Caroline's face, her scars disappearing under Lauren's fingertips.

"Caroline, I am so, so sorr-"

Her next words were swept from her mind when she saw the portrait hanging on the wall above the doorway they had just come through.

A large picture frame, at least four feet wide, was filled edge to edge with a print that Lauren recognized immediately. It was her, landing in a soft, sunlit meadow filled with wildflowers. The photo was crystal clear except for her body, where the blurred black lines of her hair and feathers gave her an other-worldly appearance. She was a black pearl in the midst of a sea of vibrant green and a riot of colors. She recognized the scene well, and was dumbfounded at seeing it here.

"Where did you get this?"

"Oh well, there've been several like these released anony-mously. There must be half a dozen by now, but this one is my favorite. Something about it, it's so... raw and honest. You never mentioned you were a model while you were staying with me before. I hope you don't mind that I hung it up?"

Caroline seemed nervous, as though afraid her choice of decoration would offend Lauren.

"No I... um, I don't mind."

"Oh good, shall I go get you those towe-"

"Caroline?"

Lauren was staring intently at her, her eyes unblinking.

"Do you have a cell phone charger I could borrow?"

A half an hour later Lauren was sitting cross-legged on Car-oline's bed. Her soaking clothes had been replaced by fluffy grey pajamas and her hair was freshly brushed and drawn back into a messy bun. Caroline had insisted she prepare some food when Lauren couldn't remember the last time she'd eaten, so she was off in the kitchen humming to herself and tinkering with pots and pans.

Lauren, on the other hand, was staring intently at the tiny black device laying on the mattress in front of her. She'd dried it as best she could and set it in a bowl of uncooked rice until just a few moments ago. She picked it up gently, the charging end of a power cable in her other hand and whispered a silent prayer as she plugged the two together.

Immediately she set it back down and held her breath. It seemed like an eternity had passed and nothing happened. No sound, no light, nothing. Lauren sighed disappointedly, trying to convince herself she didn't care. She couldn't stand to look at the phone any longer and she flopped back onto the bed trying not to cry.

Ding.

Was it real? had it been in her mind?

She waited, unwilling to look again in case she had simply imagined the sound. Her resolve lasted only seconds before she was sitting back up and grabbing the phone.

1%.

The tiny charging icon lit a fire of hope in Lauren's breast and she willed the phone to life with all her heart. The next several minutes stretched into eternity as she watched the power levels of the phone slowly rise. At long last it hit 5% and she would wait no longer.

Lauren reached out and held the power button, and her breath.

She released them both, nearly breaking back into tears when the broken screen flickered to life. The device finished powering up and immediately began to ring and vibrate like a thing possessed. Lauren watched guiltily as the number of unread text messages ticked steadily upward, and looked away when the screen flashed a warning indicating the voicemail was full.

All told she had 314 unread messages and a dozen voicemails, all from Valerie. She thought about ignoring them, considered simply calling her estranged friend straight away, but if Valerie had felt it important enough to write then Lauren was determined to read her words.

She tapped the screen and her heart sank. It didn't seem to recognize her action at all. She took a deep breath and tried again, nothing. She resisted the urge to throw the phone across the room, desperately wrestling with the angry blackness that lashed out from her mind. She could feel the rage and anger in it, but she kept herself in check.

She tried a third time. A fourth.

Hours passed as she tried every conceivable option, her solutions becoming less realistic as the night wore on. Finally, exhausted, she resorted to addressing the phone as if it could hear her.

"Work, dammit!"

Lauren nearly dropped the phone in surprise as it started to ring in her hand. She stood, uncertain of what to do as a name and number popped up on the small screen.

Sir Edward Warvington.

Lauren's mind raced, she'd not even considered that Mr. Warvington might call. She remembered the pain in his eyes when they'd parted, the stern warning that she ought not hurt his Valerie. Well, it was certainly too late for that.

The ringing continued, every ring bringing both relief and terror to her heart. Did she dare answer? what if she didn't? Would he call again?

She took a breath and hit the answer button, it worked.

She heard the phone line open, but couldn't bring herself to speak. Silence greeted her from the other end of the phone as well.

"H-hello?"

The whispered word stopped Lauren's heart. The soft, lyrical notes of Valerie's voice caught her totally unprepared. Her breath caught in her throat and she scrambled to think of something to say.

"Lauren? Lauren if this is you I'm so sorry..."

Lauren scrunched her eyes shut at the pain in Valerie's voice.

"Lauren please, say something. Say anything. Tell me you hate-"

"I'm here. Valerie I'm here."

Lauren finally managed to get the words past the lump in her throat. She heard Valerie sniffle quietly in response before answering.

"Lauren I'm so sorry, I can't ever expect you to forgive me but please understand I didn't mean to hurt you. I never, ever meant for that to happen."

"Vee Shh, It's ok I-I'm sorry too. I'm... I don't know what to do. I miss you, I'm so confused by everything else but I know I miss you."

"I was so scared you'd left the phone somewhere, thrown it away or broken it... I kept calling and texting you but I never got a response. I've called you every night since you left."

"I think I lost myself. I hated you, I hated everything. You hurt me so bad I didn't want to feel that ever again. I... did things. It's blurry, like it's not me, but it is.-"

"Lauren I know, it's been all over the news... Listen it doesn't matter, I don't believe it, any of it. And I'm not the only one, there's tons of us that still believe in you."

"Valerie you have to believe it."

There was a long pause.

"I-it's true? All those people..."

Lauren could hear a tremor of fear in Valerie's voice. But she couldn't lie, wouldn't.

"Yes. It's true. There's this.. I don't know what to call it, it's like I'm sick or-"

"Did you mean to? I mean... to... *do that?*"

She wanted to say no, but the power, the strength, the unadulterated pleasure she'd felt? Even now she struggled to muster a sense of remorse.

"I'm a monster, Vee, the things I've done? They're... unspeakable. I don't know who I was, what I was becoming and then I... saw the picture you took, that day in the meadow."

"Of course, I remember it. You were so beautiful, *are* so beautiful."

There was a long pause.

"Lauren can I... I'd like to see you, i-if I can."

She wiped her tear-streaked cheeks and smiled. Valerie's questions confirmed a hope she hadn't dared to realize. She'd never dreamt that Valerie would ever want to see her after the things she'd done.

"I'm back home, in America. I miss you so much."

"Lauren, America is a *really* big place."

"Right."

Lauren let out a stuttering, teary laugh.

"I'm at Cherry Hills Church outside of Paducah, Kentucky."

"I'm on my way."

Chapter 11

Five days.

It had been five days since Lauren's return to Cherry Hills, and Lauren didn't think she'd stopped pacing for more than a few minutes during her entire stay. Valerie was taking a boat from England. She was far too recognizable to take an aircraft, and it was only through the generous greasing of several palms that she'd managed to secure passage to America without a frenzy of media attention. Of course, as soon as her ship departed the United Kingdom, she'd gone radio silent.

Lauren was going mad from anxiety and anticipation. The unstable weather reflected her mood, and she struggled to keep herself cooped up within the confines of the tiny church. Caroline advised she stay indoors, and Lauren had grudgingly complied.

Still, she felt like a bird in a cage.

Lightning flashed in the bedroom window, illuminating the pre-dawn and burning after-images into Lauren's eyes. The storm hadn't lifted for days. If anything, the weather seemed to be growing steadily worse. Lauren didn't mind the rain or the lightning, but most of downstate Illinois would likely disagree with her. Flooding was already starting to become an issue across the bottom portion of the state, a situation Lauren was following loosely on the television.

The rain-stricken midwest barely made the news, however. Of greater interest was the deteriorating world stage.

North Korea had launched rockets carrying nerve gas on Japan and South Korea, triggering the United States to deploy soldiers to the peninsula. Iran was in the middle of a religious coup as the Ayatollah was overthrown and butchered by a group of fire-worshipping zealots decrying their loyalty to Weyland. In Europe, France, Germany, Holland, most of Scandinavia, and the United Kingdom had announced the formation of the Northern European Federation. Their governments, and militaries, were merging in the name of common defense and they were sealing their combined border to all foreign nationals.

The only place on Earth that didn't seem embroiled in war was Africa. In a change of pace, many African nations found themselves on the receiving end of a flood of Western refugees fleeing the violence.

Lauren clicked haphazardly between channels, each more gruesome than the last. Her mind was a thousand miles away, drifting in an ocean of doubt and worry.

A posh British accent brought her back to her senses and her eyes focused on the screen.

"... at 5.6 million pounds sterling, It's the most expensive photograph ever sold. The photographer, Valerie Chatwick, came to fame recently when it was alleged that she was engaged sexually with the controversial being Lauren Corvidae. She could not be reached for comment, but her spokesperson, Sir Edward Warvington, famous for his role as a fighter pilot in the second World War, released a statement saying the money would be donated to global humanitarian causes..."

Lauren's ears perked up. The short piece had revealed a host of new information, and left her scratching her head at the questions she'd not thought to ask before. Unfortunately, the report must have been finished because the reporters swiftly changed topics and fell in line with the rest of the channels.

Great.

Lauren sighed and lay back against the bed, huffing and puffing her frustration to the empty room. Finally, she could take it no longer. She slipped off of the bedspread and headed for the wide, double door to the outside world. She passed Caroline on her way and ignored the curious look she received from her.

"Lauren…"

She pretended not to hear, increasing her pace and shoving the doors open with ease. The wet, ozone tinged air hit her like a wave and filled her with wanderlust. The pine and oak, the earth and rain, all formed a perfect combination of her childhood and dragged her to the freedom of the skies like a magnet.

"Lauren you can't be seen!"

Caroline's warning fell on deaf ears. Lauren was already running, her bare feet splashing mud and water up her calves as she raced across the meadow. She relished the feeling of mud and grass squishing up between her toes, the cool water below and the warm rain coming down in sheets from above.

Her wings spread wide, Lauren leapt skyward and with a few powerful beats she was soaring just above the treetops in a wide loop above the church and it's grounds.

Her hawk-like eyes could clearly see Caroline, hands on her hips and shaking her head at her reckless behaviour. Despite her apparent frustration, Caroline had a smile on her face when she turned back to the dry interior of the building.

Lauren smiled as well, knowing she'd already won the forgiveness of her host. She turned North and let her heart carry her where it would.

Washed out roads, overflowing rivers, and partially submerged towns dotted the landscape below her, testament to days of nonstop rainfall. The land below her was serene, free of any human activity in light of the dreary weather. She enjoyed the relative freedom, diving, rolling, and cartwheeling through the air free of any prying eyes from below.

She pushed onward as the sun began to emerge from beyond the horizon. The dim, cloud-filtered rays of gray on the rolling hills and deep woods of the Shawnee had Lauren mulling over the past few months, and her current predicament. She absentmindedly put her hands on her stomach, keenly aware of the unwelcome life growing within.

Unwilling to face her difficult feelings, she turned her attention back to the land below her. She was nearing her childhood home, unless she was very much mistaken. Sure enough, first Anna, and then the tiny streets of Cobden were winding below her. Not a soul was in sight, and something in her heart demanded she land.

She touched down lightly in the overgrown yard of a faded but familiar house. Erin's windows were boarded up, the paint was peeling, and the yard hadn't been trimmed in what must have been months, but to Lauren's eyes it looked the way it did on the last night she'd seen her childhood sweetheart.

Lauren looked around the yard. A new, barely weathered light post had replaced the one she'd demolished with her truck. She shook her head to clear the fog that was building inside her and approached the door. It was locked, but that proved no great obstacle for Lauren's powerful muscles. With a sharp crack, she forced the door open and sent dust swirling into the stillness beyond.

The doorway may as well have been an concrete wall for all the difficulty Lauren had in passing through it. She forced herself to push on, to break the barrier within herself and step into the quiet, book-filled living room.

Everything was as she'd left it that night.

Books scattered everywhere, the bed a mess, the bathroom door battered and broken. She kept her composure until she reached the tub. It had been cleaned, by whom she didn't know, but all the scrubbing and bleach in the world couldn't clean the image of Erin's lifeless hand from Lauren's mind. Lauren sank to her knees, her cheek resting against the cold porcelain and hot tears burning paths of fire across her face.

"I'm so, so sorry Erin. You didn't deserve this."

The house didn't answer her, and neither did her friend.

She hadn't been at the funeral. She'd missed it while in her manic, terrified stupor at Caroline's and by the time she'd ventured back out into public she was fairly certain she'd never return to Cobden. It was a prophecy that had proven true, with the exception of the night she'd rescued her father.

Pent up guilt and shame for her weakness, for her inability to conquer her own fear and say goodbye had eaten at her, gnawed at her heart in the darkness every day since she'd died. She was a coward and she knew it, deep in her core she knew it.

Perhaps she could right that wrong, at least in some small way. The life inside her seemed to shift, to nudge her ribs at the thought of atonement. She was sickened by the thought of it, and by the way her heart jumped at the tiny movement. She hated herself, hated Weyland, hated the spark that burned in her gut, and hated that she couldn't hate the being inside her. It represented everything wrong, every crime that had been committed against her, and yet she couldn't help but know it's innocence.

Lauren clamped down on her mind, forcing thoughts of her unborn child back into the darkness and pushing herself to her feet again. Silence loomed, broken only by the soft patter of raindrops falling from her feathers.

Stop it.

Lauren wandered through the house to Erin's bedroom. Dusty blankets covered the bed in a tangled mess. A forgotten salt shaker lay spilled on the pillow and the long-dried rinds of a cut lime were scattered across the covers. Lauren's heightened sense of smell brought her heart to her throat.

The familiars scents of spice, rain, and chocolate hit her like a wave and she could close her eyes and imagine that Erin was here with her. She could practically feel her breath, her warmth, and her gentle laugh. Lauren let the feeling wash over her and crawled deep into the bedspread, wrapping herself in the blankets and burying her face in the pillows. For hours she lost herself in every good memory she could conjure, every smile and laugh that they had ever shared. But even at its height, it was a hollow shell of the real thing. She knew her high was temporary, that she'd never see her friend again.

Lauren finally let herself mourn. She released the tension and the fear she'd held onto for so long. When she finally emerged from her nest of blankets she felt fuller. Less empty and broken than she had in many months.

Lauren wiped her eyes and made her way slowly to the door. "Goodbye, Erin."

Lauren shut the door carefully and looked to the skies. She had one more stop to make.

Lightning flashed, casting odd shadows in the grey-skied afternoon as Lauren approached the small cemetery outside of town. She was having trouble seeing through the thick sheets of rain, but the cemetery looked abandoned. Unsurprising, really, given the terrible weather.

She had no clue where to begin searching, but the graveyard was quite small. Lauren touched down gently at one corner of the property, the soft ground yielding to her bare feet. She stepped in front of the first headstone and began to make her way carefully down the row.

A few minutes turned to twenty, thirty, an hour, two. Name after name and date after date wandered through her mind. *Loving father of four, Mother, Sister, Daughter.* The heartfelt epithets struck a chord in Lauren, leaving her to wonder what she would find when her search concluded.

The slow crunch of gravel caused her to duck down. She turned and pinpointed the source of the noise, but what she saw she could hardly believe. An old, battered '96 pick-up truck was making its way down the gravel road towards the cemetery. With a powerful leap, Lauren took shelter in a towering ash tree. Despite the rain, Lauren was sure she recognized the vehicle. The closer it got the surer she became. Every dent and patch of rust on the aged body of the truck was intimately familiar to her.

She watched the truck turn off of the gravel trail and glide awkwardly across the wet grass, heedless of the sacred ground below the tires. The driver let the vehicle drift left and right, seemingly unable to maintain a straight path as it worked it's way across the graveyard before sliding to a halt in front of a small rose bush a few dozen yards from where Lauren was hiding.

The driver's door opened and a woman stumbled from the cab. Bundled up against the weather, she made her way unsteadily across the grass before sinking to her knees in front of a small cluster of graves.

Lauren's breath caught in her chest when the woman collapsed, shaking, on the ground. Lauren leapt from the branch where she was perched, sending a sheet of water splashing to the ground as she took off. She drifted silently along until she circled above the woman below.

There could be no doubt, it was Allison.

Lauren dropped to the ground a few feet behind her mother, but her arrival went unnoticed. Lauren wrestled internally, unsure of how to proceed. One half of her heart ached for the only family she had. The other, wrapped in angry darkness, goaded her to lash out and destroy the source of so much of her pain. She stood, hands clenched and jaw tightened against her indecision for several minutes as the woman in front of her sobbed, oblivious to her presence.

Lightning flashed again, followed by an earth-shaking peal of thunder. The bright light glinted off of the empty bottle in Allison's hand and caused her dark, wet hair to glimmer briefly.

Lauren watched her mother's hand slowly tighten around the neck of the bottle. Allison screamed, her own thundering rage rising to match that of the storm. She punched the ground, venting her anger and pain to the uncaring graves.

Allison's fists moved to the headstone in front of her. The rough granite was soon darkened by her bleeding knuckles and Lauren took a step forward to stop her.

Before Lauren's outstretched hand could make contact, Allison smashed the bottle against the headstone and sank back against the grass, clutching her injured hands. Lauren couldn't help but flinch, not so much at the sight of her mother, but for the mirror she was looking so painfully into.

Allison turned and finally saw her daughter standing over her, her eyes widened and she was speechless.

"Lauren?"

Her soft, desperate whisper was at once a prayer, a question, and a cry for help. Lauren answered by stooping down and lifting her mother from the ground, cradling her like a child. Broken glass from countless bottles littered the grave, and the closer Lauren looked she could see dozens of tires tracks leading to this one headstone. With trepidation she read the words upon it.

Gabriel

Son, Brother, Angel. Our love for you will live on forever.

It didn't seem... enough. It felt quaint, vague, and utterly lacking to Lauren. She felt anger rising in her chest and tried to ground herself. She breathed deeply, tried to clear her mind, but the aggression within her was threatening to burst forth.

Allison drunkenly clutched at her daughter, and Lauren barely resisted the urge to drop her in disgust. Lauren could feel the volcano within, felt her composure cracking and cast around for a safe outlet.

No immediate targets presented themselves, so she lashed out at what she could find. With a snarling shout she released a mighty kick directly into the side of the pick-up. Her bare foot sent the door crumpling into the cab, and the entire vehicle tumbling sideways across the grass. It skidded to a halt with a spray of mud some thirty feet away.

Thunder drowned out her mother's helpless whimpering, but Lauren could feel Allison shaking like a leaf in her arms. She felt like a porcelain doll, weightless and delicate in Lauren's inhumanly strong grasp. The storm inside her quieted, at least enough for her to think clearly. She couldn't leave Allison here. The woman couldn't stand, let alone get herself anywhere safe. The truck was totalled, which meant wherever they went Lauren would have to provide for her. She certainly wouldn't take Allison back to Cherry Hills, there was no chance that Lauren would risk the privacy of her sanctuary for a woman who had so utterly betrayed her.

Thinking about Rome, and her mother's deceit, rekindled the fire in her gut and she was again tempted to leave her behind. Some shred of humanity within her, some as-yet-unsnuffed candle of mercy forced her to resist.

She really only had one option, if she thought about it. With a frustrated sigh she leapt back into the lightning-filled skies and headed for the edge of town once more. A few minutes of flight and she was touching down outside outside her childhood home. The small, tucked-away structure was in decent repair, but it looked much different from what she remembered growing up. The entire outside was plastered with envelopes and papers, each tacked onto countless others beneath. Besides the strange notes, hundreds of small baskets and boxes covered the yard.

It frustrated Lauren to no end, the idea that people had spent hard-earned money and time on such nonsense was embarrassing and aggravating. She picked her way across the cluttered yard to the door, which was already slightly open from her mother's departure.

Sure enough, the inside showed signs of recent habitation of a sort. Bottles and cans lay like a blanket on the floor, un-washed clothes and forgotten, half-eaten food completed the hoarder-turned-homeless appearance of the house. With every step Lauren clinked and clanked through the mess, the noise jarring her ears like nails on a chalkboard.

Lauren gave a powerful flap of her wings, sending trash tumbling across the floor and piling it up against the walls. Much better. Lauren walked to the couch and set her sleeping mother gently on the cushions. Her keen eyesight picked up a dark stain on the boards of the floor. The memory of a scared child came back to her with startling clarity and for an instant she was transported back a decade. She could almost imagine her father coming in from the kitchen with a glass of wine.

But he didn't, and he never would again.

Lauren made her way to the kitchen, took stock of the broken picture frames on shelves, the unclosed refrigerator, the fact that the power seemed to be out. She moved to close the fridge and took a peek inside. The light was out, and it was barren except for some cheap beer and a half-empty plastic jug of bargain vodka.

Lauren licked her lips, a familiar thirst stirring within her, but pushed it aside.

A scowl took up residence on her face and she shut the door, turning to the cabinets instead. Aside from some expired cans of vegetables and dusty dishes, the cabinets were bare as well. Lauren lifted a dingy glass and briefly considered going outside to collect some rainwater, but ended up rolling her eyes and simply replacing the cup.

Lauren returned to the living room to keep an eye on her mother. Allison's face was peaceful, and she was snoring loudly against the cushions.

With the couch occupied, Lauren took a seat in the aged recliner across the room. She kicked her feet up on the coffee table and sat in silent judgment over the drunkard before her. Allison's lack of control, her disgusting inability to sacrifice for her family, was the root of all of Lauren's problems.

Deep breath.

A wet retching noise brought her attention back to her mother. Allison's face was partially obscured by her long hair, but Lauren could see a puddle of vomit around her mouth. Lauren bolted upright and rolled her mother over before she could choke. Even so, Allison coughed and hacked for several minutes to clear her mouth and throat.

The smell was atrocious and Lauren felt her own stomach churn. It took all of her fortitude to keep her own bile down.

The longer she sat and stewed the angrier and more certain she became. She heaped blame on the woman in front of her until her blood was boiling over. She could feel herself losing control again. Guilt hit her like an avalanche. Here she was, tearing her mother to shreds for her addiction, but hadn't she found a vice as well? Faint echoes of hundreds of extinguished lives whispered in her mind and instead of guilt or horror, the strongest emotions that bubbled forth were lust and greed. Shame burned Lauren's cheeks, tightened around her heart. Lauren had *murdered* those people, and worse than that she had enjoyed every second of it. The power she felt, the invincibility and pleasure when she consumed their lives was a high she knew she'd never be free of.

With every killing she had felt her body grow stronger. But Lauren knew her soul, if she had one at all, was as dark as night. Laurens hands clasped self consciously over her stomach, feeling the trembling life within. What impact might her feasting have on this unplanned being?

Did it matter?

Did she care if the baby inside her died? Her brain screamed no, came up with a dozen excuses to be rid of the unwelcome parasite, but her heart couldn't commit. Faced with uncomfortable introspection, the house seemed stuffy and restricting.

Lauren returned to the outdoors and the torrential, unrelenting rain. The whispering pines and towering sycamores of her childhood home didn't seem as welcoming and safe as they once were. Nothing about the property felt the same, in fact. It was a shell of what it had been, a house but no longer a home.

She thought about leaving, would her mother even know she'd gone? Did she care? But Lauren had too many unanswered questions, too much to get off of her chest to let her mother off so easily.

A gust of wind shook the tiny house and a dozen of the letters that covered the outside tore off and flitted past Lauren's face. Her curiosity was piqued once more and she reached out to tear a few off the wall. After gathering a handful she returned to the recliner inside and settled down to read the wet, rain streaked writing.

It was raining in Washington as well.

Presley Weiss was poring over his handwritten notes. He could hear clamoring reporters just beyond the thin curtain separating himself from the podium he was about to take. Presley kicked himself for getting into the mess he was in. Secretary of State Rodney Kilpatrick's unexpected retirement a few weeks ago led to his interim appointment, at least until he got confirmed. For the umpteenth time he wished that he'd sidestepped the promotion. With a deep breath he rehearsed his talking points, 'Public Affairs Guidance' as General Malone called it.

He muttered to himself, running an unsteady hand through his dirty blonde hair. A dozen possible questions ran through his mind, he mulled over each and formulated plausible responses, then considered possible follow-ups and repeated the process ad nauseum. All too soon he could hear Press Secretary Mullens, an unpleasant, hawkish woman, introducing him as the next speaker.

"Secretary Weiss will now give brief remarks followed by a few questions."

Presley took his cue from the smattering of applause and the brief lull in the raucous room. The meeting space was crowded with reporters and dozens of camera lenses glinted unblinkingly back at him as he walked deliberately to his place behind the podium.

"Thank you, madam secretary."

Presley took a deep breath, held it a moment and then calmly exhaled.

Showtime.

"Here's what we know so far. Lauren Corvidae was last seen flying South from Chicago, Illinois. She was followed by United States Air Force assets until they were forced to suspend operations due to worsening weather conditions. In the past five days, the State Department, in conjunction with other agencies, has been conducting research into where she might have gone. We have no concrete answers yet. Based on our knowledge of her flight capabilities, we project that she is still somewhere in North America, but that's all we have so far."

The reporters were already shouting over each other to squeeze in a question around his statements. He pressed on, unwilling to be derailed so quickly.

"Weyland has been far more visible. Following the events in Chicago, he returned to London. It is unclear what relationship exists between Weyland and Lauren, but following their public conflict Weyland has issued a demand to meet with the

President, as well as various European Heads of State. At this time the President has not yet made clear whether the meeting will take place."

He was shouting by the end, and even then he wasn't sure if anyone could hear him.

"I will now entertain a few questions. Yes ah, you in the front, blue tie."

"Mr. Secretary, the fight in Chicago. People need to know what happened. Preliminary reports suggest that Lauren killed more than eleven thousand people in a 14 block radius, can you confirm those numbers?"

"It's an ongoing investigation, so details are changing rapidly, but yes our count is roughly at that number. I will stress however the cause of death has not officially been determined-"

"What does the government intend to do about Lauren? How can we fight someone like that?"

Deflect.

"Sir I'm sorry, one question per network, thank you. How 'bout you, green polo."

"Uh yes thank you, Carl Madigan CZN, same question Mr. Secretary. What is the government doing to protect American lives? Never in the history of our great nation has someone blatantly murdered sovereign citizens and gone untouched. Now we have two of these... these things running rampant."

Dammit.

"The government is exploring all options. It's certainly a unique situation, as Lauren is also a US citizen, where Weyland does not appear to be. Certainly it is the hope of the administration that swift justice be brought about."

"Mr. Secretary that doesn't really answer-"

"Next question please. Uh yes ma'am, burgundy blouse, go ahead."

Presley was sweating already, he was used to having the answers *before* he stood up in front of the wolfpack that was the mainstream media.

"Mr. Secretary, aside from the obvious danger of having two powerful killing machines running loose, the Midwest is experiencing what can only be described as a storm of biblical proportions. Twelve states from Minnesota to Alabama, Nebraska to Ohio, have been under the same storm cell for nearly a week. Record breaking flooding is occurring and millions of American lives are endangered. Is there any connection between this strange weather and the two entities?"

Finally, a softball.

"The National Weather Service is currently tracking the storm very closely. While the storm cell is behaving abnormally, there is no reason to believe it is anything other than the weather. Now, FEMA is responding as appropriate, and several Governors in the affected region have activated their respective National Guard forces. The president has made a clear commitment to helping our neighbors and federal assets are on standby for states to call upon. We understand the difficult situation, particularly with regard to travelling in the affected region.."

Natalie switched off the television, a scowl on her face. She set the remote down with a soft click on her desk and stood. She took a moment to inspect herself in the mirror on the wall, straightening the lines in her blouse and skirt and tucking an errant strand of hair behind her ear. She let her fingers linger on the golden choker around her neck for a moment.

When she was confident he would find no fault with her appearance, she walked to his office door and tapped lightly.

"Enter."

She held her breath and slipped through the doorway with her eyes dutifully downward.

"Your majesty, the United States still hasn't responded to your invitation."

Weyland didn't turn to face her. He was sitting in a high-back leather chair and facing the outside world. Natalie could hear the leather stretch as his grip tightened on the armrests.

"And the others?"

"They ah, seem to be taking their cues from the United States, your Majesty."

A long forgotten cup of coffee started to steam and then boil on Weyland's desk.

"Unacceptable. Release a statement. Tell the world that I am a merciful God, and that I will allow them time to return to the flock. Tell them also that I am a jealous and impatient God, and that to deny me is to burn."

The chill in his voice struck Natalie with fear.

"Yes, your Majesty."

She waited for him to continue, but he was silent for several minutes. She knew better than to turn away from him before he released her, so she remained where she was until he finally spoke again.

"Three days. If they have not agreed in three days then their sins will no longer go unpunished."

He sounded... tired.

"Yes, your Majesty."

Weyland sighed, giving Natalie another rare peek into his, for lack of a better term, softer side. Months of constantly being by his side had given her the ability to read him. At least to some extent. These strange bouts of melancholy intrigued her to no end. His tone felt disappointed, almost defeated even, when he spoke.

"Where does the King of the United States live?"

Natalie paused, unsure for a moment what Weyland meant.

"Um, your Majesty they don't have a king. They have an office called a president, they are elected to lead every four years by the citizens."

Weyland pondered the information, scratching his chin. He finally turned around and stood. Weyland strode over to a large map hanging on the wall.

"Where does this president rule from? Show me."

Natalie nodded, she came over and tapped the map softly over Washington D.C. Her finger felt heavy, filled with lead and danger.

"Here, y-your Majesty."

Weyland mimicked her action, placing a finger over the small dot on the map. A lump built in Natalie's throat as the map started to smolder and blacken. When Weyland pulled his finger back she could see a small circle burned through to the drywall.

"Has Lauren been located?"

"No, your Majesty. Not yet."

"Very well, you are dismissed."

Natalie nodded and left the room as quickly as she could without appearing insubordinate.

As soon as the door shut behind her she pulled out her phone and opened a text message. She typed furiously as she made her way back to her desk, glancing over her shoulder every few seconds.

Presley, he says you have 3 days - he's talking about D.C. Be careful.

Her alert sent, she set about preparing to tell the world that God was angry.

Chapter 12

Lauren rubbed her tired eyes and watched the windows of the room slowly brighten with the coming dawn. Allison was still asleep, and Lauren had a massive pile of paper beside her recliner. No, not just paper, she corrected herself. This was a pile of dreams, of hopes, and of prayers. Hundreds and thousands of handwritten notes addressed to her, desperate pleas to an angel that Lauren had never been, could never be.

When had it started? It was impossible to tell. But with every new letter she read the ice in her heart thawed and was replaced by crushing, overwhelming guilt. The earliest letters she'd found, buried beneath layers and layers of newer notes, seemed to date from around when she had first rescued her father, and returned to the public eye.

With the unrelenting storm it was hard to tell how new the outer layer was, but some at least seemed to reference her fall in Chicago. The prayers turned from self-interest to hopes for Lauren. She found fewer requests, fewer desires, and a dramatic increase in well-wishes and prayers for her recovery.

Lauren's eyes burned, but she forced herself to keep reading. She dug listlessly through the newest stack of letters that she'd plucked from outside. One in particular caught her eyes.

It was a thick envelope wrapped carefully with clear plastic wrap. The thoughtful packaging meant it had been spared the worst of the weather. Lauren flipped the envelope over and the name, written in a child's cursive, brought a flood of warmth to her heart.

To - Lauren Corvidae

From - The Helmholts

Lauren extracted the letter with trembling fingers and popped the top of the envelope open. It was thick, a whole packet of papers from the feel of it. The thin, glue-sealed barrier yielded easily to her strong fingers and a sheaf of paper greeted her. She pulled the stack out and a number of photographs slipped out as well, tumbling to the floor in front of her.

Miss Lauren,

We saw you on the news. Daddy and Mommy said that you got hurt real bad, but that you'll be ok if we have faith. Daddy got hurt too when he was younger. Mommy says he broke his back like you, and that it took a long long time to get better.

Abby said that we should go see you in the city, but Daddy said that it is not a safe place for kids like us and that you need your rest. We really miss you, and we-

Lauren had to stop. She needed a break from her shame. Folding the letter carefully, she bent at the waist and picked up the photographs scattered on the floor.

A half-dozen pictures greeted her eyes. The first was an awkward but charming family christmas card, the Helmholts were all gathered in front of their family barn in red, white, and green smiling cheesily at the camera. Lauren flipped the card over and read the back.

Merry Christmas from the Helmholts, we hope this card finds you on the mend, and we want you to know your present will stay wrapped safe until you're back this way again.

She flipped through the rest of the stack, school photos of the boys, Abby in an elegant red homecoming dress, and even a smiling snapshot of Charlie and Jennifer.

Lauren drew a shaky breath and stuffed the photographs back into the envelope, retrieving the letter once more. She'd just started to scan it, looking for where she'd left off when a snuffling, half-snort caught her attention.

Allison was stirring on the couch. Wiping dried drool from her cheek she lifted herself groggily up on her elbows. Allison's dark hair was streaked with grey now. Her face had more lines than Lauren remembered, and the dark circles under her eyes were baggy and pronounced. It was... strange. Lauren saw a woman so much older, so much more worn than the image she held in her mind.

"L'ren?"

Allison's speech was still slurred, though from drunkenness, tiredness, or some combination Lauren wasn't sure.

"Good morning, Allison."

Freshly filled with guilt from reading her letter, Lauren tried to keep the acid out of her voice. She succeeded, mostly.

Allison sat up, rubbed her eyes hard, and then put her hands in her lap awkwardly as the silence in the room stretched uncomfortably.

Lauren cleared her throat, unsure of what to say but, in a perverse way, enjoying the obvious discomfort of her mother.

"S-so you found the letters then?"

Allison gestured to the pile of papers at Lauren's feet.

Lauren answered with a nod.

"The people around here have been real uh, real nice to me... mostly. They bring me food sometimes and uh, make sure I have... water."

Lauren looked meaningfully at the piles of cans and bottles strewn about the edges of the room.

"Right. Water."

Lauren tried, she really did, but her phony patience was already wearing thin. She could feel the darkness inside goading her, pushing her buttons and getting her riled up.

Had it always been this hard to resist?

She stood and headed for the door but Allison stood as well and moved to stop her.

"Please! Please... don't go."

Allison dropped to her knees and grabbed at Lauren's clothing pitifully. Lauren felt her muscles tense, knew that she could break this wicked woman with a flick of her wrist.

Knew that she deserved it.

"Why?"

Allison's eyes widened at the question, a response that fanned the flames of Lauren's anger. Lauren grabbed the front of her mother's shirt with both hands and hoisted her up in the air until they were face to face.

"Why!"

She was screaming now, and Allison's eyes were full of terror. Lauren shook her roughly, fabric tearing and her mother's limbs flailing painfully around. Familiar darkness pumped itself into her veins and she watched her veins brighten into liquid silver. Lauren struggled to overcome her rage, to hold back the urge to destroy. It was almost painful, the act of opening her hands and dropping Allison in a heap on the floor, but she managed it with gritted teeth and eyes screwed shut.

Allison was hiccuping in terror, her whole body shaking uncontrollably.

"Lauren, I... there's nothing I can say to make up for the things I've put you through."

Lauren scoffed and headed for the door again.

"Lauren I'm trying, please it's all I know how to do is try. Hate me if you want, I understand. I deserve your hate, but... you're all I have left."

One hand on the door, Lauren turned back to look at her kneeling mother. Allison's arms hung at her sides and her face was streaked with tears.

"I've destroyed *everything* I've *ever* loved. I-"

She choked on her words and cast her eyes downward.

Lauren hated herself for it, but she knew the pain her mother felt. It was the same crushing guilt and shame that haunted her every night. The silent dread, the creeping fear that everything she would ever care about was doomed to ashes.

"Why did you leave?"

Allison didn't have to ask what her daughter meant, Lauren could see in her eyes that she understood they were talking about Gabriel.

"I'm not, I'm not healthy Lauren. I'm sick, I've got-"

"You're a drunk."

Lauren's blunt word struck Allison like a slap in the face.

"Yes, I am a drunk. I'm an alcoholic and I've let my poor choices ruin my life. I left because I murdered my own son, my beautiful little baby boy. I put these bottles to his head and pulled the trigger before he was ever born."

She gestured widely at the trash littering the house.

"I couldn't stay. I couldn't stay in this house where I'd never hear him laughing again. I couldn't look at my husband, at my daughter, knowing I'd killed my son. My Gabriel. How could I ask your forgiveness when I couldn't forgive myself? When I knew I didn't deserve it?"

Lauren blinked back her own tears and shook her head. She refused to feel sorry for the monster facing her. She focused on Gabriel, on her father, on the pain Allison had caused. No one deserved a second chance after that.

"I'm not going to forgive you. Ever."

Allison didn't even flinch.

"I don't think you should."

Lauren was uncertain how to proceed. A war raged inside her. A fight between the desperate longing she had for her mother's love and the all-consuming darkness that armored her heart. Ultimately it was her hunger that tamed the beast, the hunger she felt for love that wasn't stolen from the memories of another.

"I *needed* you. I needed you and you just, left. You were supposed to be my mom, my constant guiding light. I could have forgiven your drinking, I could have forgiven anything else. But you abandoned me, abandoned *us*, when we needed you most."

Allison didn't break eye contact, didn't even flinch under the weight of Lauren's accusation. Something about her stoic, unwavering gaze impressed Lauren more than she cared to admit.

"Lauren I know I hurt you. I'm responsible for terrible, terrible things. I've been making mistakes with you since before you were ever born. John, he was better than I deserved. He knew the truth and he stayed. He stayed through it all when any reasonable man would have left in a heartbeat. I gave him a thousand reasons to leave, just like I gave you a thousand reasons to despise me."

Lauren let her speak.

"I'd like to tell you some things. Some of what happened that you don't know about. I don't expect it will change anything, but I... feel like you have a right to know."

Lauren wrestled with herself a moment longer, then returned to the recliner. Allison clasped her hands in front of her face, unable to do more than cry happy tears for several moments. Finally Allison took a ragged breath and began to speak.

"God I don't know where to start really. Your father and I were college sweethearts, but then you already know that part. What you don't know is that while we were at college John and I had a very dear friend, James Dustin."

The wind rushed out of Lauren's lungs. Hearing his name pierced her heart like an ice cold blade. Allison could see the pain in her face and paused her story briefly.

"I'm sor-"

Lauren held a hand up for silence, her eyes shut in concentration. She could feel the armrest of the chair creak and crack under her other hand, heard it snap as the death grip she held upon it tightened. Lauren swallowed the lump in her throat, unable to speak around it.

"Don't say his name."

"Lauren...."

"I said don't say it!"

The arm of the recliner snapped off with a loud crack and Allison flinched. She looked at her daughter in fear. Lauren's heart fluttered. How many times these past few days had she hungered for that look?

Silence loomed in the room as Lauren forced herself to breath slowly, deliberately, pushing through the aggression and trying to recapture some measure of peace. She fought back tears, buried them behind walls of iron.

"I'm... sorry."

If Allison had been surprised by Lauren's ferocity, she was even more startled by her forced, even tone. She sat awkwardly, seemingly waiting for permission to continue, and fidgeted with her hands in her lap.

"Please, um, go on."

Allison cleared her throat softly, casting a nervous glance up at Lauren's face.

"Well, John, J-James and I went to highschool together, but for college we went our separate ways. John and I went off to Knox together of course, but Jim headed up to Western. He always knew what he wanted, he was studying Law Enforcement from the get-go while John and I wavered back and forth in our little liberal arts bubble."

Her tone was wistful, and her stare grew distant.

"It was Thanksgiving, the year before you were born. We were up in the city and John and I had a huge fight, I... I stormed out but honestly I had nowhere to go. I didn't even have my own car up there, Jim drove all the way out to pick me up and took me back to his dorm."

It was Lauren's turn to shift uncomfortably.

"Nothing happened, he was a perfect gentleman."

Allison's tone suggested there was more to be said, but she seemed to calculate her next words more carefully before continuing.

"He had every opportunity of course. I was half-drunk, frustrated with my fiance, and absolutely willing. But, he turned me down. He said there was no way he could ever do that to John but swore he'd never speak a word of it."

Allison clenched her fist with conviction, living the memories as she recounted them.

"His rejection was my downfall. I couldn't get it out of my head, the need to have him. It occupied my every waking moment. All I could think about was what I had been denied, and my desire was uncontrollable. It took weeks, months of whittling away at his resolve, but finally I got my opportunity. John was... he was out meeting with caterers or getting his tux sized or... something. I should remember that part but... well, obviously he deserved better."

At last Allison began to show some small hints of remorse, her tone saddened and her cheeks burned red.

"I told him I didn't feel well, asked Jim if he would come look after me while John was out. He didn't have a chance, I was waiting for him like a hunter. I used to be so beautiful, and I knew his weakness for lace and lavender. When we were done I remember he cried, told me he could never forgive himself. That he had to come clean. I begged him not to say anything, suddenly afraid that I had wasted my opportunity to be with the one man who trusted and loved me above all others. I was convinced that John would leave me, call off the wedding. But it was so much worse than that."

She was crying now, and seemingly incapable of meeting Lauren's accusing eyes.

"He was crushed, but refused to blame me. It destroyed the boys' friendship, shattered it into a million pieces. John couldn't accept that it had been my idea, my plan, that James hadn't stood a chance. Jim had John by a foot, and at least forty pounds, but John, bless his heart, he was bound and determined to have a fist fight."

It was hard for Lauren to imagine her father, a diminutive, mousy fellow, squaring up against the mass of muscle and experience that she remembered of her former guardian. The two women shared a smile at the thought before Allison continued her tale.

"Anyway, we found out I was pregnant three weeks later, and we were married inside of two months. Then, well, then you came along at the end of the summer and he just dropped it. He made me swear never to tell you, and from the moment you were born you were his daughter in every possible way save for blood. God he loved you so much. You were the only thing that made him truly happy, if he could make you smile he would move mountains."

The estranged women talked for hours. As the morning lengthened it was almost, *almost* like they were family again, or at least once-close friends. In the hours they spent talking, Lauren learned things about her father she would have never dreamed of, and things about her mother she could scarcely have imagined. By noon they had discussed the misadventure of driving to the hospital on the day Lauren was born; how Allison and John's wild, passionate college-fling-turned-rocky-marriage began; and a dozen other stories ranging from the comedic to the tragic.

It was after the laugh-filled recounting of a botched date that Lauren first noticed Allison's hands were shaking. Shaking quite badly, actually. Lauren almost commented on it, second guessed herself, then decided to go for it.

"When did that start."

It was less a question, more a statement.

"I uh, well it's difficult to say. We both drank in school, of course, everyone did. John was always a lightweight, but I always had a sort of.. pride? I guess? In how much I could drink. But it never seemed like a problem, never seemed like it was out of my control until the big falling out between Jim and John. I want you to know, I *need* you to know that I wasn't always this way."

Allison had a determined look on her face. Hard, desperate eyes set against scarlet, shame-filled cheeks.

"I was a *good* mom while I was pregnant with you. I gave up smoking cold turkey, didn't touch a drop of alcohol the whole nine months. I ran every day, I ate so much goddamn kale I thought I was turning into a cow."

She was crying again, but she never took her eyes off of Lauren's.

"You were going to be my redemption. My chance to prove I was a good person, my penitence for breaking the heart of a good man. I knew from that first day, when I saw that little plus sign, that I could save our marriage. John was over the moon, he didn't care that you weren't his biological child, only that you were his precious unborn daughter. I finally had something to give him, something that would make up for my betrayal."

Lauren's cold, armored heart stirred faintly at her mother's passion.

"But then you were born with your um... gift. John and I never had a chance to decide for ourselves what we wanted to do. The story broke in less than a day and our lives, and my hopes for a normal family, went up in smoke immediately. John was uncomfortable with it from the start, he warned me that it wasn't going to be good for you, for us, but I insisted that we share you with the world. I've never regretted anything more. For a few years it was great. A gilded life of luxury. But it was fool's gold. John was right. People began to want more.

The ivory tower we thought we were living in started to crumble, and I crumbled with it. By the time I could admit I had a problem I was too far gone to turn back, too terrified that I wouldn't be strong enough to fight it. So I didn't even try."

Lauren dug deep, trying to force herself to feel sympathy for her mother. But she came up short. Allison's addiction brought up her own uncomfortable guilt, which was converted into kindling for her temper within the dark forge of her soul.

"Then, after Gabriel..."

Lauren tensed, here at last was the phrase she'd waited for all morning. For years really. Was she ready to hear her mother's words? Her excuses? She doubted it. Allison opened her mouth, tried to speak, but couldn't bring herself to make a sound. Instead she stood unsteadily and made a beeline for the kitchen. Lauren let her go, keenly aware of the cabinet doors opening roughly and slamming shut as her mother ransacked the kitchen.

The longer her fruitless search went on, the more pathetic it became. Finally Lauren rose as well and followed the sounds to the kitchen, arriving just in time to watch her mother pull the vodka from the back of the refrigerator.

"Allison..."

Allison stopped, her back turned to her daughter. She paused a moment, spun the cap off the bottle and took a long slow pull. Instantly she seemed more at ease, less shaky. With a big, shoulder-lifting sigh she faced Lauren once again.

"Lauren I lied to myself every day of the pregnancy. Some days I told myself it would be alright, and others I told myself that I didn't care if it *wasn't* alright. What if I had another 'gifted' child? Could I handle it? Maybe I was better off if something 'happened,' you know?"

Lauren took an involuntary step backwards. She flinched at the external echoing of her own morbid thoughts. Allison mistook her reaction for disgust and dropped her head in shame.

"I know. I never dreamed how wrong I could be. Gabriel brought your father and I together in a way that just... hadn't happened with you. Not through any fault of yours, but because here we had a kid that *needed* us. And then the day he died, God the day he died might have been the hardest day of my life. I just, broke."

"Where did you *go*, though? You just left, abandoned us without a word."

"Honestly I don't remember the first few weeks. I was so drunk I'm not sure where I was or what I did. My first sober memory was waking up in a ditch outside Woodstock in the pouring rain, off the side of the road in my totalled car. I remember a state police officer cutting my seatbelt and pulling me out of the car, booking me and driving me to the station."

Lauren was surprised, the nonchalant manner in which her mother recounted the potentially fatal accident was far from normal. The pair stood awkwardly in the kitchen for a while, neither overly eager to continue the conversation it seemed.

"Anyway, I was too drunk to speak clearly but once they found out who I was they seemed pretty unsure what to do. I was still in holding a few days later when Jim showed up, flashed his badge, and had me in the back of his SUV in a matter hours. He told me he was taking me to the city to get some help, reached out to the diocese, and had me linked up with the church that evening."

Allison took another swig from the bottle she held in her now-steady hands. Lauren briefly considered suggesting she put it down, but the hypocrisy of it prevented her. There was something about this old house that made her feel young and unsure again. Maybe it was Allison? Maybe it was the weight of her childhood or the unrealized dreams that pervaded the air. Whatever it was, it was stifling.

"I think I need some air. I'm going to go for a run, will you... will you be alright here while I'm gone?"

Allison put a hand on her heart, overwhelmed by Lauren's simple question. She could only manage a weak nod, and Lauren didn't stick around long enough for her to recover her voice. Instead, she turned crisply and stepped back out into the rain.

The warm air conspired with the cold rain to fill the forest with faint, wispy curls of mist. Lauren ventured out into the once-familiar foliage along a now overgrown path. Her bare feet padded carelessly across rocks, branches, and mud with equal comfort and ease.

The long-remembered sounds of birdsong and buzzing insects were either missing or simply drowned out by the rainfall around her. Dripping leaves and low, rumbling thunder filled her ears and swept her mind away as she strolled through the woods.

It had been so long since Lauren really *walked* somewhere. She couldn't recall the last time she had gone anywhere on foot purely for the fun of it, she certainly didn't know the last time she'd been for a run. Flying had long ago replaced running as her favorite pastime and therapy of choice, but the nostalgia of this place beckoned her. She picked up her pace, splashing through the muddy trails at a speed that would have made her younger self green with jealousy.

Her muscles were stronger, her body seemingly impervious to not only the rain but any passing branch that reached out to slow her progress. She thought back to her youth, recalling a time when such things posed an actual threat, albeit a temporary one. Lauren lifted a hand and ran her finger gently across her cheek, tracing the line of a forgotten cut.

Lauren was so wrapped up in her own thoughts as she ran that she very nearly stumbled into a pair of hikers. Her incredibly acute hearing picked up the sounds of bickering just in time. She was travelling too quickly to stop in the mud, so she simply leapt upwards. With a gentle assist from her wings, she landed as softly as she could in the upper branches of a large sugar maple. The branches shook, sending a deluge of water down onto the trail as two raincoat clad figures rounded the bend.

"Well, I'm telling you we're off track."

The woman's voice, emerging from the hood of her purple jacket, was heavy with irritation. The man behind her was nearly a foot taller and dressed in what appeared to be military surplus rain gear.

"Honey, we're not off track. There was a blaze a quarter mile back and we have been following the directions perfectly-"

"Well then where is this damn house you're insisting on seeing? We've been 'nearly there' for two hours."

Lauren could pick out the scowl on his shadowed face and hear the faint whisper of his sigh before he responded.

"Yes dear, we're going more slowly because of the mud. I told you it's not about time it's about pace count and I still put us at least two miles out."

Lauren raised a silent eyebrow. Where they talking about her house? And if so, why? She contemplated dropping down to ask them, but Caroline's warning was still fresh enough in her mind to convince her not to. Nonetheless, she found the exchange below quite engaging.

The woman huffed along grumpily, her almost comically large backpack leaning ever-so-slightly off kilter to the left. She had a pair of stout walking poles, but in the mud they seemed as much a hindrance as a help.

The man on the other hand had his pack positioned carefully in the middle of his back and seemed much more at ease under its weight. Lauren began to reconsider whether his gear was surplus, or simply the heirloom of a previous career.

As Lauren watched from her perch she saw one of the woman's walking poles slip precariously, sending her tumbling to her knees in the muck.

"God *damn* it!"

Her companion whipped around, instantly at her side to help her up.

"Are you ok? Let me grab your back-"

"I already told you, you're not carrying my damn pack. I'm not gonna be like those bimbos at the Grand Canyon making their boyfriends carry their shit for them."

The man, suitably chastised, helped her to her feet. Her legs were absolutely covered in mud. The pair stood quietly for a few moments while the woman fumed and the man did his best to not interfere.

"Hey."

The lady glared at him.

"What."

"I fuckin' love you."

She cracked a smile and rolled her eyes.

"I fuckin' love you too. Let's find this stupid house."

"Ok, you're sure you are ready to go? We can take a breather..."

"Come on, weren't you in the Army? You need a break already?"

The woman laughed, a rich, vibrant sound, and set off down the trail.

"You *know* what I meant dear."

He hustled after her.

"If we aren't there in an hour, I'll give you a backrub tonight!"

Her laughter intensified.

"Oh honey, you're doing *that* regardless..."

Lauren watched the two until they were out of sight. The man, whoever he was, was correct. The couple were still approximately two miles from her childhood home, though Lauren was sure they'd be there in less than an hour. More like 30 minutes at their current pace.

That didn't give her much time to get back and make sure that Allison knew to keep her mouth shut. Lauren's heart suddenly pounded with fear. What if Allison said something? What if she got too drunk to control herself? Lauren's cover could be blown in a heartbeat.

Lauren spread her wings and leapt into the air. Better to skim the treetops and risk being seen than to let them beat her home. A few minutes of flight time later and Lauren was approaching the clearing around her house. As she crested the last of the trees, the pine needles just inches below her collarbone, she pulled herself into a tight circle and cursed under her breath.

A shiny green sedan was sitting, half-covered in mud, in their driveway. She could pick out rental plates on the front of it, and no one was in sight. She hovered a moment and then dropped into the trees, perching like some great crow as she peered at the house.

Damnit.

Lauren knew she was in trouble. She'd left her mother hungover at best, still half-drunk most likely, and actively consuming straight vodka. In short, she was screwed and she knew it.

Lauren squinted as movement passed in front of one of the windows. Her keen eyesight picked out her mother and a stranger, another woman. From her vantage point she could only seen the guest from her midsection down, she was wearing a forest green top and a pair of jeans. Whoever it was, her mother seemed to be carrying on a very animated conversation with her. Allison was laughing, gesturing widely, and kept looking out the window almost... expectantly?

With every passing moment Lauren grew more nervous. There was a growing knot in her stomach that refused to dissolve. A minute ticked by, then another. She was going to be caught, the question was simply whether or not it would be by the stranger already here, or the two on the trail headed her way.

Lauren strained her ears, but the storm made it impossible for her to pick anything out from where she sat. Finally, the women moved again. The stranger joined Allison by the window, both of them gazing out into the woods. Lauren caught sight of a mess of walnut curls and her jaw dropped to the floor.

Valerie.

With her mother.

Together.

In her house.

Lauren's heart did a wild backflip and then stopped dead. She leapt from the tree and swooped down to the door in a flash. Lauren yanked on the door just a little too hard, tearing it unintentionally from the hinges.

"Hi!"

Lauren cringed at how squeaky her voice sounded and her entire face flushed scarlet. Her eyes were wide, nervous pools, sending a million unspoken questions to her.. friend? Lover? Ex?

"Hi honey, was your walk good? I was just catching up with your friend, Ms... Prescott was it?"

Lauren forced a wide smile and forgot how to breath.

"Please, *call me Vicki*.Yes, uh Lauren I was just telling your mum how we met while you were touring in Europe and became good friends!"

Valerie gave her a meaningful look and a sly wink behind Allison's back.

"Yes Ve-she and I are friends! This is my friend, mom!"
Brilliant.
She was being weird, she could feel it.
Too weird?
Too weird.

"Uh yes, um, that's what she was saying. A-are you ok? You look really flushed and red."

"I was flying!"

Allison raised an eyebrow at her daughter's obvious statement, clearly wondering if the three words were all she should expect.

Be casual.

"V-Vicki and I um, we have a lot to catch up on. Vicki, can I speak to you in private for a moment? Please?"

"Of course!"

Valerie's bright, peppy attitude and poorly disguised accent were at once unbearably adorable and terrifyingly obvious to Lauren. Allison, on the other hand, seemed genuinely not to notice. Lauren flashed a too-wide smile at her mother, grabbed Valerie by the hand, and whisked her away into the kitchen.

"What are yo-"

Valerie halted her hushed whisper with a deep, warm kiss. Lauren was too shocked to respond right away, but Valerie threw her arms around her neck and lifted herself up to wrap her legs around Lauren's midsection.

Instinctively, Lauren returned the embrace, supporting her companion and adding her own fire to the kiss. After several moments Valerie finally came up for air, her eyes sparkling and her lipstick smeared across one cheek.

"I missed you so m-"

It was Lauren's turn to interrupt, and she took it with gusto. She turned to the wall and pressed Valerie up against the light blue drywall. She ignored the thump they caused, enraptured by Valerie's suddenly arched back and the way their bodies pressed warmly together.

Lauren snaked an arm up Valerie's side and pulled gently at her hair, revealing her neck and moving her lips there. Her attention drew a whisper-quiet half-moan, half gasp and she felt Valerie's fingers gripping her own hair in return.

"Hey, I heard something go bang, is everythin- Oh my God! I'm so sorry!"

Allison's voice jolted the pair like lightning and Lauren took a wide step backwards. She lost her footing, stumbled, and fell. Her bottom impacted the linoleum with enough force to make an embarrassingly loud crash, but she managed to save Valerie. In fact, she was holding Valerie up rather comically in her outstretched hands.

Chapter 13

Allison looked like a fish out of water, her cheeks as scarlet as those of her daughter. She seemed unsure of whether to stay or go. To speak or remain silent.

"I am *so* sorry. I didn't. I'm just. I think maybe I should. I'm gonna go now!"

Lauren was mortified.

Allison turned and rushed from the room, leaving the two women staring at each other, cheeks burning in embarrassment.

"Oh my god, oh my god!"

Lauren couldn't seem to form any other sentence. she was exchanging a wide-eyed look of disbelief with the woman she cupped in her hands like a doll. Valerie was equally stunned, seemingly incapable of producing any sound at all.

A can rattling in the next room, no doubt kicked by Lauren's mother in her haste to leave the awkward situation behind, startled Valerie into action at last.

"Wait!"

Lauren looked at Valerie in alarm, what did she mean 'wait?' What could there possibly be to say? Shouldn't they talk about this first?

"Wait, please!"

Valerie scrambled to her feet, extending a hand and yanking Lauren upright as well. She took a brief moment to smooth her shirt and tuck her hair behind her ears before heading for the doorway.

"Ms. Corvidae?"

Valerie pulled up short as Allison poked her head back around the wall, her eyes anywhere but the two of them. She had a weak, nervous smile on her face and her entire face was a deep red.

Valerie took a deep breath and cleared her throat softly. She extended a hand towards Allison, her other arm firmly around Lauren's shoulders.

"Hello, I'm Valerie Chatwick. It's a pleasure to meet you."

Allison's gaze rose uncertainly to the level of the out-stretched hand, then further to Valerie's flushed, nervous face. She took a step around the corner, her reluctance obvious.

Valerie's gesture went unreciprocated for several long, si-lent seconds. Lauren widened her eyes at her mother, look-ing pointedly from her to Valerie's outstretched hand. Allison caught her cue and hastily grabbed for Valerie's hand before she could change her mind and retract it.

"Yes, um, yes right. Valerie. I *knew* you looked familiar, I believe I saw you on the news?"

Awkward.

Lauren coughed lightly, quite certain that Valerie would pre-fer to be recognized in *any* other context. The handshake be-tween the two seemed to stretch far past any normal greeting, each party apparently unwilling to break first. Finally Allison pulled her hand back, letting it hang limply at her side.

"L-Lauren is this your, uh...g-girl...friend?"

Emboldened by Valerie's courage, and the gentle squeeze of Valerie's arm, Lauren set her jaw tightly and nodded. Some-thing inside her was building, preparing to burst forth.

"Yes. Yes, mom, it is."

Allison nodded slowly, eyes slightly narrowed. Lauren could practically hear the gears in her head whirring and see smoke pouring from her ears.

"Ok. So, you two are, uh, seeing each other... romantically?"

Lauren's superhuman hearing heard Valerie's breath catch as she drew it in, heard the beat skip in her heart and felt the tremor in her fingertips.

"Yes. And if you have a prob-"

Lauren was interrupted by a massive bear hug from her mother. The gesture deflated the self-righteous anger in her breast and took her utterly by surprise.

"Oh sweetie I'm so happy for you. For *both* of you!"

Lauren exchanged a stunned look with Valerie, who was trapped in Allison's embrace alongside her. Valerie face was impossible to read, a cocktail of surprise, joy, and was it... anger? Sadness? Lauren could see her eyes tear up and felt her own follow suit.

The tension evaporated, mostly, and within moments all three were crying, laughing, or both.

"Y-you're not...?"

"Mad? Upset? Oh Lauren don't be ridiculous! I've worried for so long that you'd have trouble finding... companionship. With your gift I knew it was going to be harder for you, and it isn't always easy for the rest of us!"

"You don't *care* that your daughter is *gay*?"

Valerie's question was sharp, accusatory, skeptical. The warmth in the room cooled a bit.

"Valerie!"

Lauren quirked an eyebrow at her lover, what was *that* about?

To everyone's surprise, Allison burst out laughing.

"Oh sweetie, my daughter has fucking wings. She cures the sick with some kind of magical power. You honestly think *gay* is going to upset me?"

Valerie still looked sour as Allison reached out and patted her arm with amusement.

"I've had suspicions for *years*, actually. I've expected this since her, ah, special friendship in high school. Besides, her happiness was always far more important than who she chose to love. I've been... less than great at showing it, I'm afraid, but I will always choose to love my daughter. No matter what."

Lauren was speechless. A huge burden was lifted from her heart, a weight she'd not realized she was still carrying. Her elation was ruined by Valerie's obviously mixed feelings.

"Excuse me a moment."

Valerie extricated herself and walked into the next room, leaving the Corvidaes baffled.

"Hey, what the hell?"

Lauren's call went unanswered.

"Lauren I'm sorry, was it something I said?"

She shook her head at her mom and headed for the next room. Before she could reach the doorway Valerie reappeared. She plastered herself to the wall in fright.

"There's someone here. Oh my God what if I was followed? I'm so sorry!"

Sure enough a loud firm knock sounded on the front door a split second later.

"I-t's ok, uh just wait here. I'll distract them, tell them to go away. Just, just wait... ok?"

Lauren could tell that Allison knew she wouldn't stay, and she didn't have the nerve to lie to her. She softly shook her head instead.

"Mom I... can't. I can't stay here, no one can know."

Allison's shoulders drooped.

"I love you Lauren. Please, give me a chance to do better. To be better."

Lauren shook her head, leaned forward and gave Allison a kiss on the forehead.

"I forgive you, mom."

She choked on the word, but the resumed pounding on the door drowned the sound out.

"I'm coming!"

With one last look, Allison slipped away into the living room. Valerie and Lauren heard the door open and an exchange of pleasantries. Lauren breathed a little easier when her powerful hearing picked out the voices of the hikers she'd run across in the woods.

"Come on, we're getting out of here."

She held a hand out to Valerie, who looked on the verge of tears again.

"Hey, are you... ok?"

Lauren was whispering, but even so she was terrified that they might be caught. Valerie nodded and took Lauren's hand, allowing herself to be led out the back of the house and into the rain.

"Hold on tight, ok?"

"What?"

She didn't give Valerie a chance to object, scooping her up easily in her arms instead. Lauren planted a quick kiss on Valerie's cheek and leapt skyward. She drove her wings hard and fast, propelling them up into the clouds in a matter of moments.

She hoped they'd avoided notice.

Valerie let out a terrified half-scream and clung to her savior tightly. Both of her eyes were screwed shut and her face was buried in Lauren's neck. Her welcome warmth flooded Lauren with a heady mixture of emotion and desire.

"Hey, hey it's ok I've got you."

"Lauren, d-d-don't drop me! Are you sure this is ok? We're not too far up right?"

She couldn't help it, Lauren laughed and squeezed Valerie a little tighter. Lauren was quite sure she could have carried

Valerie for days and not broken a sweat. Her new strength was nearly as intoxicating as the smells of cinnamon and lavender in Valerie's hair. Her frustration with Valerie washed away as they soared through the sky.

"Open your eyes, it gets better."

Valerie shook her head no and redoubled her grip.

"Don't worry. I won't let go."

Valerie cracked an eye open. As she caught a glimpse of the ground a few thousand feet below her eyes snapped wide. A moment of stark terror yielded to hushed amazement.

"Oh God, Lauren it's beautiful… "

They flew in comfortable silence, the only sounds their shared heartbeats and the roar of the wind, which made normal conversation difficult. They were getting close when Lauren noticed that Valerie was shivering fiercely.

"You ok?"

"Mhmm."

Valerie nodded sleepily, but when she unburied her head to do so Lauren noticed that her lips were a deep purplish blue. On closer inspection, so were her fingers. The rest of her exposed skin was pale and cool.

"Valerie? Valerie!"

"S'cold…"

Lauren dipped into a steep dive. How could she have been so stupid, of course it was nearly freezing up here. Every soaking wet wisp of cloud that she passed through had her kicking herself.

Finally, the girls were soaring just above the treetops, the temperature at least 20 degrees warmer.

"We're ok, you're ok. Almost there."

She repeated her reassuring mantra, juicing Valerie with healing energy as well.

The last few minutes of their flight were hell on Lauren's nerves. At last though, they touched down in the field behind

Cherry Hills. Lauren came to a jogging stop right outside the door and shoved it none-too-gently open.

"Caroline? Caroline it's me, can you put some tea on please?"

"Mmm I'li tea..."

"I know baby, we're gonna get you some ok?"

Lauren went directly to Caroline's room and set her soaked companion on the thick bedspread. A moment later Caroline appeared, concern etched on her face.

"Lauren? Oh! Who is... well it's none of my business I suppose. I've got the kettle on, let me get you some towels."

Caroline's discretion was much appreciated and Lauren was grateful when she returned with a stack of dry fluffy towels. Caroline slipped back out of the room after giving the pair of them a meaningful look and a wry smile.

"Hey dear, we uh, we gotta get you out of these wet clothes ok?"

Valerie was sleepily mumbling something, but Lauren' couldn't catch what it was. She took a deep breath to steady her nerves.

You're just making sure she doesn't catch a cold. This is fine, everything is fine.

Lauren let out the breath and pulled Valerie to the edge of the bed. In her semi-conscious state Valerie was incredibly cooperative as Lauren peeled off her khakis.

"Tha's th'spirit. C'mere."

Valerie reached up, lips puckered as her head emerged from her polo when Lauren finished stripping it off of her. Lauren narrowly avoided her grasping hands. Putting a firm hand on her collarbone, Lauren pushed her back down on the bed.

"You're uh, not quite right in the head right now baby. Just lay back and rest ok?"

Lauren's cheeks burned as she put the dripping wet clothing in a small pile at the end of the bed. The garments were not only soaked, they were ice cold from the altitude.

She took a pause to clear her head and turned back to Valerie with a towel in hand. She carefully laid the towel across Valerie's midsection, covering her from her bust down past her hips.

Now the challenging part.

Lauren reached behind the towel, grabbing hold of Valerie's underwear and sliding it quickly down her legs, carefully avoiding lingering anywhere she shouldn't and being certain to keep her eyes averted lest something slip.

After a similar encounter with Valerie's bra, Lauren wrapped her up more thoroughly in towels and tucked her under the large comforter. Valerie's resistance crumbled almost immediately and within a few minutes she was sound asleep and snoring softly. Lauren sat beside her, careful not to disturb her slumber.

"She's very beautiful, isn't she?"

Lauren started and turned, Caroline was standing in the doorway with two steaming mugs of chamomile. Lauren smiled so wide it hurt her face, and turned back to Valerie when she answered.

"Yes. Yes, she is very beautiful."

Lauren tucked an errant strand of Valerie's hair behind her ear, her finger hovering just a moment on her slowly warming cheek.

"I'm sure she will be fine, not only because of your powers either. When I was a young girl living in Nebraska I got hypothermia much worse than this and I'm happy to report that I made a full recovery. I was, however, delirious for hours."

Valerie chose that moment to softly mumble something about unicorns.

"It certainly does make for an amusing story afterward though."

Lauren breathed a little easier. Hearing Caroline so relaxed about the situation eased the tension in her shoulders and let her relax as well.

"You know, Lauren, invincible and unshakeable as you may be, if you continue to sit on that bedspread with soaked clothes you will be sleeping in wet blankets."

"Shit!"

Lauren leapt up and looked down at her sopping sundress - and the wet splotch on the bed where she'd been sitting.

"Ugh, dammit all."

I guess that will be my side of the bed.

Lauren blushed, catching herself in the assumption that they would be sleeping together. Of course, she reminded herself, Caroline had made the same assumption. She knew it was too early for that, that the pair had a lot of ground to cover.

"I'm gonna grab a shower, can you please let me know if she wakes up?"

"Of course."

Even with her doubts, Lauren's steps were lighter and she couldn't help but smile as she headed for the bathroom.

Unsure of how long she might take to recover, Lauren lingered longer than she needed to in the hot steam of her shower. She took the opportunity to contemplate exactly what it was she hoped to hear from Valerie, how her feelings for her had changed.

And which had stayed the same.

Lauren was wrapped in a towel, softly brushing and straightening her feathers with her long delicate fingers when she heard a soft tap at the door.

"My lady?"

Ah, Caroline. Lauren wondered at the tiny flutter of disappointment in her heart.

"Come in."

"Ma'am, your guest is awake. I've given her some tea and she seems to be feeling much better. She would like to see you, I imagine."

Lauren beamed back at her host, nearly forgetting to reply out loud.

"Great!"

"I thought you might need this, since I didn't see you grab anything when you came in."

Caroline presented a short purple dress. Strapless, and extending just past Lauren's knees, the dress added a raven-like luster to Lauren's dark, shiny wings. She turned a few times in the mirror, tousling her hair this way and that.

Ok, you got this. Casual. Be casual.

Caroline gave her a conspiratorial wink and excused herself. Lauren turned back to the mirror, smoothing non-existent wrinkles and lamenting the paleness of her complexion. She gave the bust of her dress a little shove, adding volume in just the right places, and carefully avoided admitting to herself why she'd done so.

Really though, the only thing Lauren was accomplishing was delaying the inevitable. Finally she peeled her eyes off the mirror and forced herself to take several deep breaths and head back to the bedroom.

Valerie was sitting up. She had a borrowed tank top on, and her lower half was still wrapped in a nest of blankets. In her hands she held a steaming mug that she was presently blowing on softly. She froze upon seeing Lauren in her dress, her wide, hungry eyes making Lauren blush.

"Lauren!"

She could feel the hesitation in her voice. Valerie's uncertainty resonated within Lauren and she was suddenly unsure. Unsure of how she felt, how she *should* feel.

And what she should say.

Here at last they were alone together once more and rather than clear, her mind was muddy and confused.

"Lauren I... I owe you an apology for how I acted at your house. That was very unfair of me."

Lauren grasped the life preserver of Valerie's topic and clung to it.

"It's... ok. You seemed really upset though and honestly, I guess I thought you would be happy?"

Valerie's face crumpled in sadness.

"Lauren I am happy, I'm happy for *you*. It's just..."

Valerie broke eye contact and wouldn't meet Lauren's gaze, so she walked over and joined her companion on the bed, sitting cross-legged next to her.

"Just what? I'm here, you can talk to me."

"It wasn't that easy for all of us! We didn't... we didn't all get hugs and 'I love you' and acceptance."

"Oh."

Valerie was sobbing softly as a deep and hidden wound was laid bare. Lauren felt like an ass, her memories at Valerie's house made much more sense now. What was it she had said?

"St. Agnes. My family is very religious."

Lauren wrapped Valerie in a hug, letting her cry against her shoulder and wrapping her wings protectively around them both.

"So your family, they didn't...?"

"Want anything to do with me."

"I'm so sorry, Valerie."

"I told my mother in the hospital, I wanted her to know before she... left. She got sick when we were still young, Colin and I, but she hid it until I was nearly done with finishing school. Colin was in his last year at Hamilton's when we really realized how bad it was. I brought my camera with me, I wanted to capture the beauty of the moment. I was sure it would be beautiful..."

Valerie's voice took on a razor edge.

"So, I told her. My father and brother as well. My father had a meltdown, chased me out of the hospital before I could say goodbye, before I even heard her response at all. I had to take a bus home from the city, and when I got there the house was locked. I must have beat on that door for hours before I gave up."

"He locked you out of your own house?"

"He made no bones about it, he had no daughter. Certainly not some queer girl."

"Where did you go?"

"That first night I slept on Sir Warvington's porch. He found me about five in the morning when he headed over to our place. He fixed me breakfast, made sure I had a bed, and dried my tears. I think it was the only day he missed work in all the years of my life."

She let out an unexpected laugh.

"He met my father that day in the driveway of our home, with me tucked away in the backseat of his old car. He screamed at my father so loud it scared the birds out of the field. Split his lip as well, and swore he'd never set foot at the Chatwick estate so long as his Vee wasn't welcome there."

Lauren thought of the kind old man she'd met outside London. It was hard to imagine him in a fight of any kind, let alone with someone half his age.

"And he was true to his word."

Her face fell again.

"Three days I spent with Sir Warvington. I had a place to sleep, but I was homeless. My mother was dead, and I was dead to the only family I knew. The only reason I knew about the funeral at all is because it was in the paper. Word gets around in a small town, after all. Sir Warvington and I showed up to this.... *hideous* silence. I remember everything was black. The clothes, the veil, the casket..."

Valerie's gaze lengthened into a thousand yard stare. Her volume dropped and her tone flattened as Lauren listened.

"I... brought my camera with me. I'm not sure why, other than it was the only thing I had with me when I was kicked out... and of course it was my very favorite gift I'd received from her. It seemed like the only thing I had left, really. I remember thinking if I could just get one last photo of her, I'd have something to hold on to. I set up the shot, I was looking through my lens at her. She looked, *so* beautiful. Like a porcelain doll. But I couldn't take the shot. I don't know why. Something held me back. Well, my father fixed that. I didn't even hear him coming up behind me. He knocked me to the ground, knocked my camera to the ground too. I heard she shutter snap and the next thing I remember my brother had him in a headlock. People were shouting, my uncles were holding Sir Warvington back, Colin had father on the ground... it was *quite* unbecoming of a proper British family."

Silence.

Lauren was enraptured. She felt every word of the story, lived and breathed them as though they were her own.

"What... what happened next?"

"I grabbed my camera and ran. By the time I could think straight I was a fews miles away, clutching the cracked frame and shattered lens of my most prized possession. The entire roll of film was ruined, of course. All but that frame. Washed out, with burn marks all over it, it's still the single most important photograph I will ever take, and my greatest regret."

Lauren sat with goosebumps on her arms despite the warm air of the bedroom. She considered what she'd heard. Valerie was stronger than she'd ever imagined, and her story also put Lauren's own life in better perspective.

They sat in silence once again while Lauren processed internally.

"Lauren, I never meant to hurt you."

Lauren blinked in surprise, the sudden shift giving her a moment's pause.

"Deep down I think I know that, but you did."

Valerie looked crestfallen.

"I just... I want to understand *why* you would tell your boss about us? Why you would tell the world-"

"Lauren I didn't! I swear on my life I didn't! I didn't know that Reggie had cameras at his dock, and I never suspected he'd release that footage..."

Ah shit.

With Valerie cleared of wrongdoing, Lauren was once again the 'bad guy.' At least in her own mind. The unfamiliar weight of remorse fell heavy on her shoulders and prompted an uncomfortable realization. When had she stopped caring? It was hard to pinpoint.

The reality of what she'd done over the past few days felt subdued. She tried to feel guilty for the lives she'd taken, to stir up some semblance of a normal reaction, but she felt only the inky darkness.

Lurking.

Waiting.

Simmering gently beneath the surface of her heart.

She'd *killed people.* A lot of people. And Valerie hadn't even done anything wrong. She was supposed to feel... something, right? So why didn't she? A deep, unnerving feeling of 'wrongness' tried to find purchase in her hardened heart.

"Penny for your thoughts?"

Lauren snapped out of it, suddenly aware of the scowl on her face and the way she was clenching her fists. She slapped a smile on her face and tried her best to be convincing.

"Sorry, I just. I should have given you a chance to explain."

"You were right to be upset-"

Her smile faltered.

"Do I scare you, Valerie?"

Lauren fixed her piercing black eyes on Valerie's, scanning for any hint of fear.

"Y-yes. A little. But I don't think you'd ever hurt me. I trust you."

"What if you shouldn't? Trust me I mean. I don't... I don't understand exactly what's happening. I have this... this *hunger* inside me."

Valerie gulped. The soft, nearly silent motion pricked Lauren's keen ears. She listened harder, Valerie's heartbeat was also elevated. Lauren doubled down, unwilling to break the silence first and doing her best to look serious.

"W-where are we? Last I remember we were flying and I was so *cold...*"

It was an abrupt, artificial change of topic.

Lauren didn't resist.

"We're safe. This is Cherry Hills. It's the church I came to when my wings first came in. Miss Caroline took excellent care of me. It's as close as I have to a home of my own anymore, I suppose."

As she spoke, a peal of thunder rattled the windows. Valerie, still wrapped in her arms, started at the sound and let out a pitiful little squeak. Lauren bit her lip to keep from laughing. Lauren rubbed Valerie's back and felt her tensions ease once more. Valerie was looking nervously through the glass at the gray skies and pounding rain.

"You don't get tornadoes here, do you?"

"Sometimes, yes. One of the perks of the Midwest."

Valerie squeezed tighter.

Definitely a perk.

"Is it possible? Are you actually afraid of something?"

"Ha, ha."

Valerie turned her face up to Lauren's and treated her to an adorably pouty glare. Lauren couldn't resist, she met Valerie's lips with her own. The kiss was shallow, uncertain, and Lauren pulled back right away to gauge her companion's reaction.

Valerie's cheeks were flushed with heat, her lips gently parted and her eyes glazed with passion. Her breath was heavy and Lauren felt her muscles tighten. She was straining to hold herself in check like a racehorse in the chute, eager to be set free.

Reassured that Valerie's desires were the same as her own, Lauren saved her the trouble of deciding. Lauren brought a hand around to cradle Valerie's upturned face, drawing their lips together once more.

"Don't worry, I'll keep you safe."

A thousand miles away Presley Weiss was riding out a storm of his own. He was sitting at a large, round table several stories underground at the Pentagon. A dozen senior military officers, the Vice President, and a handful of staffers were sitting quietly in the wake of the slideshow that had just ended.

"General Malone, just... what's the bottom line?"

Justin looked worried, in all the years that they had known each other Presley had never seen so much as a bead of sweat cross the general's brow, and now he looked like he'd just run a marathon despite the artificially cooled air of the bunker.

"Conservatively, based on the figures from Athens and London, we're looking at 40-70% losses in the event of failure."

"Losses? You mean just the forces at the Capitol?"

Malone's jaw set.

"No, Mr. Secretary, in the D.C. Metro area."

The air was sucked out of the room.

Presley did a bit of mental math, then did it again.

"Jesus, Justin, that's... you're saying two and a half million people?"

"At least."

Vice President Lynn Charles, a thin, wiry woman in her late forties, squirmed uncomfortably in her chair. She looked past her steepled fingers at the map of the Washington D.C. laid out in the middle of the table. A projector in the ceiling showed the metropolitan area plastered with lines, tactical symbols, and a series of concentric circles of red, orange, and yellow.

"Two and a half million Americans... God help us. There has to be another way. You're talking about a device ten times the size of Hiroshima!"

General Malone was frowning, but did not back down.

"Mrs. Vice President, ma'am, this may be our only chance to preemptively strike at the being. Consider the cost in terms of human life if we *don't* do something-"

"What if it doesn't work!"

Presley didn't make a habit of interrupting his friend, but until this critical question was answered he couldn't refrain. No one save the Vice President would meet his gaze as it travelled around the room.

"What if it doesn't work. What if we make him angry, instead of destroying or disabling him? God forbid, what then? Does two million turn into three hundred million? Nine billion? What assurance do we have that we aren't about to declare ourselves extinct?"

General Malone was annoyed, but the steel in his eye suggested he wouldn't budge. He remained seated for his reply, but gestured widely at the large world map that covered one wall of the briefing room.

"Mr. Secretary, respectfully, there are only two paths here. The first is the path of submission, the path we are on now. If we continue to huddle in fear, powerless to oppose this monster, it will continue to destroy human lives, culture, and erase our history on a whim."

The seated officials grumbled, but no one objected. None could argue that Weyland's power was already absolute.

"The second, the path of rebellion. The path of independence. I, for one, refuse to simply roll over for this monster. Operation Elegant Gesture is our best hope, our *only* hope."

The Vice President let out a scornful laugh.

"I'm sorry, 'Operation Elegant Gesture,' is that what we're calling this... this suicide mission? This massacre?"

General Malone looked taken aback.

"Well ma'am it's not exactly a suicide-"

"Yes. Yes it is. Forgive me, but did you not just finish explaining to me that 80 special forces operators dying and potentially tens of thousands of civilians being injured was the absolute best case? Did you not just tell me that in all likelihood we are sentencing millions of Americans to a fiery, agonizing death in the middle of American streets?"

Presley was torn.

"Mrs. Vice President, I am with General Malone and the Joint Chiefs on this. This is our only real chance at bringing Weyland down. We have a unique opportunity, brought to us at great personal risk to a dear friend of mine, to take our best, most calculated shot at him. We may never get another chance like this, we had no reason to believe we'd ever get this one even. And, at the end of the day, if this mission fails, we will know that there is no mortal way to stop him. That no stronger measure could have been taken."

"Are you willing to sign the order, Presley? Are you willing to put pen to paper and write a check for the lives of millions of your fellow countrymen?"

The Vice President clearly expected a delay, but General Malone answered instantly and without question.

"I am."

Tension crackled like lightning in the air between the two. Finally it was the Vice President who backed down. With a heavy-hearted sigh she returned her gaze to the table in front of them.

"Ladies and gentlemen if we do this, we may well go down in history as traitors to all mankind. We will, at best, have defied the very constitution we all swore to uphold. Not simply by pursuing military action on American soil but by extrajudicially sentencing Americans, innocent Americans, to death as collateral. We'll be bypassing Congress, the Supreme Court, every check and balance that exists within our government. Are you prepared, should we survive, for the legacy we will leave behind?"

Unanimously, the decision around the room was yes. Their minds made up, the group set to the task of bringing blood and fire to American soil.

"Ma'am, with your permission I'd like to introduce the leads on each phase of the operation. General Ajoku, Special Forces Command, will be heading up ground operations; General Rogers, First Army, will take charge in the event we elevate to phase two; and finally, General Van Zwieten, Air Force Space and Missile Command, will be the lead if... well if it comes to that."

The three men stood, introduced themselves, and took turns explaining their part of the operation in greater depth. The longer they spoke, the deeper the sense of melancholy grew in the room. By the time General Van Zwieten stood and began to deliver his remarks, the room felt like a morgue.

Would it be enough? Was it even possible to destroy Weyland?

Presley prayed that it was.

Chapter 14

Lauren couldn't remember the last time she'd felt so at ease. She could feel Valerie tucked against her chest, the weight of the covers over both of them, and the faint light of the morning creeping in through the window and across the bed. She carefully memorized the soft rustle of Valerie's every breath, the way their hearts beat in sync and the feel of their skin touching.

She willed the moment to last forever, begged time to stand still and eternity to halt in its tracks.

But time marched on.

She would not wake Valerie, could not spoil the perfection that was this moment, so she decided instead to dwell on the night before.

The two, largely undisturbed by Caroline, had enjoyed a fairly innocent evening. Certainly, it was far less heated than their encounter at the Liebeslied, let alone the Chatwick Estate. Still, passion smoldered beneath unsure, hesitant kisses and a long, loving embrace.

In the end, most of the evening was spent simply holding each other closely and talking. Pouring their hearts into one another and catching up on the time they had spent apart.

It felt like a dream, really, even the weather seemed to have calmed somewhat. The raging storms of the past few days had been replaced by warm rain and distant thunder. The sun was actually peeking through the clouds, a welcome reprieve from the dreariness she'd grown accustomed to.

Lauren took a deep breath, inhaling the moment as much as the air around her.

Valerie snuffled and tightened her grip as Lauren's shifting chest shook her gently. She held her breath, trying not to rouse her sleeping lover. After a few moments though it was obvious that Valerie was on the path to wakefulness. Her nose crinkled as she slowly rolled over, her hair wild and her leg twitching out into a deep stretch. Her change in position brought her face just inches from Lauren's own.

She took a moment to enjoy the beauty she saw there. Valerie had a thin line of drool down the left side of her mouth, and her warm brown hair covered half her face, but Lauren was fully enamoured by her natural state.

Lauren saw an opportunity too ripe to pass up. Valerie's red, succulent lips were simply too close to resist. Craning her neck slightly, Lauren dipped in for a kiss.

She took the opportunity to test a theory she'd been kicking around as well. The moment their lips pressed together, Lauren tried to exercise her powers by giving Valerie a slow trickle of positive energy. She felt the turbulent energies stir within her and a kind of buzz between them as they kissed.

Valerie's eyes shot open in surprise, cool green pools glinting in the sun.

"W-what was *that?*"

Lauren smiled nervously.

"The kiss or...?"

"Was it? Just a kiss?"

Damn, she was caught. Lauren shook her head.

"Sorry. I was, well I was trying something with my powers. I'm sorry."

"No, no. Don't be. That was... *intense.* Jesus, I feel so *alive!* Is this how you feel all the time? Like your whole body was just electrified?"

Lauren was overjoyed that Valerie was receptive, but still kicked herself for not asking permission before experimenting on her girlfriend. She knew it was wrong. Knew that Valerie deserved a say. But even now and with someone she loved she was struggling to *feel* the way she felt she ought to, to feel remorse.

Her face must have shown some hint of her inner turmoil because Valerie reached up a hand to gently cup her chin, concern in her eyes.

"Hey, you ok?"

"Yeah, I'm sorry. I've been a little off that's all."

Valerie rolled onto her side, propping herself up with one arm and looking down at Lauren. She had a mischievous gleam in her eye and a suspicious flush in her face.

"Well, now that you are officially *out* and officially my *girl-friend.*"

Lauren blushed hard at her teasing, but felt a long-forgotten warmth start to fill her from within.

"I have to tell you," she kissed Lauren's cheek.

"That after that little shot of," another kiss, this time on her nose.

"*Whatever* you just gave me, I am definitely not feeling off."

Valerie leaned back and smiled before bending down to kiss Lauren's lips once again. She broke contact and allowed her face to drift past and nuzzle Lauren's ear. She lowered her voice to a whisper while she nibbled gently at her earlobe.

"In fact, I would have to say I'm feeling *on.* if you catch my meaning..."

Lauren was caught between giggling as Valerie's breath tickled her neck and sighs of arousal as her lover's lips traced a line from her jaw to her collar bone.

"Valerie... w-we're in a Church!"

Lauren had no real reservations about the location, but she was still new enough to being intimate that she was scared, uncertain.

Valerie, on the other hand, was not. She also seemed more than willing to lead Lauren on this particular journey.

"I'm sure I don't know what you mean, I can be *very* devout."

Valerie punctuated her words with kisses, each deeper and more passionate than the last. With a sudden burst of playful energy she climbed up, straddled one of Lauren's legs. Leaning forward, she grabbed Lauren's hands and pinned them beside her head.

Lauren could feel Valerie's thigh pressed high between her legs. The firm, steady pressure was like a drug driving her into madness. From her perch, Valerie was also comfortably seated with Lauren's leg between her own, their entwined limbs strategically placed to maximum effect.

She knew at any point she could lift Valerie off of her like a doll, but the brazen way that Valerie held her hands to the bed left her feeling deliciously helpless.

"Really now, I didn't know you were a believ-ahh!"

She gasped as her companion leaned deep into another kiss, maneuvering in such a way as to make both of their thighs slide back and forth.

Lauren rocked instinctively with the movement, riding the building wave of passion between them. Valerie leaned back, her eyes closed with pleasure, and Lauren once again saw her opening. With a wicked grin, Lauren pumped a much larger surge of energy into Valerie everywhere their skin touched.

Valerie bit her lip to hold back a moan, her eyes rolling and her entire body shaking.

Lauren took her experiment a step further.

Lauren slipped softly into Valerie's mind. She reveled in the ecstasy she found there, experiencing Valerie's pleasure as well as her own. She collected her own ecstasy and channeled it into Valerie, allowing her lover to feel every bit of pleasure she was creating in Lauren. Stars popped before her eyes and her toes curled as their mutual pleasure grew more and more intense each time the sensations looped through them.

Valerie's back arched and she held white-knuckled to Lauren for support. Her mouth was open but she was speechless with desire. Finally the wave broke and she shuddered to a stop, panting heavily.

But Lauren wasn't done yet.

She slid a hand up Valerie's quivering thigh and under the hem of the soft, jersey shorts she was wearing. Valerie's breath stuttered as probing fingers revealed she had nothing beneath the thin garment.

Lauren knew the theory, or could guess at it, but she was painfully aware that she was still exceptionally new at this. She made up for her lack of experience with an abundance of enthusiasm and soon Valerie was hunched over her, hands entwined in Lauren's hair and gasping for breath.

"Sto-st-o-stop, too m-much, too much."

Lauren complied, leaving Valerie to rest her sweat-slick brow against Lauren beating chest. She was more than content to bask in the glow of what was certainly the most magical morning of her life, but Valerie lifted herself back into a sitting position as soon as she was able.

"H-holy hell baby."

Lauren smiled.

"Did you enjoy the uh, ride?"

She knew the answer, she'd felt it herself, but it brought a glow to her face to see Valerie's emphatic nod. Lauren patted her chest gently, indicating that Valerie should return. She put on a fake, exaggerated pouting face.

"Come back baby, I'm cold."

Valerie laughed, that infectious, hearty, unashamed sound that Lauren so desperately loved. But rather than return to Lauren's side, she shook her head no and shimmied down the bed. She paused in her journey towards the foot to grasp Lauren's hand and kiss it, a just reward for the attentions she'd received from it. She entwined her fingers with Laurens, who blushed at the slickness of her hand.

Valerie came to rest between Lauren's legs, her shoulders even with Lauren's knees and her upper body propped up on her elbows. Lauren's mind raced.

She *knew* what was coming but she had no idea what to expect. Valerie ran a hand through her hair, shaking out the curls and then tucking them back behind her ears before flashing Lauren a winning smile.

"My turn."

"Valerie..."

Lauren was self conscious, never in her life had someone been this *close*. What if Valerie didn't like what she saw?

Valerie's head disappeared between her thighs, taking with it all thought left in Lauren's mind. Lauren gripped her lover's head as gently as she could, careful at all times to be mindful of her strength. She pumped every ounce of pleasure she received back into Valerie and the two of them soared the clouds together.

When the pair finally landed, after what seemed an eternity to Lauren, Valerie crawled exhausted back up to Lauren's arms. She made the trip back up to Lauren's head before collapsing in a tangled heap with her. Lauren's vision swam but she met Valerie's lips with a grateful kiss.

She wrinkled her nose at the unexpected taste. It was tangy yet mild, and not at all unpleasant.

"Sorry!"

Valerie wiped her mouth before sheepishly returning to Lauren. She kept a distance between their lips, looking uncomfortable.

"N-no, no it's ok it's not bad just... different I guess?"

Valerie smiled uncertainly, looking up through her lashes into Lauren's eyes. One hand was resting gently on Lauren's stomach, the other propping her head up as she lay beside her.

"Lauren, I think I love you."

Lauren's eyes widened and her heart slid off the rails. Her mind and body were singing in sync, flooding with endorphins and pushing her to respond. But the darkness inside her hissed like a coiled snake deep in the pit of her stomach. She ignored it, unwilling to let it taint the joy of the moment.

"I think I love you too, Valerie."

The rumble in Lauren's midsection intensified, culminating in a hard thump against her stomach wall. The impact was easily felt by Valerie, who jumped and pulled her hand back from Lauren's stomach as though she'd been bitten.

"W-what the heck was that?"

Her gaze ping-ponged back and forth between Lauren's face and her bar stomach. Lauren rested a hand protectively below her belly button, her eyes wide with surprise.

"Valerie, I uh..."

There it was, reality coming back to punch her in the chest. Lauren sat up as she broke into tears, clutching her stomach with both hands. Valerie wrapped her in her arms, sending Lauren further into hysterics.

"Lauren, baby, what is it?"

"I'm pregnant."

Lauren barely breathed the word, unwilling even to raise her voice to a whisper.

Valerie stiffened, but didn't let go.

"P-preg...nant?"

Lauren nodded, tears flowing freely from her chin down to the bedspread. She took shelter in Valerie's arms, clung to them like a drowning woman to a life preserver. She felt suddenly filthy, unclean. The glow of their lovemaking was perverted, consumed by the shame of Weyland's attentions. She hated herself for thinking of him in this moment, hated him for destroying her even now. She dove into the darkness within, and it embraced her with open arms. Immediately her pain began to cool and grow numb, along with every other sensation.

Lauren could feel Valerie's breathing change, her muscles tighten and release, even her heart changed it's patterns. She held her breath, ready for the hammer to fall. But it never came..

"Weyland?"

Lauren flinched at his name, then nodded.

Valerie tightened her grip, squeezing Lauren in her arms and pressing their foreheads together. Her simple act of comfort and protection was a lifeline for Lauren. She returned the embrace, her shoulders shaking with silent tears.

"How long have you known?"

"A week or so, I should have told you..."

"I'm not sorry."

The conviction in her voice gave Lauren pause. She felt her chin lifted by Valerie's strong hands and found herself staring intently into the blazing emeralds of Valerie's eyes.

"I'm not sorry. You shouldn't be either. This may be your burden to bear, but it doesn't have to be your burden to bear alone. You did *nothing* wrong."

Lauren broke eye contact.

"I didn't ask for.. to... for this. He-"

She couldn't finish her sentence, the word stuck in her throat and her eyes burned with shameful tears as comprehension dawned on Valerie's face.

Valerie's voice dropped low and she reached a hand out to Lauren's shoulder.

"He... raped you, you mean?"

Lauren nodded,

"I don't know h-how long I was... with him. He had me trapped, dreaming. When I woke up, this... this girl, Natalie, was p-putting burn cream on m-my-"

Valerie wrapped her in a hug.

"Hey hey, you're ok, you're safe now. I've got you."

"Sh-she s-said he came for me every morning, I didn't want to believe it. He t-told me the dream was what I unconsciously wanted-"

Their bodies shook with the power of Lauren's sobs. Valerie broke their embrace and held Lauren at arm's length.

"Hey! You listen to me! You. Did. Nothing. Wrong. That monster did this to you. *To* you. You didn't deserve this, you didn't do anything that gave him the right to do this. This is his wrong, his *crime*."

Lauren nodded, wiping her eyes and sniffling loudly.

"Vee, what the hell am I going to *do*?"

"Lauren, no one can decide that for you. No one *should* decide that for you."

Valerie was right, Lauren knew, but it did little to warm her heart. The peace and hope that had been building all last night and this morning were chilled by the darkness she'd welcomed back. Her split second of weakness had coated her soul once more with frost.

Lauren shivered in the cool air. With the flames of passion reduced to embers, the chill of the morning brought goose-bumps to her bare shoulders and legs.

"Come on, let's get you up! We can't stay in bed all day, and I will be stunned if Caroline didn't hear that last uh, tussle, of ours."

Lauren groaned, what on earth was she going to say to Caroline? Their climactic morning had been far from silent.

"Oh god, I can't. Just leave me here, go on without me."

She buried herself in blankets, burrowing into the relative safety of wool and cotton. She felt Valerie's hands in hot pursuit, chasing her feet through across the sheets in an attempt to rouse her from her nest.

"Lauren! Come on, you're too strong this isn't fair!"

Valerie finally caught hold of Lauren's left ankle, but she could do nothing to slow her progress through the covers. Lauren had only to evade her a few moments longer when Valerie let go and seemed willing to surrender.

She poked her face out of the blankets to get a better look at Valerie, but didn't see her.

Hmm.

Lauren pulled her head free and looked around. she spotted Valerie, now standing beside the bed, just in time to see her gather the last of the corners of the blankets together and give them a mighty tug.

"Hey!"

But the very cloth she'd sought refuge in was the net within which she was now captured. She struggled to free herself but Valerie was too quick. She dragged Lauren from the bed to the floor where she fell with a loud thump.

Valerie dropped the blankets and raised her fists in triumph. the action pulled her white tank top up over the waistband of her blue shorts, giving her the appearance of a 1970's track star.

A light tapping at the door, accompanied by Caroline's soft voice, interrupted their mirth.

"Are we decent, ladies?"

Valerie looked at Lauren with embarrassment, her hands covering her smile and her cheeks burning.

"Y-yes, yes ma'am!"

The door slowly opened and Caroline peeked her head inside. She smiled at the unusual situation within but refrained from comment.

"Your breakfast was getting rather cold, so I've put it in the oven for you when you're ready."

"We're ready!"

Lauren's response was muffled by the blankets she'd nearly escaped.

"Oh! My first genuine American breakfast!"

"Well dear it's nothing fancy. Just grits, eggs, toast, bacon and potatoes and some sausage gravy. Cooking isn't my strong suit, but I suppose we do alright, don't we Lauren?"

Lauren, who was by now standing sheepishly in her dress, crossed her arms to cover her partially exposed bust.

"Give yourself some credit Caroline, you're a wonderful cook."

Caroline looked over her glasses at the pair, a wry, grandmotherly smile on her lips.

"Mhmm, well I'll just pull the food back out and see you at the table shall I? Don't forget to wash your hands."

Caroline ducked back out of the room to an outburst of giggling from both women.

Lauren felt lighter already. She looked curiously at Valerie, who noticed her staring and shuffled awkwardly from one foot to the other a moment before blushing and speaking out.

"What?"

"Nothing just, how do you do that?"

"Do what?"

"Make me feel."

"You mean feel better?"

Right.

"Yeah, sorry, feel better. How do you do that?"

Valerie smiled and held a hand out to Lauren.

"I must have learned it from you love."

A few minutes later found the women, still holding hands, stepping into the kitchen. The small wooden dining table, designed for two, was set for three. The extra place setting gave the table an air of abundance and each plate was indeed piled high with food.

"I hope you're hungry!"

They both answered in the affirmative and tucked into their plates of food. The room was fairly quiet while they ate, the sounds of sipped coffee and the clink of forks and knives mixing with birdsong and storms. Seconds, and thirds, later, when the plates were stacked into the sink and the pans and pots put away, Caroline spoke again..

"So, tell me a little about yourself, Ms. Chatwick."

"Ah well, um, there's not a whole lot that hasn't been on television lately I'm sure..."

Caroline quirked an eyebrow as she poured another round of coffee.

"My dear I don't believe half the nonsense I see on that wicked little box. Haven't for years. Not, at least, since they started producing lies and blasphemies against our Sacred Lady."

Lauren choked on her coffee as Valerie gave her a very, very surprised look. Her raised eyebrows and wide eyes fell on Lauren's blushing face just as she buried it in her mug once more.

"Yes, I can imagine that would make it difficult to follow. I admit I'm a bit confused about the *Sacred Lady* myself."

Caroline took no offense to the surprise in Valerie's tone, but sat quietly and waited for her guest to continue.

"I'm a photographer and former journalist at the BBC. I was a global reporter, generally following large humanitarian pieces around the globe. Floods, famine, hurricanes, and then of course Weyland."

Caroline made the sign of the cross over her chest.

"B-but I never spent any time in the States, really. Not very many crises, I suppose. More of the poorer countries and territories... places that couldn't help themselves, if that makes sense."

Caroline nodded, took a sip of coffee, and set her mug down.

"Well, I must tell you, I admire your photography very much."

"Y-you've seen some of my work?"

"Oh yes! It's gotten quite famous as I'm sure you must know by now-"

"Well I mean, I knew they'd caught on in London, and a few galleries were interested but... honestly most of the value is just because of the subject."

Lauren reached her foot out underneath the table and ran it up Valerie's calf, making her jump.

"No, no. While I agree that the subject is important I dare say that you have an incredible gift for photography. In fact, I have one of your prints hanging in the chapel right now."

"No..."

"Yes! I do! In fact I was rather hoping you might, ah, sign it for me?"

Valerie looked surprised and at the same time delighted.

"Uh, yeah of course! I honestly don't think anyone has ever asked me that before!"

Caroline led Valerie from the table with Lauren trailing bemusedly behind them. She felt a spark of her former contentedness. The familiar warmth of a home and a family started to creep back into her heart.

Valerie had just lifted the canvas down from the wall when Lauren strode through the doorway to the chapel and leaned against the frame, happy just to observe her two friends excitement.

"... really don't mind? I know it must be obnoxious of me to ask you, my guest-"

"Mrs. Adams, it is my *distinct* pleasure to sign this for you."

Lauren's stomach was full, but she felt the familiar rumble of another hunger within her. Her smile faltered and she felt a bead of sweat form at the base of her neck as the darkness stirred. Wasn't she experiencing joy and love right now? Why wasn't the beast within her content?

Enticed, perhaps, by the lightness of her heart, oily tendrils reached up within her chest and tapped at her heart's door. So far, she'd subsisted on the lives she'd taken in Chicago. Her stay here in Cherry Hills, and the peace surrounding it, was made possible in no small part because of the stockpile of memories she'd drained unintentionally from the heart of the city.

But it had been days now since she consumed the last light from within her stolen memories.

Lauren forced herself to remain calm, ignored the way her arms itched and her mouth watered. She dipped a toe into the haunting remnants of the fallen, searching out the familiar, delicious warmth she'd grown so dependent on. But she felt nothing but icy sadness, crushing anger, and boiling hate.

The longer she searched the more desperate she became. Lauren scanned frantically through the minds of the dead, lowering her standards from love to simple happiness, debasing herself until even a shred of contentment would do.

"Lauren? Lauren are you ok?"

Valerie's voice, sharp with concern, cut through the fog in her mind. Lauren wanted to respond, to reassure Valerie, but she couldn't break from her hunt. Not until she'd found something, anything.

There.

A tiny ember of warmth nestled within the ashy remnants caught her attention. She dove into the glowing coal of light and found herself at a fifth grade talent show. She was watching a little girl, her niece? No. Daughter. Her daughter was playing the violin in the middle of a stage in a half-filled school auditorium. Her host's chest swelled with pride as the spritely blonde girl flawlessly executed a difficult piece of baroque composition.

Lauren devoured that pride, cringing internally at the precious recollection she was destroying, but utterly incapable of stopping herself.

It wasn't much, but it was enough to trust herself re-engaging the real world. She snapped her eyes open to reveal Valerie and Caroline worriedly examining her. Lauren was covered in cold sweat, her hands cold and clammy against the warmth of Valerie's palm.

"Hey, you scared us. What's wrong? Do you need to lie down?"

Lauren shook her head no and took a few deep breaths. Her heart was no longer racing, and the monster was back in it's cage. For now.

"I'm ok, I think I just need some fresh air."

Valerie nodded solemnly and practically dragged her by the hand to the door of the church.

"Come on, we'll go for a walk-"

"No!"

Valerie looked like she'd been slapped.

"Wha-why?"

"Sorry um, I'm just gonna take a lap or two. I don't want you to catch a chill again, that's all."

"Lauren, I want to be there for you, I want-"

"Sweetie you're here for me, I know you are. I'll be back I promise I just need an hour or so-"

"An hour! I'm supposed to sit here and worry about you for an hour?"

Valerie's indignance would, in any other context, be adorable. Unfortunately, Lauren's hunger was already clamoring for release once again.

"Baby please, I need this. I'll be right back."

Lauren left a kiss on Valerie's cheek as she extricated her hand and leapt into the sky. Lightning illuminated her shadowy form as she rose through the rain. Every downbeat seemed to stir the storm into action and by the time she hit the clouds the rain was coming in sideways.

Within moments Cherry Hills was a tiny dot in the distance. Like some great hawk Lauren soared above the trees, each of her magnified senses straining, hunting. Lauren headed south-east until she hit the Ohio River, then followed it's winding path eastward. The river split a few miles from where she began, and she was unsure where it went from there. She chose the right fork at random, hunger making it difficult to think straight.

The miserable weather keep the roadways beside the river fairly clear, but even as the mild morning whipped into a torrential storm she could see the occasional vehicle.

Alone.

Isolated.

Vulnerable.

She shook her head, determined that innocents wouldn't die for her hunger. For her fix. There *had* to be another way.

Lauren caught sight of a bus on the horizon below her.

Then again, she reasoned with herself, was anyone truly innocent?

Her wings tucked and she plummeted from the sky, a silent arrow of darkness. She pulled her dive high and tight, rocketing through the air and easily outpacing the cumbersome vehicle. Lauren cut into a deep turn, circling her prey.

KY DEPT OF CORRECTIONS

Jackpot.

The darkness inside her roared to life. All doubt and guilt fled and she banked her turn and landed softly, silently, atop the moving vehicle. Lauren raised a hand and brought it crashing down on the metal shell of the bus. Her hand easily pierced the thin metal sheeting and she peeled back a large section of the roof.

In an instant she was inside, her eyes blinded by hunger and her arms glowing an eldritch silver. Her victims never even had a chance to scream, her power poured through the metal frame and by the time the bus skidded to a halt a few hundred feet down the road, it's lifeless occupants were nothing but dried husks.

Fourteen souls to appease the beast.

Lauren noted the guard uniforms worn by three of the men, but felt nothing. Her muscles flexed and tightened as pure, unfiltered carnal pleasure rebounded through her body. She shivered, not from the cold but from the ecstasy of devouring their lives.

Her need was sated, but not her desire.

She had the wherewithal to know she needed to dispose of her kill or risk the safety of her home, so she exited the vehicle the same way she entered. Lauren picked up some altitude, scouting a reasonable location to dump the evidence, and caught sight of a large body of water a few miles distant.

She returned to the pavement with a smirk and reached under the bus. Lauren lifted it up easily, grabbed onto the axle, and surged back into the sky. She couldn't contain the joy she felt carrying the vehicle through the air like a toy, and laughed aloud at her raw power.

By the time she hit the edge of the lake she wasn't even sure she cared if the bus was found. Still, the thought of Valerie was enough to convince her that she should finish cleanly.

Lauren made it to the middle of the lake and dropped the bus into the murky, wind-whipped water below. Flood lights across the lake caught her eye and led her northward to investigate.

Several layers of tall, razor-wire-topped fences and guard towers looked to her like the wrapping paper on a christmas present.

The maximum security Kentucky State Penitentiary was a fortress of steel and stone, but it yielded to her like paper. In less than a half hour she'd cleared the building of life. Nearly nine hundred inmates as well as the contingent of three hundred staff and guards. Even the soaked, flooded yards of the prison were nothing but black barren dirt when she returned to the skies outside.

Lauren was radiant, her glow so powerful that it illuminated the ground around her in the dark gloom of the morning. Curious, she walked to a puddle and examined herself.

Her arms were pure mercury from her fingertips to her shoulder blades, her chest was crisscrossed with deep silver veins that radiated from a deep black core around her heart, and she could see the reflection of her glowing eyes like tiny molten suns surrounded by tendrils of liquid metal.

At last the beast was quiet. With that silence came the realization of what she'd done. She knew it was wrong, she knew that hundreds of families would find their innocent loved ones lives snuffed out meaninglessly.

But she *could not* muster the will to care.

Lauren dug up her most painful memories. She thought of Gabriel, of Erin, of her father and James. The pain was there, but dull and faded like an old photograph. Darkness numbed her from within and she realized the armor she'd built around her heart had no opening, no back door through which she could cling to her own precious life.

It terrified her.

What was left of her screamed out in fear and loneliness, searching for a lifeline to find her way back from the hell she'd built around herself.

Lauren's mind gave life to her body and directed her homeward, back to the only people she had left who loved *her*. She gripped her stomach as she flew, when was the last time she'd felt it?

She was nearly back to Cherry Hills when the being inside her finally gave a faint but reassuring flutter. Some small measure of tension released from her shoulders at last.

Lauren wasn't sure how long she'd been gone, but as she touched down in the grass outside the church the door swung wide and Valerie splashed out to greet her.

"Lauren!"

Valerie wrapped her in a hug, already soaked in the few seconds she was exposed to the weather. Lauren flicked her wings back open and shielded both of them from the worst of the storm. Valerie's embrace ignited warmth within her once again. She tried not to let on that she needed it far more than Valerie did.

"You're going to catch a cold Vee, I told you I was coming back! You should have waited inside where it's warm and dry!"

Valerie didn't let go, instead she buried her head in Lauren's shoulder and gripped even tighter. Lauren closed her eyes in gratitude, warming herself by the fire of Valerie's touch.

"I'm sorry I left like that, I just needed to... to sort something out, that's all."

Valerie turned her face up to Lauren's, her frustrated scowl competing with a relieved smile.

"We're supposed to sort things out as a team. I don't know how it works in America, I admit, but in Britain being in a relationship means working through things *together*."

Lauren allowed herself an annoyed eye roll, which did not go unnoticed by her companion.

"*Yes dear.*"

Valerie narrowed her eyes.

"You did *not* just 'yes dear' me!"

Lauren's amused smile was met with a playful shove. She picked her girlfriend up, lifting her in both arms like a new bride, and headed for the door.

"And you can't just waltz in and sweep me off my feet and expect me to forgive you!"

"Yes dear."

Caroline met them at the door. In one hand she held a mop, in the other a long pink rain jacket.

"Nope, uh-uh. You two are an absolute mess. You wanted to go out and play in the rain, go play in the rain!"

Lauren took a step back. Certainly she was kidding.

She wasn't.

Caroline extended the pink jacket to a sheepish Valerie, who took it reluctantly. She looked pointedly at their feet, all four were caked in mud and grass, and then brandished her mop like a broadsword.

"Shoo!"

Chapter 15

Dawn found Weyland watching the sun rise over the London skyline. Over millennia he had built this simple act into a habit, then a ritual, and now an obsession. It was... calming, in a way. Some aspect of his psyche, some long-forgotten grain of sand on the floor of an endless sea of history, drove him to savor this moment each day.

Weyland closed his eyes as the first rays lifted past the horizon and warmed his skin. He lost himself in the imagined smell of Kikuyu grass and Mahogany flowers.

For hours he stood in perfect, total stillness. He dwelt on ancient plains, chased long-dead prey through forgotten jungles, and climbed ancient ziggurats shrouded in the mist-draped mountains of memory. Millions of sunrises chased each other across his exposed skin. One constant in the ever-changing world he was surrounded by.

But reality intruded on his memory.

His half-smile faded into a frown. Nothing was ever as perfect as the creations of his mind. No matter how many times he tried to guide them, mankind seemed always to invite its own destruction. But he was the shepherd, and at times it was his duty to cull the flock.

Today was such a day.

"Natalie!"

She appeared instantly, good. His chosen mouthpiece's training was going well. It had been more than two weeks since he'd last had to discipline her, and she'd been careful to cover the scars well. He despised ugliness, though he found it everywhere. She was wearing what passed for professional attire in this age. Weyland found the skirt and blouse combination most pleasing to the eye, and whatever human had invented 'high heels' was certainly enlightened. It promoted the greatest characteristics of the female form while also inducing the twin weaknesses of pain and an inability to run effectively.

Nothing pleased him so much as her collar, however. The thin gold band send blood rushing through his veins. Pride, like that of a renowned horse breeder, filled him.

Natalie prostrated herself as she knew was proper, and waited obediently for him to speak.

"You passed my message to the United States?"

"I did my lord."

"And their response?"

"They did not respond my Lord, but their President is speaking publicly this morning. Many of the governing body will be with him…"

Her hesitance was annoying, she should fear nothing so much as him.

"And?"

"And, my Lord, you are reportedly the subject of his speech. He is expected to denounce you as a false God."

Weyland's anger flared, the tight weave of the carpet smoldered and Natalie's skin flushed red with the sudden heat.

"Where?"

"Lexington, Massachusetts, it is a site of historical importance to the United States. I-it is where their revolution began."

Revolution. The word boiled his blood.

"Is it close to the place we discussed?"

Natalie nodded.

Weyland grabbed his servant by her hair, ignoring her gasp of pain, and willed himself across the globe. He appeared with a thunderous explosion in the middle of a crowded street, sending shattered cars and broken pedestrians alike tumbling through the air half charred. In the space of a heartbeat the peaceful boulevard turned into a swirling storm of screaming and wreckage.

Weyland still had a firm grip on Natalie's smoking ponytail when they arrived. He didn't wait for her to recover before lifting her above the ground, her face next to his own.

"Where?"

Natalie had both her hands wrapped around Weyland's closed fist, the pain from her burning palms surpassed by the pain in her scalp. When her answer was not forthcoming enough he shook her violently.

"Where!"

He relished the panicked, wide-eyed fear in his subject a moment longer before releasing her to fall to the ground.

"P-please, please my Lord give me just a moment to determine our exact location."

She stumbled to her feet and over to a glass and steel structure that stood beside the street. The tiny building was the entrance to an underground tunnel, and on one wall it had a large multicolored map. She returned at once, pointing a quivering finger to the Northeast.

"How far?"

"Several hundred miles, my Lord."

She gulped in trepidation, how pitiful.

Weyland dragged his herald across the intervening miles, stopping regularly to hone in on the correct location. By the time they arrived in concord his servant was all but useless. She was a shivering, heaving wreck, so he left her on the banks of the river they'd appeared beside.

A small crowd, perhaps two hundred people, were gathered around a podium at one end of a narrow wooden bridge that crossed the river. The gathering noted his arrival, but surprised him when they did not immediately break and run.

Weyland noted the unusually bulky clothing, the hardened stares, and the muscular physiques of the predominantly male group.

Warriors.

Weyland's stride did not falter, but he was stunned at the audacity of these mortals. The crowd parted for him, putting on a show of whimpering and cowering, but he was not so easily fooled. He toyed with the idea of vaporizing them, but their courage should be rewarded with a much slower death.

Besides, he admitted to himself, he was just a bit curious at what these men and women hoped to accomplish.

"You are an invader on the sovereign soil of the United States."

A strong, powerfully built man addressed him from the podium. In his younger days he must have been a formidable soldier, but age had drawn his muscle into disrepair. It had done nothing to diminish the strength and brightness of his eyes, or the harshness of his tone.

"No. *You* are invaders. Insects, permitted to live but by my grace."

Weyland pretended not to notice the crowd closing behind him. He cast his attention into the glinting lenses of the dozens of television cameras that were trained on him instead. During his short return to the world he'd come to realize that this, truly, was what had replaced him. What had replaced the Old Gods. Tiny flickering boxes of sound and color, transmitting information, opinions, and distractions directly into the minds of his flock.

"For too long you have wandered aimlessly. You have strayed from my guiding hands and from the purpose I have given you-"

"We do not need you. We do not *want* you."

To be interrupted by the upstart was more than Weyland's short temper would allow. With a narrowing of his eyes the grass around him smoldered and the stage burst into flames. He left a ring of safety around the President. Their False God was watching, and it was important that the billions of eyes watching him through it understood his role, his power.

"I have long been the guiding light behind humanity's achievements. Since a time before your most distant ancestors I have watched you. I have shaped you. I have led you into purpose."

The crowd continued to part, partially from heat and partially to allow him to make progress towards the speaker. Finally he was mounting the steps of the small platform, only the President seemed unwilling to give way.

"You will kneel to me."

The man squared his shoulders. Weyland could see his chest rise, his hands ball up, and his jaw set and knew his next words would be insolence.

"I will not."

Weyland turned to the cameras again.

"See that I am a merciful God. See that I am a just God. I offer sanctuary to the penitent, but I will not hesitate in the destruction of the unfaithful."

As he spoke the President staggered beside him. His skin was turning a blotchy red and he clutched at his throat. Rather than fall to his knees, he gripped the podium for support, gurgling in his attempts to speak.

"You *will* bow to me. This world is my right by birth, hard-won in combat, and sealed by the fates themselves. Your impudent, insubordinate, ruler will pay the price for his crimes. But you need not-"

The President was starting to steam, his eyes, lips, and fingernails turning a dark, ugly red. With the last of his strength he lunged at Weyland, but he fell to the floor without reaching him. His act, whether a cue or simply a call to action, mobilized the entire crowd.

In a rolling wave the men and women surrounding him pulled concealed weapons from their garments. Assault rifles, shotguns, even sidearms were leveled at him in a heartbeat. There was no hesitation, the crowd opened fire immediately and Weyland laughed as their rounds impacted uselessly against him.

"And yet you will not be cowed!"

Weyland's gloating was interrupted by a loud hissing noise. His inhuman speed allowed him to turn just in time to see a rocket impact his leg and blossom into an explosion. The blow did nothing to him, but shattered the stage he was standing on which made him stumble to catch his footing. He traced the sound of the rocket back to a low stand of trees just as another salvo of half a dozen more flew in and detonated around him.

Weyland growled. He flashed over to the pocket of warriors, sending the stand of trees into a towering inferno that drowned out the screams of the soldiers trapped inside.

The crowd had broken into squad sized elements, each laying down a steady staccato of firepower in his direction as they pulled back. By now, the closest group was more than fifty feet away.

A few hearty cameramen were still filming. Weyland found himself respecting the courage of the unarmed journalists, but derided their foolishness. Weyland, rapidly losing his temper, forced himself to remember how much more difficult it was going to be to subordinate the world without at least some measure of cooperation. Still, he could not resist torching the upstart mortals one handful at a time.

Neither could he resist a hungry, wicked grin.

Weyland saw Natalie, limping, being half-dragged and half carried to the East. A tall, lithe hispanic woman with a bullet proof vest and rifle was helping her towards the river. Secure in the knowledge that his delicate slave was out of the immediate firing line, he set about punishing the sinners before him.

"Do it. Escalate to Phase Two."

"Mrs. Vice president, there are still troops in the kill radius-"

"Now!"

"Aye ma'am."

Vice President, no, not anymore. *President* Lynn was sitting in a bunker deep inside the Cheyenne Mountain Complex in Colorado. Secretary Weiss, members of the cabinet, and the Joint Chiefs of Staff were all present, keeping a watchful gaze on the same monitors to which her eyes were presently glued.

The images, fed directly from a dedicated satellite, were paired alongside live news coverage of the unfolding events from around the world.

"Fire Team Retribution, this is Cheyenne Star, prepare for coordinates, over."

A brief moment of static followed the command.

"Cheyenne Star this is Retribution, go ahead, over."

"One, niner, tango, charlie, hotel, break. Zero, six, seven, two, break. Zero, four, five, one. How copy, over?"

"Good copy. One-niner-tango-charlie, hotel-zero-six- seven, two-zero-four-five-one, over."

"You are clear to engage, fire for effect, over and out."

The room held its breath while fireteam Retribution pulled the trigger on a dozen 155 millimeter howitzers just outside of Concord, Massachusetts.

Ninety agonizing seconds ticked by. Ninety seconds of America's finest dying on the sword of keeping their enemy in the crosshairs.

The finely tuned artillery team used a combination of angles and fuse lengths to stagger their shots, each system dropping three high-explosive rounds onto the target area simultaneously. Thirty-six explosions, each more than capable of leveling most structures on earth, impacted within a fifty meter radius of Weyland. Dirt and debris blocked the lenses of the satellite, all but two of the cameras providing live coverage when suddenly black.

"Nothing could have survived that. Not a chance, ma'am."

But President Lynn would not dismiss their enemy so swiftly. She held a hand up for silence, peering desperately at the monitors for any hint of movement.

"Task Force Minute Man is at 12% strength ma'am... Vitals on three are falling but the other nine appear stable. I'm getting incoming radio traffic from them now."

"Put it up."

"... Movement within the crater. Hostile is unharmed, I say again Hostile is-"

The radio cut with an uncomfortable suddenness.

"We've lost vitals on fou-eight more. Ma'am, he's still up!"

General VanZweiten, a thin, elderly man with short-cropped blonde hair and hazel eyes, wordlessly lifted a briefcase from his side and popped it open on the table. He handed the President a key from his pocket and lifted another from around his neck.

The room fell silent as the pair turned the keys in unison and punched in a series of numbers and letters.

"May god have mercy on our souls."

Weyland was panting, not from exhaustion but from excitement. The rush of combat, of war, electrified him. The last few soldiers were clinging to life, barely, and one lone reporter was trying to crawl his way out of a crater, his one remaining leg dangling useless and broken.

Weyland granted the warriors swift deaths, but he approached the reporter more playfully. With a flick of his wrist he cauterized the bleeding stump of the man's leg and with a foot he not-so-gently flipped him over. The man, who still clutched his camera out of some haywired mix of habit and instinct, held it out like shield, trying to protect himself.

"Can the people see me? Through the television?"

On second thought, Weyland wasn't sure the man could actually hear him at the moment. Sure enough blood and some clear fluid was leaking from the man's ears and nose. Still, there was a tiny blinking red light at the front end of the machine so Weyland erred on the side of caution.

"Know this. I am the Lord your God. You will bow to my whims and in return for your worship I will guide you as I always have, or you will suffer the destruction and ruin of blasphemy."

He turned and left the man to die, heading for the river, and his slave, instead.

Three shots impacted the center of his forehead in quick succession, followed by a half dozen to the center of his chest.

The soldier. The Latina woman from before was kneeling in waist deep water. Her rifle shouldered and nothing but courage on her face, she stood her ground against him, braced by the cold, fast moving river.

Natalie was crouched behind her, hands over her ears screaming.

"Natalie, come."

Natalie started to obey, but the warrior took her hand off the foregrip of her weapon and held it out, stopping her.

"You don't own her."

Weyland smiled wide.

"Oh but I do. And I own you too. I own anything I want, everything I want."

He took a closer look. Good bone structure, clearly in physical shape, thin but not entirely lacking in the chest. And that attitude, that... defiance. Yes, she would be a *very* amusing new toy.

"What is your name, child?"

"Staff Sergeant Carlita Santos, and I ain't ya' child."

Her off-hand returned to the weapon.

A half-dozen states away Lauren stirred beneath a small mountain of blankets.

"Lauren... wake up baby..."

Her only reply was a low mumble, but Valerie was insistent.

"Come on sleepy head, you're burning sunshine. Well, sort of."

Lauren smiled, she could hear the listless sigh in Valerie's voice just as easily as she could hear the raindrops beating down on the roof above.

"Mhmm, you come back to bed instead."

Lauren snaked a hand out from under the covers towards her girlfriend. When her grasping fingers finally made contact it was with a bulky winter coat. She poked her head out from under her pillow.

"Baby? What are you doing?"

Valerie was wearing an odd assortment of winter clothes and rain gear, wrapped to the gills in layers and layers.

"I wanna go out!"

Lauren laughed.

"What do you mean you want to go out? It's *miserable* outside."

Valerie pouted. Her bottom lip puffed out and she crossed her arms in front of her chest.

"It rains all the time in England! You don't think we just sit inside, bored out of our minds every day do you?"

Lauren rolled over.

"I thought that's *exactly* what you guys do."

Valerie stomped a foot playfully.

"Ok fine, that's what we do. But it's horrid! Take me out?"

Lauren allowed herself another smile and sat up in the bed. A strange pain shot through her stomach, like a pulled muscle, but it only lasted a moment it was gone as quickly as it had appeared. She put a gentle hand on her belly, looking down in alarm.

"Ooh! Did she kick?"

Valerie hopped down in the bed beside her and put her hand on Lauren's.

They waited a minute to no avail.

"I guess she's sleeping."

"That's twice you've said 'she,' do you know something I don't?"

Valerie sheepishly fiddled with her hands.

"I don't know, just feels like a girl, doesn't it?"

Lauren hopped out of the bed and extended a hand to Valerie.

"Let's go for a walk."

A few minutes later and the pair were outside, trudging through the rain and the mud in the forest outside the church. There was an odd tension in the air, not between them but all around. Like the world was holding its breath. The air was stuffy and warm, but the rain cold and harsh.

Lauren shook an uncomfortable tingle at the base of her neck, returning her girlfriend's excited smile. Everything was fine. Still, a knot she couldn't explain was forming in her stomach.

Valerie was jumping in puddles, running her hands through the leaves above them, and smiling from ear to ear. Twenty minutes down the path she turned to face Lauren, who was trailing a few feet behind.

"I wanna go up again."

"What?"

"Lauren I want to *fly* with you again. I-if you'll let me…"

Lauren quirked an eyebrow.

"I dunno Vee, you got so cold last time. You scared me half to death!"

"Please? Pretty please? I got all dressed up!"

Lauren couldn't keep from smiling.

"Your wish is my command."

Valerie jumped up and down with joy, clapping like an excited child on Christmas.

They kept walking until they happened upon a clearing with a small pond in the middle of it. The tiny pool was almost double its normal size, over-filled by the constant rain. They came to a stop on a small patch of crushed rock beside a bench, thoughtfully placed beside the pond in some long-ago act of conservation.

Lauren ran a hand along the mossy old wood of the backrest.

"I wonder how long it's been here? How long it's been sitting empty."

She felt Valerie's hand slip into her, their fingers intertwining.

"Ready?"

No.

Lauren tried once more to stifle her unease. She cast around for a distraction, and was struck with an idea.

"Do you know how to skip stones?"

She bent at the waist and retrieved a handful of the rounder, flatter rocks she could find.

"Do I know what?"

"How to skip stones, I don't know if that's just an American thing or… I don't know."

"Love, we English *invented* Ducks and Drakes."

"Ducks and what now?"

"Ducks and Drakes, the proper name for it. The first bounce is a duck, the second a drake, and so on and so forth. I remember Colin used to take me to play at the Thames. That's where there game was invented, he always used to say. We played with two pence coins by the banks..."

Valerie had never expanded on what happened to her brother before, so Lauren was inclined to let her speak.

"After mom's funeral he couldn't stand to look at my father anymore than he could stand that old house of ours. We always knew he'd leave with the military, but it felt more like running away to me. He used to write, still does on holiday. But... he went and fell in love across the sea and can't pull himself back."

"He fell in love?"

Valerie nodded.

"With Australia. He tells me she's beautiful, and wild, and free. A whole continent of mystery and wonder. How can I blame him? I fell in love with my own adventures, I suppose."

Valerie's buzz was well and truly killed, her cheerful excitement replaced by morose introspection. Lauren steeled herself against her discomfort, and determined to cheer her up.

"Ok, you ready?"

It's alright, you've got this.

Valerie's face lit back up, though not quite as brightly as before.

"Listen, Vee, just promise me if you get uncomfortable or you don't feel well... anything at all and you'll let me know ok? We'll come right down and that'll be the end of it.

Valerie's smile faltered.

"Of course, is everything ok?"

Lauren nodded, and did her best to look convincing. She knew this is what Valerie wanted, and she didn't want to ruin it. She scooped Valerie up in her arms delicately, gave her a quick kiss on the cheek, and leapt into the air.

The cold wind whipped over both of them, driving the rain into a stinging sheet. Lauren pushed for altitude, rocketing upwards into the low-hanging clouds.

"Hold on tight, this part is going to be cold."

Valerie's face, obscured by her scarf and hood, was alight with wonder. The wind was too loud to hear her reply, but she nodded fervently. As they plunged into the menacing gray mountains above, Lauren cradled Valerie, holding her tightly but being careful not to squeeze too hard.

Before long they were breaking through, the clouds shifted from gray, to white until suddenly there was nothing but clear blue sky and radiant sun above them. She slowed her climb until she was hovering a few feet above the highest cloud.

Mile after endless mile of rolling, pristine hills and valleys of purest white as far as the eye could see. It was still early, but the sun was well above the horizon.

The sunlight poured over both of them, washing them with renewed energy and warmth.

"My God Lauren, it's beautiful."

She looked down at Valerie and saw tears in her eyes.

"Are you ok?"

Valerie nodded.

"I'm just... speechless. I can't imagine being able to come here, to see *this* anytime you want."

She certainly had a point. Not to mention a way of framing things that made Lauren more grateful. But the splendor of the moment was spoiled by Lauren's discomfort. The nagging at the back of her mind was becoming more insistent, and finally she was sure she knew what it was.

"Valerie I have to tell you something."

Valerie's cheerful upturned face didn't make this easier. Her unsuspecting smile and the redness of her nose gave Lauren pause.

"I think something is *wrong* with me. I... You know I've hurt people."

That precious smile on Valerie's face faltered and she shifted her weight uncomfortably.

"Lauren, I know but-"

"No. You have to understand. It's like there's this hunger inside of me. Like I can't feel anything at all unless I..."

Lauren's words trailed off as her mind tried to understand what she was seeing. They were suddenly awash in a harsh orange light. A second Sun had appeared far to the East, drowning the familiar daylit skies. Lauren's eyes burned, and she could feel her cells regenerating themselves rapidly but even so the impossible brightness of the event was bleaching her retinas.

"Wha-"

Valerie turned to look but Lauren forced her to look away.

"Don't!"

Valerie stiffened at being handled so roughly.

"I'm sorry, there's a... a light? But it's burning my eyes. I think it would hurt you."

The glow lasted several long seconds before slowly, gradually, fading.

Lauren squinted, willing her powerful senses to unravel the mystery she'd just seen. A dark but growing smudge was all the could make out.

She inhaled sharply as the knot in her stomach tightened suddenly into a sharp pain, like she'd felt before but much worse. She flinched, but kept her grip on Valerie.

"Lauren are you ok?"

She couldn't speak at first, only shake her head no.

"I think we need to land, hold on to me."

A moment later and they were plummeting from the sky like a comet. When they emerged below the clouds once again Lauren could see the wind had blown them a few miles off course. But Cherry Hills was easily visible and Lauren banked into a head-on approach.

Lauren hit the ground running, but only made it a dozen steps before she faltered and fell to her knees. She kept Valerie off the ground, but only just.

"Lauren? Lauren baby get up!"

Valerie extricated herself from Lauren's grasp. She was hunched over, her wings in the mud and her hands clutched over her stomach. She shook her head and waved her lover off. Valerie headed for the church instead.

"Mrs. Caroline!"

Valerie cleared the rest of the lawn in a heartbeat.

"Mrs. Caroline? Mrs. Caroline it's Lauren, something's wrong!"

Caroline appeared, a handkerchief around her head and a broom in her hand. She pulled the headphones from her ears as Valerie cleared the door.

"Good heavens child, what's the matter?"

Valerie gasped for breath, took Caroline by the hand, and dragged her out into the rain, her cleaning supplies forgotten.

"It's Lauren, something is wrong."

The women sprinted across the lawn to Lauren's side.

"What are her symptoms, did she say anything?"

"She was acting a little strange, talking about a 'hunger inside her' or something. We were up in the air and then there was this flash of light. She wouldn't let me look at it, said it was dangerous."

Caroline dropped to her knees in front of Lauren.

"Lauren, it's Caroline honey can you talk to me?"

Lauren didn't respond, she was too focused on breathing and trying to control the pain.

"We need to get her inside."

Valerie nodded in agreement and they each lifted one of Lauren's arms over their shoulder. They were nearly to the door when the ground seemed to slip out from beneath them. They stumbled into one another as the mud-soaked ground buckled and rolled below their feet.

"What the fuck was that?"

Caroline shared a wide-eyed look with Valerie as the rumbling stopped and they pulled Lauren into the church. Caroline took the lead, directed Lauren to the bedroom and laid her out on the covers. Mud, water, and feathers were everywhere, but none of those were what froze Valerie in her tracks.

Blood.

She knelt, taking a closer look. Yes, there was no mistaking it. A steady trail of bright red drops led from the doorway to the bedroom. Valerie pushed her fear aside and returned to Lauren's side. Her eyes were scrunched shut and she was holding her stomach, breathing heavily through gritted teeth.

With Lauren distracted, Valerie tapped Caroline's shoulder and pointed silently to the blood.

"Ok my Lady, I know this isn't what you want to hear, but we need to consider the possibility that you should be in a hospital."

She shook her head.

Caroline's lips tightened into a thin, frustrated line. She set a hand on Lauren's stomach, but felt nothing. When she spoke, she did so in a careful, even tone.

"When is the last time you felt the baby?"

Lauren's eye snapped open.

"T-this morning? Maybe? I-I'm not sure. Why? Is that bad? Is something wrong?"

Caroline gifted Valerie with a sideways glance.

"Lauren, I'm *not* a doctor, I don't know how to help with this. But..."

"But?"

"But, I think you need a hospital my Lady."

Internally, Lauren was screaming. Not only was she in incredible pain, but now the two people she wanted most to be with her were both pushing her to do something she knew she couldn't. There was no way she could go to a hospital without Him knowing, she knew it in her heart of hearts.

"Lauren?"

"I know! Damnit, I know!"

Lauren pushed herself up on the bed, clenching her jaw tight to keep the pain at bay.

"Do you really think she should move?"

"She needs a doctor!"

"I'm right here!"

They were silent.

Lauren stumbled to her feet, slipped on the muddy floor and caught herself in Valerie's arms.

"Honey please, sit back down."

Lauren pushed her aside and stumbled to the door. She braced her arms against each side of the heavy wooden frame as another spasm rocked her midsection. Wood splintered beneath her tightening grip.

She was about to leap skyward when Valerie threw her arms around her, wrapping her in a bear hug from behind.

"Please, take me with you."

Pulling herself free was the hardest thing she'd done in months, maybe years, but Valerie would be far safer here. She turned, returning the embrace and planting a quick kiss on Valerie's lips.

"W-why does this feel like goodbye?"

Lauren didn't answer, instead she raised her wings and stepped backwards. One last long look and she propelled herself skyward, wheeling quickly Northwest.

Chapter 16

You're almost there. You're almost there.

Lauren's prayer became her mantra as she careened through the rising winds. Miles burned past at a prodigious rate, but it her path was erratic and uncoordinated. Her navigational issues, though primarily based in the pain she felt, were further aggravated by the sudden and dramatic increase in the severity of the weather.

Where the past few weeks had been stormy and gray, the skies were now an ugly black tinged with green. She'd lived in the Midwest long enough to know tornado weather when she saw it, and for the first time since growing her wings the skies seemed a place of very real danger.

By the time she passed Cobden it was raining sideways; by Springfield it was hailing the size of golf balls; and when she finally passed Peoria the lightning was so thick it illuminated the ground like a strobe light.

Lauren guided herself by instinct as much as anything else, but as her strength failed so too did her altitude fall. She was barely a thousand feet from the ground, tracing the highway and blind to the rest of the world.

She impacted the pavement just outside of Galesburg, Illinois, cracking the roadway and forcing cars to slam on their brakes to avoid hitting her.

Most of them did.

A semi-truck, whether blinded by the rain or unable to slow itself quickly enough, rammed headlong into her kneeling body. The front of the vehicle crumpled like tissue paper and Lauren found herself half buried in twisted metal and hot escaping oil. Lauren wasted no time tearing her way out of the wreckage, emerging to a gathering crowd of onlookers. Dozens of cellphone cameras were trained on her, tracking her every move and no doubt broadcasting it to the world. To Weyland.

She stumbled forward, and caught a glimpse of her dress. The front from her pelvis down was a solid red streak. She shoved it out of her mind, and drove on. The sea of people parted before her.

Some dropped to their knees in adulation, some fled, but the vast majority of the watchers were simply that - watchers.

Silent observers with unblinking cameras, detached from the woman just feet away.

Familiar darkness, her constant companion, crept forward in her heart. She knew the solace it could bring, but she refused to yield.

Her stumble turned to a walk, turned to a run as sore muscles picked up the well worn pace of memory. Lauren tucked her wings and lengthened her strides, bare feet slapping lightly on the pavement. She retreated inward as she ran, severing the links between her mind and the world around her. There was only the run, only the ground beneath and before her.

She spotted it just as the tornado sirens started to wail.

St. Mary's.

For the second time this morning a bright orange glow illuminated the skies. If she had to guess, this one was either much larger or much, much closer. A bright blaze just over the horizon bathed the entire town in an eerie light. This time it was only seconds before a shock wave passed through the ground, and much more intensely than the first.

The glass sliding door of the emergency room, as well as multiple windows in the buildings around her, cracked and blew out into the street from the fury of the quake.

But nothing would deter her. She charged headlong into the hospital, skidding to a halt in the entryway of the emergency room.

Dazed workers were recovering from the unexplained earthquake, picking up the contents of their desks and righting overturned trolleys all around her. Those staff members who noticed her seemed too surprised to do anything other than stare until one plump, older woman snapped to attention and started barking orders.

"Ma'am, are you-"

"I'm pregnant, somethings wrong."

As if to punctuate her statement, Lauren hunched over suddenly to vomit. Bent at the waist, she noted the pool of blood between her feet.

"Right! Get me two techs and a wheelchair, prep the O.R., page Dr. Janga, and alert the NICU."

She took command of the hectic waiting room and conducted the staff like an orchestra.

Two young men and a wheelchair appeared almost immediately and Lauren sank into it gratefully, closing her eyes as they began moving her deeper into the hospital.

"Amelia, you have the room."

The old woman hustled to keep up with them, intent it seemed on accompanying Lauren.

"Room four please, Allen."

The wheelchair turned sharply into a crisp, sterile room already starting to fill with nurses and equipment.

"Ok darlin' you're gonna need to get up on the table here, can you stand?"

She shook her head no.

The two men and the old woman lifted her gently and laid her on the table. The act of straightening back out unleashed a fresh new wave of hell in the form of a brutal tearing feeling inside her.

The woman tried to soothe Lauren's screams. She placed a hand on her forehead and locked eyes with her. Something about her was familiar to Lauren, but she couldn't place just what.

"How far along are you? Hey, hey focus on me honey, how far along?"

"I-I'm not sure. A few months I think."

"That's ok, that's ok. What's your normal kick-count?"

"My what?"

Lauren wished she was worse at reading people's faces, wished she didn't notice the sadness creeping into the woman's eyes.

"You're ok dear. We'll get everything straightened out. We're gonna put an IV in now, and hook you up to just a few little monitors ok?"

The nurses were indeed hooking her up to various external monitors when the woman returned with a needle connected to a thin clear tube and a bag of liquid.

"Ok little sting here sweetie..."

Lauren braced herself but felt nothing.

The woman's eyes widened with surprise. She held up a bent needle, looking it over for defects.

"Wait here just a minute, we didn't want that one anyway now did we dear?"

She reappeared with a much larger needle, but her frustrated sigh indicated to Lauren that it had also failed to pierce her skin.

"Honey you can't um, you can't shut this off can you? I can't get a needle through that skin of yours."

Fuck.

Lauren shook her head, tears in her eyes. She drew a long shaky breath and tried to let it out slowly.

"N-no, I don't know how."

The woman's face stayed passive, but her voice was laced with even greater concern than before.

"Oh that's... that's ok. That medicine is mostly for you anyway dear. Lord above knows you don't need it right?"

She managed a thin smile before turning back to the staff. A tall young man was entering the room in scrubs, his hands held up at a funny angle so as not to compromise their cleanliness. On either side he was flanked by an additional doctor, all mimicking his stance.

"We can't do anything subdermal Doctor, how do you want to proceed?"

"Let's start with intranasal Pitocin, and get an intrauterine monitor in immediately."

He walked to the bedside, stopping near Lauren's head and looking down at her.

"Good morning ma'am, I'm doctor Yerevan Janga, I'll be helping you as best I can this morning. Nurse Peggy tells me you're pregnant, is that right? Now, I need you to listen carefully and answer me as well as you can, ok?"

She nodded and he smiled down at her warmly.

"Ok good, now I don't want to make you uncomfortable, but I'm going to touch you ok?"

Lauren jumped when he started to lift her dress and he immediately stopped. Weyland's horrifying, hungry face tore it's way into her mind and she quaked at the memory of his bedroom in Greece.

"Ma'am? I have to get these clothes out of the way, I need access or I can't help you."

Lauren nodded as another wave of pain throbbed through her.

He was quick, professional, and gentle, sliding her dress up until he could see her stomach and then placing both hands on it. He pressed and prodded, asking her questions and making short unintelligible comments to his fellow physicians in a slow, steady stream.

"Do you know when your projected due date was?"

"No."

"Have you used any drugs, alcohol, or other chemicals since you've been pregnant?"

Did eating people's souls count?

"No."

"Ok good, good. Two for two so far. No more than six months. I can't tell the orientation either. Extreme fetal distress-"

"Fetal distress? What does that mean, does that mean what I think-"

"Ma'am, You have to remain calm ok? The best possible thing for your baby right now is for you to remain as calm as you can. Where is that Pitocin please?"

A nurse appeared with a small bottle of nasal spray and jammed it unceremoniously into Lauren's nose. She jerked back, shaking the whole table.

"What is that?"

"It's pitocin dear, one of the safest drugs out there. It will help with the pain and the bleeding ok? You just need to take a deep breath."

Lauren complied, inhaling a lungful of fine mist. Immediately her eyes went fuzzy and her head felt heavy. Colors swam around the room and her limbs felt distant and unwieldy. Dull, fuzzy stinging sensations ran up and down her nerves, concentrating in her lower abdomen.

Then the contractions hit.

Lauren screamed as her uterus tightened into a fist. The death grip on her organs subsided after several impossibly long seconds, leaving her panting and drenched in sweat.

"...can't remove it via c-section either, we don't have anything that could cut through her skin, let alone the uterine..."

Another contraction, and another after that. Tiny dots
popped and disappeared before her eyes as she gripped the
metal arms of the bed hard enough to crumple them like
soda cans.

"... minimal heart rate, oxygen levels are at 80% and falling
doctor..."

Lauren's vision was going in and out of focus but she could
make out doctor Janga's face a foot or so from her own.

"... to push. Your body is rejecting... you're going to have
to push."

Lauren pushed as hard as she could, nearly blacking out.
The next time her vision collected itself she lifted her head
and looked down. She could see Doctor Janga again, the front
of his lab coat was a dark red and a nurse was handing him
something that looked like a huge pair of tongs.

The building was shaking hard enough to rattle the metal
implements in their trays beside the bed when suddenly the
room went dark. Lauren was certain she'd blacked out until
the lights flickered and came back on. The nurses and doctors,
though focused on her, were clearly nervous.

"... out of time. Is the incubator prepped?"

One last screaming push and the doctor was standing, cradling a blueish-gray object less than a foot long. She barely
got a look at it before he turned his back to her and placed
the tiny, unmoving bundle into a large clear plastic box beside
the bed.

Doctor Janga stepped back and two others stepped in to
take over.

Almost immediately one of the technicians jumped back
like he'd been bit by something.

"Ow! Jesus what the hell was that?"

He was shaking his hand out and massaging his forearm with a stunned look on his face.

"It friggin' shocked me man."

"Allen, focus!"

The technician returned to the incubator and as various wires and cords were attached to the struggling new lifeform monitors started to light up in response.

Lauren's vision was starting to clear, her body recovering rapidly from her internal injuries. Even the drugs seemed to be wearing off, so she tried to sit up.

The room swam and several nurses moved to restrain her.

"Lemme up. Ou' my way."

Peggy appeared by her shoulder.

"Sweetie you have to stay in bed ok? The doctors need time to work."

Lauren shook her head and swung her legs clumsily over the side of the bed.

One of the monitors started to let out a high-pitched keening sound.

"Paddles!"

One of the tech's grabbed a pair of tiny, undersized defibrillator pads and Lauren watched them disappear out of sight.

"Clear!"

There was a bright flash and a popping noise like a firecracker. Every light and machine in the room flickered wildly and several of the fluorescent tubes in the ceiling exploded.

"Allen? Allen!"

The technician was twitching on the floor, paddles still in hand and a patchwork of angry red lines covering his hands.

The heart rate monitor started beeping again, a series of unpredictable, erratic tones.

The attention shifted and Lauren seized the opportunity to exit the bed. Her legs still felt heavy and numb, and she fell immediately to her knees. Shaking her head she stood unsteadily and pushed her way through to the incubator.

"Help him!"

One of the technician's had grabbed her by the shoulders and was shaking her.

"You have to help him he's hurt!"

Lauren shoved him aside. She had only one goal and would not be distracted.

There it was, there *she* was.

The tiny being was maybe eight inches long. Her skin was thin enough to see the bluish veins underneath and her little heart could be seen raising her chest with each weakened beat.

All the wires and leads connected to the tiny person were blackened and melted, the bedding was blackened and even the plastic tub had a large crack in it. As Lauren watched, her daughter started to convulse, her tiny lips moving and her chest heaving. She watched the dull purple of her veins darken into a deeper blue.

"What's wrong? what's happening to her!"

The staff were staring at her, horrified and silent.

"What's the matter with you people! Do something!"

She bent down and lifted Allen from the floor with both hands, only then noticing that her arms were glistening silver up to her elbows. A quick glance downward confirmed that major arteries through her body were again bright, mercurial silver.

She pumped life back into the technician, awakening him with a gasp.

"Fix. Her."

The monitor started to flatline again and she dropped the man, leaving him to recover beside her.

Lauren took a deep breath and reached delicately into the incubator, placing her fingers gently on the tiny life within.

She dug deep inside herself, willing her powers to work. She could feel the energy there, could manipulate it easily and felt it flowing through her body and out her fingertips.

But it had no effect.

She pushed harder, a splitting headache filled the front of her skull and still she pushed.

Nothing.

Lauren lifted her hands with a frustrated scream.

"B-Bring more paddle things, do the paddle thing again!"

Allen turned and ran from the room, returning a few moments later with another defibrillator set. He handed her the box with shaking hands and then retreated several steps.

Lauren's temper flared.

"I don't know how to use this you jackass!"

She shoved them back in his direction, but he held his hands up and shook his head no. Lauren's eyes narrowed menacingly.

"I wouldn't be afraid of what *might* happen to you with these paddles. I would be afraid of what *will* happen to you if you don't. And not just you, everyone in this hospital."

The second technician shoved Allen forward, and he stumbled into her. With clumsy, trembling fingers he peeled the melted electrodes off of Lauren's baby and replaced them with new ones from the portable kit he carried, one on the chest and the other on the back. He connected the long bright wires to the small box and a blinking light indicated that a shock was ready almost immediately. The box let out a brief warning tone, prompting Allen to hastily remove his hands.

Another second ticked by and the box let out a high-pitched whine and an obvious jolt of electricity. The tiny infant jerked for a moment, then the box sizzled and popped, smoke pouring out of it.

The hospital shook with a fury that matched Lauren's own.

A roaring sound, like a thousand angry freight trains filled their ears. A gust of wind blew the door to the operating room inward and Lauren could see papers, hospital gowns, even a desk go careening past in the hallway.

The tiles above them broke loose but they didn't fall. Instead they were ripped skyward as if by the hand of god, revealing a massive black scar on the face of the heavens. A tornado, hundreds of feet across and easily the biggest Lauren had ever seen, was bearing down on the tiny hospital.

Wind shredded the buildings around them, sending cinder blocks, cars, and people spiraling upward to disappear into the blackness.

Rain blasted the town with enough force to leave welts. Hail tore like bullets through car windshields and windows. And all the while lightning danced through the streets like a thing possessed. The screams of the nurses and patients were drowned by the incomparable power of the storm. Lauren stood her ground, unwilling to move, unwilling to leave her daughter.

Boards, bricks, and other unattended objects became missiles in the storm. They battered Lauren, and the wind tore at her feathers, but she paid them no mind until a stray stone impacted the tiny box cradling her baby. The thick plastic cracked deeper, driving Lauren to action. She hunched over the box, wings spread protectively, and shielded it from the storm with her body. the glow from her chest and face was enough to illuminate the scrunched, struggling face below her.

Gale force winds buffeted them, but inside the tiny sanctuary she was safe.

Gale.

Lauren closed her eyes, it was a perfect name.

Gale.

Something heavy and metal crashed into Lauren's exposed back, making her stumble at last. Even she couldn't stay here forever. Gingerly, she reached out her hands to lift Gale from the soft cushion where she lay.

No sooner had she plucked her from her resting place than the sky lit up like a spotlight. Lauren watched in stunned amazement as columns of lightning several feet across poured in solid streams from the clouds and down into the ground.

The pillars writhed and moved like snakes, carving molten paths along the ground around her. The columns of electricity, nearly a dozen in total, swirled and danced chaotically. Lauren watched with growing trepidation as they undeniably started to close in around her.

Her hands grew hot, and Lauren glanced down to see Gale covered in tiny arcs of lightning. Her back was arched and her tiny, undersized hands clenched and unclenched. Gale shook violently, shuddered, and lay still.

Lauren flinched in pain as energy shot along her nerves. Power filled her body and a buzzing filled her ears until an arc of lightning burst forth from her chest into the sky. Her eyesight was bleached out until all she could see was a blaze of white.

When the blinding flash finally subsided and Lauren's chest finally relaxed she felt her heart stutter and stop, and then restart several times before resuming it's normal beating. Her lungs gulped fresh air as her muscles spasmed and drew her to her knees.

She blinked to clear the afterimages from her eyes and stared at her hands. Where her baby had been there was nothing. Red lines covered her like the branches of a gnarled tree. Flashing light drew her gaze to upward in time to see the columns of lightning pour upwards into the sky, pulsing like a heartbeat across the clouds.

She stared in awe at the rapidly dissolving funnel clouds around her. In seconds the winds had died to a low roar. The hail stopped, replaced by cool, soft rain that mixed with Lauren's uncomprehending tears. A stray puff of wind caressed

Lauren's cheek, whisking her tears away with an unexpected gentleness.

Before she could gather her thoughts, an explosion unlike anything Lauren had ever known rocked the air around her. The suicide bomber in Sarajevo was a firecracker compared to the ear-shredding pressure wave she experienced. Lauren was thrown a few dozen feet, crashing into one of the few walls left standing.

There, in a crater at least fifty feet across, was a blazing figure of fire. Lauren knew his form, knew intimately the powerful physique, but she'd never seen Weyland like this before. His dark black skin was replaced by a casing of molten orange and white, like fresh stoked coals in a forge. His eyes, tiny orbs of darkness, were the only part of him that did not radiate light and heat. The air around him sizzled audibly. The ground around him cracked and burned, concrete glowing red hot and asphalt bursting into flames. The heat was so intense that the air around him rushed upward and pierced a hole in the clouds above.

His chest heaving with anger, Weyland strode slowly forward. As he moved, great cracks split in the ground beside him, and everything near him melted away to ash and cinder.

"We have unfinished business."

Lauren felt fear tapdance through her mind. The hairs on the back of her neck raised and she realized that the terrible destruction she had seen from Weyland up until this point was, as he had warned her, but a fraction of his wrath.

Still, she refused to let him see her fear. Lauren opened her mouth to speak but before she could utter a sound Weyland raised his hand for silence. His gesture was accompanied by another earth-shaking explosion that knocked her onto her backside. The ground around him was literally boiling like soup, concrete, steel, and glass evaporating into clouds of acrid gas.

"Do. Not. Speak. If I want to hear you I will tell you what to say."

Lauren scooted backwards. She recognized the look on his face. The hateful hunger there sent a chill through her spine.

"Understand this, you will *never* make me look for you again. I have been extraordinarily lenient with you, but my patience is at an end. I already reduced your precious Chicago to ashes, and when we are finished here I'll track down the rest of the vermin you've been hiding with."

His powerful fists clenched with an audible crackle.

"You are *mine.* You will always be *mine.* Everything you are, and think, and feel, is *mine* to do with as I please. Moreover, you carry *my* child."

Lauren's eyes narrowed. How dare he. Her hackles raised and she clenched her fist hard enough to break through the pavement below her fingers.

Weyland seemed to sense her pending rebellion. His eyes narrowed and the air itself ignited around him, surrounding him in a halo of barely visible flame.

"You insolence is intolerable, but not incurable."

A wave of heat unlike anything she'd ever known washed over Lauren. She felt the outer layers of her skin crumble to ash and dissipate. But her powers had grown since last she'd faced Weyland, and her abilities prevented all but the most superficial damage. Her dress sizzled and blackened against her body, hissing as the moisture of the storm was boiled out of it in an instant.

"You will acknowledge our place as Gods of this world, just as you will acknowledge your place below me as my consort and raise our child to obey my will."

Lauren scrambled to her feet.

"I don't want to be a God, I don't *need* to be a God! And I sure as hell don't want you."

Weyland balked in confusion, the flames of his wrath dimming briefly.

"You don't have a choice, Lauren-"

"I do have a choice! We all have choices! It may be the only thing we have, but we have choice. Don't you dare try to take that from me."

Weyland disappeared in a flash and rematerialized inches from her face. The heat pouring off of him vaporized her clothes and set her hair and feathers smoking and wilting.

"Do I truly need to remind you, again, that I will take what I want? That you are *nothing* before me? To do with as I please?"

Lauren lashed out with a backhand to Weyland's face, but he caught her wrist mid-strike. The heat from his strong fingers made her flesh sizzle like bacon in a pan.

"Amazing. Your willingness to die is as stunning as your beauty. Unfortunately, your stupidity to think I would let you go so easily is even more so. You are mine, Lauren, as is the child you... "

He paused, his grip loosening as he cocked his head to the side. His eye flitted back and forth from her belly to her face several times before narrowing.

Lauren smiled, a wide, genuine, ear-to-ear grin.

"Where is it!"

His powerlessness, even at the high cost of losing her daughter, filled her with a perverted joy. He gripped her shoulders and shook her like a ragdoll, but all she could do was laugh. He lifted her with a growl and pressed his ear to her stomach, listening hard. A moment paused with nothing but the sound of her mirth, when he finally grew tired of waiting.

Lauren felt the air rush from her lungs as he threw her to the ground with enough force to create a sizeable splash in the lava below his feet. The molten stone stuck to her bare skin like hot glue, searing her flesh and generating enough pain to stop her laughter.

Lauren moved to stand but Weyland put a heavy foot on her chest, crushing her down into the mire.

"Where. Is. It."

"She."

Lauren could barely fill her lungs enough to get out the single word. It hit Weyland like a truck, staggering him.

"S-she? No, that can't be right, you're lying. I was promised a son!"

He pushed harder, until the liquid stone was lapping up Lauren's sides and splashing onto her chest and neck. She craned her head to keep her face above the surface, fear once again setting in. She didn't want to find out what drowning in magma might feel like.

"No matter. Girl or not, she is mine and I demand to know where you have hidden her."

A growing glow drew Lauren's gaze past Weyland's shoulder and into the deep mountains of black clouds that still hovered over the town. The pulsing lightning was beating faster now, a giant, tangled knot of electricity forming in the heart of the storm.

"Her na-name is Gale, and she is no more beholden to you than I am."

Her declaration was punctuated with a massive lightning bolt from the sky. The column of energy hit Weyland in the center of his back and drove him to his knees. The moment his weight lifted from her chest, Lauren tucked her wings and rolled away. Her wings sprung back open, flinging droplets of rock in every direction as she found her footing and leapt skyward. She was a dozen feet off the ground when Weyland appeared in mid-air in front of her. She couldn't turn in time and he wrapped her in a bear hug.

She felt the familiar twisting sensation as they jumped across the globe. When they crashed to the ground it was not the melted slag-heap of her birthplace but the center of of a crowded street under a blazing desert sun.

Crowds of hijab and thawb clad women and men dispersed in chaos as the street erupted in fire and smoke. Those unfortunate souls caught too close when the pair appeared were broken and burned without any hope of escape. Lauren saw stars as her head bounced off the ancient stone street. Weylands hands were wrapped around her neck, his fingers tightening slowly and his lip curling into a callous snarl.

"Fear not, *bride*, you have an eternity to remember your place. Just as I have an eternity to breed a son from you."

Lauren's eyes burned with flash-dried tears and she felt herself draw inward as her vision blurred around the edges. She could feel his eagerness, feel his weight bearing down on her.

She could feel his sadistic excitement.

But she was not the helpless girl of a few months past.

Lauren's eyes blazed with fury as she reached her hands up to Weyland's wrists. She pried at his muscular forearms but to no avail, he was still too strong.

Weyland brought his face down to her, his strong hands holding her head still, and forced his searing lips on hers. She kicked and hit him. Tried to scream, to bite his lip, to pull her lips away from him. When he finally drew back She spit uselessly at him and he freed a hand from her neck to shove her face into the ground. He leaned in again and whispered in her ear.

"You *belong* to me."

Rough hands grabbed her and started to roll her over. She met his hands with her own, her muscles tearing with the strain of holding him back. His power was too great, she felt her joints groan and snap as he twisted her to his whims.

As her shoulder dislocated, Lauren felt herself detach further. She was aware of the hundreds of eyes watching the terrible scene unravel from a safe distance, aware of the screams of the dying and injured. She saw herself as a broken baby bird, fallen too soon from the nest and surrounded by a swarm of tiny ants. A sea of life too small to make any impact, but complicit in her destruction nonetheless.

As it had before, the monster lurking in the shadows of her soul called to her when she was most vulnerable. She relented, giving way not for Weyland but for the inky blackness within herself.

She had barely cracked open the door to her heart when the darkness, so long contained, poured in and filled her with strength. The inky pool rebounded off the walls of her soul, rushing to fill the voids and tears it found there and armoring her against the pain she felt.

A surge of strength rushed into her as she reached deep within the ground. She gave the darkness free reign and it leeched the life from the very earth around her. Weyland's advance stalled as she absorbed the countless lives of the city. She could almost see it, a network of life invisible to the naked eye but running from every blade of grass and beetle to the hawks in the skies around them. Thin but undeniable threads ran back and forth in a vast web of connection.

She played the part of the spider, hunting down every trembling life in that web and draining it dry. Cars careened off roads, construction workers fell lifeless from scaffolding, and children slipped silently from swings in parks all over the city. Tehran bled dry in a matter of seconds. She devoured them indiscriminately - every man, woman, child, animal, even the grass and the trees.

Weyland realized too late that his victim was drawing her power from the people around them. He ripped them across the world again, leaving the city in ruins and leveling several hundred yards of rainforest where they arrived next.

But the jungle, for all it lacked in humanity was teeming with life. Lauren used the first few seconds after their transition to shove Weyland aside. She buried her fists into the dark, rich earth.

She needed more.

Weyland sought to starve her. He blazed with renewed intensity, vaporizing the forest for as far as the eye could see. Lauren stood as the web around her blinked out of existence. Weyland was breathing heavily. His fists were clenched in anger but he maintained his distance. Waiting, no doubt, to strike.

"So what then, little pet? You just want to watch the world burn now?"

Lauren looked inward, what did she want? She struggled to find the spark of humanity that had weathered every storm so far, but it's light no longer hid within her heart. The question hung unanswered while she pondered.

Ultimately, she knew, there was only one thing she wanted from Weyland.

"All this for what? For the cockroaches you choose to love?"

He spread his hands wide, indicating the destruction around them.

"You are a higher life form Lauren. *We* are higher life forms."

Lauren weighed her options, judged the distance between them and gauged the strength in her wings.

"She must be truly something, the pet of yours. Perhaps I'll taste her myself on the days I get bored of you. I imagine she's far less durable, not that I care particularly if I break your toy-"

Lauren lunged at him with a feral growl.

He caught her in the air, using her momentum to swing full circle and drive her into the ground again. His left hand gripped her waist and his right her throat, but her clutching, clawing fingers found his face as well. He lifted her up and slammed her into the ground over and over, but she did not relent. She tore at his eyes with all her strength, pressing her nails into the hard, unyielding flesh.

He gave out a yell of his own and they appeared in the center of London. A quarter-mile section of the Thames turned to steam in an instant and dozens of structures crumbled outward in the wake of their arrival.

"This is where she lives, yes?"

Lauren didn't answer, but Weyland wasn't really waiting for a response regardless. The flames of his wrath raced against her own powers to extinguish the light of the city.

Tens of thousands of lives were snuffed out in the space of a few heartbeats. But where Weyland remained the same, Lauren grew more powerful with every soul she harvested. Weyland reached out to grab her, but she dodged him, maintaining her connection to the dying city.

In desperation Weyland hunched over and clenched his muscles. All the heat and fire shrank into him in an instant, causing him to glow so brightly that Lauren's couldn't bear to look at him. A brief silence, deeper than any Lauren had ever known, was broken a split second later by an atomic fireball that left London a crater several miles wide and more than thousand feet deep.

Millions of lives gone, erased from history in the blink of an eye.

But as Weyland unclenched his fists and stood upright again he was met with Lauren's smiling face. He took an involuntary step backward, his cocky, self-assured facade finally cracking.

"Impossible."

Lauren was silent, walking across the glowing earth towards him.

"I-I will not be denied! You are mine by birthright! I-it is fated!"

Lauren glared at him, but still she did not speak. The gap between them shrank, twenty feet, eleven, five.

"Is this what you want? I will burn this planet to ash! You and I will be the last living creatures on a dead rock. I will boil the seas, scorch the skies, I will-"

They were face to face now. Though he had her by more than a foot it was he who trembled, not she. His blustery speech trailed off as she stared him down.

"Are you truly the God you claim to be?"

He took a deep breath and did his best to appear menacing.

"I am."

"Can you bring back my father? My brother? My best friend?"

He paused.

"I told you, n-no one can do this, it is beyond-"

"Then you are a pathetic God!"

He flinched as she screamed in his face.

Lauren shoved him, making him stumble backwards.

"Lauren, take your place beside me. I can give you anything else-"

Lauren slapped him across the face. The thunderclap from her impact sent a cloud of dust blowing out in every direction around them. Weyland took the blow, his head jerking to the side, but he stood his ground.

"What can you *possibly* give me that would compare."

She practically spit the words at him, turning away before he could even begin to speak.

He chose to answer her statement as a question.

"I built you a world of dreams before, I can build you another. You can be with your family once again. At least until the pain eases."

Lauren froze, she hadn't considered his other gifts. To be reunited with her loved ones, to live in peace in a world not ruled by constant pain, fear, and rejection, was a tempting price for her soul.

Weyland sensed her indecision. He reached a hand gently out and rested it on her shoulder.

"In time, you will see that this is the only way."

His touch reignited the fire in her belly. She spun, her hand shooting up and gripping him by the wrist.

"Perhaps I want something else, some more."

"Anything."

His sincerity, whether rooted in fear or some perverse sense of duty, only drove her further into madness.

"I want my *vengeance.*"

Weyland tried to jerk his hand back, but her fingers remained locked around him. She felt the darkness within reach hungrily down her arms and sink its fangs into Weyland.

Lauren let out a shuddering, uncontrollable gasp. Her knees felt weak and her eyes half-closed in pure ecstasy. The energy she drew from Weyland was pure, raw, *limitless.*

Weyland's eyes widened with disbelief and he tore at her hand, but no matter how hard he pried he could not free himself. Lauren felt like she'd hooked up to a power plant. Every passing second was the most intense, powerful, mind-blowingly magnified moment of her life.

"Let go of me!"

Lauren was too distracted, too high to respond.

Weyland's energy was different from those she'd tasted before. It was richer, fuller, more complex. She'd absorbed a hundred lifetimes from him already and barely felt she'd scratched the surface.

The pair bounced around the globe together as Weyland sought to escape her with growing desperation. Lauren's uncaged powers and Weyland raging fire left hollowed seas of death, empty skeletons of burning cities wherever they landed.

But she would not relent. She wasn't sure if she could.

"Please, Lauren."

She opened her eyes. It was as though she'd been blind her entire life. They were standing in a ocean of sand, with nothing but dunes for miles in every direction. Even so, the incredible vibrancy of the desert captivated her. She could just as easily perceive the colors of individual grains of quartz around them as she could pick out the feathers in a buzzard some thirty miles distant.

Weylands voice was an intricate weave of vibrations and minute temperature fluctuations in the air as much as it was words.

"Lauren...."

She snapped out of it, focusing her eyes on her prey. She could feel thousands of years of history, of memory, filling her mind and slaking her thirst. But he was an endless font of life and energy.

She noticed his skin had dulled again to the broken rock and magma appearance she'd seen before, but the black was dull and drab around the edges, and the fire within him seemed dimmer. Her own arm, by comparison, was a violent mosaic of black stone and silver fire from her fingers where they locked around his wrist up to her elbow. She did not dwell upon the change, but something about it thrilled her.

His spirit was broken, and he knelt before her with his shoulders low. His eyes, filled with pain and fear stared up at her. Lauren leaned in close to him, her face next to his and her lips beside his ear.

"You are *mine*. You will always be *mine*. Everything you are, and think, and feel, is *mine* to do with as I please."

She felt the flutter in the air as his chest tightened, heard his eyelids blink and felt the vibration of him swallowing the lump in his throat. The sweetest sound, was the rattling gasp that slipped past his lips as she drained him completely. She tore through his lifeforce with reckless abandon, pulling it apart and letting pieces fall all around her like a lion pulling the choicest meats from a fresh kill.

She finally let go of his thin, wasted arm. It flopped to the ground beside his dessicated corpse.

Perception flooded her body, it was all she could manage to stand in place. Her body was awake in ways it had never been. Every sense was raw and new as she found herself in a world infinitely more complex than she could have possibly imagined.

Reality flickered in an out, replaced with momentary visions of other worlds, of her childhood home, of Valerie's face the first night they made love, and a thousand other moments from her life and the lives of others.

It was utterly overwhelming.

Had he felt this way? Weyland's incredible arrogance suddenly seemed natural, a matter of course.

Lauren took a deep breath, tracing the currents in the air to their beginnings across the world. She looked down at herself, the black, cracked stone of her skin was fading back to the cool cream of her normal complexion. The silver streaks remained, though, brighter than ever.

She clenched her fist, testing muscles that felt capable of lifting mountains. She watched in wonder as the sand around her melted to liquid glass. She shook her head, accidentally dismissing the heat waves pouring off her cracking skin.

She concentrated and in an instant the ground around her glowed red-hot for as far as she could see. The skin on her arms turned to thick plates that looked somewhere between cast iron and polished obsidian, with deep cracks of molten silver running between them.

With another deep breath Lauren furrowed her brow in concentration. Unseen by the eyes of mortal men she disappeared in a fiery explosion, leaving behind nothing but a cracked field of smoldering glass.

Epilogue

Lauren reappeared with far greater force than she intended. Nonetheless, she smiled at the success of her test-run on her new power. She was pleasantly surprised that she hadn't experienced the nausea and discomfort she expected either, perhaps it only affected passengers.

She re-examined herself, noting that the thick plating that covered her body had once again dissolved to reveal her silver-threaded skin.

She knew she ought to be cold, that her naked form ought to be freezing at this altitude, but she was supremely comfortable.

The top of the mountain she'd landed on had been blown apart by her arrival. Even now she could see rocks tumbling thousands of feet into the forests and fields below her. The lush greenery of New Zealand spread out before her majestically, unspoiled by men and machines. Her keen vision could make out minute details from leagues away, and she scoured her surroundings for signs of human habitation.

Content at last that no one had witnessed her arrival, Lauren pondered her next move. It only took her a few minutes to come to the conclusion she knew she'd arrive at.

Weyland's last offer hung in her mind, taunting her.

She cast around for a place to sit, frowning at the devastation she'd caused. She settled on a particularly large chunk of granite that her violent arrival had revealed. Lauren approached it and placed a hand on the cold stone. She did her best to heat the stone in a controlled manner, and after a few minutes of trial and error she managed to melt a crude seat into the rock.

She stood back and observed her handiwork. It was rough, but it would do. The boulder itself was larger than her childhood home, and the small alcove she'd carved into it was barely larger than a refrigerator. Still, she could sit comfortably out of the elements and she would be invisible from almost any angle, should anyone seek her out.

Lauren smelled a familiar scent and cast her eyes skyward just as dull gray clouds started to appear above her. Rain sprinkled down softly all around her, drawing a small smile onto her face as she perched upon her new throne.

Lauren closed her eyes, digging deeply into Weyland's memories. She sifted through them until she had a fair idea of how to utilize the power she sought most desperately.

His ability to build worlds of fantasy.

She didn't know how much time had passed when she finally decided she had enough information. It could have been hours or it could have been weeks.

Finally though, she told herself, she was ready.

Lauren took one last look out at the narrow slice of the world she could see from her hidden vantage point. A deep breath later and she closed her eyes once more.

Lauren's senses went dark and then, suddenly, she could smell hay and fresh trimmed grass. Her ears picked up a soft bleating in the distance and she cautiously opened her eyes.

She was sitting in a pile of hay in a familiar barn.

Lauren stretched, noting with extreme satisfaction that her wings were gone, replaced with normal shoulders instead. She jumped out of the hay and did a slow spin, relishing the freedom she hadn't felt in years.

"Lauren, honey?"

Valerie's voice called from outside, and Lauren rushed excitedly to the door. She pulled open the massive wooden entrance and stepped blinking out into the sunlight of the English countryside.